DARK

and

SHALLOW

LIES

DARK

and

SHALLOW

LIES

GINNY MYERS SAIN

First published in Great Britain in 2021
by Electric Monkey, part of Farshore
An imprint of HarperCollins*Publishers*
1 London Bridge Street, London SE1 9GF

farshore.co.uk

HarperCollins*Publishers*
1st Floor, Watermarque Building, Ringsend Road
Dublin 4, Ireland

Text copyright © 2021 Ginny Myers Sain

The moral rights of the author have been asserted

ISBN 978 0 0084 9478 0
Printed and bound in the UK using 100% renewable electricity at
CPI Group (UK) Ltd

3

Typeset by Avon DataSet Ltd, Alcester, Warwickshire

This book is dedicated to my Summer Children,
all the STAGES theatre kids.
But, most especially, this is for our Caitie.

What's past is prologue.
– *The Tempest*

He's tearing through the brush behind me.
Breathing hard and calling my name. Even with
the wind and the driving rain, he's all I hear.
So I push myself faster. We break out on to the
wide-open flats, and I feel him closing in on me.
There's nowhere left to hide except inside the dark.
So I turn off my flashlight and
let the blackness eat me alive.

1

The last time I saw my best friend, she called me a pathetic liar and then she punched me in the mouth. The shock of it almost kept me from feeling anything until it was over. And I had no idea what Elora was thinking in that last moment. Because she didn't say. And I'm not a mind reader.

Honey is. My mother was. I guess. All the women in my family, right up to me.

But not me.

I'm thinking of that night last summer as I stand on the front porch of the Mystic Rose and stare at Elora's missing poster, trying to catch my breath. I'm wondering why they chose that picture. The one with her eyes half-closed. She hated that picture.

Jesus.

She *hates* that picture.

I've been steeling myself for this moment since I got that phone call back in February. Trying to imagine what it would be like to come home and step off the boat into a La Cachette without Elora. And I knew it would be bad. But I hadn't been prepared for the poster.

The words MISSING GIRL printed in red caps.

The sheriff's phone number.

My chest tightens. I drop my backpack to sink down and sit on the front steps so I can pull myself together. Clear my head of that weird flash that hit me out of nowhere.

Elora running from someone.

Being chased through the rain.

Swallowed up by the dark.

A few seconds to shake off that terror. Her terror. That's all I need. Then surely I'll be able to breathe again.

The screen door slams, and I hear footsteps on the porch behind me. It's Evie. "Hey, Grey." She perches beside me on the steps, like a bird, and offers me half a stick of gum dug out of the pocket of her cutoff shorts. "Miss Roselyn said you was comin' this mornin'. You just get in?"

La Cachette, Louisiana, is the self-proclaimed "Psychic Capital of the World," so I always find it odd that every summer visit starts with people firing off questions they should already know the answers to.

How was school dis year?

Still makin' good grades?

Gotcha a boyfriend yet?

"Yeah." I unwrap Evie's offering and nod toward the backpack at my feet. "Got off the mail boat a few minutes ago." The gum's a little stale, and I wonder how long she's been carrying it around.

"We didn't know if you'd come this year . . ." Evie's voice trails off, and she glances at the curling edges of the MISSING poster. At the picture in the center. Half-closed eyes and a long dark ponytail. That bright blue tank top with the faded yellow stars. And a knock-you-on-your-ass smile.

Elora.

"She's my best friend," I say. "My –" But I can't choke out the words.

"Your twin flame," Evie finishes for me, and I nod. She settles on to the step and slips her hand into mine. "So you had to come."

Evie's gentle sweetness is as familiar as the worn smoothness of the porch step. And the smell of the river. I'm glad she was the first one to find me.

Sweat stings the corners of my eyes, and I pull up the collar of my T-shirt to dab it away. Barely eight thirty in the morning and already a million degrees with 500 percent humidity. I lived down here full-time till I was almost nine years old, so you'd think I'd be used to it, but it always takes me a while to reacclimate after spending the school year up in Arkansas with my dad. I mean, it's hot there, too . . . but not like this.

Nowhere is hot like this. Or wet like this. Spending the summer in La Cachette is like living inside someone's mouth for three months out of the year.

I pull my eyes away from Elora's picture in time to watch the back half of a big black snake disappear into a clump of tall sedge grass beyond the boardwalk. It's too far away to say for sure if it's a moccasin. But I figure it probably is.

That thick body gives it away. And I know they're always out there, sliding back and forth beneath our feet like the slow roll of the tides. Every once in a while, one of them finds its way up on to the boardwalk and into someone's house, where it meets its doom at the business end of a long-handled hoe. Or a shovel.

I don't like to think about the snake, or where it might be heading, but it's better than staring at that poster while the words *missing girl* burn deep into my brain.

"You okay, Grey?" Evie asks. She's twisting a strand of almost-white-blonde hair around one finger.

"Yeah," I say. "It's just weird, you know? Everything's different –"

"And nothing's different," she finishes.

And that's it exactly.

Evie reaches down to scratch at a bug bite on one bare foot, and I can't help noticing how long her legs have gotten since last summer. Plus, she's gotten boobs. She's finally growing up.

Evie turned sixteen last September, the youngest of us all . . . but not by much.

People down here call us the Summer Children. We started our lives as a complete set.

Ten. The most perfect number. The number of divine harmony. The number at the heart of the universe. Ten commandments. Ten plagues of Egypt.

Ten babies born to eight different families.

A real population boom for little bitty La Cachette. One hundred tiny fingers and one hundred tiny toes. All of us arriving that same year, between the vernal equinox in March and the autumnal equinox in September.

Me and Elora. And Hart.

Evangeline.

Serafina and Lysander.

Case.

Mackey.

Ember and Orli.

I wonder if the others have changed, too. Like Evie. I wonder if Elora had.

Shit.

Has.

Suddenly, there's this ache inside me that feels big enough to fall into. And, unlike me, maybe Evie is a mind reader, because she puts one arm around my shoulders and gives me an awkward squeeze.

Only, I know she isn't a mind reader. Evie is clairaudient. She hears things. Messages. Words. Snatches of whispered conversation. Music sometimes. Like a radio in her head. That's her gift.

And my mother wasn't a true mind reader, either. Not really. She saw color auras. That was her thing. Which explains how I got my name. Imagine looking at your perfect baby girl and seeing her swimming in a sea of grey.

The color of fog and indecision.

The color of nothing special.

The color of everything that's in between.

"We're glad you're here, Grey." Evie's words are so soft. She always talks quiet, like she's afraid of drowning out the voices in her head. If it were me, I think I'd talk loud, so I wouldn't have to hear their whispering. "We've been waiting for you," she adds. And I know she means all of them.

Well, all of them except Ember and Orli, of course, because they've been dead forever.

And all of them except Elora.

Because Elora's been gone a little over three months now. One night back in February, she walked into the swamp and vanished. Almost like she'd never been here at all.

"You seen Hart yet?" Evie asks.

"I haven't seen anyone," I tell her. "Except you."

"He's not doing so good, Grey." There's something strange in her voice, and she looks away from me. Out toward the river. "I mean, it's been real hard on everybody, but Hart . . . he . . ." Evie shakes her head and chews on a ragged cuticle. "You'll see for yourself, I guess."

It feels wrong, the two of us gossiping about Hart before I've even had a chance to lay eyes on him. I know he wouldn't like it.

"Is Honey up?" I ask.

"Yeah," Evie says. "She's in the back room unpacking a bunch of new yoga DVDs. I just came over to bring some muffins for the boat people."

To everyone else, my grandmother is Miss Roselyn. But I call her Honey. She runs the spiritualist bookstore, which happens to be the only real business in town. The Mystic Rose sells books, sure, but also amulets, crystals, incense, candles, healing herbs, and now yoga DVDs, apparently. On busy weekends Evie's mama, Bernadette, makes a little money by sending over fresh baked goods and sandwiches for Honey to peddle to the hungry tourists.

"I better let her know I'm here," I say. "She thinks I'm coming in on the ten o'clock boat."

There are no roads that lead to La Cachette. To get here, first you drive to the end of the world, then you get on a boat and keep on going. Two hours south of New Orleans, Highway 23 dead-ends in Kinter, a tiny almost-town where you can buy groceries, gas, and round-trip "scenic" boat rides to the Psychic Capital of the World. From there, the journey downriver to La Cachette takes another half hour.

The town, if it's even big enough to be called that, sits on a low-lying island, absolutely as far south as you can get in Louisiana, just above the spot where the Mighty Mississippi splits into three fingers and then splinters into a hundred more before it finally floods out into the bayou, eventually reaching the Gulf of Mexico. Ol' Man River on one side and nothing but waterlogged swamp on the other.

As Hart likes to say, one way in. And no way out.

I glance at an old wooden sign nailed to a post out on the boat dock.

WELCOME TO LA CACHETTE, LOUISIANA
ELEVATION 3 FT.
POPULATION 106 LIVING SOULS

The only time the number changes is when someone gets born.

Or dies.

Somewhere inside my head, a voice jeers that they'll have to repaint it. Because of Elora. But I close my ears. Don't let myself listen.

Just then, Honey calls to me from inside the bookstore. "Grey, you gonna come in here and see me?"

Evie gives me a little smile as she stands up to leave. "She knows." A whisper of a breeze moves through, and I hear the tinkle of wind chimes from someplace nearby. It's a nice sound. Almost like laughter.

Evie's smile fades. "Miss Roselyn always knows."

She turns and starts down the boardwalk in the direction of her house, right next door. But I stop her with a question that I hadn't planned to ask.

"Do you think she's dead?"

Evie stares at me for a few seconds. She's twisting that long strand of white-blonde hair around and around one finger again. She blinks at me with pale blue eyes, then answers me with a question of her own. "Do you?"

"I don't know," I say. "I hope not."

I don't tell Evie the rest of it, though. I don't say that Elora can't be dead, because, if she is, I don't know how I'll keep breathing.

Evie reaches up to swat away a horsefly that's buzzing around her head, and when she opens her mouth to speak again, I want to tell her I'm not asking for her opinion. I want to know if she *knows*. For sure. If she's got that radio in her head tuned to Elora's frequency. But all she says is, "Welcome home, Grey."

Honey yells at me again from inside the bookstore, so I stand up and grab my backpack. Then I spit Evie's gum into the tall grass before I head inside.

A bell jingles when I open the door, and Honey shouts, "Back here, Sugar Bee!"

I'm careful with my backpack as I weave my way through the crowded shop. Incense burns on the counter, and every bit of space is crammed full of books and bottles and jars and colorful rocks. Herbs dry in little bundles on the windowsills.

I pause a minute to breathe in the comfort of a hundred familiar smells, then I push aside the bead curtain that marks the doorway to the back room. Honey stops unpacking boxes to come give me a big hug. She has on a purple flower-print dress and sensible white tennis shoes. Dangly earrings. A yellow headscarf covers her white curls. I can't decide if she looks any different than she did when I left last August. It's like whatever age Honey is, that's the age she's always been to me. It's only when I look at photographs that I see she's getting older.

"There's my girl!" She plants a big kiss on the top of my head. "Oh! Look at your hair!" she says, even though I've had basically the same short pixie cut for years. "You look so sophisticated!" That makes me smile. "I thought you weren't coming till later," she scolds. "I would've made breakfast."

Twice a day Monday through Friday and three times a day on weekends, an ancient ferry shuttles passengers back and forth between Kinter and La Cachette. The first trip of the day is always at ten o'clock. Sometimes, though, if you're lucky, you can talk Alphonse, the mail-boat captain, into letting you ride along on his early morning run. Today I was lucky.

"I'm not that hungry," I tell her. "I had a granola bar." Honey raises one eyebrow, silently judging my dad for putting me on the boat without breakfast.

"Evangeline brought over some fresh muffins," she tells me. "Bran. And some blackberry, I think." She leads me back into the shop and points out the basket by the register.

I dig around until I find a big blackberry one. I'm in the middle of peeling away the wax paper when I notice the stack of flyers sitting on the counter.

HAVE YOU SEEN THIS GIRL?

Underneath the big block letters, there's another picture of Elora. This time she's sitting on the edge of the picnic table out behind her house. She's wearing cutoffs and an orange bikini top. Her long dark hair is loose, sunglasses perched on the top of her head like a crown. Her mouth is open, and she's been caught midlaugh.

I recognize the photo immediately. It was taken at the beginning of last summer. Before everything went wrong between the two of us. Only a sliver of bare shoulder at the edge of the picture hints that someone is sitting next to her. Someone who's been cropped out of the image.

Me.

The best friend she cut out of her life, just the way someone cut me out of that photograph.

I'm stuck for a minute, trying to remember what she was laughing about. Staring at Elora. And the space where I should have been. When I finally look up, Honey is watching me.

"You feel her," she says. "You've always said you didn't have the gift, but I've never believed it."

"No." I wrap the muffin back up and set it aside. "It's not like that. I just keep expecting her to show up, you know?"

I want to ask Honey the same question I wanted to ask Evie. I want to ask if she knows – for sure – whether Elora is still alive. But I don't. I'm afraid to hear the answer.

Honey is an old-school spiritualist at heart. A true medium. She believes that the spirits of the dead exist and that they have the ability to communicate directly with the living. If they want to.

For Honey, they communicate mostly through visions. She reads tea leaves and stuff like that, but that's just for the tourists on day trips down from New Orleans. The real stuff she keeps to herself these days. She says nobody wants to listen to the wisdom of the dead any more. They just want to know when their boyfriends are going to propose. Or if they'll win the lottery. And the dead, Honey says, don't give a shit about stuff like that. They have bigger fish to fry.

I tear my eyes away from Elora's frozen laugh, and Honey is still watching me. "Every year you remind me more of your mother," she tells me, and I know the resemblance she sees goes deeper than our chestnut hair, our big green eyes, and the freckles scattered across our noses. "Always keeping the most important pieces of yourself tucked away somewhere."

The little bell over the door jingles, and I look up, thinking maybe it really will be Elora standing there and this whole thing will be over. We'll rip down the missing posters and toss the flyers in the trash. Then I'll tell her I'm sorry, and she'll forgive me. And everything will be the way it's always been.

The way it's supposed to be.

But it isn't Elora. It's Hart.

And I guess that's the next best thing.

I take a few steps back. Because this is where everything ends. We both know it now. And that's when the rain finally comes. The sky splits open and it comes all at once. It comes in buckets. Rivers. The kind of rain that washes away the blood and carries away the evidence. No clue. No trace. No goodbye.

2

Before I even have a chance to say hello, Hart's made it around the counter and has me wrapped up in a hug so tight it hurts. His arms are strong. Familiar. And I finally let myself melt into the safety of home. The soft sound of the bead curtain tells me Honey has slipped into the back room to give us some privacy.

"Evie told me you were here." Hart's voice sounds different than it did last summer. Deeper. Or maybe just sadder. I talked to him on the phone in February, when he called to tell me about Elora. But that conversation had been so weird. Short and confusing. We weren't used to talking to each other on the phone. And we were both upset. He hadn't offered a lot of details, and I'd been too stunned to ask questions. As soon as I hung up, it almost seemed like maybe it wasn't real. Like I'd imagined the whole phone call.

But now it's definitely real. This hug makes it real.

Hart is the oldest of us all. The first of ten. Born in late March, almost three months before Elora and I came into the world on the same day in June. He's technically Elora's stepbrother, but the "step" part never mattered to us. And I've always thought of him as my big brother, too. Sometimes he played with us. Sometimes he tormented us. Occasionally he kicked someone's ass on our behalf. But he was always there. Hart's mama married Elora's daddy when we were six years old, but in our minds, that only cemented what we already knew – that the three of us belonged to each other.

Three peas in a pod.

Three coins in the fountain.

Our very own three-ring circus.

Hart and Elora and Grey. Grey and Elora and Hart.

Hart was just a month shy of seventeen when Elora disappeared back in February, but when he called me that next day, he sounded so much younger. He sounded like he had when we were little.

He sounded scared.

"How you holding up?" I ask him. Evie was right. He looks like he hasn't eaten or slept in weeks.

"It's rough, Greycie." He pulls back to look at me. "How 'bout you?"

I shrug. "It's better, being here, I think."

I'd wanted to come right at the beginning – I started packing as soon as I got that phone call from Hart – but my dad wouldn't let me. We had a screaming, door-slamming fight about it that lasted most of a week. I couldn't afford the time off school, he'd said. Not at the tail end of my junior year, with track season getting ready to start.

Scholarships, you know.

Hart moves to sit on the tall stool behind the cash register, and I see him glance at the flyers. He runs his fingers through the wild dark curls on the top of his head, but they're untamable. I bet he hasn't so much as touched a comb since sometime in February. His eyes are red, and his fingernails look like he's bitten them down to the quick. Hart spends most of his life outside, but somehow he looks pale underneath his deep fisherman's tan.

He jerks his head toward the stack of flyers. "I took that picture," he says. "Remember that day?"

I nod. "I was trying to remember what she was laughing about."

"Who knows." He tries to smile. "Elora was always laughing."

I wait for him to correct himself. Elora *is* always laughing. But he doesn't. He leaves her in the past.

"There's still no news?" I ask him. "Nobody knows anything?" It seems wild to me that someone could vanish like that. No clue. No trace.

No goodbye.

How is that possible? Here, of all places?

Hart shakes his head. "There's no sign of her anywhere, Greycie. They've never found –"

He hesitates, and I feel sick. I know what he means. I know what they've been looking for out there in the bayou. They haven't been looking for Elora. They've been looking for something awful and ugly. A floater. A bloated, decomposing body that's risen to the surface of the foul black water. A body identifiable only by a bright blue tank top with faded yellow stars.

Or part of a body, more likely. Gators don't leave much behind.

The room starts spinning, and I grab the edge of the counter to try to make it stop. My knees threaten to buckle.

Hart is instantly on his feet. He takes my arm, and I let him pull me against him again. "Hey, easy, Greycie." His voice is low and gravelly, and the familiar sound of it soothes me a little. "You're gonna be okay. Just breathe." I nod against his chest, feeling guilty for making him comfort me. Especially when I know he's so broken, too.

Hart is a psychic empath. Honey says it's the greatest psychic gift but also the worst. She says it will tear him up if he's not careful. It's not just that he knows what other people are feeling. He actually feels it, too. Every bit as strong as they do. It gets inside him somehow. And I know what it costs him, constantly taking on everyone else's pain. I untangle myself from his arms and move away to give him some space.

"What were you guys doing out there? That night." I have so many questions. He didn't really tell me much on the phone. After we hung up, I called Honey and she told me what she knew. But the details she had were pretty sketchy.

Hart looks at me and sighs. "You wanna get outta here?" He glances around the shop. "Before the first boat comes? I'm not in the mood to deal with tourists."

Everyone in La Cachette has a love-hate relationship with

the tourists. They hate them. But they love their cash. It's the only thing that keeps most of them alive. That and maybe a bit of fishing. On a Saturday with good weather, a couple hundred people might make the trip from Kinter to La Cachette and back on board the old shuttle boat. Along the way, the captain drones into a crackling microphone, pointing out things of interest on the riverbank.

Spoiler alert: there aren't any.

I stick my head into the back room and tell Honey that Hart and I are heading out for a bit. She nods. "It's good for you two to be together. Healing."

I don't know about healing, but I know I need to be with someone who loves Elora as much as I do. It doesn't make her any less gone, but it makes me less lonely.

Outside, Hart and I both turn left. We walk in silence, and for a few minutes, things feel almost normal. I like the familiar *slap-scuff-slap* of my flip-flops on the boardwalk. It's a summer sound – a La Cachette sound – and I know the rhythm of it as well as I know the rhythm of my own name.

La Cachette is made up of two dozen or so little houses – all of them on stilts – connected by a half-mile stretch of elevated wooden walkway. Every bit of this town was built to let the floods and the tides and the mud flow right underneath us. Down here, there is no water and there is no land. There's only an uneasy in-between. When it's dry, we have yards. Sort of. When it's not, you wouldn't know where the river ends and the town begins.

Right now, the tide is coming in and the water is slowly

rising beneath our feet. I blink against the glare bouncing off the river. And off the gleaming white paint. The whole town gets a new coat each spring. Every square inch of it. All the buildings. The boardwalk, too. Even the dock. All the same bright white. Living their whole lives a few feet above the relentless muck, everyone down here craves that kind of clean, I guess.

The Mystic Rose sits smack in the middle of the boardwalk, right across from the boat dock, and Hart and Elora's place is on the downriver end of town. The very last house. A quarter mile and a whole five-minute walk away. In between, every single structure has a swinging sign hanging from the front porch or painted lettering on the windows advertising a buffet of psychic services – everything from séances to palm readings to past-life regressions. There's even one lady who claims she can contact the spirits of your dead pets, and that – for a nominal fee, of course – they'll relay messages to her. In perfect English.

The sign that hangs out front of the little house where Elora and Hart live is made from plywood cut in the shape of a heart. It's painted bright red with fancy gold letters that spell out PSYCHIC LOVE READINGS – MISS CASSIOPEIA, ROMANCE COUNSELOR.

If you bring Hart's mama something that belongs to a boyfriend or a wife or a fiancé, she can hold it in her hands and tell you if their love is true. I've seen her do it a million times, and she's never wrong. People even send her things by mail from all over the country. A girlfriend's pencil or a husband's cuff link. Their front room is papered with wedding invitations from happy customers. I don't doubt her talent, but her name is Becky. Not Cassiopeia. In La Cachette, the line between what's real and what isn't gets blurry sometimes.

The boardwalk ends just past their house, and that's where Hart and I are heading. There's an old pontoon boat rusting away in the mud down there, washed up by some hurricane I can't remember the name of. Elora's daddy, Leo, chained it up so it wouldn't float away in the next flood, and that's where it stayed. I guess he thought maybe he'd fix it up someday, but he never did. Then, the summer we were all seven, we claimed it as our hangout. And it's been ours ever since.

It was our pirate ship that first summer. Evie's mama sewed us a skull and crossbones flag to fly. Another summer, it was our spaceship. When we got older, that's where we'd go to sneak cigarettes or pass around a can of beer. Most of us had our first kiss there, too. Some of us more than that. I know for a fact that Elora lost her virginity there with Case the summer we were all fifteen.

Hart jumps down into the bow of the old boat. It's not that far, maybe four or five feet below the boardwalk, but my legs aren't nearly as long as his, so I climb down the rickety wooden ladder to join him.

"Hey, Shortcake," he teases. "You think you're little 'cause you live in Little Rock? Or is that just a coincidence?" I roll my eyes. It's an old joke – and a bad one – but the familiarity of it feels good, and when I reach the bottom of the ladder and step off into the boat, Hart's almost grinning at me. I've always loved the way his eyes crinkle up at the corners when he smiles, and it makes me happy to see the old him, even if it only lasts a second.

We sit together on one of the cracked and peeling bench seats. The boat's canopy is long gone, and I'm grateful for the shade of a single bald cypress tree that rises from the murky water of a pond a few feet away. I slip off my flip-flops and pull my knees up to hug them to my chest.

"You seen Willie Nelson this year?" I ask.

Hart nods. "Yup. See him almost every day, seems like. Still big as a barge and ugly as sin."

Willie showed up three or four years ago. A monster gator. Probably thirteen feet at least. Somebody probably would've shot him for meat by now, except the tourists like taking pictures of him. Sometimes he'll disappear off into the bayou when it's flooded out, but soon as the water starts to recede, he comes crawling right back here to this pond. Year after year. Because this deep hole never goes dry. Once, Leo caught us throwing hot dogs to him, and he threatened to beat the shit out of all of us – Willie included. Since then we've coexisted in a kind of cautious truce. He sticks to his side of the muddy pit, and we stick to ours.

Hart leans down and picks up an old nail that's rusting in the bottom of the boat. He pitches it out into the center of the gator pond, and I hear it hit the water with a plink. We watch the ripples spread across the surface, and for a few minutes, it's so quiet between the two of us that the angry buzzing of the water bugs is almost deafening.

Finally, he takes a deep breath. "We were out hunting fifolet. Like we used to do when we were kids, remember?"

I nod. We all grew up hearing stories about the mischievous ghost lights that appear in the bayou. Strange, eerie balls of floating blue gas. Cajun folklore says they'll lead you to Jean Lafitte's pirate treasure, if you're brave enough to follow. But sometimes the fifolet play tricks, leading people farther and farther from safety until they're lost forever deep in the swamp.

I shiver as the old fear creeps through me, and Hart nudges me with his shoulder. "It's only a story, Greycie."

"I know that," I tell him. But those stories have always scared me.

"It was the second Saturday of the month, so everybody'd gone upriver to Kinter for bingo. All the adults, anyway. And there wasn't shit to do. It was Elora's idea. She wanted to go huntin' fifolet." He shrugs. "So we did."

I wait while Hart pulls a beat-up pack of cigarettes out of his T-shirt pocket. He shakes one out and lights it before he goes on. "It was really dark that night. Thick clouds blockin' out the moon. And we walked for a bit, but we didn't see any lights. Didn't see anything at all. Didn't hear anything, even. It was weird. The quiet."

I shiver again, imagining that strange silence. Down here, the daytime can be still enough to hear a pin drop. But the bayou is never quiet at night. It's a cacophony of bugs and frogs and owls and bellowing gators. Sometimes they carry on so loud you can't sleep inside the house with all your windows closed and the AC humming on high.

"We had some beer, so we drank that. Evie got freaked out. She wanted to go home. But Case wanted to play flashlight tag." Hart pauses to take a long drag off his cigarette, then he exhales and stretches one arm over the edge of the boat to flick away the ash. "And nobody really wanted to play. We were over it, you know? But Case was pissed. Half-drunk. You know how he gets. He wasn't ready to go home yet."

Case has the most gorgeous hair I've ever seen. Deep, dark red. And the temper to go with it. He's okay most of the time, but he can be mean as a cottonmouth when he's been drinking. He and Elora have been a thing since we were twelve years old. She'll step out with other guys occasionally, but she's never had any real boyfriend besides Case. Not true love, she told me once. Not by a long shot. Just something to do.

Someone to do.

Hart finishes his cigarette and stubs it out before he goes on. "So we played flashlight tag for a while. Out there at Li'l Pass. Then it was Mackey's turn to be it, and he found us all real quick. Everybody except Elora."

"What'd you do?" I ask him.

"Called the all clear. But she didn't come out. We figured she wouldn't have gone far, so we started lookin' for 'er." He runs a hand through his sweat-damp curls. "But this huge storm blew in outta nowhere. Craziest thing I've ever seen. We stayed at it, though. All of us. Searched out there for hours in a goddamn downpour."

I feel sick, remembering that flash of Elora that came to me earlier. That moment the sky split open and the rain came. Just the way Hart describes.

"I left the rest of 'em huntin' for her out there at Li'l Pass. Where she disappeared. Came home and got the four-wheeler. Looked everywhere I could think of. Rode all the way back to Keller's Island, even. Ended up soaking wet. Mud up to my neck. Covered in bug bites."

"No way." I shake my head and swallow my rising panic. "She wouldn't have gone way back there. She's scared of that place."

We all are. There's no way she would have gone there. Not in the dark. Not alone.

Not at all.

Not to Killer's Island.

"I know," he says, "but, shit, Greycie. She had to go somewhere."

I hug my knees harder to my chest, remembering how Hart used to make fun of Elora and me. How he used to tease us that Dempsey Fontenot was coming for us. But he doesn't make fun of me now. He just shakes out another cigarette and lights it up, pulling the smoke into his lungs and breathing it out slow and steady before he goes on.

"Then, after midnight, when everybody got back from bingo, the men all went out lookin'. Airboats and huntin' dogs. ATVs. Searchlights. All of us callin' her name till we were hoarse. Clear through till mornin'." He chokes a little. "And there was absolutely nothin'. Not a goddamn sign of her."

He pulls the bottom of his T-shirt up to mop his sweaty

forehead, but it doesn't do any real good. The shirt is already soaked through. I'm melting in shorts and flip-flops. And here he is in jeans and boots. I've never seen Hart in shorts, unless we were out swimming.

"So that's the story," he tells me. "Leo called Sheriff early the next mornin'. Pretty soon they had boats all up and down the river. Search teams scouring the bayou. Two hundred volunteers in hip boots wading through inch by inch back there where she disappeared. Just like on TV." He puts the cigarette to his lips again. Inhale and hold. Breathe out smoke. "Still nothin'."

Hart's focused on something off in the distance, and I let myself take a minute to look at him. Really look at him. He's all dark tangled curls and sun-browned skin and hard angles. Faded jeans and an old grey T-shirt stretched tight across broad shoulders.

Hart is what Honey calls "a tall drink of water," which is her way of saying he's hot. I think. And she's not wrong. Even now, rough as the last few months have obviously been on him.

For a couple years, when we were younger, I thought we might be something else to each other. Things got confusing between us. He even kissed me once, the summer we were thirteen. Elora never knew that. She would have been so pissed. It's the only secret either of us ever kept from her. It never went anywhere, but sometimes I still find myself fighting the urge to reach out and run my fingers through those beautiful curls.

And I'm fighting it hard as hell right now. I'm fighting it so hard my fingers itch.

But I settle for asking a question.

"Do you feel her?"

Hart runs one hand over the stubble along his jawline and nods, then he takes another long, slow drag off that damn cigarette. Only this time, his hand is shaking something awful. It's bad enough that I worry he'll drop the cigarette in his lap and set himself on fire.

"Yeah." There's a long, slow, smoke-filled exhale. "I feel 'er all the time, Greycie. That's the thing. I feel her every fuckin' minute of every miserable day."

"What do you feel?"

"Fear," he says. "I don't feel anything but fear."

"I feel her, too," I tell him.

He really does drop the cigarette then. And it lands in his lap, like I predicted. But it doesn't set him on fire.

"Shit," he mutters, and he knocks the cigarette into the bottom of the boat and grinds it out with the heel of his boot. "Jesus, Greycie. For real?"

He's staring at me.

I hadn't planned to tell him about the strange flashes I've been having. I hadn't planned to tell anyone. I've never had the gift. And I've never wanted it.

I don't want it now.

But I can't hide this from him. Not from Hart.

"Yeah," I say. "For real."

"What do you feel?" he asks me.

"It's like you said," I tell him. "Nothing but fear."

Run and hide. Hide and run.
I'll count from ten, then join the fun.
Say a prayer and bow your head.
If my light finds you, you'll be dead.
Ten, nine, eight, seven, six, five, four, three, two, one.
Ready or not, here I come.
I'm Dempsey Fontenot.
You better run.

H art and I both jump when the shuttle boat blasts its horn. It's the last Saturday in May. A three-day weekend. Perfect weather. Hot. But not as suffocating as it will be in another few weeks. The people of La Cachette should do good business today.

Aside from running the Mystic Rose and doing her own readings, Honey also acts as a broker for all the other psychics and spiritualists in town. For a commission, of course. Day-tripping tourists get off the boat and pour into her shop first thing, looking to buy a cold bottle of water and maybe a postcard, and Honey gets them lined up with appointments all up and down the boardwalk. Advice about lovers. Energy cleansings. Conversations with dead pets. Whatever they're in the mood for. It can get hectic, and I know she's glad to have my help during the busy summer season.

Across the pond, Willie Nelson has dragged himself out of the muck, and he's sunning in the long grass like he doesn't give a rat's ass about the tourists. Or their money. And I swear,

Hart's watching that alligator with this expression on his face that looks an awful lot like envy.

He scuffs at a rusty spot in the hull with the toe of one boot, then he turns to look at me. "Tell me what's going on, Greycie. With you." There's a wariness in his voice that matches the deep worry in his hazel eyes. And now I'm wishing I hadn't even mentioned it.

"I don't know." I shrug. "Maybe nothing."

"Dreams?" he asks, but I shake my head.

"Definitely not dreams. I'm wide awake."

"So . . . like . . . what? Visions of some kind?"

"Not exactly. They're just . . . flashes. You know?" This sounds so bizarre. Or at least it would in Little Rock. In La Cachette, this is what passes for normal conversation. "It's like I'm seeing bits and pieces of that night through her eyes. Thinking what's she's thinking and feeling what she's feeling. None of it makes sense, though. It's all jumbled and out of order."

Hart is digging dirt out from under the edges of his fingernails. He's hunched over. Elbows resting on his knees. "But these flashes, you think they're Elora?"

"I know they are."

"What do you see? Exactly." His voice is easy. But I don't buy it. "Or feel? Or whatever." His jaw is tight. Muscles taut.

Hart is afraid. He's afraid of me. Of what I know. Of what I'm going to tell him. And I don't want that kind of power. I've never wanted it.

Not over Hart.

Not over anyone.

"I'm not really sure," I admit. "Dark. And water. The storm. That sudden rain." I have to make myself say the next part. "She's running from someone, I think. Somebody's after her." I hear Hart's sharp intake of breath, and I hate myself for being the cause of it. "Mostly, I just feel that fear. Like you said. This awful fear that almost stops me breathing."

Hart reaches for my hand. His fingers curl around mine. They're rough and calloused. And they feel like home. "Yeah," he says. "Me too."

"But I still think maybe she's alive," I say.

"Greycie –"

"No. Listen," I insist. "In all those snatches or flashes or whatever, when they come to me, she's always alive. She's scared. Lost, maybe. Or hurt, even. I don't know. But she's always alive. I never see her . . ." I can't say it. But Hart does.

"You never see 'er die."

There are voices and footsteps up on the boardwalk, and Hart and I pull back from each other. He lets go of my hand, and I wipe my sweaty palm on my shorts. Could be tourists looking for Willie Nelson.

Could be. But it isn't.

It's them. They've found us. The rest of the Summer Children come down the ladder one right after the other, like circus acrobats under the big top.

Serafina.

Lysander.

Mackey.

Evangeline.

They're laughing about something and talking together. And just for a second, I feel like an outsider. Then Mackey takes both my hands and pulls me to my feet. Sera is hugging me and saying how much she missed me, and Sander is batting those long eyelashes of his. And there's Evie, still barefoot, looking like she isn't quite sure what she's supposed to do – as usual.

That outsider feeling evaporates, and I know I'm right where I belong. The only place I've ever belonged.

I just wish so hard that Elora was with them. I feel her absence in the burning pit of my stomach. She's a deep ache in my bones.

But then there's this voice in the back of my mind saying, even if she were here, she wouldn't talk to me. She'd just sit there on the railing, glaring in my direction. Or maybe she'd laugh in my face again. Tell me to go to hell.

It hadn't been just that last night. Things had been messed up between us all last summer. And that was mostly my fault. I know that now.

Mackey throws one arm around my shoulders and gives me a big, warm grin. "It's good you're home, Grey," he says. "We're all together."

The others nod and agree, and we all settle into our regular spots. Evie passes out stale gum to everyone. Just another long and lazy summer day, right? It almost could be.

Except when I look over at Hart, he's staring off at Willie Nelson again, like he'd crawl out of the boat and join him in the pond if he could. He looks lost.

Hollow.

And I feel the echo of his emptiness way down inside my own soul.

Because I know Mackey means well, but it's not true. We aren't all together. We haven't all been together since we were four years old. Not since what happened to Ember and Orli. Without them, we're incomplete.

And now we're missing Elora.

Evie asks me some random questions about school. We chat for a few minutes about my classes. Mackey asks about track, and I tell him I ran cross-country for the first time this past season. He grumbles something about how they don't have enough runners for a cross-country team.

Mackey, Case, and Elora all go to high school upriver in Kinter. There's a school boat. Evie and Hart and the twins, Sera and Sander, are homeschooled.

There's no cell phone service way down here. No internet, either. So this is how summer always begins for me, with the catch-ups and the recaps. Occasionally, Mackey might send me an email from school up in Kinter. Or Elora might call every so often from the payphone up there. But mostly, my Little Rock life and my La Cachette life stay separate. Two totally different universes.

When I'm down here, it's like my friends and my world back in Arkansas don't exist. It doesn't work the other way around, though. Even when I'm up there running track and going to the mall and studying, La Cachette always takes up space in my head. It's like I never really leave the bayou. Not entirely. My feet stay wet. The smell of the swamp lingers in my nose. And when I finally get back down here at the start of every summer, everything is just the way I left it. Like no time has passed at all.

Or at least that's the way it's always been before.

"This is total bullshit." The chitchat stops, and everyone turns to look at Sera. She gazes right back at us. Defiant. "Are we gonna talk about 'er or not?" She gives Sander a look that clearly says, *Can you believe this?*

Serafina and Lysander are basically carbon copies of each other. Folks around here call them the Gemini. Twins born in late May. Both of them mind-blowingly talented artists and smarter than the rest of us put together. I forget how many languages Sera speaks. Five, maybe? Sander doesn't speak at all – never has – but he has plenty of other ways to communicate.

The twins come from an old Creole family. Home for them is out on Bowman Pond, about ten minutes away by airboat. But their mama, Delphine – they call her Manman – makes good luck gris-gris and love potions that she sells from a little card table she sets up on the dock most weekends. People swear by them. She tells tourists the charm magic was passed down from her great-great-great-granmè, who was a famous New Orleans voodoo queen. A friend of Marie Laveau's.

Maybe that part's true. And maybe it isn't.

Sera spits her gum into the water. Her hair is the color of rich, wet river sand streaked with copper, and she wears it in a long braid down the middle of her back. Almost to her waist. The madder she is, the more that braid swings back and forth when she talks. And it is really swinging now.

"We gonna sit here all day dancin' around her name?" she

demands. "Not talkin' about what happened won't make things different."

"Don't be mad, Sera," Mackey soothes. He's a little guy. Not much bigger than me. Dark skin and soft brown eyes. An easy smile. He can't stand for anybody to be upset. "We can talk about her." He turns to look at me. "We talk about her all the time, Grey."

"What's the point?" Hart's voice has an edge that I'm not used to hearing from him. "We've been over that night a million times."

Sera doesn't back down, though. She never does. "Not with Grey, we haven't."

Evie bites at her lip and glances over at Hart. "Grey doesn't have the gift," she pipes up. Then she looks embarrassed. "I'm sorry, Grey. You know what I mean. It's just . . ." She shrugs. "You don't. Right?"

I feel Hart's eyes on me. I feel all their eyes on me.

"Grey deserves to hear us speak Elora's name out loud," Sera argues. "It's a sign of respect. She was her twin flame, after all."

Her *was* isn't lost on me.

There were three sets of twins in the beginning. Serafina and Lysander. And Ember and Orli.

But also Elora and me.

Elora and I were born to different families, but on the very same day at the very same hour. Almost the exact same time, down to the minute. There's an old story that tells how human beings originally had two faces, four arms, and four legs. But God was afraid of being overpowered, so he split them all in half. That's why we all have one twin soul out there in the world.

People say the moment you meet your twin flame is the moment the earth beneath your feet begins to shift. There's one midwife down here to deliver all the bayou babies, so our mamas labored together in Honey's big upstairs bedroom. They laid Elora and me side by side in the same bassinet. And I guess that's when the earth shifted for both of us, when we were only minutes old.

"Go ahead, Mackey," Sera prods. "Tell Grey what you told the rest of us. She's tough. She can take it."

Hart gets up and moves away from me. He stands at the front of the boat, his back to all of us, one boot up on the rusted railing. Then he pulls out that pack of cigarettes and lights another one up.

Mackey watches him for a few seconds, then he swallows hard and turns in my direction. And suddenly, I know exactly what he's going to say.

"I had a death warning. That night. About Elora."

Hearing him say it out loud is like a kick in the teeth.

Mackey's family history here goes way back. Further back than anyone's, probably. *Cachette* is a French word. It means "hiding place." Back in the days before the Civil War, this area was a hideout for enslaved people who had escaped their captors.

Mackey's family were some of the first ones who made their way here. They faced down venomous snakes and swarms of mosquitoes, plus ripping thorns and sucking mud – but they were free, so they stayed and made this inhospitable place their home. And to hear Mackey tell it, every single one of his ancestors could feel when death was about to come knocking, which it must have done pretty often in those days.

Mackey frowns and runs one hand over the top of his head. His hair is shaved down almost to his scalp. It's what he calls his "summer haircut," which means it's about one-sixteenth of an inch shorter than he wears it the rest of the year.

"We were playing flashlight tag," he goes on. "And Evie was it. She was counting down that rhyme. About Dempsey Fontenot. You know the one."

I do know the one. I get a little dizzy when I remember how it came to me earlier. How I felt Elora's fear of the old taunt.

"And it was pitch black, so I couldn't see. But then Elora ducked behind this tree with me. And I felt it. Strong as anything."

"Did you tell her?" I ask him.

"I did. I had to." He hesitates. "But she laughed it off."

I picture her, head thrown back, laughing into the dark. Elora could be like that. If she was in the mood to have fun, she might not take anything seriously.

Hart takes one last drag off his cigarette and flicks it out into the murky pond. I see how tense the muscles in his neck are.

Evie is watching him. I pat the empty seat next to me, and she comes to sit in Hart's vacant spot. Evie's always been younger than her years, and long legs or not, she's still the baby. Our baby. Everyone's little sister. I slip my arm around her, and she rests her head on my shoulder. She smells like honeysuckle, and it calms me, breathing in her summertime sweetness.

"It's the water that bothers me," Mackey mumbles. "Drowning. That's what I felt that night. Death in the water." I look over at Hart, but he's still got his back to me. To all of us. "Elora was so pretty, you know?" Mackey's voice breaks. Another chalk mark next to *was*. "I can't stand to think of her dying like that. In the water."

Sander pushes his hair out of his face – soft waves the color of river sand and copper, just like his sister's – then puts an arm around Mackey's shoulders.

"She didn't die in the water." Hart sounds drained. Exhausted. "Search teams combed the bayou from one end to the other. River, too. They'd have found something."

"Yeah," Mackey says. "Sure, Hart. You're probably right. Sometimes I get things confused."

But not very often.

"Ember and Orli were in the water." My voice sounds funny in my ears. Far away. Everyone turns to look at me. Everyone but Hart. We don't hear those names spoken out loud very often. People down here don't like to talk about what happened back then. Thirteen summers ago. Two identical little girls snatched off the boardwalk early one morning, just this time of year. Right under everybody's noses. "They found them floating facedown, back of Dempsey Fontenot's place," I go on. "Back at Keller's Island."

Killer's Island.

"Dempsey Fontenot's long gone," Mackey reassures me. "That doesn't have anything to do with whatever happened to Elora."

And it's true; they never found him. He'd already cleared out. But it's not really true that he was gone. Not in the ways that really mattered. When we were kids, Dempsey Fontenot was the reason we avoided the dark of the tree line. He was the reason Elora and I ran the distance between her house and Honey's at night, instead of walking. He was every campfire legend we ever told and every slumber party ghost story we ever whispered. It didn't matter that nobody ever saw hide nor hair of him again. For the eight Summer Children who were left alive, Dempsey Fontenot was a permanent resident of La Cachette. He walked the boardwalks. Same as we did.

"What if you're wrong, Mackey?" Sera asks, and for a second I can't breathe. "What if it does have something to do with Elora?"

I remember what Hart said, about how he went back there that night. To Keller's Island. Looking for Elora. He must have been afraid he'd find her there, floating facedown in that stagnant drowning pool, out behind what's left of Dempsey Fontenot's burned-down cabin.

He must have thought *maybe.*

We all look at each other, and Sera puts words to what every single one of us is wondering. "What if he came back?"

Hart finally turns around to face us, and I'm waiting for him to say that it's not possible. That we're being silly. Like he would have when we were kids.

But he doesn't.

Behind him, across the pond, Willie Nelson slides into the

water without making a sound. Silent. Ancient. Deadly. The kind of predator you would never see coming.

"What if he didn't come back?" I say. My voice is thin as fishing line, and I feel Evie shiver against me in the steamy midday heat. "What if he never left?"

Slicing rain stings my skin like a thousand tiny knives. The mud is pulling at me. Sucking me down. If I don't do something now, this is where they'll find my body.

I take advantage of the silence – everyone caught off guard – to conjure up that little flash of Elora.

That slicing rain.

And the sucking mud.

I try to focus on what she's running from. What – who – she's afraid of. Could it really be Dempsey Fontenot, our long-lost childhood boogeyman?

It's no use, though. I can't see Elora's face, let alone the face of whoever is chasing her down through the storm.

If I've suddenly become a psychic, I've become a really shitty one.

Sera turns to Sander and whispers something to him in Creole. I wonder what she said, but I don't speak much Creole. Just a word or two I've picked up from the twins over the years. Curse words, mostly. Evie speaks some French, but it's not quite the same. Case, too. But what he speaks is Cajun French, so it's a little different.

And that's when I realize that Case isn't here.

"Where's Case?" I ask, and everybody gets really interested in the cypress needles scattered around the bottom of the boat. Evie sits up and pulls away from me. She's watching Hart again, twisting that white-blonde hair around her finger and chewing on her lip.

"He's around," Mackey tells me. "We just haven't seen much of him lately."

"Why not?" I ask, and they all exchange looks.

"Case won't come around if I'm here." Hart's arms are crossed in front of his chest, and ropy blue veins stand out against his skin. "The two of us got into it a while back."

That's nothing new, really. Hart and Case run up against each other from time to time, like dogs fighting over territory. Their little pissing contests never last long, though. And then they're friends again.

Sera is the one who spells it out for me. "Hart thinks Case did something to Elora."

"No." I shake my head. "No way." Case is a hothead. We all know that. But he wouldn't hurt Elora. He's head-over-heels for her. Has been since we were kids. I find Hart's eyes, but I can't read what he's thinking. He's turned off the lights and pulled the shades down. "Case loves Elora," I say.

Mackey reaches over and lays his hand on mine. "We all loved Elora, Grey."

Nobody corrects him.

We all *love* Elora.

Tourist sounds drift down from the boardwalk, and it's like some kind of spell has been broken. Sera gets to her feet. "We need to go," she says, and Sander stands up, too. "Time to make some money."

"Me too," Mackey says, and he seems grateful for the excuse. On busy weekends, Mackey and his brothers take paying customers out on airboat rides. "Swamp Photo Safaris," they call them. Turns out the ability to see death coming isn't a psychic talent that people really appreciate. Or pay for.

The three of them say their goodbyes, and Mackey gives me a hug. Then they hurry up the ladder and head off down the boardwalk, leaving Evie looking back and forth between Hart and me. She stands up, but she doesn't follow the others.

"I could stick around," she offers. And there's something hopeful in her voice. "I mean, if you guys want company."

"That's okay," I tell her. "I need to get back and spend some time with Honey."

Hart nods. "I gotta get to work."

Sometimes he hangs around the river dock up in Kinter making a little money here and there helping guys off-load cargo. It's backbreaking work, but nobody bothers him. And they pay him in cash. I figure he makes just enough money to keep himself in cigarettes.

But Hart doesn't head toward the ladder.

And neither do I.

Evie hesitates another few seconds, shifting her weight back and forth to stand on one long leg and then the other, like some kind of flamingo.

Finally she gives up and says, "Okay. I'll see you later, Grey." We share a hug before she turns toward Hart. "Bye,

Hart," she tells him, and I feel a tiny twinge of jealousy when he smiles at her.

Evie has always worshipped the ground Hart walks on. Ever since she was born. But there's something new about the way his name sounds in her mouth this year. Something that's different from last summer. And all the summers before that. Something about the way her eyes linger on his face – and the rest of him – a split second longer than they should.

I guess she really is growing up.

When she's gone, Hart lets out a long, ragged breath, then he leans against the boardwalk piling.

"She has a crush on you," I tell him. "Evie."

"Yeah," he says. "I know." Of course he does. I wonder what that must be like, to actually feel someone's heart beat faster when they look at you. "I helped her out with something. That's all it is. Evie's a sweetheart. But she's just a kid."

I let go of that jealous feeling, because I guess he hasn't noticed the new boobs.

"You really think Case could have done something to Elora?" I ask him.

"It isn't just me who thinks it. Sheriff must have questioned Case a dozen times. Investigators from the state police, too. They never officially named him as a suspect, but it was pretty clear they were looking hard in his direction. Probably still are."

"But do you really think it could be him?" I can't wrap my brain around the idea, because Case is one of us.

"I don't know." Hart shrugs. "He was out there that night. If she pissed him off bad enough. Or if he had some reason to be jealous . . ."

Case has a jealous streak a mile wide. That's not exactly a secret. But he's never hurt Elora before. Or anybody else, really. Punched holes in a few walls, maybe. Slashed some guy's tires once at a party up in Kinter. That's about it.

"I don't think he'd do anything like that," I say. "Not Case."

Not to Elora.

"Yeah. Well, I've seen a lot of people do shit you wouldn't have thought they'd ever do." Hart goes to pull out another cigarette, but there aren't any. He growls in frustration, then he crumples the empty pack in his fist and drops it in the bottom of the boat. "I never thought my mama would blow my daddy's head off in our kitchen." I grit my teeth against the pain in his voice. The shock of that sentence.

We were only five years old that summer when Hart came knocking on my bedroom window in the middle of the night, eyes wide and face pale as a ghost. I remember sliding open the window to let him crawl in. The two of us curled up in my bed together under one of Honey's thick quilts.

His daddy was dead, he told me.

Blood and brains all over the wall.

Hart's father was an abusive bastard. Everybody knew it. And it was self-defense. No question. Elora's mama had died when we were babies. Cancer. So when Becky married Leo a year later, Hart and Elora became brother and sister, and everybody agreed that a little bit of good came out of an awful situation.

Hart's never gotten over that night, though. I don't see how anyone could. He still carries it with him. It's not just that he witnessed it with his eyes. He felt it, too. It soaked into his soul, the way the blood soaked into the wallpaper.

The stain is still there.

"What about Dempsey Fontenot?" I ask. "Do you think –"

He shuts me down. "That's a bunch of nonsense. I only went back to Keller's Island that night 'cause I was half outta my mind." He lays a hand on my shoulder. "You don't need to be afraid of Dempsey Fontenot, Greycie. Don't get yourself all spooked."

But it's too late. Suddenly I need to be with Honey.

"I should go," I tell him. "Seriously."

Hart takes my hand and helps me up the ladder, then he climbs up behind me.

We walk back toward the Mystic Rose together, dodging tourists on the way. I notice Miss Cassiopeia's sign is flipped to CLOSED, and I wonder if she's been open at all these last three months. I guess maybe nobody wants a reading from a psychic who can't even find her own missing stepdaughter.

When we stop to say goodbye in front of the bookstore, Hart digs something out of his jeans pocket, then he takes my hand and folds whatever it is into my palm.

I open my fingers to reveal a necklace. Part of a set I gave Elora last year in honor of our golden birthdays. Sixteen on the sixteenth. A delicate silver chain with a single blue pearl.

Pearl because it was our shared birthstone.

Blue because the regular white ones had seemed too plain for Elora.

It's one of the few good memories I have of us last summer. The way she gasped when she opened the little box. "Oh, Grey," was all she said.

"I wanted to find the ring that goes with it," Hart tells me. "I looked all over. But I didn't see it anywhere." One corner of his mouth twitches up a little. "You know what a disaster her room is." Then his face turns serious again. "She probably had it on that night, though. She wore it all the time."

She wore it all the time. Even after what happened between us at the end of last summer.

I need that to mean something.

I shake my head. "I don't want this."

"Come on," he pleads. "Take it. Please, Greycie?" Hart puts a finger under my chin and tilts my face up toward his, so I can't avoid his eyes. "For me?"

Jesus. How am I supposed to say no to that?

"It's hers." I feel tears creeping up on me, but I'll be damned if I'm going to start sobbing. Not with all these stupid tourists milling around.

"She'd want you to have it. What you guys had – have – that connection . . ." Now it's Hart's turn to get choked up. "You two were –" He stops. Flustered. Looks down at his boots.

"Lit from the same match," I finish, and Hart looks back up at me. "It's something Honey used to say. About Elora and me. That we were two flames lit from the same match." I'd reminded Elora of that when I gave her the ring and the necklace last summer. Our very own magic words.

Hart and I study each other for a few seconds. I let him

fasten the chain around my neck, and he gives me the very beginnings of a grin before he turns to go. "Later, Shortcake," is all he says. But his fingers brushing against my skin and the low, throaty sound of his voice are enough to remind me that I've been on the brink of falling in love with Hart for basically my entire life. And occasionally, I trip.

I watch him walk away. There's the kiss of a breeze. The musical laughter of wind chimes. When I look toward the little house Evie shares with her mama and her uncle, Victor, I see the homemade chimes hanging right outside her bedroom window. Colorful bits of hand-strung glass and metal. A flash of white-blonde hair lets me know that Evie has been watching me from behind her pale blue curtains.

Watching us.

And it makes me sad for her.

If our little Evie has a crush on Hart, she's really barking up the wrong tree. In that way, Hart is the most solitary person I've ever known. He's never dated anyone, and no matter how hard I try, I can't imagine him ever falling for a girl.

Not shy, nervous Evie.

And definitely not me.

I turn and run. I run like I have someplace to run to. Even though I don't. I run like there's somewhere to go. Even though I know there isn't.

5

Inside the Mystic Rose, Honey is showing two girls not much older than me a collection of carnelian stones that are supposed to enhance sensuality and boost passion.

"Now, this little beauty," she says, holding up the darkest red one, "this one is guaranteed to get a fire going." She winks at the taller of the two. "If you know what I mean."

The girls are giggling quietly, heads close together as they examine the stones and make their selections. They communicate in the secret language of best friends. Nudges and raised eyebrows. Embarrassed smiles half-hidden behind hands. And watching them is like peeling off a scab.

I head back to my tiny bedroom off the kitchen and find Sweet-N-Low, Honey's ancient wiener dog, asleep on my bed. I lie down next to him and scratch his belly. He's deaf in one ear, mostly bald, and noxiously gassy. Honey says he reminds her of her third husband, Eldon – one of the dead but not entirely departed.

I look around the familiar room – everything just where

I left it last August – but my eyes keep wandering back to a framed photograph that sits on my bedside table. Elora and me at our tenth birthday party. We're holding hands, both of us sunburned and happy, leaning over a pink-frosted sheet cake. Cheeks puffed out and eyes closed tight. Caught in the very moment of making a wish.

Our birthday is just a few weeks away, and the idea of turning seventeen alone settles on my chest with a suffocating weight. I close my eyes and find the little blue pearl hanging around my neck, then I try with everything I have to pull up one of those images of Elora. One of those terrifying flashes. Maybe if I can conjure up some clue –

But there's nothing. At least at first.

And then it's there. Just for a split second.

Elora is running –

    I'm running –

        for my life.

Rain.

And howling wind.

Moonlight on dark hair.

My stomach lurches and I feel sick. I'm sure I'm going to throw up.

I suck in a breath and open my eyes, and Honey is standing in the doorway watching me. She comes to sit on the edge of my bed and smooth my hair.

"Not everyone is born into their gifts," she tells me. "Some people have to develop them over time."

"Just a dream," I lie. "I fell asleep for a second. That's all."

But Honey doesn't give up. "Your mother was still coming into herself . . . into her abilities . . . when she crossed over. And she was a lot older than you are."

My mother killed herself. But Honey never says it like that.

I was eight years old when she did it, and after, I remember asking Honey if she could talk to my mother for me. If she could ask her why. But Honey says the dead are picky about who they talk to. They get to choose who they communicate with, if they choose to communicate at all. And my mother has never reached out to Honey from the other side.

She's never reached out to me, either.

Since my mother died – or crossed over or whatever – I've spent the school years up in Arkansas with my dad and the summers down here with Honey.

That's one of the things Elora and I went round and round about last summer. She couldn't wait to turn eighteen and get the hell out of here. And I couldn't wait to turn eighteen and finally come home. Full-time. I imagined myself helping out in the shop, then running it on my own. Someday.

Honey is still watching me. She tucks a piece of hair behind my ear, and I somehow find the courage to ask the question I couldn't ask her earlier.

"Has she reached out to you?" I hear the fear in my voice. "Elora's ghost? Or spirit or whatever?"

Honey chuckles a little. "Oh, goodness, no, Sugar Bee. Why would Elora want to talk to an old lady like me?" Then her voice turns serious. "Besides, if Elora has crossed over, she may not have the energy to reach out to anyone yet. Sometimes it takes a while for spirits to gather themselves. And even then, they may only have the strength to communicate with one person, so they have to be choosy about which channels they open up." Honey is quiet for a moment before she goes on. "It would make much more sense for Elora to contact someone she was close to in life. Someone she already had a deep connection with."

I know she's talking about me, but I'm not ready to share those strange flashes with Honey yet.

"Did you know Mackey had a death warning?" I ask. "About Elora? The night she disappeared?" I shiver a little in the air-conditioning. "Death in the water."

Honey sighs and pulls the blanket over me. "I heard about that," she admits. "But a death warning is just that. It's a warning. That's all. It means death is close by. But it's not a sure thing. Not always."

I remember an old story about Mackey's uncle knocking on the front door one morning to give Honey's first husband, my grandfather, a death warning that had come to him over breakfast. Death from below, he'd told them. And sure enough, my grandfather had been bitten by a huge water moccasin that very afternoon while he was out hunting. He nearly died that night. But come morning, he was still hanging on. He ended up losing his big toe, but he didn't lose his life. Not until a heart attack took him a couple years later. And nobody had warned him about that.

Honey's hand is still in my hair. It's making me so sleepy. I can hardly keep my eyes open, and an old nightmare comes creeping in around the edges of my consciousness.

"Do you remember anything about Dempsey Fontenot?"

Honey tucks the blanket around my shoulders. "Well, I never knew much about him, to tell you the truth. He lived way out there all alone. Kept to himself, mostly." She pauses, like she's trying to choose her words. Being careful. "He had some odd ways. There were stories . . ." She stops and smooths my hair again. "I don't guess folks cared much for him, even before what happened."

"Do you think he got Elora?" The words come out thick and sleep-coated. Heavy in my mouth. "Like he got Ember and Orli?"

"No. I don't think so," Honey says, and for a long while, there's only the hum of the air conditioner in the window and the soft sound of Sweet-N-Low snoring beside me. By the time she adds the next part, I'm almost too far gone to hear it. "I don't imagine poor Dempsey Fontenot ever got anybody."

He hauls me up by my arm – like I'm a catfish
he's pulling out of a pond – and I come roaring
back to myself. I fight against him. I kick and I
claw and I bite. I spit rain and mud and curse
words. But he's too strong, and there's not enough
life left in me. I'm choking. Fighting to breathe.
Out of the water but still drowning.

6

When I wake up, the light coming in the windows is different. I've slept the whole afternoon. Which means I've missed lunch. And I'm starving.

I hear Honey humming to herself in the kitchen while she makes dinner. "Crazy" by Patsy Cline. She promises it won't be long, so I head out front to the steps to wait.

Five thirty. The shuttle boat is blowing its horn for the final upriver trip of the day. The last of the tourists are heading back to Kinter, where they'll climb into their cars and drive north to New Orleans for a night out on Bourbon Street.

At the river dock, right across from the bookstore, Sera and Sander are helping their mama pack her little bottles and charms into boxes. They finish loading everything into their boat, and Delphine wanders over to chat with one of the fishermen who's just come back in for the day.

I wave to Sera and Sander, and they exchange one of those looks they have. Then Sera digs something out of her backpack, and they start in my direction. As soon as I see the artist's sketchbook tucked under Sera's arm, something that tastes like dread tickles at the back of my throat.

Sera and Sander are psychic artists. The dead communicate with them, like they do Honey. Only it's different. The twins draw things. People. Places. Objects. Images that come into their heads out of nowhere.

A lot of weekends they sit out there on the dock with their mama, and for twenty bucks they'll sketch the exact place your lost wedding ring is hiding, or a perfect spitting-image likeness of your dead son or your grandmother – people Sera and Sander have never even laid eyes on. I've seen folks clutch those drawings to their chests and sob. And when that happens, they always tip extra.

"We have something to show you," Sera says, and the two of them join me on the steps. Sander does his best to give me a reassuring smile. "We didn't say anything earlier because we haven't told Hart yet. Or any of the others."

"Okay," I say, even though I don't like the idea of keeping secrets. Especially from Hart.

Sera flips open the sketchbook, and I stare at the shape drawn in charcoal. "You recognize it?" she asks, and I nod.

"It's the big black trunk from Honey's shed."

I haven't seen it in years.

When we were little, we used to play magician. Hart would be the magic man, and Elora his beautiful assistant. The others would be our captive audience. And I'd be the one to climb inside the trunk, trying not to breathe while Elora covered me with a blanket to make me disappear.

Eventually, it was the trunk that disappeared, though, pushed into a back corner of the storage shed and covered over with a decade's worth of junk and spiderwebs.

And now Elora's disappeared.

And the trunk's come back into my life. Almost like magic.

"I'm not sure what it means," Sera says. "I've been trying to figure that out since I drew it. But I know it has something to do with Elora."

"It could mean she ran away," I say, and I feel a little hope surge through me. "Packed up and left." I look up at Sera. "Right?"

Sera and Sander exchange another look. "Maybe," Sera says. "But we don't know that for sure."

"Why haven't you shown this to Hart?" I ask.

"Grey, you don't know how low Hart's been." Sera gives her head a little shake, and that braid swings behind her back. "He feels responsible, I think. Like he should've been lookin' out for Elora. That night." Sander nods in agreement. "We didn't want to get him all worked up when –"

"When you can't say what it means."

"Yeah."

"Can I keep this?" I ask.

"Sure," Sera says, and she rips the page out and hands it to me. "There's more, though." She passes the sketchbook over to Sander, and he flips through until he finds what he's looking for. Then he places the open book in my lap. "Sander did that one."

I shiver when I see the bold pencil lines. Like someone walking over my grave, Elora would have said.

"This one is about Elora, too?" Sander nods and runs his fingers over the sketch.

The page is filled with a figure. The shape is human. Arms and legs. Normal enough. All except the face. That's not normal at all. Because where the mouth and the eyes and the nose should be, there's nothing. No features. And the more I stare at that emptiness, the more it scares me.

I flip the notebook closed.

"We don't know what that one means, either," Sera says, and she shoots another look at her brother. "But Manman thinks she does."

"What does she say?" I hand the sketchbook back to Sera. I don't want to hold it any more.

"*Étranger,*" Sera tells me. "A stranger. Someone we don't know."

Fifty or so people live in the little houses that dot the boardwalk. That many again, roughly, out in the swamps nearby.

And I know every single one by sight. By name, too. And they all know me. There are no strangers here.

Not in La Cachette.

Delphine yells something in our direction. A Creole word. And the twins stand up. So I stand up, too. "We have to go," Sera says.

"Thanks for sharing these with me," I tell them.

Sera studies me for a second, then she asks, "You really don't feel her at all?" The question throws me for a loop. I'm not ready to tell them about those flashes I've been having, so

I shake my head. The twins stare at me with two identical sets of amber-colored eyes.

"Your mama had deep power," Sera starts. "Manman says –"

Delphine yells at them again. "*Asteur!*" And that word I know. It means *now*.

Sera yells back that they're coming, then Sander hugs me goodbye and Sera leans close to whisper in my ear. "There's bound to be some magic in you, Grey. You need to know that."

Then the two of them hurry across to the dock and into the boat. That leaves me staring at the drawing in my hand and wondering what Sera meant. About my mother.

And about me.

Honey calls me in for dinner, so I fold up the sketch and slip it into my back pocket. She's made my favorite. Fried catfish with dirty rice. Homemade pralines for dessert. Sweet-N-Low sits between our chairs, drooling in a puddle and hoping someone will drop something. And it all tastes like heaven, but I can't enjoy the feast. Because I keep thinking about that big black trunk.

As soon as I help Honey clear the plates, I make an excuse to get away. It's starting to get dark when I slip out the kitchen door and follow the short bit of boardwalk that leads to the little storage shed out back. It's low tide, and I can smell the sickly sweet odor of exposed mud and rot.

The door to the shed is never locked – none of the doors in La Cachette are ever locked – so it opens right up when I turn the knob. There's a bare light bulb in the ceiling, but when I pull the string, nothing happens. It must be burned out.

I should've grabbed a flashlight. The sun isn't all the way down yet, but there are no windows in the shed, so that just leaves the last of the grey light coming in the open door to see by.

I push my way through the junk and the cobwebs toward the back of the shed. The light is fading fast, and I can barely make out the writing on the cardboard boxes stacked shoulder high.

CHRISTMAS DECORATIONS

CAMPING GEAR

OUIJA BOARDS

You know. The kind of stuff everybody keeps in storage.

I move the boxes one by one until I can see behind them, to the spot where the trunk should be. And I'm not surprised when it isn't there.

"You huntin' somethin'?" A deep voice echoes in the almost-dark just as a shape moves into the open doorway, blocking out the dying light.

I whirl around fast, knocking over one of the boxes and sending Christmas ornaments spilling across the dusty floor.

The shape in the doorway is huge and silhouetted against that little bit of light from outside, so I can't make out any facial features. There's just an empty nothingness.

Étranger. The stranger.

I take a step backward, pressing myself into the boxes behind me. Then there's a flash of light. The smell of sulfur. A glimpse of dark red hair.

Case holds the lit match up near his face, and the featureless monster disappears.

He takes a step toward me, and that's when I notice what he's holding in one hand. It's a long pole with four barbed prongs on the end. Sharp. Deadly. A frog gig. They're illegal, but some people down here still use them for hunting in the shallows.

"Heard you was home," he says. Then he looks around the shed and repeats his question. "Lookin' for somethin'?" His eyes sweep the floor, searching the shadowy corners.

"No," I lie. "Just putting something away. For Honey." I bend down and scoop up the scattered ornaments. I don't know why my hands are shaking.

Case is my friend.

The match goes out, and we're left in the dark again.

"Case," I say, and I try to make my voice sound even. Calm. But he doesn't let me finish.

"I didn't do it, Grey. Whatever dey told you I done – whatever Hart said – I never laid a goddamn hand on Elora." There's something hurt in his voice. Something real. Something that reminds me I've known Case my whole life. "Shit. I know ya know dat." I hear his Cajun accent bleeding through. Rough as he can be, Case always sounds like music when he talks. There's a long pause, then, "Jesus, Grey. I loved 'er."

"She loved you, too."

Dammit.

I correct myself. "She loves you, too."

"Bullshit." Case shakes his head and leans against the doorframe. "Don't play dat game, Grey."

"What do you mean?"

He laughs, but it's the kind of laugh that's splintered around the edges. Like a thing that's been dropped. Or stepped on. "Elora was in love, yeah, but it sure as shit wadn't wit' me."

"Who?" It's the only word I can choke out.

Case strikes another match, and for a second I see his eyes. They're green, like mine, but in the match's orange light, they glow hard and bright like the night shine of some nocturnal animal.

"No clue," he says. "I figured if anybody was to know, it'd most likely be you."

But I don't have any idea, and right now, the fact that Elora might finally have been in love – really in love – and I didn't know anything about it is just one more deep wound.

"How do you know there was somebody else?" I ask, and Case laughs again. Then he turns his head to spit behind him into the mud.

"Didn't take a fuckin' psychic to see it. Trust me."

Suddenly I'm thinking back to last summer. How Elora started pushing me away, almost as soon as I got here. I was suffocating her, she said. She needed some space. Time alone. Things she'd never wanted before. At least, not from me. And I'd been angry. Hurt and ugly. So I'd latched on harder – refused to give her what she needed – instead of taking the time to figure out what might really be going on with her.

What if she'd been hiding a secret romance?

"I don't know anything," I tell Case. He blows out the last match, and darkness sweeps over his face again. "I need to get back inside. Honey's waiting for me."

Case steps out of the doorway, and I move to squeeze past

him. But just as I'm about to step out on to the boardwalk, he grabs me by the arm and jerks me back. Hard. He moves like lightning, raising the frog gig and bringing it down with a stabbing motion in front of my feet. I gasp and try to pull away, but when Case lifts the gig, there's just enough light to see a thick black snake squirming on the end of it.

"Whoa dere," he says. "That's a cottonmouth, sure." And I recoil like I've been bitten. "Gotta be careful pokin' round out here in da dark." His voice is thick and slow as bayou mud. "Dat sucka nearly got ya." Case shakes the dying snake off the gig into the long grass beside the boardwalk. "Careful where ya steppin', chere."

Chere. Pronounced like *sha.* It's a Cajun word. A term of endearment. Like darlin'. Sweetie. Sugar pie. Nobody ever calls me "chere" in Arkansas. Only in La Cachette, and usually it makes me smile.

But not tonight.

"T-thanks," I stammer. My heart is beating ninety miles an hour. I look back down at the boardwalk, and I can make out a trail of ooze and mud standing out against the fresh white paint. Marking the places where the snake has touched.

When I look back up, Case has vanished into the dark. Silently. Like he came.

I follow the boardwalk around the side of the house to sit on the front steps again. I can't stop shaking, and I don't want Honey to see me like this.

Across from me, on the dock, I catch another glimpse of dark red hair. Seems like Case didn't go far. Now I'm more angry than scared. What gives him the right to come skulking around here trying to freak me out? It's an asshole move.

"I know you're over there," I call out. The safety of the well-lit front steps is making me brave. "You planning on staying out here all night?"

Nobody calls back, but someone steps out from the shadows and into the light.

Dark red hair. But not Case.

It's Wrynn, Case's little sister.

Wrynn is nine, but she seems way younger. Scrawny and bug-eyed, she always looks startled. Like life has taken her by surprise.

"*Comment ça va*, Grey?" she says. *How's it going?* A question that doesn't need answering. She gives me a little wave with one hand. I wave back, and she hurries over to sit beside me on the steps. Like I invited her for tea.

Wrynn's barefoot. She has on cutoff shorts and a ratty old camouflage T-shirt, probably a hand-me-down from one of her brothers. Her hair spills across her shoulders and down her back.

"I was catchin' lightnin' bugs," she tells me, and she holds up a glowing jelly jar.

"Be careful running around out here without shoes on," I warn her. "Case killed a cottonmouth out behind the house just now."

Wrynn gives me a funny little smile.

"Case is out with Daddy. Huntin' frogs with Ronnie and Odin way over at Lapman Pond. Won't be back till mornin.'"

The fear I felt in the shed pricks at me again, and goose bumps pop up on the backs of my arms.

Case's gift is bilocation. The ability to physically exist in two places at once. The ancient Greeks talked about it. And some of the Catholic saints were supposed to have been able to do it, too. It's documented and everything.

Here in La Cachette, everybody knows that Case can do it. His grand-père – his daddy's daddy – had the very same talent, they say. Elora used to swear she'd experienced it firsthand. She'd know for sure Case was at home asleep, but then she'd come sneaking out of a late-night party up in Kinter – always with some boy – and there'd be Case. Standing in the driveway. Pissed as the devil and real as anything.

It's enough to make my head spin.

"Grey?" Wrynn's voice is small and sad.

"Yeah?"

"You miss Elora?"

"Of course," I tell her. "I miss her a whole lot."

"Me too." The words come out in a rush, like she'd been waiting for permission to breathe them out to someone.

Wrynn is the only sister in a house crammed absolutely full of boys. She's been Elora's shadow since she was old enough to walk. And Elora has always been so good to Wrynn, paying attention to her and helping her with her hair and playing pretend with her when nobody else could be bothered. Wrynn has a wild imagination, and she always has some game going. Dragons and wizards and princesses.

"Wanna hear a secret?" she asks me, and I nod.

Wrynn leans close to whisper in my ear. She smells like grape soda. I feel her breath on my cheek, and her long red hair brushes my shoulder.

"Everybody wishes dey knew what happened to 'er." Something shifts in Wrynn's voice, and she doesn't sound sad any more. She sounds afraid. Her words are hushed and breathless. "But dey don't wanna know. Not really." She pulls into herself and shudders.

Wrynn's bottom lip quivers, and she sucks it into her mouth and works at it with her crooked baby teeth. She's chewing so hard I'm afraid she'll draw blood. When I put my arm around her, I feel her bones rattling. I'm surprised I can't hear the sound of her pointy little shoulder blades knocking together, right through her skin.

Wrynn isn't afraid. She's scared about to death.

From over at Evie's house, the sound of wind chimes moves through the night air. Twice as loud as it was earlier.

Insistent.

"Do you have a guess, Wrynn?" I ask her. "About what might have happened to Elora?"

Wrynn looks at me and nods. "Only it ain't a guess." Her eyes are dead serious. "I waited one hundred and one days, so I can tell da secret now." Something skitters in the back of my mind, like a spider. Some bit of a story I've almost forgotten.

"What happened to Elora, Wrynn?"

She buries her face against my side. "It got 'er, Grey."

"What got her?"

"Da rougarou."

I remember the legend then. The Cajun werewolf. We used to scare each other silly with stories about a snarling wolflike creature that prowled the fog-covered swamplands on two legs. Hart used to tell us that if we left our windows open on full moon nights, the rougarou would come slinking in and rip us to pieces, right in our own beds. Then he'd eat us up. Bones and all. Nothing but blood-soaked sheets for someone to find come morning.

"That's not real, Wrynn," I reassure her. "There's no such thing as the rougarou. It's made up."

"It ain't made up," she whispers. "It's da truth. Cross my heart."

"Wrynn –"

"You gotta listen to me. I saw it, Grey. I saw it dat night." She grabs my arm, and her sharp little fingernails dig into my skin. Like claws. "I saw it wit' my own eyes."

"Saw what?" I ask. Wrynn's face is pale as death in the porch light. "What did you see that night?"

Her answer is whispered right into my ear, warm and close, so there's no mistaking the words.

"I saw da rougarou kill Elora."

Teeth. Nothing but teeth. Teeth piercing skin.
Then muscle. Then bone.

7

Everybody down here knows the story. If you're unlucky enough to see the rougarou, you have to keep that secret for one hundred and one days. If you don't, you'll become the monster yourself. So I guess Wrynn's been counting down the days.

One hundred and one since Elora disappeared.

One hundred and one days since Wrynn saw whatever she saw. Or whatever she thought she saw. Whatever she imagined.

I push that flash aside – the teeth – and tell Wrynn that she can't be right. That there is no rougarou. That those stories are no more real than her tales of unicorns and fairies. She looks at me like I've let her down, but she doesn't say anything else. She just takes that jelly jar full of lightning bugs and heads off in the direction of her house, moving barefoot through the tall swamp grass. Silent as an apparition.

Case and Wrynn's people don't live on the boardwalk. Their house sits up on a narrow strip of high ground, back toward

Li'l Pass. Their mama, Ophelia, is the best cook for at least a hundred miles. They're pure Cajun, through and through. Real Acadians.

I don't have a drop of Cajun blood, but I always loved having supper with Case and his family. Étouffée and jambalaya. Homemade pistolette rolls. Giant cast-iron kettles of bubbling gumbo. Enough to feed everyone in La Cachette twice over. After we stuffed ourselves silly, we'd all move out to the front porch and his daddy would play the fiddle or the harmonica and all the boys would sing. Even Case.

Joie de vivre.

The joy of life.

Good food and good music. Good times. Good people.

I feel ashamed for being afraid of Case. Hart is wrong about him. He has to be. Because Case is one of us. One of the Summer Children.

Inside the house, I pull Sera's folded drawing out of my pocket and tuck it into the bottom of my underwear drawer. It's a cliché, but I'm too tired to think of a better hiding spot. I barely manage to brush my teeth and pull on a clean T-shirt before I crawl under the covers.

My first night home.

Honey comes to sit on the edge of my bed again. She scratches my back and hums me a song. It's a ritual that's been ours ever since I was born, I guess.

"Good night. Sleep tight. Don't let the mosquitoes bite," she tells me. "Love you, Sugar Bee."

"Love you," I answer, and Honey kisses me on the forehead

before she flips off the light and heads upstairs to bed, closing my door behind her.

But sleep plays hide-and-seek with me, the way Elora used to. No matter how hard I try, I can't find any way to rest. Maybe it's those wind chimes of Evie's keeping me awake. I hear them outside, singing in the dark.

Or maybe it's more than that.

Maybe it's the constant ache of the Elora-shaped hole somewhere in the middle of me. Memories of long summer nights spent wishing on stars in her backyard. Or singing along to the radio in Honey's kitchen while we churned homemade ice cream.

Or it could be all my questions that won't let me drift off into oblivion.

I keep thinking about that trunk that isn't there.

And Sander's drawing. The stranger without a face.

It's almost two o'clock in the morning when I give up and crawl out from under the covers. I pull on a pair of shorts and tiptoe through the shop. Sweet-N-Low comes waddling out to investigate, but when he sees it's me, he loses interest and heads back to bed. Then I open the front door nice and slow, so the little bell doesn't jingle, and slip out on to the front porch.

As soon as my feet hit the slick dampness of the painted boards, I realize I haven't bothered to put on shoes. And I think of that water moccasin Case killed earlier.

Careful where ya steppin', chere.

I take a good look around before I sit down on the front steps to stare out toward the water.

Nobody would call the lower Mississippi a beautiful river, but it looks prettier at night than it does in the harsh light of day. And the constant movement of it has always soothed me. I can't see much of it tonight, though. The fog is too thick.

The night is alive with the sound of wind chimes. When I look next door, I see that there are two of them now, hanging right outside Evie's bedroom window. I don't know how she sleeps with all that ringing and clinking.

I've only been out there a few minutes when I hear something else, too. The soft sound of someone crying. I freeze and squint into the darkness, in the direction of the dock. And there it is again. Muffled sobbing wrapped in a blanket of mist. The thick, damp air plays tricks, distorting the sound. It seems to come from nowhere in particular. And from everywhere all at once.

Then it stops.

I hold my breath until it comes again. And this time, there's something familiar about it. I stand up and take a few steps out on to the boardwalk, and I'm instantly walled in by the suffocating fog.

I turn in a slow circle. "Elora?" I whisper.

The crying stops. A little gasp.

"Elora?" I whisper again. A long sniffle. But no more crying. "Is that you, Elora? It's Grey."

And then a voice, like a bony hand reaching through the dark.

"Grey?"

My heart leaps into my throat, and my eyes find something

in the darkness. The ghostly glow of a floating orb. *Fifolet*, my brain whispers. But then I see it for what it is, and I move toward the shine of the lamppost out on the dock. There's another long sniffle, and I follow the sound around to the back side of a stack of wooden crates. And there she is. Wet and shivering and staring up at me with unblinking eyes.

Only it isn't Elora at all.

White-blonde hair glistening with fog. Pale blue eyes.

"Evie?"

She covers her face with her hands. Doesn't answer.

I kneel down beside her. Rough boards against my bare skin. "Are you okay?" Still no response. "Are you hurt?"

Her teeth are chattering. Chin quivering. "No," is all she says, and I can't be sure which question she's answering.

"What's wrong, Evie?" I wrap my arms around her, but she pushes me away. "What are you doing out here?"

Her face is frozen, like she's slipped on a mask.

An Evie mask.

"Evie," I try again. "Tell me what's going on."

She scrambles to her feet and backs away from me.

"I'm fine, Grey. I promise. Just leave me alone." Her voice is desperate. "Please."

Evie can trace her lineage all the way back to the Casket Girls, the first French women sent here to help populate the fledgling city of New Orleans. They arrived half-starved – filthy, sick, and deathly pale – and they stepped off the ship carrying casket-shaped chests that held their few belongings. The men on the docks were shocked at the ghastly sight of them. "*Filles à la cassette,*" they whispered. They thought they were vampires.

Now, standing here in the dark and the fog three hundred years later, smelling the damp of the river and looking at Evie – pale and tear-streaked and glassy-eyed – it's easy to understand why the men were frightened.

"Evangeline?" Evie's mama is calling to her from their front porch. Bernadette's voice is hushed. Nervous. "You out there, Evie girl?"

"Evie," I try again. "If something's wrong, let me help you."

Another voice cuts through the dark. Louder. This one is steeped in alcohol, soaked with irritation. "Evie! Get your ass in here, girl!" It's her uncle, Victor. Her mama's brother. "We ain't got time for your shit tonight!"

"You know what's awful, Grey?" Evie wipes at her face, then she wraps her skinny arms around her chest and shivers hard. "The dead? They lie. Just like the rest of us."

Then she's gone, absorbed into the dark edges of the night. And I'm left alone and confused.

I should go inside. But I don't. Instead, I walk all the way up to the edge of the dock. I close my eyes and stand above the dark, rolling surface of the great, wide river.

Elora is a water witch. She feels the magnetic pull of water in her bones. Lots of times that magic pulls her right back here. To this very spot. To the edge of the dock. To stand above the Mighty Mississippi, arms spread wide, and let its unstoppable life force seep into her soul.

There have been so many summer nights when I've woken up long after midnight, for no reason I could ever lay a finger on, and felt myself drawn out on to the front porch. And Elora would be here. Right at the edge of the water. Silver moonlight on long, dark hair. She'd feel me close. Just like I'd felt her, even in my sleep. She'd turn and smile at me, and I'd hurry down to meet her, still in my nightclothes, so we could sit on the dock, pressed close together, and feel the river's power – Elora's power – move through both of us.

Those are the nights I felt the most magical.

The least grey.

The sound of Evie's wind chimes carries through the fog and echoes off the river. It bounces between my ears. After a few minutes, I can't hear the lap of the water against the dock any more. Or even the frogs and the bugs. All I hear are those tinkling chimes.

And Elora's musical laugh.

I open my eyes and try to see the other side of the river. But I can't. It's too wide and too dark. The water goes on forever.

I have this idea that if I could just turn my head fast enough, Elora would be standing right there. I feel her so strong. Just beside me. I don't turn my head, though. Because I don't want to be wrong.

Then there's a sharp splintering sound. Suddenly, I'm falling.

The board I'm standing on gives way beneath my feet. I feel it crumble like it's happening in slow motion. I lose my footing and pitch backward, clawing at the air with my hands as my feet go out from under me. But there's nothing to grab on to. I go down hard, and it's a relief when my hip meets the solid wood of the dock with a sharp and painful crack. One leg is dangling over the deep, fast-moving water, and one arm is twisted behind me at an awkward angle. I scramble back and hug my knees to my chest. My heart must be close to exploding. I hear it thumping in my ears. Louder than Evie's damn wind chimes, even.

Right where I was standing seconds ago, the plank has totally disintegrated, eaten away by rot and termites. When I reach out to touch it, the spongy edge turns to powder under my fingers.

The boards have been rotting away under their coat of pristine white.

I look around. The hair on the back of my neck stands up. This strange feeling comes over me. An odd tingling sensation.

I'm being watched. That's what it feels like.

I tell myself I'm being ridiculous, but I stand up and move away from the black wood and the black water, back toward the safety of the boardwalk. Honey's front porch light. Then I turn and head inside. And I lock the door behind me.

All I want is sleep. But when I crawl back into bed, it's still no use.

I keep feeling that falling sensation.

And I'm trying not to look at the framed photograph on the table. Trying not to touch the little pearl around my neck.

Trying not to think about Elora.

Eventually, I get up again. Four a.m. Maybe this time it's the tender bruise forming on my hip that won't let me rest, but it's the relentless whispering of those wind chimes that calls me to the window. The fog has drifted off, and the moon is out. A full moon, or close to it.

A rougarou moon.

I sweep my eyes across the landscape, scanning the emptiness of the bayou behind the house. Nothing but flat and wet all the way back to Li'l Pass.

Then I see it. And I stop breathing.

A shape blending into the dark.

Someone is out there.

Motionless.

Watching me.

Étranger. A stranger.

He couldn't be more than fifteen feet away. Only the thin glass of the windowpane and that little bit of night separating the two of us.

The figure looms tall and mysterious. But all I really see are his eyes. They glow with a kind of icy blue fire.

We stare at each other for a long minute. Both of us caught. Still as stones. And I feel half hypnotized. Then whoever is out there turns and melts into the blackness. He moves with the lithe-limbed grace of a night animal.

And I'm alone again.

My whole body is shaking. I slide down to huddle against the wall underneath my window. And I wait for the lonesome howl of a wolf. But all I hear is my own breathing.

And the nervous murmur of wind chimes.

I swallow the panic along with the rain and keep running. Blind. Arms stretched out in front of me. Hoping not to feel anything. Hoping if I do feel something, it won't be him. Not him. Not him. Please don't let it be him.

8

I spend the next few hours on the floor. Frozen. When daylight comes, I drag myself to bed. My body gives in and sleep finally finds me. It's close to noon when I wake up. Despite that little jingling bell, I've slept right through the first wave of Sunday-morning tourists in and out of the Mystic Rose.

With bright sunshine streaming in the window and the chatter of customers floating back from the bookstore up front, everything that happened last night seems far away. Like maybe it was a dream. Or a nightmare.

But I know those eyes were real. There was someone outside my window last night.

Étranger.

A stranger.

Even with the sunshine and the chatter, that memory chills me all the way down to my bones. It gives me what people down here call the frissons.

In the kitchen, Honey's left a plate of homemade biscuits on the table for me. But just as I pick one up, that flash of Elora hits me hard. I feel her panic.

She's running.

I'm running.

Blind. Through the rain. Outstretched arms.

I grab the back of a chair to steady myself until the terror passes, then I offer my biscuit to Sweet-N-Low, and he rewards me with a kiss.

My mouth is bone dry, so I open the cabinet to reach for a glass. But I get distracted by a big picture frame that's hung on the wall as long as I can remember. It's the kind with all the little slots for different-sized photos. I've seen it a million times, but I've never really looked at it.

It's the picture in the center that I'm staring at now. I'm sitting on my mother's lap on the front steps of the Mystic Rose. The photo must have been taken not long after Ember and Orli were killed, because I'm wearing a watermelon-pink sundress that Honey made for my birthday that year. I guess I was wild about that dress, because I have it on in almost all the snapshots taken that fourth summer of our lives.

My mother's long chestnut hair is pinned back with one delicate hummingbird hair clip. Silver with beautiful painted eyes. There were two of them, originally. She wore them all the time. And I loved them because they were a set. Like Elora and me. But one of them got lost at some point. Before this picture was taken, I guess. I still have the one she's wearing in the photo, though. It's tucked away in my bedroom, but I never wear it.

I let my gaze linger on my mother's face. I've always thought our green eyes were identical. A little too big. A little too round. Hart used to say I reminded him of a tree frog.

But our eyes don't look the same in this picture.

Mine look innocent. My mother's look haunted. Hollow, maybe. Like there's nobody left inside.

I think about what Sera said yesterday. *Your mama had deep power.*

If that's true, it's the first I've heard about it. Of course, there are a lot of things I've never known about my mother. Starting with why she took her own life when I was only eight years old.

I can't stand to be in the kitchen with those haunted eyes, so I head out into the shop.

Honey is busy arranging tiny bottles of essential oils on a silver tray. BUY ONE, GET ONE FREE. Her face wrinkles up in concern when she sees the dark circles under my eyes. "Long night, Sugar Bee?"

I nod and crawl up on the tall stool behind the register. "It's hard being here without her, that's all."

It's not like I made a conscious decision not to tell her about my late-night visitor. Or about what happened before that. Evie crying in the night. My near-death experience on the dock. I hadn't even realized I was going to lie – at least by omission – until I did it. But once the decision is made, I don't know how to undo it. I've been home twenty-four hours, and I'm already juggling secrets like knives.

Honey nods. "Anything we lose comes around in another

form," she reminds me. "But that doesn't mean we don't grieve."

I still want to believe Elora's alive somewhere, but with every one of those terrifying flashes, that hope gets harder and harder to hang on to. It's like trying to hold an ice cube while it melts and drips between my fingers.

"Do you think she's dead?"

Honey stops rearranging bottles to look at me. "Are you asking me what I think? Or what I know?"

"The second one, I guess."

Honey sighs. "I wish I could tell you for sure, Grey. But it doesn't work like that. If it did, we'd all be lottery winners, wouldn't we?" She squeezes the last delicate bottle on to the tray. "It isn't like placing an order at a restaurant or picking something out of a catalog. I tried to explain that to the sheriff. The dead tell us what they want us to know. Not what we want to know for ourselves."

"I miss her," I say, because it seems like the only thing I can say for certain.

"Oh, Sugar Bee," Honey says, and she lays her hand on my cheek. "I know you do. And I wish I had the answers you need. It's so hard when someone goes away and leaves a hole."

I don't mean to ask the next question. It just falls out of my mouth.

"Did my mom love me?"

Honey turns back to the tiny bottles. She picks up an orange one and holds it up close to squint at the label. "You were her whole world, but there were things that were hard for her to live with." She puts the little bottle back in its place. "Things that ate away at her until there wasn't much left. Especially the last few years."

Before I can ask what things she's talking about, the bell over the door jingles and the next group of tourists comes in to poke around. We offer them water and sandwiches and books on astrology. They pay for a thirty-minute reading, and Honey asks me to watch the register before she leads them over to the little alcove in the corner and pulls the privacy curtain.

When the bell jingles again, I look up, ready to say, "Welcome to the Mystic Rose, gentle spirits." Like Honey taught me when I was barely old enough to talk. But it's only Hart.

It makes me a little sick to see him, because I already know I'm not going to tell him about my stranger. Or about those drawings the twins showed me. The missing black trunk.

He wouldn't want me protecting him. He'd be pissed as hell. But I can't stand to cause him any more hurt.

Not until I have an idea what it all means.

Hart saunters up to the counter like I'm an Old West bartender and he's here to order a double shot of whiskey. He rests his elbows on the glass top and runs his fingers through his hair.

"I've been thinking about what you told me." He looks around the store and lowers his voice. "About those visions you've been having of Elora." I have to lean in so I can hear. He smells like chicory coffee and cigarettes. "Her runnin' from somebody."

Our heads are almost touching. His hair brushes my cheek, and it scares me to be this close to him. I'm worried that he'll be able to feel me. The fact that I'm hiding things. Or maybe just the way my fingers occasionally long for those dark curls on his forehead.

"It's gotta be Case," Hart says. His eyes have clouded over. There's a bayou lightning storm building inside him. "That's the only thing that makes sense. Him and that damn jealous temper of his."

I try to fight it off, but that fear I felt in the shed comes slithering back like a cottonmouth. It prickles at the backs of my arms and climbs up my neck to wrap itself tight around my throat.

"He came to see me last night," I admit. "Case. He told me he thought Elora was cheating on him. That she was in love with someone else." Hart jerks his head up and frowns. His face has gone white. "And he wanted me to tell him who."

"See what I'm sayin', Greycie? Now that's a buncha bullshit, right there." Hart clenches his jaw tight and runs another hand through his hair. "But hell, if Case even thought it was true . . . if he got that idea into his head somehow . . . that's more than enough motive for –"

"For murder," I say, and he nods, but I still don't want to believe it. "Can't you feel anything from him? From Case?"

"Shit yeah," Hart tells me. "That's the damn problem. There's too much there. Guilt. Anger. Hurt. Jealousy. Fear." His muscles twitch in frustration. "Take your pick. The guy's a fuckin' mess. I can't wade through it all."

"None of that means he killed her," I offer. "I feel all those things, too. Every single one of them."

"Yeah." Hart's face softens. "I know you do, Greycie."

I take a little step back.

And I remind myself that Hart only feels the emotions. He can't know the cause.

"But none of that means he didn't kill her, either." Hart's face hardens up again. "There are things Case is hidin'. I feel that for sure."

I have the urge to put even more space between us. Because there are things I'm hiding, too.

But having secrets doesn't make you a murderer. Besides, whoever that was outside my window last night, it definitely wasn't Case.

"What about a stranger? Someone we don't even know. Maybe –"

"Nah." Hart shakes his head. "It's not like she disappeared from the parkin' lot of a grocery store. What would a stranger be doin' way down here? Way out at Li'l Pass? Late at night like that? It doesn't make sense."

"What about Dempsey Fontenot, then?" I ask. "What he did to Ember and Orli –"

"This doesn't have anything to do with Dempsey Fontenot," Hart says. "I wish you'd never brought him up. You've got yourself seein' ghosts."

"But what if –"

"For Christ's sake. That's ancient history." He bring his hand down hard on the countertop, and all the little bottles rattle. "Let it go, Greycie."

The bell jingles, and a young couple strolls into the store

holding hands. I mumble, "Welcome to the Mystic Rose, gentle spirits," and Hart moves over so he can pretend to look at the candles while I help Ian and Mandy from Lake Charles make their selections. Then I ring up their purchases – some incense, a book on wild herbs of southern Louisiana, and one of those ever-popular red carnelian sex rocks.

Awesome. I hope they get their money's worth.

When they're gone, Hart comes back to the counter and leans in close to me again. He reaches up to touch the little blue pearl on Elora's chain. Rough fingertips graze the skin at the hollow of my neck, and my insides go all liquid.

"Can you get out of here?" he asks under his breath.

"Yeah," I tell him. "Soon as Honey is done with her reading."

He nods. "I'll wait for you out front."

I watch Hart disappear through the door, and I wonder what Elora would say if she were here to see the pathetic way I'm pining after her brother. Sometimes, when I was supposed to be working in the shop, we used to sneak away and hide in the tall grass out behind the storage shed. Elora and me. Bare legs entwined and fingers laced together. We'd eat peppermints stolen from Honey's candy dish while she'd poke fun at my hopelessness when it came to boys. Occasionally I'd try to mimic the cadence of her voice, to see if I could wield that musical charm the way she did. But she'd always say I sounded like a dying goose. And then we'd both laugh until we cried.

Elora could flirt with anyone. It was the same as breathing to her. But I've never had that kind of easy magic.

I've never had any magic at all that wasn't borrowed from her.

When I step outside ten minutes later, Hart is standing on the dock looking at something. I take a second to study him. Long legs. Strong back. Cowboy boots and faded jeans. Tight white T-shirt. Loose black curls. My girls up in Little Rock would eat him with a spoon.

But he's different this summer. Harder, maybe. More unreachable.

He turns around to catch me staring at him, and I hurry across the boardwalk.

"Wonder what happened here." He's pointing at the place where the wood gave way underneath me. Somebody has put up a safety rope to keep people back.

"I almost fell in," I tell him. "It's all rotted."

"Holy shit." His eyes go wide. "You could have been killed. When? What happened?"

"Really late last night. I heard something, so I went to check it out." The whole memory is so surreal. "And the board just –"

"Goddammit." Out of nowhere, Hart wheels on me and wraps his fingers around my upper arms. His voice is low and tight, like a stretched rubber band. "You shouldn't be out here late at night, Grey." There's something in his tone that's half-angry and half-frightened. It reminds me of when I was a kid and Honey caught me playing with matches in the shed.

"You're hurting me," I say, but mostly he's scaring me.

Hart gives me a shake. "You wanna end up like Elora? It's not safe. Not out here. Okay?"

"Yeah." I've never seen Hart like this. I'm caught off guard. "S-sure," I stammer. "Okay."

"I need you to listen to what I'm sayin.'" Hart relaxes his grip on me, but he doesn't let go. "There are things out here in the dark, Greycie." He finally releases me, and I stagger backward a step or two. He's still got ahold of me with his eyes, though. "Dangerous things."

I nod. "I'll be more careful. I promise."

"I can't lose you, too." Hart sits on an old wooden crate, and it's like I'm watching him disintegrate, just like that rotten board. "Please. Greycie." If I touched him, he'd turn to dust.

For the first time in my life, I think Hart's about to cry. But he doesn't. He just stares out at that wide, muddy river. And it's a long time before he says, "She's not coming back. You know that, right?"

"Hart," I beg him, "don't. Please." But he ignores me.

"Somebody killed her. And I think you need to prepare yourself to deal with that. You know? And if it wasn't Case, then I have no fuckin' clue who it could have been."

And there it is.

Out loud.

We sit in silence for a really long time. Minutes creep by in slow motion like river barges. Hart pulls out a cigarette and lights it in one fluid movement, then we watch the little tugs moving up and down the Mississippi. He tips his head back to blow smoke into the air, and it reminds me of the vapor from an old-fashioned steamboat funnel.

"We had a fight," I confess. "A really bad one. That last night. Back in August of last year."

Hart finishes the cigarette and crushes it under the heel of his boot.

"What about?"

I shrug. "Everything. Her wanting to leave. Me wanting to come back. A whole bunch of other stuff." I focus on the cigarette smoke hanging in the still afternoon air. I detach myself and try to drift away like that. "It'd been building all last summer. She was feeling suffocated, I think. By this place. By me." Hart is staring at me now. "And I didn't handle it well."

I can't be your one and only, Grey! God, we're not six years old any more. I need more than that! Shit, maybe you do, too.

"She was sneaking off a lot. Lying to me. Leaving me out of things." I take a deep breath. "That's why I was thinking, maybe Case was right. Maybe there was someone else. Someone secret. Because things weren't the way they'd always been between us." It feels weird to finally say that to someone. I've kept it locked away for so long, afraid that telling would make it true. "She didn't love me the way she used to."

Hart lets out a long puff of air. I see the damp curls lift off his forehead before they settle back against his skin. "She still loved you, Greycie. Whatever was going on between the two of you last summer, Elora loved you more than she loved anybody in the world. I know it for a fact."

A thick silence settles into the space between us, and Hart gets up to leave. But I grab his hand to stop him. "Wrynn told me something last night. It's silly, but –" I feel my face flush. It's so stupid. I shouldn't even have brought it up, but now Hart's staring at me. Waiting. "She said she saw the rougarou kill Elora."

"You don't believe that, do you?"

"Of course not," I tell him. "But –"

"It's Wrynn," he says.

"I know. But she must have seen something. Right?"

"Greycie, Wrynn wasn't even out there that night. She's tellin' you one of her stories." Hart tries to smile, only his eyes don't crinkle up at the edges. "But do me a favor, Shortcake, and stay inside tonight anyway." He turns and heads off down the boardwalk. "Rougarou or no rougarou, I don't want you out here in the dark."

When he's gone, all I can think about is air-conditioning. But Evie is waiting for me on the front steps of the bookstore. I figure she's been watching us again.

Hart and me.

A breeze blows through, and I lift my face to find it. The sound of tinkling wind chimes cuts through the stifling afternoon heat. Now three homemade creations dangle from the overhang of the roof, right outside Evie's bedroom window. The newest one is made from old silverware. Forks and spoons clink against colorful bits of polished river glass.

"Those are really pretty," I tell her. "I bet Honey could sell them for you in the shop." Evie's uncle, Victor, is a shrimper. He has his own boat, but he doesn't make much money, and I know they mostly do without. Like everyone else down here.

"Oh . . ." Evie turns to look at the chimes. "I could never sell them." Her voice is even softer than usual, almost like she's afraid they'll hear. She offers me another half stick of that stale gum, so I take it and sit down beside her.

"Is Hart gonna be okay?" she asks. And there's that new sound in her voice again. Like she takes special care of his name when it's inside her mouth. She's always had this intense hero-worship thing for Hart. Most of us have, honestly. But that naked longing in her words? That's definitely new.

"I don't know," I say. "I really hope so."

"Me too." Evie takes a deep breath, and I feel her relax against me.

"Evie, can't you tell me what was wrong last night? Did anybody hurt you or –"

"Nobody hurt me, Grey. I promise." She slips her soft hand into mine, and I give it a little squeeze. "It was the Flower Moon last night. Did you know that?" Her head is warm and lazy on my shoulder. "That's what you call the full moon in May. And it's magic. The most powerful moon of the year. 'Cause everything's in bloom."

"I didn't know that," I say.

"The Flower Moon means change comes soon. That's a thing my mémé used to tell me."

"Why did you say that last night?" I ask her. "About the dead telling lies?"

Evie pulls at a long thread on her shorts. "Because everybody lies, Grey. Don't they?" Those wind chimes sing out again, relentless as the biting flies. "It's just the dead are harder to ignore."

Honey calls me inside then, and I spend the rest of the afternoon helping her in the bookstore, scheduling appointments and working the register. Mackey stops by to drop off some

French mulberry that his mama harvested, and we drink sweet tea from mason jars while he tells me about some girl up in Kinter that he has a crush on. I smile and tease him, but really, I'm stuck thinking about Evie. What she said about the dead telling lies. And what she was doing out there on the dock last night, crying into the fog.

For dinner, Honey cooks more of my old favorites, and it makes me feel loved.

Comfortable.

Safe.

And I'm grateful for that.

Before I get into bed, I turn off the light and move to the window to search the inky blackness. But there's nothing there. No ice-fire eyes staring at me from the shadows.

No rougarou howling at the moon.

I double-check the window latch before I crawl under the sheets and close my eyes. But when I roll over on my side, I wince, so I sit up and flip on the lamp. Bruises ring my upper arms. Blotchy blue-and-purple fingerprints.

There are things out here in the dark, Greycie.

I turn the lamp back off and lie down again. Evie's wind chimes whisper through the room like a ghost, and I wonder what Hart is so afraid of.

Exactly what kind of monster is hiding out there in the night?

Something grabs my ankle – cold, wet fingers –
and I scream and go down hard. I hit the mud
like it's concrete, and it forces every bit of
air out of my lungs.

Three or four times that night, I jolt awake in a cold sweat, struggling for air, with those disjointed flashes of Elora flickering across my mind like a badly edited movie. I get out of bed and go to the window.

But there's never anything there.

The next day is Monday. Memorial Day. Honey and I close down the bookstore that morning so we can pay our respects at the cemetery up in Kinter. We open up that afternoon, though. And Honey lights extra candles for the dead.

When night falls, Sera comes by to invite me to a bonfire out at their place. We all pile into their airboat with Sander in the driver's seat. Me. Sera and Sander. Mackey. Evie. Hart. It's so close to being right. But none of us can ignore the fact that Elora isn't with us.

Or Case.

The six of us huddle around the fire together, trying to push back the darkness. But it won't be held at bay. Mackey plays his guitar. We sway to the music, but nobody sings along. Hart is moody. He drinks too much. Gets moodier. Sera and I sit on a rough plank bench, with Evie smooshed between us, and watch the flames change color. But I keep looking back over my shoulder, scanning the dark for blazing eyes.

When Evie gets up to go pee, I turn toward Sera. "I'm worried about her," I say. "Evie. Something's going on with her." Sander stops poking at the burning logs to turn around and listen.

Sera nods. Her river-sand-and-copper hair hangs in long, loose waves tonight. Glowing and gorgeous. She's combing it with her fingers. "Evie's been through a lotta shit this year. That's all. She'll be okay."

"We've all been through a lotta shit this year," Mackey says from the other side of the fire.

"I'll drink to that," Sera adds, and she lifts her plastic cup in a toast. Tilts her chin up toward the stars. "This one's for Elora."

We all nod and mumble. "For Elora." Hold up our own cups. On the edge of the circle, Hart lights up a cigarette. Turns his face to the shadows. And I wonder if he's crying.

Later, back at home – before I crawl beneath the quilts – I find myself drawn to my bedroom window again. But the darkness is empty.

No stranger. No blue eyes blinking back at me like ice on fire in the moonshine.

There's nothing the next night, either. Or even the night after that. And before I know it, two weeks have melted away in the swampy heat.

Elora is still missing.

And my hope is fading. The cold lump of dread in my stomach feels heavier every day.

Hart keeps watch.

Case keeps his distance.

And Evie keeps making those pretty wind chimes.

Sera whispers to Sander in Creole – even more than usual – while Mackey does his best to pretend like everything's normal.

And each night, I wait by the window and look for a secret stranger who isn't there.

The Flower Moon wanes. Still no rougarou.

I dream about those wild blue eyes, though, whenever I manage to fall asleep. And even when I'm awake, I can't shake the feeling that someone – or something – is just out of sight. Watching me. Sometimes when I'm outside, I feel it so strong that I turn around quick, sure the stranger will be standing right there. Burning me with those fiery eyes.

But there's only flat, empty bayou stretched out behind me.

I keep having flashes of Elora, too. They come more and more often. Sometimes they hit me out of nowhere and I end up frozen, fighting the wind and water and the mud. The terror. When it passes, I look up to catch Honey studying me.

But I still don't know who Elora's running from. Or how it all ends.

So by the middle of June, I'm no closer to knowing what happened to my twin flame than I was that first morning I stepped off the mail boat.

Elora and I were born on June 16. We're just two days

away from turning seventeen. So far, nobody's mentioned my birthday, though. Our birthday. And that's fine with me. The thought of blowing out candles alone gives me a pain so deep in my chest that I'm sure my lungs have imploded.

It's early evening when Honey sends me out back to the storage shed. She needs an extension cord for the Himalayan salt lamp she wants to show off in the bookstore window.

But when I step outside, the shed door is cracked open and boot prints stain the white paint of the boardwalk. They remind me of the muddy track that cottonmouth left. The one that ended up dead on the end of a frog gig. And it makes me uneasy. Because I know someone's been in the little storage building. Maybe is in there now.

I hold my breath and creep toward the door. When I put one eye to the crack, I see someone crawling around on his hands and knees inside the shed, looking for something on the dusty floor. From my angle, all I can see are jeans and a worn pair of boots. It could be anybody in Plaquemines Parish.

But then then I get a glimpse of dark red hair.

"Fuck." The word comes out in a low growl. Whatever Case is looking for, I guess he didn't find it.

I turn and head back into the kitchen as quickly and quietly as I can. Sweet-N-Low is passed out on his pillow in the corner. Snoring. Some watchdog. Case could be robbing us blind, for all he cares.

I peek through the curtains and keep an eye on the shed. It's only a few minutes before Case comes sneaking out. He eases the door closed behind him, then he hops down from the boardwalk and takes off through the mud in the direction of his house, like somebody lit his feet on fire.

I think about the summer we were all twelve. Case taught Elora and me how to play baseball. I can still see him sidling up behind her with a big grin on his face, arms reaching around her middle to show her how to hold the bat. I'd been so jealous of the easy way she'd flirted, even back then.

Then she popped the very first ball he tossed in her direction. And that's when it hit me.

Bam!

Like the crack of the bat.

Exactly where things were headed between the two of them. I never saw it ending up here, though.

I only wait a minute before I head straight back to the shed. I leave the door wide open, to let in all the light, and I drop down to my hands and knees to feel around on the floor. Like Case was doing. I look in the corners. Under the edges of boxes. But I come up empty-handed, so I grab the extension cord for Honey and pull the door closed behind me.

I drop the extension cord on the kitchen table before I head back out again to pull on my boots. I take the wooden steps down into the wet grass, and I feel the familiar squelch of mud beneath my feet.

I didn't find any answers in the dark corners of Honey's storage shed, but maybe I'll find some in the last place anybody saw Elora.

Back at Li'l Pass.

In between the place where the La Cachette boardwalk rises

out of the muck at the river's edge and the vast wetlands that lie beyond, there's a long, narrow strip of high, solid ground. Lil' Pass runs right behind it. It's not much of a waterway. Way too small and shallow to navigate, even in a kayak. Or a pirogue. We played back there all the time when we were kids. Jumping across the water and chasing each other. I've been avoiding going out there, since I got home this summer. To the place Elora disappeared. Tonight, though, it's almost like the spot is calling to me.

It used to seem like a long way, but now it takes me less than ten minutes to cover the distance. Clumps of skinny trees are scattered across the landscape. Patches of tall grass here and there. A few things people have dumped. An old clothes dryer with the door half off. A molding living room recliner. A flatbed trailer with no wheels.

This is where they were that night.

I look around, and that strange feeling comes over me again. That feeling of being watched. I tell myself I'm being ridiculous. Maybe there never was anyone outside my window. Maybe I imagined my stranger.

The way Wrynn imagined her rougarou.

I crawl up on the old dryer to stand on top and take it all in, like some kind of animal in a documentary about the savanna.

And I don't see a damn thing.

I don't know what I expected. I could get down and comb through the grass. But I still wouldn't turn up anything. Hart said the searchers went over this whole area with a fine-tooth comb. If there'd been a clue here, they would have found it.

"She ain't out here."

"Jesus!" I almost jump right out of my clothes, but it's only Wrynn. "You scared me half to death."

She's wearing shorts. Mud splashed all up her skinny legs. No shoes. And she's eating CheeWees right out of the bag. Her fingers are stained orange from the fake cheese dust.

"You're lookin' in da wrong place," she says.

"I'm not looking for anything," I tell her, sitting down cross-legged on top of the clothes dryer.

"This ain't where it happened." She offers me a CheeWee, but I shake my head. Wrynn shivers hard. "Gives me the frissons, sure, thinkin' about dat ol' rougarou." Her eyes are huge. She takes her thumb and one bright orange finger and rubs at something hanging around her neck. A silver dime with a little hole drilled in it for the string. It's a talisman to ward off evil. Lots of folks down here still hold with the old superstitions.

"Wrynn –" I start.

"You need to be lookin' over dat way." She licks CheeWee dust off her index finger and points. "Not way out here."

I follow Wrynn's finger with my eyes. The boardwalk glimmers bright white, like the sun-bleached ribs of a snake stretched out along the river.

"Elora was on the boardwalk that night?"

"Yep. Dat's where he kilt her at." I see the tiny red hairs standing straight up on her pale arms. "And you best watch out, Grey, or he'll get you, too."

She reaches into the pocket of her shorts and brings out a handful of little objects. "Take 'em," Wrynn tells me, and I hold out my hand. Polished pennies. Pop tops. Bottle caps. Paper clips. It's an odd little collection.

"Scatter 'em on your windowsill," she explains. "For protection. Dat rougarou, he'll have to stop and count 'em, see? Cain't help hisself. And he ain't too bright. Cain't count no higher than twelve, dey say. So every time he comes to thirteen, he gets all confused. Has to start over. He'll stand dere stuck. Countin' all night long. And then when daylight comes up, he'll have to hightail it home."

"Little Bird!" Case's voice makes us both jump. "Time to be gittin' on in." He's standing not five feet away. I wonder how long he's been there. And where he came from. "Dark's comin' on soon."

Wrynn gives me one last look – like she has more she wants to say – but I expect she knows better than to argue with Case, so she turns and takes off toward home.

Case stands there staring at me for a few seconds, then he takes a step in my direction. "You scared of me?" he asks, and I shake my head. Case smirks, then he turns his head to spit into the grass before he starts off after Wrynn in the direction of their house. "You git on inside now, chere," he calls back over one shoulder. "It ain't safe out here come nightfall."

I shove Wrynn's little collection into my pocket. The sun is sinking toward the river, and the mosquitoes are eating me alive. Case isn't wrong. I need to head home.

But suddenly, one of those flashes hits me hard. Elora's fear jams my frequencies, and my brain starts to short-circuit. I close my eyes tight, but that doesn't stop me seeing what she saw.

Or feeling what she felt.

I stumble again when I hit the water, but I don't go down. Li'l Pass isn't so little any more. There's no jumping it now. The water is up to my knees, and I fight the current to stay on my feet.

I see the bounce of his flashlight beam, and I hear him yelling my name again. Over the wind and the rain and the rushing water. And I'm not completely sure if I'm hearing him outside my head. Or inside.

And that's it.

I try to hang on to that little bit of Elora, like reaching for her hand, but she's already gone again.

My eyes fly open, and I suck in air so hard I choke.

Then I freeze.

I feel it. The air has changed. It's electric. It pulses and dances around me.

I'm not alone. Someone is watching me from behind one of those skinny trees. A glint of light-colored hair and a flash of movement. That's all I catch.

"Evie? Is that you?"

There's no answer, and every muscle in my body tenses. I wait, but there's nothing. A breeze whispers through the long grass. The blades bend and sway and murmur to be careful.

I slip off the clothes dryer, and when my feet hit the ground, my legs feel like Jell-O. I take a cautious step toward the trees.

"Evie?"

Nothing.

"Quit playing around, Evie."

I glance over my shoulder toward the boardwalk. How long would it take me to run that distance? If I needed to.

If I had to.

Something moves behind the trees again.

"Who's there?"

Shit.

This is all wrong.

I start to back away, but my foot ends up in a muskrat hole and I go down hard on my backside.

And that's when he steps out from the shadows. He must have been there the whole time. Watching me.

I hold my breath and brace for something terrible.

Fangs and claws. Or worse.

But he's not a monster. Or at least he doesn't look like one. He's ordinary. About my age. Tall and slender. Faded jeans and an old green T-shirt. No shoes. Blond hair the color of dirty sunshine. It hangs down in the front, hiding his face.

And I don't recognize him.

Not until he lifts his chin and tosses that hair out of his eyes.

And those eyes are anything but ordinary. They shine bright blue, like ice that's lit up from the inside.

Like ice on fire.

Étranger. The stranger outside my window.

He smiles at me then. And I should try to run. Scream for help.

But I don't. I can't.

I'm frozen.

Hypnotized by those eyes.

And that smile.

He offers me his hand, but I don't take it.

"I didn't mean to scare you, Grey." His voice is like the ocean, and I feel myself relax a little, against my will. I try to fight it. I need to get away. I need to put some distance between myself and this stranger.

I need to –

But I don't.

The wet air crackles with electricity.

It hums.

Pops and sizzles.

"How do you know my name?"

The sun slips lower. I'm losing the light.

"Elora told me."

His eyes never stray from mine.

"Elora."

I'm not sure if I said her name that time. Or if he did.

I'm still sprawled on the ground. He holds his hand out to me a second time. My head feels fuzzy. Like it's full of cotton. I can't think of the right questions.

I can't think of anything.

"Who are you?"

"Zale," he says, and I search my memory. But that name doesn't mean anything to me.

"How did you know Elora?"

Something sad crosses his face. Those eyes darken a little.

"She was a friend of mine," he says.

Was.

Everything feels so strange. Off-kilter.

Sideways.

"I won't hurt you, Grey. I promise. I just wanted to make sure you were okay."

He takes a step toward me, and I scramble backward until my spine is pressed against the old clothes dryer. The touch of metal against skin shocks me. Just a sharp zap of static electricity. But it wakes me up, and it's like I come back to myself. Whatever spell he's got me under, I don't like it.

I don't trust it.

I don't trust him.

"I have to go," I tell him, and I push myself to my feet.

Surely this is where he steps in front of me. Blocks my path. Bares his teeth and eats me alive.

Only he doesn't. He just nods and says, "I'm glad to finally meet you, Grey."

I don't say anything back. I just turn and start for the boardwalk off in the distance. But I don't let myself run for home. Everybody knows you don't run from a wolf. You move slow and easy.

So I count my steps and keep going.

And when I glance back over my shoulder, he's gone.

The closer I get to the boardwalk, the harder it gets to slog through the mud. It sucks and pulls at my boots. I almost lose one. I have to stop and play tug-of-war with the soggy ground. But I win. There's a sickening sound when the mud lets go.

I hit the wooden steps just as the light dies. The white paint is peeling. Turning grey. Curling up and pulling away at the edges of the boards. I hadn't noticed it before. Rot and mold peek through.

Decomposition.

But the wood holds.

At home, I push open the back door and slip off my muddy boots. Honey looks up from the stove, where she's working on dinner. I'm grateful for the light and the clean kitchen. For the artificially cool air and the smell of red beans and rice.

When I go to Honey, she turns and wraps both arms around me. Mud and all. And she doesn't ask any questions. Which is so great. Because I have no clue what just happened. Sweet-N-Low drags himself over to lick at my ankles, and I don't even bother to shoo him away. I just try to catch my breath while I stare over Honey's shoulder at that photo frame on the wall. Me in that watermelon sundress. My mom with that one hummingbird hair clip.

And the haunted eyes. Now that I've noticed them, they're all I see.

Later, after dinner, I still feel weird.

Slightly disoriented. Hungover. A shower sounds so good.

I peel off my tank top, then I slip out of my jeans. They make a jingling sound when they hit the bedroom floor. Wrynn's collection. I fish the shiny little objects out of my pocket so I can toss them in the trash. But then I think about Zale. Those strange eyes of his. The way he watched me. So intense.

Tiny pinpricks on my arms. The back of my neck.

Gives me the frissons, sure.

Evie's wind chimes kick up in the night breeze. She's been

busy the last few weeks. There must be at least fifteen of them dancing outside her bedroom window now. The tinkling sound of them burrows its way inside my brain. Sometimes I think I hear them ringing, even when there's no breath of air on the bayou. Like a leftover echo inside my head. The ghost of a song.

Elora had a good luck charm. A little silver Saint Sebastian medal. Case gave it to her as a love token that twelve-year-old summer. His mama had gotten it for him when he made the sixth-grade baseball team at school up in Kinter, because Saint Sebastian is the patron saint of athletes, and I remember the way Elora batted her eyelashes at him when she slipped it into her pocket. From then on, she carried it with her all the time. All the protection she ever thought she needed.

I wish I had a charm of my own now. I reach for the blue pearl around my neck.

But it's not enough to make me feel safe.

So I count the shiny objects in my palm. Three pennies. Five pop tops. Two bottle caps. And three paper clips.

Exactly thirteen.

Then I lay them out on the windowsill. One by one.

The wind is merciless. It's like being hit with a two-by-four. Over and over and over. I grab one of the spindly little trees and hang on. But I don't take my eyes off him. I can't. Because there's nobody else left in the whole world now. It's down to just the two of us. Him. And me.

10

The next day, the Mystic Rose is slammed. June is always peak season for day-trippers down from New Orleans. They do way more looking than buying – nobody goes home with that ugly Himalayan salt lamp – but Honey still needs me all day. So I don't get a chance to see Hart. Or anybody else. And that's fine with me. I need some time to think through what happened last night.

The whole time I'm working, though, I keep seeing Zale. His eyes, especially.

That strange blue fire.

And I hear the echo of his voice inside my head.

I have a couple flashes, too, while I'm wiping fingerprints off the glass countertop and again while I'm dusting the crystals. I'm looking through Elora's eyes. I see the storm and the bayou so clear. I feel the force of the wind. But I can't ever see who it is she's so terrified of.

What's the point in having this stupid gift if I never see anything useful?

Honey makes pork chops and gravy that night, and I'm helping her wash the dishes when I finally ask, "Are there any new families around here? Since last summer?"

She gives me a funny look. "Why?"

I shrug. "I saw someone I didn't know yesterday. Looked like a local. Not a tourist."

Honey wipes her hands on the dish towel. "What kind of someone?"

"A boy."

"Oh. Well, let's see." She hands me the towel to dry my hands. "Some new people moved in last fall. Bought the old Landry place, out near Blackbird Point. Cormier, I think their name is." She covers the leftover pork chops with foil and puts the plate in the fridge. "I know they have a couple girls. Seems like they might have a little boy, too."

"A little boy?"

"Maybe six or seven years old."

"Oh." Honey has no idea that when I say a "boy" these days, I don't really mean a six-year-old. "Anybody else?"

"No. Not that I know of." She shrugs. "But there's an awful lot of swamp out there. Plenty of places to hole up and not be bothered, if you've a mind to live that way."

I nod and put the clean silverware in the drawer. Like it's no big deal.

But I keep thinking about those ice-fire eyes. The burning blue of them.

"You know, tomorrow's your birthday," Honey says after a few minutes. "I thought maybe we could get away for the day.

Get Bernadette to watch the store. Go up to New Orleans. Do a little shopping. Maybe take Evie and Sera –"

"I don't wanna do anything."

"I know it's hard," she goes on. "But it's still your birthday. You deserve –"

"My birthday's canceled this year."

Probably forever.

Honey sighs. "You sure that's what you want, Sugar Bee?"

"Yeah," I say. "I'm sure."

Honey turns back toward the sink. She wrings out a wet cloth and wipes crumbs from the countertop. "It might be a nice time for you all to celebrate Elora. To mark that special relationship in some way. Honor her."

"You mean honor her memory."

"It might help. That's all I'm saying." Honey's voice is gentle. "It might bring you some peace."

"I don't need peace," I tell her. "I need to know where she is."

I escape to my bedroom and lie down in the cool air. My mind keeps going back to that drawing of Sander's. *Étranger*. The stranger with the missing face.

Someone we don't know.

It could be Zale. The stranger outside my window. But what if it's Dempsey Fontenot, come back home to steal another summer girl? Or Case? His familiar features distorted by rage and jealousy.

Or Mackey. Or Hart. Or Evie or Sera or Sander.

Because I know they all must have their own dark corners.

Or what if it's Elora herself? How well did I really know my best friend?

Or . . . what if it's me?

Because I'm starting to think that I'm the biggest stranger of all. I've been home just over two weeks, without Elora, and I can already feel myself changing. I'm keeping secrets from Hart. And from Honey. Telling half-truths.

And I can't really even say why.

Later, when I get up, I hear the shower running in Honey's upstairs bathroom. I head into the kitchen to get some milk. I don't let myself look at that picture. The one of me and my mom. Instead, I cross to the back window and part the curtains to peek out into the night.

I see the storage shed, and I think about Case again. Crawling around in there on his hands and knees.

I grab a flashlight and head out back. The wind has really kicked up, and Evie's chimes are singing so loud.

Feels like maybe there's a storm blowing in.

I push open the door to the shed, then I drop down low and shine my flashlight around the dusty floor. The rough wood bites at my palms and my knees. But I keep looking. I didn't find anything yesterday. But this time, something tells me not to quit.

So I don't.

I check every spiderwebbed corner and lift every single box to look underneath. I'm about to give up when something shiny catches my flashlight beam. It's wedged down in a crack between two of the floorboards. I pry at it with one fingernail, but it's stuck tight.

I dig a screwdriver out of the toolbox on the counter, and I use that to pry at it some more. And it eventually comes free.

I hold it in my palm and shine my flashlight on the little silver circle.

Saint Sebastian stares up at me. Patron saint of athletes.

Elora's good luck charm.

The one she's carried in her pocket every single day since we were twelve years old.

My hand starts to shake, and it makes it hard to turn the medal over. But I have to. I have to know. For sure.

And there's Case's name engraved on the back. So there's no mistaking what this is. Who it belonged to.

It isn't the name that stops my heart, though. It's the dark red smudge across the name. Something dry. The color of rust.

I drop the Saint Sebastian medal like it's on fire.

I want to scream, but I only gag on my own tongue as I scramble to my feet. There's no air in the shed. I stand there for a long time with the little silver medal lying on the floor in my flashlight beam. Like I'm hitting it with a spotlight.

Finally, I force myself to pick it up. I choke back vomit as I slip it into my pocket and step out on to the boardwalk. I take a few steps toward the back door.

There's a flash of lightning. The low rumble of thunder. Clouds roll fast across the black sky, and Evie's wind chimes cry into the night.

They tell me that I'm not alone. Out here in the dark. Something is moving through the cypress trees. Whispering through the tall grass.

I feel it coming closer.

Breathing.

And waiting.

Watching me.

I try to move toward the kitchen door. Just a few feet away.

But I can't make my feet work.

Another flash of lightning.

Night becomes day, and I see him clear.

Zale stands in the open as the storm gathers around him. He's barefoot and shirtless. And his blond hair is blowing in the wind.

When he raises his arms to the sky, more jagged lightning splits the dark in half. Electricity surges through me. My whole body tingles with its power.

He's at least fifty yards away. But somehow I hear him whisper my name.

And it sounds like a storm on the ocean.

I can't let him find me. I drop down to my hands and knees in the middle of the storm. In the middle of Li'l Pass. My mouth is barely above the water, and I dig my fingers and toes into the mud to keep from being swept away.

11

There's a huge clap of thunder. Loud enough to shake the boardwalk under my feet. And the next thing I know, Honey is grabbing my hands and pulling me into the brightly lit kitchen. As she closes the door behind us, rain comes in huge pounding drops. Thunder rattles the windows, and lightning explodes across the bayou like artillery fire. Sweet-N-Low ducks for cover under a stool.

"Grey." Honey takes my face in her hands. "What were you doing out there in this weather?" I'm shaking too hard to answer. "You know better than that."

My great-great-grandfather was electrocuted. He'd sought shelter from a storm in the open doorway of an unlocked church, but the thunderbolt found him anyway.

Lightning got a taste for our family then.

It hunts us, Honey says. So we have to be extra careful.

She takes off her robe and drapes it around my shoulders, then she parks me in a chair at the little kitchen table while she makes me a cup of herbal tea. I take the steaming mug, and Honey sits down across from me with one of her own.

After a few sips of chamomile and lemon, I'm finally able to make my voice work.

"Did you see him?"

Honey gives me a funny look. "See who, Sugar Bee?"

"I thought I saw someone. In the dark."

She gets up and goes to the window, then peers out into the night and comes back to the table, shaking her head. "I can't imagine anyone would be out and about with a storm like this comin' on."

For a few minutes, Honey just sits across from me in her nightgown, watching me sip my tea. Finally she says, "Troubles are always heavier when you carry them alone, Grey."

I don't meet her eyes. I'm busy counting the tiny pink flowers on the white tablecloth.

She sighs. "Maybe it's too hard on you, being here this summer."

I jerk my head up. "No. I need to be here."

"Then you need to be honest with me." Honey's voice is firm. But also familiar and warm. Like the old pink robe draped around my shoulders. "You've been seeing Elora, haven't you?"

It seems pointless to keep lying, so I nod.

Honey takes a deep breath and leans back in her chair. But she doesn't look surprised.

"Tell me about it," she says. And suddenly, I want to.

"It's not really that I'm seeing her. More like I am her." I struggle for the right words to explain it. "Like I'm seeing what she saw that night. But it's just bits and pieces. I can't make any sense of it."

"How long has this been going on?" Honey asks, and I shrug.

"A little while."

"Since you got here?"

I shake my head. "It started before that."

"Oh, Grey." Honey reaches for my hand. "Why didn't you tell me?"

"I don't know. I wasn't sure, I guess. And I didn't want it to be real. I was hoping it would go away."

Honey nods like she understands. "Clairvoyance. The ability to see beyond eyesight. Your great-grandmother was clairvoyant. Sometimes she couldn't say exactly whether she saw things or just felt them clear enough that it was like she saw them."

"Is that how it is for you, too?" I ask.

"No." Honey shakes her head. "I'm a medium, not a see-er. I relay information from those who have crossed over. That's all I can do. I only know what the spirits choose to share with me. But clairvoyants are different. They just know things – about the past or the future – all on their own."

The rain beats down on the roof, and thunder rumbles long and low.

"I don't want to know things."

"You can ignore it, but that won't make it stop." Honey takes a sip of her tea. "Our gifts can be heavy burdens to bear."

"Seems more like a curse than a gift," I mumble.

"It's a hard way to go through life. Being different. Having power that doesn't come with any instruction book." Honey glances toward the picture frame on the wall. The one with the photo of my mom and me. "Too hard, sometimes. For some people."

I want to ask her what she means. What it has to do with my mother. But I'm afraid she won't tell me.

Or that she will.

"I've never had the gift before," I say. "Why now?"

"Oh, you've always had it, Sugar Bee." Honey gives me a little smile. "Everyone has some kind of psychic gift. It's just that some people are able to unwrap their gifts more easily than others. It's like singing. Everyone is born with the ability to sing, but not everyone joins the church choir."

"So why is it coming out now?"

"Because now you need to know what happened to Elora. And sometimes, when everything else fails us, we have to rely on those gifts we've kept buried deep inside ourselves." She squeezes my hand. "It doesn't surprise me. You two have always been so connected."

Hurt washes over me like the rain running off the roof outside the kitchen window.

"It wasn't like that any more. The way it used to be. Between Elora and me." I swallow the lump in my throat. "Something happened last summer."

Honey shakes her head. "Twin-flame relationships are magnetic," she says. "They're pure white-hot energy. Push and pull. Attract and repel. They can be explosive. Dangerous, even."

I've heard all this before, but I don't have the will to interrupt.

"Sometimes things get too intense for one of you to handle. So one of you runs. Or pushes the other one away. But you can't stay apart long. Twin flames will always feel that hard pull toward each other." She gives my hand another squeeze. "It's fate. You and Elora were meant to be together. You're two halves of a whole. Two flames –"

"Lit from the same match," I finish, and Honey nods.

There are hot tears on my cheeks, and I reach up to brush them away. I blink hard, but I can't stop them falling.

"I don't know how to be me without her."

"She's still with you, Grey." Honey leans in closer. "Whether she's dead or alive, Elora is part of you. Don't give up on that."

When I don't say anything, Honey offers to make me a bedtime snack. But I shake my head. "I just need to go to sleep."

I stand up to leave, but she puts a hand on my arm. "Having great ability isn't something to be afraid of, Sugar Bee. But it is something to be careful with."

I'm not sure what she means at first, but then I remember Sera's words.

Your mama had deep power.

I feel the pull of my mother's haunted eyes. But I don't let myself look in their direction.

"Don't allow what you can do to change who you are," Honey warns me as she picks up our mugs and carries them to the sink. "That's the most important thing to remember."

In my room, I pause at the window to search the darkness. But nobody stares back at me from the pouring rain.

Evie's wind chimes sing out loud and clear in the storm. They clink and clank against each other with a ringing fury that carries over the wind and the water. Not even the constant rumble of thunder drowns out their strange music.

I take Case's bloodstained medal out of my pocket and wrap it in a tissue. I know I should give it to someone. Turn it over to the sheriff or something. And I will.

Soon.

Because I figure Saint Sebastian is proof of what Hart has been saying all along. Case has to be the one that Elora is afraid of. He must be the one chasing her down through the rain in all those mixed-up flashes I've been having.

There's no real way to deny that now.

Then, after he killed her, he took his medal back. The one she slipped into her pocket when we were only twelve years old. The summer of batting practice.

Baseballs.

And eyelashes.

He stole it from her while she lay there. Dead at his feet. Or maybe dying.

But then what?

How did Saint Sebastian end up lost in Honey's shed?

If my power is so great, why don't I know the answer to that question?

I slip the medal into my underwear drawer, and my fingers find the corner of Sera's drawing. I unfold the paper and carry it over to my bed. I crawl up on top of the quilt to sit cross-legged and study the image.

That big black trunk.

The trunk that currently isn't in the shed where it should be.

I think about how I used to hide inside it. And it hits me that it's exactly the right size.

The right size to hold a body. The right size to make a girl disappear.

Like magic.

The room starts spinning. Suddenly I'm imagining Case folding Elora's long legs into that black trunk and closing the lid. I get up and shove the drawing back into the drawer, then I run to the bathroom and drop to my knees in front of the toilet. My stomach heaves and heaves, but nothing comes up. I'm shaking all over, and my face is on fire, so I curl up on the bath mat and rest my cheek against the smooth tile.

And then I guess I fall asleep, because when I open my eyes again, it's pitch black. No bedroom light. No bathroom light.

The power must be out.

I hear the storm raging outside, pelting the window with rain and what must be little hailstones. They make an eerie rattling noise against the glass. Like a tiny army trying to break in.

The tile is hard and cold, and my arm is numb from being pinned under my weight. It's uncomfortable but undeniably real.

And then all that disappears.

The solid tile of the floor dissolves beneath me and –

The bayou is flooding out. Water runs over my back and

swirls around my ears. Deeper and deeper. I try not to breathe it in. But I have to breathe. I gasp for air and water rushes in instead. I'm coughing and gagging, and every time my body cries out for oxygen, all I get is more water.

Panic stabs at my insides. It slices me up and leaves me in ribbons.

I can't see.

I can't think.

I can't breathe.

I can't –

My throat is on fire. The water burns my lungs like I'm sucking in gasoline.

I lose my grip on the mud, and I feel myself being pulled along with the torrent.

Tumbling.

Spinning.

Arms over head over knees over elbows.

Mud in my nose. My mouth. My eyes. There's nothing to grab on to. Nothing solid in the whole world.

And then it all goes black.

My head slams against the base of the toilet, and I scramble to my hands and knees on the dark bathroom floor. My chest hurts. Everything hurts.

I can't see. I can't think. I can't breathe. I can't –

My stomach heaves. I sputter and choke. My throat burns again as the water comes up.

I'm vomiting and coughing.

Water.

Water everywhere.

It comes up and up and up. It gushes from my throat. Pours out my nose.

My ribs ache. I retch and gag and listen to the splash of water against ceramic tiles. It spreads across the floor and pools around my fingers. And it keeps coming.

I vomit up water from my stomach. I cough it up from my lungs.

Again and again and again.

So much water. Enough water to drown a person.

Enough water to drown Elora.

When it finally stops, I fold in on myself and hold my aching sides. The smell of the bayou fills up my nose. I grab the edge of the sink and pull myself to my feet. My legs are shaking, and my bare feet splash through the puddle as I feel my way out of the bathroom.

Blind.

I can't be in the house any more. There's no air in here. I need to be out.

Outside. On the front porch. Where maybe I can breathe.

It's late. After midnight. I stumble my way through the dark bookstore, and Sweet-N-Low comes padding out of the kitchen to see what's up. I hear the jingle of his collar, so I put one finger to my lips, like he's a person, and whisper to him to go back to bed.

Then I open the front door. Slow and easy. So the bell won't wake up Honey.

And everything goes silent.

The wind. The rain. The thunder and lightning.

It all just –

stops.

No movement. No breeze.

Dead still.

But I can hear the faintest tinkling of wind chimes.

When I slip out on to the front porch, my feet skitter on tiny pieces of ice. Hailstones the size of green peas. I pick some up and hold them in my hand, but they're already melting in the summer heat.

I cross the boardwalk and step out on to the dock. Hart would be pissed.

But Hart isn't here.

I avoid the rotten, roped-off area and move to the other side of the platform to stand over the dark Mississippi.

I wonder if maybe I've become a water witch.

Like Elora.

Suddenly a strange energy swirls around me. The damp air hums and crackles, and the hair stands up on my arms and the back of my neck. Evie's wind chimes whisper louder and louder until they ring like church bells.

And I know it's him.

When I look back over my shoulder, he's standing right behind me. Blond hair and ice-blue eyes that shine with a deep-lit fire.

He's so close. If I put out my hand, I could touch him.

I should be afraid.

But something in the water murmurs not to be.

I turn to face him, with all the strength of the great, rolling river at my back, and I can't even explain it. This weird calm settles over me, and I don't feel any fear.

"I didn't mean to scare you, Grey."

I wonder if all our conversations will begin with those same seven words.

His smile is genuine. Open.

Up close, there's nothing about him that reminds me of Sander's drawing. The faceless stranger. *Étranger* is all emptiness. And there's so much blazing light in Zale's eyes.

He's not wearing anything but a pair of faded jeans. His skin is beautiful. Golden. And that blond hair of his is storm-blown. It shines like silk in the moonshine. It occurs to me that he'd look right at home on the cover of one of those cheesy romance novels. The kind Honey keeps stashed in her nightstand. The ones I'm not supposed to know about.

"Who are you?" I ask him.

"Zale." I notice a little bit of a gap between his front teeth. And somehow that makes him seem more real. "But I already told you that, didn't I?"

I swear that ocean-deep voice could sweep me out to sea. But I refuse to let it.

"How did you know Elora?"

Something like sadness crosses his face, and he looks past me, out at the river.

"I told you, she was a friend of mine. That's a thing we have in common, Grey. You and me."

"Do you know what happened to her?"

He shifts his focus back to me again, and my stomach drops like I'm riding a roller coaster.

"I didn't kill her, if dat's what you're askin' me."

There's the faintest hint of a Cajun accent. It's not nearly as strong as Case's, but I still hear it flowing like water under his words.

"How do I know that?"

He shrugs. "I guess you don't."

But I know who killed Elora now.

Don't I?

That bloody Saint Sebastian medal is sitting in my underwear drawer with the murderer's name engraved on the back.

"Where did you come from?"

"I was born here," he says. "Same as you were."

But that doesn't make sense.

"Then how come nobody knows about you?"

His eyes darken, like when a cloud passes in front of the sun.

"I've been gone a long time," he tells me. "Just came back around last winter."

"But nobody even knows you exist."

"You know." He smiles at me again.

"And Elora knew," I add.

"Yeah." He nods. "Elora knew about me." Something changes in his voice, and I hear the reverberation of deep loss. It sounds so familiar. "Elora knew me."

"You've been watching me." It isn't a question. I've felt those eyes on me so often these last two weeks.

"I just needed to make sure you were safe." He tosses his hair back out of his face again.

"Why?"

He shrugs. "I figured that's what Elora would want me to do."

I'm struggling to fit the pieces together.

"Safe from what?"

"I don't know, Grey. I wish I did."

A lightning bug lands on my hand. It sits there blinking like a lighthouse beacon.

"Why should I believe you?"

He tilts his head to one side, like he's thinking hard about that question. "You probably shouldn't," he acknowledges. "But I hope you will. I think maybe we can help each other."

"I don't even know you." None of this feels quite real.

"But you do know me, Grey. In a way. You always have." He grins, and it lights up the night. "I'm one of you."

"What do you mean, one of us?"

Everything in my life has become some kind of riddle.

"I was born right here," he says. "Not quite seventeen years ago." And that's when I get it. "My birthday's comin' soon. The middle of September. Just before the fall equinox."

The earth has started to spin in the opposite direction.

"You're one of the Summer Children."

He nods, and none of the rules I thought I knew apply any more.

Zale is probably just a few days younger than Evie. That makes him number eleven.

I can tell he means it to reassure me. But for the first time since he appeared on the dock tonight, I'm frightened.

In numerology, eleven can be the number of power and wisdom. But it's also the number of imperfection. It's chaos and disorder. A world in disarray. The undoing of the ten. Everything out of balance.

My muscles tense.

"You don't need to be afraid of me," he says. "I promise."

But I'm not sure any more. I look up, and my eyes find Honey's darkened bedroom window. Suddenly I'm aware of how alone I am out here.

With this stranger.

I move to step around him. To head back toward the front porch. The light of home.

"Grey. Wait." Zale reaches into his pocket, then he holds out his fist. "I have a gift for you." I hesitate, and he opens up his fingers. Something small and silvery catches the moonlight. My hands fly to my mouth, but they can't hold in my gasp of surprise. Zale gives me another little smile. "Take it," he urges. His voice is so gentle, like Honey's hand in my hair. "It's yours now."

I reach for the shiny thing with trembling hands, then I slip it on to my finger.

Elora's ring.

Silver with one tiny blue pearl.

"Where did you get this?" There's an accusation in the words, and I know he hears it.

"Elora gave it to me," he says. "The last time I saw her. But it belongs on your finger. She'd want you to have it."

I'm staring at my hand. At Elora's lost ring. "Why should I trust you?" I ask him. Because it seems like a thing I should want to know.

I feel the burn of those blue eyes on my skin.

"Because Elora trusted me." I raise my chin to look at him. "And she told me the two of you were lit from the same match." I'm staring now, mouth open, because he couldn't have known that. Not unless Elora had said those words to him. Our special words.

The tinkle of wind chimes floats across the boardwalk.

"That ring was really important to her," he says. And whatever little bit of glue is holding me together, I feel it start to melt under the heat of Zale's ice-fire gaze. "It was the most precious thing she had to give. Because it came from you."

His words flow over my soul like fresh water out of the ground.

"She loved you, Grey. So much."

My heart falls out of my chest and splashes into the river. I look over my shoulder to watch it float downstream until the current sucks it under.

Because everyone keeps saying that. That Elora loved me.

But if that's true, why did things end the way they did last summer?

I'm off and spinning again.

Spinning and spinning and spinning.

I grab for something to hold on to. An anchor. Any little bit of hope.

"Do you think there's a chance she's out there somewhere?" I ask. "Alive?"

"No." Zale shakes his head, and I watch that blond hair fall across his eyes. I'm glad when he reaches up to push it back. Because I need that light. But his answer cuts deep. "She's gone, Grey. I feel it."

"Me too," I whisper, and a sharp-toothed hole opens up somewhere in my heart. It eats me alive when I say those words out loud.

It isn't a sudden realization. The permanence of Elora's loss has been stalking me all summer. I haven't been able to admit it to Hart, but how long have I known it, deep down?

Since I picked up Case's bloody medal a few hours ago?

Since I got off the mail boat that first morning home?

Since the visions started?

Since that phone call from Hart way back in February?

Or since the night before that? The very night Elora went missing – even though I didn't know it yet – when I woke up in the dark, sick and dizzy with loneliness that hit me like a sudden flu.

I'm shivering now. Shaking so hard I'm afraid I'll crack open. I've never felt this kind of cold before. A cold so deep it hurts.

"I need to go inside," I mumble. "I need –" I stop and suck in a rattling breath. Choke back a wail. Because all I really need – all I want in the whole world – is Elora.

And Elora is dead.

I'm frozen solid as Zale walks me back toward the Mystic

Rose. We stop in front of the bookstore, and he reaches for my hand. As soon as Zale wraps his fingers around mine, a tingling heat surges up my arm and lodges somewhere in my chest. Under my ribs. When he looks at me, I see all the way down to the bottom of those eyes. And they are deeper than the Gulf of Mexico and ten times as blue.

Something flutters loose inside me.

And my heart starts to beat.

"Be careful, Grey," he tells me. Evie's wind chimes start up. There's a warning in them this time, and when Zale speaks, something in his voice echoes that sound. "This town is poison. Elora knew that. She'd want me to make sure you know it, too."

I start to tell him he's wrong about that. That La Cachette is my home, and as much as Elora might have wanted out, it was her home, too. But before I can form the words, Zale squeezes my hand and fades into the dark. I look down at my fingers, and I can still feel the strange tingle of his electric touch.

I step inside the Mystic Rose and close the door behind me, and the rain comes again. Not angry, like before. Gentle. Like tears. The lights flicker a few times, then come back on, and the air conditioner shudders once and begins to hum.

I blink against the brightness as I cross to the half-price shelf to search out a small blue book that I know is hiding there. *Secrets of Numerology Revealed.* I find it and turn to the section on number eleven.

I see all the things I already know. Power and wisdom . . .

but also chaos. The unbalancing of ten. A universe spiraling out of control.

But then there's this: In the tarot, eleven is the card of Strength and Justice. It represents the courage to stand strong in the storm and face your own worst fears.

I close the book and slip it back into its spot. Then I flip the light off on my way out of the shop.

In my tiny bathroom, there's a puddle of muddy water on the floor. I clean it up with a dirty towel, but the smell of the swamp still hangs in the air. I go to the window and slide it open just enough to let in the damp breeze and the scent of rain.

The whisper of wind chimes.

Wrynn's little trinkets are still lined up on my windowsill, so I count to thirteen.

Thirteen shiny charms –

Thirteen years old the summer Hart kissed me –

Thirteen Junes come and gone since Ember and Orli were drowned –

Then I slide the window closed and lock it.

There's been a shift. I feel it. Everything is different.

I think about the first time I saw Zale – outside my window – in the bright shine of the Flower Moon.

The Flower Moon means change comes soon.

I hold Elora's ring to the light, then I take a deep breath and tell myself that Elora is dead. And I can't be afraid any more.

Not of the rougarou.

Not of the dark.

Not of this power that is growing inside me.

Not of the questions.

And, most of all, not of the answers. No matter how ugly they are.

I kick at the hand at my ankle and realize it's just a twisting root. But I don't have the strength or the will to get up. Then something thick and slimy moves against my leg. And I'm on my feet before I have time to think about what it might be.

12

And then it's June 16. The day I've been dreading for months. Seventeen years since they laid Elora and me side by side in that bassinet up in Honey's bedroom.

The rain is still falling. And that seems right.

My birthday has always been my favorite day of the whole year. Better than Christmas, even. Because Elora and I always spent it together. A holiday just for us. But now all those shared birthdays press against my memory until I'm suffocating under the weight of them. The matching party dresses we had when we were five. Yellow taffeta and lace that made us itch in the bayou heat. A pirate-themed treasure hunt when we were nine. A weekend camping trip up at Grand Isle when we turned thirteen. Finally teenagers. And last year. Elora's eyes when she unwrapped that pearl ring and necklace.

Sera and Sander and Evie and Mackey all make excuses to drop by that afternoon. Sander gives me a sketch he did. Elora and me sitting side by side on the front porch steps. "He drew it from memory," Sera whispers, and I manage to tell him that it's perfect.

Mackey cracks jokes. Tries to make me smile. All Evie can offer is a half stick of gum, but I take it, because I can see how desperately she wants to make me feel better.

At least all of them have the good sense not to mention what day it is.

Honey honors my request and doesn't bring it up, either. She gives me plenty of space all day, and I appreciate that. But there's still this pressure building inside me.

I feel it when I touch the little blue pearl on the chain around my neck.

It swells every time I twist Elora's ring around my finger. I keep thinking about what Zale said. About how it was the most important thing she had to give. Because it came from me.

By nightfall, that pressure is crushing me, and I need to escape.

Late that evening the rain finally stops, so I grab a flashlight and head out the door. Honey and Sweet-N-Low both look up, but they don't ask any questions. And that's good.

Because I wouldn't have any answers. I have no idea where I'm going.

My feet know, though. They carry me through the blackness toward the downriver end of the boardwalk. Toward the old pontoon boat. When I get there, I see movement down below me, in the dark. Something big. I suck in my breath from the surprise of it and almost lose my balance.

"Careful, Shortcake." I click on my flashlight. Hart is sitting in the driver's seat, boots propped up on the railing. "That's a long drop for a little girl."

I slip off Elora's ring and hide it away in my pocket before I stick my flashlight between my teeth and make my way down the wooden ladder.

When I step into the boat, it moves underneath me and I almost lose my footing again. Hart holds out a hand so I can take it and steady myself.

The old pontoon usually sits in the mud at the edge of the gator pond – but it's high tide, plus the water is up from all the rain – so tonight it's floating, tethered to the dock by a rusting chain. Like a neglected dog tied up in somebody's yard.

Hart has a case of beer, and by the looks of the empty bottles scattered around his feet, he's already well into it. He uses the base of his cigarette lighter to pop the top off one, then he hands it to me. He's shielding his eyes from the flashlight beam. "Jesus," he grumbles. "Turn that thing off, will ya?"

I click off the light and take the seat across from him.

Hart is sopping wet. Soaked through. I figure he's been sitting out here for a long time. Since before the rain stopped, for sure.

All day maybe. Probably. Just letting the water fall on him.

"What are you doing out here?" I ask.

"Celebrating." He's drunk. If the empty bottles hadn't told me that, the thick sound of his voice would have. "And waitin' for you."

I watch Hart shake out a cigarette and smoke it in slow motion between swigs of warm beer. Every time he reaches out to flick away the ash, my eyes trail after his hand. I'm half hypnotized by the glowing orange embers hovering in the dark.

Willie Nelson hisses loud and angry from across the pond, and the sound of an airboat drifts in from somewhere back in the bayou.

I hear Hart clear his throat, then he pulls a beat-up envelope from his back pocket and hands it to me. It's bent in half and all wet. He flicks open his lighter and holds the flame so I can see. The envelope is purple, and my name is scrawled across it in pencil.

"It's just a card. But I wanted you to have somethin' tonight." I can tell he's embarrassed. "Picked it up at the Chat and Scat in Kinter."

That actually makes me smile. A wet gas station birthday card. Typical Hart.

I can't stand the idea of reading it right now, though. Even a cheesy Hallmark knockoff might be enough to sink me this evening.

"Thanks," I tell him. And I slip the soggy envelope into my back pocket.

"You believe in past lives, Greycie?" Hart's already working on another beer. He'll be totally wasted before long.

"Why?"

He runs one hand through his wet curls before he takes another drink, and I feel that familiar itch in my own fingers.

"Somethin' my mama told me. She thinks all of us – you, me, Elora, Sera and Sander, Evie, Mackey, Case, Ember and Orli – all ten of us – are linked like that." I add Zale's name to his list in my head. Mysterious number eleven. "That's why we pull so hard on each other."

Hart digs the cigarette pack out of his shirt pocket and shakes out another one. It'll be a miracle if the thing is dry enough to light.

But he holds it between his lips.

Flick.

Whoosh.

Pull in air.

Slow burn.

"Like maybe you and Elora were mother and daughter once. But another time, you stormed the beaches at Normandy together." He slaps at an mosquito. "Shit. Maybe Case was my goddamn grandpa in another life. Or my boss." He laughs low and quiet. "For all I know, Evie coulda put a bayonet through me during the War of Eighteen fuckin' Twelve."

I finish my first beer and immediately get handed a second one.

"I like that idea," I tell him. "All of us recycled over and over in each other's lives."

"Me too." Hart looks up toward the dark sky, then he takes a long drag off his cigarette. I wish he could breathe out hurt, the way he breathes out smoke. "Maybe next time I can save 'er."

We sit in silence while I finish my second beer, and Hart offers me a third. But it turns out there aren't any more. Which is probably good, because my head is spinning now, and Hart's words sound sloppy. But I can't tell if it's his tongue that's not working right, or my ears.

He stands up and moves toward the back of the boat to rummage around under one of the seats, then he holds up a half-empty bottle of whiskey and grins at me in triumph. "For special occasions," he announces. And I guess the saddest birthday party in the world counts, because he unscrews the top and turns to pitch it into the dark like a baseball player. Then he tips the bottle up and takes a long swig without even flinching.

"Hart."

He doesn't respond. He just stands there for a long time. Staring out at the water.

Still.

Watching.

Waiting.

If it weren't for the whiskey bottle dangling from one hand, he'd remind me an awful lot of Willie Nelson.

Finally he turns around to look at me.

"Don't come back here, Greycie. Next summer." I stare at him. "Elora didn't want you here. That's what last summer was all about. At least mostly. All that shit that went down between the two of you. She didn't want you to come back here. Ever. She didn't want you to have any reason to."

I feel stung. Like he's slapped me hard across the face.

"She wanted to get rid of me."

Hart shakes his head. "Dammit, Greycie. You aren't listening. She wanted to save you."

I hear the words, but my brain won't process them.

"Save me from –"

He cuts me off midquestion. "From this godforsaken place."

"Why?"

"Jesus." He lets out an exasperated sigh, and it makes me feel stupid. "Because she was scared for you. Of what you might become if you came back here." He washes the words down with another long swallow of whiskey. "Because she fuckin' loved you."

Something Zale said last night swims up through the beer and the confusion to bob up and down on the surface of my memory.

This town is poison, Grey. Elora knew that.

That night on the dock, at the end of last summer, things had gone so wrong. It was my last night in town, and I'd wanted us to spend it together. Just the two of us. Like always. That was our end-of-summer tradition. Elora had been acting so weird for months, but I figured . . . if we could just have that one good night . . . then everything would be okay. Then she'd run off somewhere for most of the evening. And when she finally showed back up, she was evasive and distant. Not in the mood to talk. So I accused her of being selfish, and she accused me of smothering her.

Grow the fuck up! We're separate people, Grey! We're allowed to have our own lives! I'm getting out of here soon. I promise you that. And don't expect me to ever come back to this shithole town. Not even for you!

Her words tore my heart out. And the hurt of it set me on fire with rage. I called her a bitch. And then I said the worst thing of all. The one thing I knew would cut her to the bone.

I told Elora that she'd never get out of this place. Not if she lived to be a hundred. Because she'd never have the guts to face life out in the real world.

Not on her own.

Especially not without me.

I looked my twin flame right in the face and told her that she'd die here. In La Cachette. And there was nothing she could do to change that.

And that's when she called me a pathetic liar. And punched me. Right in the mouth.

It was her fist that caused the bruise under my jaw, but it was her words that drew blood.

There's nothing special about you, Grey. And there's nothing special about us. A few years from now, I won't even remember you ever existed.

For almost a year, those parting words have been the first thing I hear when I open my eyes in the morning, and the last thing I hear before I fall asleep at night. They ring and echo in my head every single second of every day, like Evie's wind chimes.

They've been the rock in my rock bottom.

And now Hart's telling me she didn't mean them. Not really.

And I don't know where that leaves me.

Except drifting.

Hart makes his way back to me. He squats down low and puts a warm hand on my bare knee to steady himself. "You shouldn't have come home this year. I shouldn't have let you." He tips his head way back and drains the very last drop from the whiskey bottle. "But I needed you so bad, Greycie." His voice cracks, and my heart cracks right along with it. "God, I fuckin' needed you." The pain in his eyes makes me ache. "I needed to be with someone who loved her as much as I did. Ya know?" He wipes at his mouth with the back of his hand. "But you got no business bein' here. There's nothin' good here any more."

Hart's face is swimming back and forth in front of me. I try to focus on him, through the alcohol and the tears that are welling up in my eyes. He's the only anchor I have left. And I finally let myself reach out and touch those beautiful curls.

"You're here," I tell him, and I guess I'm not too drunk to get embarrassed, because I add, "And Honey. Evie. All the others."

"Yeah. Well, don't come back for me." Hart lurches to his feet and throws the empty whiskey bottle with everything he has. It slams into the boardwalk piling behind me and shatters into a million pieces. "Because I'm gonna end up a piece-of-shit loser in the end. An abuser and a filthy drunk. Worthless and mean and alone." There's cottonmouth venom in his words. The low warning hiss of a snake that's let itself get cornered. "Until somebody finally puts me down. Like an old rabid dog."

"Hart," I beg him. "Don't."

"Just like my mama had to do my old man."

The boat moves and I feel seasick. Because that isn't what I want for him.

"You could leave," I tell him. "You could get out of here and go somewhere different." Hart shakes his head.

"This place is a riptide. And we're all caught in it. Nobody ever gets outta here." He looks down at me. "Well, nobody but you. The rest of us, we're stuck here. For good." One corner of his mouth twitches up. "Except for maybe Sera. I could sorta see her going to college somewhere. Studyin' French literature and drinkin' eight-dollar coffee at some hole-in-the-wall place full of stuck-up, pretentious assholes."

He's trying to make a joke of it, but I can't stand to listen to this. "Hart –"

"Nah." He cuts me off again. "I'll never get outta here. And we both know it. There's no place else for me to go. It's too crowded out there. Too many damn people in the world."

Too many damn feelings in the world. That's what he means.

He'd never survive all their pain. He hadn't even been able to go to school up in Kinter. Becky pulled him out halfway through kindergarten so she could teach him at home. The little cinder block building packed full of big emotions had been too much for him to handle. He'd started hurting himself. Slicing at his little arms with chunks of broken glass and sharp bits of plastic. Pulling his hair out. Chewing the skin off his lips.

I push myself to my feet. The boat rocks under me, and I lay a hand on Hart's chest to steady myself. I feel his rhythm. That constant thumping under his ribs.

The boat rocks again, and we both stand there trying to find our balance together. It feels like forever since I've stood on solid ground.

The night presses in, heavy and wet.

Hart studies me with dark eyes, and everything inside me melts together into a solid lump that settles somewhere low in my stomach. I feel the sudden heat of it.

He grins and cocks his head to one side. I blush in the dark and try to take a step backward, but I'm too late. He grabs my hand and my heart races.

Shit.

The bemused look on his face tells me that he knows exactly what I'm feeling. No use trying to hide it.

Hart hooks a lazy finger through my belt loop and pulls me against him. His other hand reaches around behind me to snake its way under my tank top. Rough fingers on my skin. I gasp out loud as my bones dissolve.

"Greycie." My name catches in his throat as he bends low to brush his lips against mine. It's not much of a kiss at first. More of an accident born of closeness. Like we're both tumbling toward each other, and it's our mouths that break the fall.

But then he pulls me harder against him. And I don't resist.

He tastes different than he did at thirteen. Back then, he was all Dr Pepper and Big Red gum.

Now he's seventeen.

Jack Daniel's and Marlboros.

And it turns out his tongue definitely works.

Hart presses himself into me. Wet clothes and hot skin.

We take our time with each other. Slow but not gentle. I feel his teeth on my neck. Biting and sucking and pulling at me. Dismantling me bit by bit.

Stubble burns my cheek and his palms press hard against

my back, sliding around to my sides to let his thumbs play over my hip bones.

I pull his bottom lip into my mouth, testing it with my teeth, nibbling on it as my fingers tangle in those sexy curls. I hear him moan, and a deep shiver runs through his whole body. He pulls back for a second to look at me.

"Fuck, Grey," is all he gets out before we're on each other again.

We kiss until my lips are swollen and my arms ache and all I feel inside is this desperate wanting. It swells and builds like a cresting wave. And that is so much better than anything else I've felt lately. It beats that broken feeling all to hell.

Because I'm not thinking about Elora. Or about my mother's haunted eyes.

I'm only thinking about what I need. And what Hart needs. What feels good. And this feels good. Hart feels good.

Hart is what I need.

We need each other.

So bad.

When we finally stop to breathe, Hart untangles himself from me and takes a few steps backward. He's blinking at me now. Almost like he's trying to remember who I am. His mouth opens and closes like a fish when it's pulled out of the water. Then he sinks down to sit on one of the peeling bench seats.

And I don't know what to do. I'm not sure what he wants from me in this moment. So I sit down across from him and wait for my heart rate and breathing to drop back to normal.

That good feeling is slipping away fast, and the lost, hurting feeling comes rushing back in to fill in the void. Except it's different this time.

It's bigger.

Deeper.

It's like we let ourselves feel one thing, and now everything is more raw. Even closer to the surface.

Elora's absence stretches out between us like the Grand Canyon. Hart's sitting inches away from me. I can still feel his lips on my neck. His fingers against my skin. But I don't know how to reach him.

His breath hitches, and this strangled sound tears its way out of his throat. Hart drops his head to his hands, and I see his shoulders shake.

But no tears leak out.

I'm watching him build a wall, brick by brick, to try to hold them in.

"She's gone, Greycie," he finally chokes out. "Dead."

I cringe hard and my stomach twists. But I give him the honesty I know he needs from me right now.

"I know, Hart."

"I fucked up." His voice is rough. Sandpaper on rusted pipe. "I let her down so bad. I was supposed to take care of her. Keep 'er safe. I shoulda been there. I shoulda –"

And then the sobs come. Great, huge, racking sobs that rattle his whole body and leave him gasping and choking while I watch. Paralyzed.

I've never seen Hart cry. Not one time. Not ever. But especially not like this. I've never seen anyone cry like this.

Like every sob is scraped up from somewhere deep inside him, made up of equal parts blood and guts.

I ache to put my arms around him. I want to comfort him. Say something. But I know he won't let me. Sometimes Hart can't stand to be touched. There's too much feeling in it. Besides, there's no easing a hurt that deep. To try to make it better would be an insult. I know because I've been walking around for months, slowly bleeding out from a mortal wound of my own.

Eventually, the sobs slow and his shoulders stop shaking. Hart draws a long, ragged breath. And then he mumbles that he's sorry.

But I can't be sure if he means for falling apart. Or for kissing me.

I figure it's probably both.

So I tell him it's okay.

"Come on," he says. But he won't look me in the eye. "I'll walk you home."

Hart takes my hand and pulls me up off the seat. Then puts one foot on the bottom rung of the ladder to hold the boat steady for me. He offers me his hand again as I move from the boat to the ladder, and I'm grateful. I still feel really off-center. From the beer.

And the kiss.

When I reach the boardwalk, Hart starts up after me. He's about halfway up when I hear a sickening crack. The ladder gives out under his weight, and he drops too fast to grab hold of anything. It isn't far to fall. Maybe three or four feet. But the pontoon has drifted out to the end of its short chain, and

Hart lands half on the boat and half in the flooded muck.

Before I can even blink, something huge explodes out of the shallow water right next to the old boat. There's a violent thrashing. Mud flies in every direction. Something bellows, low and angry. A throaty grunting sound that any good Louisiana girl would know right off.

"Gator!"

The scream doesn't even have time to leave my mouth before I hear the snap of powerful jaws.

"Shit!" Hart tucks his legs up as he rolls on to the boat and Willie Nelson gets a big ol' bite of air and rusted metal. "Fuck!"

My heart is pounding, only not down inside my chest where it belongs. It's moved up into my mouth. I feel it pounding against my teeth.

Willie bellows and thrashes again, and Hart hollers at me to get back from the edge of the boardwalk before I fall in and get eaten. He's sprawled out on the deck, and he kicks the metal side of the boat three or four times as hard as he can.

Pissed as he is, the banging sends Willie Nelson slinking back into the sludge. I track him with my flashlight and watch as he sinks beneath the surface.

"Hart!" I shout his name, but he's breathing too hard to talk.

"I'm okay," he pants. "Just gimme a minute."

My bones disintegrate, and I sink to my knees on the boardwalk. It's only a few seconds before Hart somehow manages to haul himself up to sit beside me. He's wet and muddy and still sucking in great gulps of air. His eyes are wide, and his curls are heavy with swamp water.

"Wood must've been rotten," he says. "Probably scared the daylights out of ol' Willie Nelson." He tries to laugh, but it doesn't quite work. "Me crashing down right on top of him like that."

I reach across to run my hands over his chest and arms. Just to make sure he's whole. But Hart flinches away. He pulls the pack of cigarettes out of his shirt pocket with shaking hands, but they're all soaked. "Goddammit," he mutters. Then he tosses the ruined pack into the mud before he gets to his feet. "Come on."

I follow Hart toward the Mystic Rose. We're about halfway there when I look out at the river and see someone night fishing, right at the edge of the water. Lantern shine bounces off dark red hair. Case is out in that patched-up pirogue of his. What my friends in Arkansas might call a canoe. I hear him whistling to himself. An old Cajun tune I almost know the name of.

I come close to throwing up when I think about that Saint Sebastian medal hidden in my underwear drawer. And I know I can't keep that secret much longer.

But I can't tell Hart tonight. He's already in too many pieces.

It only takes another minute or two to reach the Mystic Rose, but when we stop on the front steps, I look across to the dock.

And there stands Case. Real as you please.

Fishing off the edge. Like he's been there for hours. And Hart and I both know that was him we passed on the walk here.

Whistling in the dark.

But here he is now, too. Goading us.

Goading Hart. Daring him to say something. Hoping to get something going.

Case doesn't even turn around to look at us, but I feel Hart bristle beside me. His muscles tighten, and he puffs out air through his nose like an angry bull.

"Don't." I lay a hand on his arm, but Hart is already wound up. Ready for a fight. "Please," I beg. "Not now. Not tonight."

Hart gives me a long look, then he sighs and leans against a porch post. He glances at his watch. "After midnight," he says. "Your birthday's over."

Evie's wind chimes ring like funeral bells. Every day there are more of them. There must be close to twenty now. Each one different from the others.

"I need to go to bed," I say. And Hart nods.

I reach for the front door, but he stops me. "What are you hiding, Greycie?"

I don't look at him. "Nothing."

I feel the burn of Elora's ring in my pocket.

"That's bullshit," he says, and the disappointment in his words makes me cringe. "You don't think I can tell?" He shakes his head in disbelief. "You think I can't feel it when you sit next to me? When you touch me? Jesus." He lowers his voice. "You think I can't taste it when you fuckin' kiss me like that?"

"Hart –"

"Look, Greycie. I know everyone has secrets. And maybe, when you get right down to it, I don't wanna know yours any more than you wanna know mine."

As stupid as it is, it bothers me that Hart has secrets, too.

Things he's hiding from me. Because we never used to be like this. Not back when we were Hart and Elora and Grey. Or Grey and Elora and Hart. Back then, we all told each other everything.

Now that we're just Grey and Hart – Hart and Grey – it's all changing. All these hidden things are flowing in like mud to fill up the Elora-shaped space between us.

Hart reaches for my hand, but I pull away. He looks at me and sighs again. "Listen, if there's something you know . . . something that I need to know . . . I'm countin' on you to tell me. Straight. Okay? No matter what."

"Yeah," I tell him. "Okay."

But it's a promise I know I can't keep. At least not quite yet. Not when all I have are questions.

I watch him walk away for a minute, and as I turn back, I catch a flash of movement. A glimpse of white-blonde hair disappearing around the corner of the little house next door.

Evie.

She's been playing spy again. I think about calling her over, but I don't have it in me tonight.

Inside, I find Hart's soggy birthday card in my back pocket, but I still can't bring myself to open it. Like he said, my birthday's over.

I bury the card in my underwear drawer before I dig Elora's ring out of my pocket and slip in on to my finger.

"Happy seventeenth birthday to us," I whisper.

But the ringing of wind chimes is the only response.

I hear the cocking of the gun. Just behind my head. There's so much noise. Rain and wind and the thumping of my heart. But that single metallic sound echoes louder than any of them. It's the flipping of a light switch. Click. And everything else fades to black.

13

It's early the next morning when that image of the gun comes to me.

Or more the sound of it.

Click.

I'm in the middle of getting dressed, and that sound is so clear – so real – that I whirl around to look over my shoulder.

Just to be sure.

My head is pounding from last night. Two beers is two more than I'm used to. I feel like total crap. But I can't stand lying in bed and staring at my ceiling any more.

Honey has arranged for Bernadette to watch the shop this morning so the two of us can go upriver to Kinter, but I figure she won't be ready to go for at least an hour.

What I could really use is a good, long run to work out the stiffness in my aching muscles and to clear my jumbled head, but there's nowhere to run down here. So a walk will have to do.

I swallow some Tylenol and head out through the bookstore.

Sweet-N-Low whines and follows at my heels, and I feel bad, because he probably has to pee. But I hear Honey moving around upstairs, so I figure she'll take him out pretty soon.

When I step out on to the porch to pull on my mud boots, I'm greeted by the tinkling cacophony of Evie's wind chimes. They're spread out all along the side of the house now, and she's standing on a kitchen chair, tying another one up. This newest one is made of metal bits and scraps. A couple keys. A little toy car. A measuring spoon. A set of big hoop earrings.

"Don't those things keep you awake at night?" I ask her.

"No." She's balancing barefoot on the chair – stretched up on her tiptoes, arms extended over her head – tying off a fishing line loop. "They help me sleep."

Evie's hair is dull and stringy, and when she glances in my direction, her eyes look a little wild. I guess I'm not the only one who can't rest easy this summer.

I turn and start down the boardwalk, toward the old pontoon boat. Just out of habit. But then I think about Hart.

That kiss last night.

And what he said to me after. On the front porch.

What are you hiding, Greycie?

I stop and change directions, heading for the back steps instead. Li'l Pass seems like a safer destination.

I think about asking Evie if she wants to come with me, but she's still standing up on that chair, chewing on her lip and looking for an empty spot to hang the next wind chime.

Besides, I'm kind of hoping maybe someone else will join

me. I spin Elora's ring on my finger. Three times. Like making a wish.

There are a lot of questions I need answers to.

I make my way around the house and down the wooden steps in the back. The ground is saturated from all the rain, and my feet sink deep into the mud. The only cure is to keep moving, so I put one foot in front of the other until the earth finally starts to feel more solid underneath me.

It doesn't take long to hike back to Li'l Pass, but the throbbing in my head is already subsiding some by the time I kick off my boots and climb up to sit on the old flatbed trailer.

Only eight o'clock, but it must be close to ninety degrees already.

I don't mind the heat, though. Not today, anyway. Seems like lately I haven't been able to shake the chill in my bones, despite the stickiness of summer.

I close my eyes and tilt my face up to let the sun reach all my cold places. I soak it up like a lizard on a rock.

Suddenly there's the low hum of static electricity. The air crackles with it. I feel it vibrating against my skin. When I open my eyes, Zale is standing a few feet away. And I'm not totally surprised, because some part of me was thinking he might show up. But seeing him again still knocks the wind out of me for a second.

I can't get over the blue of his eyes.

He's still barefoot and shirtless, and I wonder if he ever wears any damn clothes.

"You look like you could use some company," he says. But he

doesn't move any closer to me, and I realize he's waiting for me to say something. To give him permission.

He doesn't want to spook me.

"Yeah," I say. "I guess I could."

When he smiles and closes the distance between us, my stomach feels funny.

Nervous. But not scared.

"I sure missed dat view," he says as he climbs up to sit beside me on the trailer. "All those years I was gone." I follow his gaze across the wide, flat grass, toward the La Cachette boardwalk. It sparkles bright white against the Mississippi River, curving behind it like a serpent.

And I know what he means, because I miss the river so much during the rest of the year up in Little Rock. I get homesick for that always-moving brown water, almost like missing a person.

"How old were you when you left here?" I ask him, and he shrugs.

"Little. But old enough to remember."

Fog is drifting in at the edges of my brain. Softening the sharp corners. Making everything fuzzy. It feels so good, but I have to hunt for the words I need to ask my next question.

"How come nobody knew about you?"

It's something I've been thinking about a lot since our conversation out on the dock the night before last. Our whole lives, the Summer Children have counted our number as ten. Even after Ember and Orli died, we've always said there are ten of us.

And all this time we were really eleven.

Seems like we should have known.

Zale shrugs. "My folks kept to themselves, I guess." He's still watching that distant river. "Not much reason to go into town. Never was much for us there. I never even knew about the rest of you, till Elora told me."

I try to imagine what that would be like. Growing up cut off from other people. Way back in the bayou somewhere.

"Plus I was so young when we left Louisiana," he adds. "My daddy died, and I grew up in Florida with my mama. Down on the edge of the Everglades." He turns in my direction and grins. And it makes me a little dizzy. "So dat's my swamp."

"Why come back here, then?"

A few seconds slip by before he answers.

"I guess I just thought it was time."

"Why stay hidden, though?" I'm still trying to make sense of it all. And Zale doesn't seem to mind the questions. "Why not let people know you're here?"

He shrugs again. "It's a hard thing, knowing who to trust."

"Then why trust me?" I ask him, and he answers without any hesitation.

"Because of the way Elora talked about you." He smiles at me again. "It kind of felt like I already knew you."

I feel like I'm at disadvantage, because I don't know anything about him. I think maybe I want to, though, because his voice is doing more to soothe my aching head than the Tylenol ever could. It has such a pretty sound to it, but there's something lonesome about it, too.

Like the call of a mourning dove.

"Were you in love with her?" I ask.

"I definitely was," he says. "You were, too. Weren't you?"

I blush, because you couldn't know Elora and not be in love with her.

"Was she in love with you?" I ask. I need to know if he's the one who made Case jealous enough to kill her.

But he shakes his head.

"We weren't lovers. It wasn't like dat between us." There's that familiar music in his voice again. Just a few notes of an old Cajun melody that I know as well as I know my own heartbeat. "We saved each other is all."

I don't understand what he means.

"I was out fishin' one night back in January. Just at the edge of the river. Middle of the night. Nobody awake. And my line got all tangled, so I bent down to sort it out, and when I looked up again, there was this girl standin' up there on the dock. Right where we were standin' the other night."

"Elora."

I whisper her name like an incantation, and the long grass whispers it back.

"Full moon," he says.

A rougarou moon.

"And I could see her plain. The kind of beautiful that steals the breath right out your chest. Couldn't take my eyes off 'er. She was standin' dere right on the edge."

"The river was calling her," I say, and Zale nods.

"Only I didn't know dat then. So I watched her for a minute. And then she went over."

I feel that fog at the edges of my brain, and I try to push it back.

"What do you mean, went over?"

"She went over the edge. Into the water."

I gasp out loud, and my stomach clenches like a fist. It's a fifteen-foot drop, at least, from the dock to the dark, churning river below.

Deep and fast-moving and treacherous.

"You saved her life that night."

He shrugs, like it's no big deal. "When I fished her out of the river dat first time, she cussed me up one side and down the other. Wouldn't even tell me her name. But I still came back the next night, just in case. And we did the whole thing all over again. And again. And again. And again. I must've saved her a dozen times. A dozen different nights."

"She wanted to die that bad?" I can't stand to think of Elora like that.

Hopeless.

"No." Zale shakes his head, and his eyes flash extra bright. "It was just the river she needed. That letting go. So I kept dragging her into the boat. I'd sit out dere in the dark and wait for the splash. Like I was a deep-sea fisherman and her some kind of Mississippi mermaid."

"Mississippi mermaid." I like the way the words feel in my mouth, but they sound better in Zale's ocean-deep voice. Each *m* is a wave against the sand.

"Toward the end, she stopped fallin'. Stopped needin' to, I think. And I didn't see her near as much after dat. But we'd still meet out on the dock sometimes. After the town went to sleep. Three, four o'clock in the mornin'. And we'd just sit together till the sun started to come up."

My heart aches.

I should have been there. I should have been the one to save Elora. To sit with her in the darkest part of the night.

Not this secret stranger.

"Why did you reach out to me?" I ask him. "What is it you want?"

He stares at me for a second.

"Like I said, I think maybe we can help each other." Zale looks back out toward the distant river. "I saw her dat night," he admits. "The night she disappeared. I just had this feelin'. Somethin' about Elora. And then that storm blew in. So I set out in the rain to make sure she was okay. And I found her standin' right dere on the dock. Just like the very first time I saw her."

"She must've sneaked away." I'm thinking out loud. "From the others."

Zale nods.

"Slipped off while the rest of 'em were playin' flashlight tag. That's what she told me. Left 'em out dere lookin' for 'er."

And that makes sense. Because it sounds just like Elora. She would have loved the drama of it. Everyone worried and calling her name.

"Did she say anything else?" I ask him.

"Just goodbye. She was leavin', she said. For good."

"That was something she talked about a lot," I tell him. "Getting out of La Cachette."

"It was more than talk dat night. She was waitin' for someone." My insides flip-flop, and I grip the edge of the flatbed trailer. "And she was nervous. In a hurry."

"Who was she waiting for?" I hear the desperation in my voice.

The longing for an answer. Any answer.

But Zale just shrugs. "She wouldn't say."

"Did she at least say where she was going?"

He shakes his head. "We only talked a few minutes. Just long enough to say our goodbyes. And Elora kept her secrets close to her own heart. But she gave me dat blue pearl ring as a friendship token. For savin' her all those nights."

I look down at the ring on my finger. The little silver band reflects the bright June sun.

"And then everyone was out lookin' for her," he adds. "And I was thinkin', good for her. She fooled 'em all. Ran off. Like she said she was gonna. Only –"

"Only you don't think that any more."

Zale shakes his head. "It doesn't feel right. Somethin' tells me she never left La Cachette."

I think about that bloody Saint Sebastian medal. The ugly picture it paints of Elora's last moments. With Case. If he found her there – on the dock, waiting for someone else – maybe it doesn't matter who it was she was running away with.

Maybe all that matters is Case's reaction.

My breathing changes, and I feel this squeezing pain in my chest. Like my heart is being crushed into dust. But it's at war with the insistent voice inside my head that's still telling me this is all impossible. That there's no way she can be gone.

Dead.

Not Elora.

I know it's true – some part of me has known it ever since that night back in February when I woke up and felt it, clear as anything – but I still can't make any sense out of it.

Because if she were really dead, surely I would be, too. How do you go on living with only half a heart?

Suddenly I can't get enough air. I'm panicking. Gasping for breath. My vision is blurry. I'm trembling.

Zale reaches over to take my hand, and I feel the electric shock of his skin against mine. My whole arm tingles. I pull my eyes away from Elora's ring. Zale's hand on mine.

And I find myself in the blue of his eyes.

For a split second, I think about Hart.

Dark curls. Teeth bared against the skin of my neck. Rough fingertips on the small of my back.

That gnawing need.

His.

And mine.

But then I feel the gentle heat of Zale's touch spreading out through my whole body. It isn't hot. I don't feel that burn. Like I did with Hart last night.

But finally, I'm warm again. And I let myself breathe in deep.

I think about something Honey always says when she does a tarot reading.

It may not be what you were expecting, but that doesn't mean it isn't what you need.

That reminds me that we're supposed to go up to Kinter this morning. Honey has a hair appointment. And I've totally lost track of time. How long have we been out here?

I don't have any idea.

"I need to head back," I say. And Zale nods.

I don't want him to let go of my hand. But he does.

"Maybe I'll see you this evening." Something in his voice sounds hopeful.

"Yeah," I tell him. "I'll come back out tonight."

And I'm surprised by how much I'm already looking forward to it, because I know it doesn't make any sense. I just met Zale. And he still seems only half-real to me. I'm curious, though. About this stranger who loved my twin flame. This secret friend who sat with Elora in the dark of the night when I couldn't be here to save her from herself.

I cover the ground between Li'l Pass and the boardwalk as quick as I can, hoping like heck I'm not in trouble. When I get back to the Mystic Rose, Honey is already out on the dock getting the boat ready, so I hurry inside to trade my mud boots for flip-flops and grab my sunglasses.

Like most people in La Cachette, Honey has a little flatboat with an outboard motor that she uses to scoot up to Kinter and back. You can't really take a tiny boat like that out on the river, though. The Mighty Mississippi is too everything. Too fast. Too treacherous. Too full of logs and submerged dangers. Too crowded with enormous cargo ships and barges.

You have to go the back way.

Up through the bayou.

I think about my friends in Little Rock and their sweet little grandmothers. Delicate, grey-haired Southern belles with strings of pearls and pastel sweaters dyed the colors of Easter mints. I bet not one of them could pilot a flatboat through the thick of the swamp. But Honey makes it look easy. One hand on the tiller and the other hand on her head to keep her bright blue scarf from blowing away.

On the ride up to Kinter, Honey plays wildlife guide, pointing out the big swamp rabbits grazing in the Bermuda grass and the pink spoonbills feeding at the water's edge.

I can't really hear her, though. My mind is too full of Elora.

And Hart.

And Case.

And Zale.

The things I know.

And all the things I still don't.

I'm so lost in my thoughts that I don't even realize we're there until I feel the boat bump against the wooden pilings.

Most everyone in La Cachette pays a few bucks a month to keep a car parked at the bayou dock up in Kinter. So once Honey gets things squared away with the boat, we haul ourselves into Eliza, a dented old Toyota pickup with faded red paint and no air-conditioning.

"This is the truck I bought your mama when she headed off to college," Honey tells me. Like she does every single time. "Good ol' Liza Jane." She pats the steering wheel. "Your mama drove her up to LSU in Baton Rouge that fall. Only eighteen years old."

And only twenty when she got pregnant and dropped out to come home so Honey could help raise me. Before my mom died, I'd met my dad a handful of times. I can't complain about him, though. We talked yesterday. On my birthday. And I told him everything was fine.

Dad does the best he can by me, but – even half my lifetime later – Little Rock is just Little Rock.

La Cachette is still home.

Honey parks Eliza outside the Kut and Kurl, and I wander across the street to the tiny public library to pass the time. It's only been a couple weeks, but it seems like forever since I've seen civilization. Not that two-stoplight Kinter really counts. Still, it feels weird to be in the library. The lighting is too bright and the AC is too cold.

I wander through the fiction section for a while, but I already have too much summer reading to do for school. I'm supposed to be slogging through *The Tempest*, and I haven't even started. So I can't commit to anything else. I make my way over to the periodicals section, just to see if I can find something worth flipping through, but I'm not really into *Field & Stream* or *Southern Living*.

Then I notice a newspaper tucked down in between the magazines. It's a copy of the *Advocate Times Picayune* from up in New Orleans. I figure that's better than nothing, even if it is dated almost a month ago, so I pull it out.

And there it is, right at the top of the page.

AS THIRTEENTH ANNIVERSARY APPROACHES, STILL NO JUSTICE IN PSYCHIC TOWN DOUBLE CHILD MURDERS

I gasp so loud that some old lady across the aisle shushes me.

My legs are shaking something terrible, so I sink into an ugly orange chair to stare at the color photo under the headline.

I was only four years old when Dempsey Fontenot did what he did to Ember and Orli. I don't have any memory of ever having laid eyes on him. Definitely not in real life. Not even in a picture, either. In my imagination, he always looked like a monster.

Here he is though, staring right through me in the Plaquemines Parish library. Looking almost normal.

A long, slender neck.

Sun-blond hair.

And the most striking, unmistakable eyes.

They're ice blue.

Backlit with fire.

I cover my ears. Tell myself this is the worst of it.
Even though I know it isn't. I close my eyes and try
to breathe. While I still can.

 **14**

M y heart stops beating in my chest.

The face is slightly different. But those eyes? They're the exact same.

When I glance up, Honey is waving at me from the entryway, so I stuff the newspaper back where I found it before we head down the street for lunch at the Lagniappe Café.

Lagniappe is one of my favorite Cajun words. It means "a little something extra," and the café's owner is famous up and down the river for her pies.

But all through lunch, it's like I'm not really there. I'm hovering above myself, watching some other girl eat my food, while I can only wonder what it tastes like. I hear myself say things, but I couldn't tell you what. And I manage to make my arms and legs work, but I couldn't tell you how.

Because the whole time, I keep thinking about those eyes.

Dempsey Fontenot's eyes.

Zale's eyes.

On the ride back down toward La Cachette, I finally ask.

"Why didn't people like Dempsey Fontenot? I mean before."

Honey sighs, and at first, I think she isn't going to answer me. But then she does.

"There were stories. That's all it takes, sometimes, to get people riled up."

"What kind of stories?"

"It's been a long time, Grey." Honey slows the boat so we can hear each other better. "But people said he could . . . do things."

"Everybody down here can do things."

"What they said Dempsey Fontenot could do was beyond anything we'd ever seen."

"What do you mean?" I press.

She sighs again. And hesitates. "They said he had the power of the sea and the sky. That he could bring storms. Lightning and rain. Hail."

"Was it true?" I ask. It sounds so unbelievable.

Or at least it would in Little Rock.

"I imagine there might have been some truth in it," Honey says.

"And people didn't like that?"

"Even in La Cachette, there are things beyond imagining. That kind of power frightened folks."

"Why?"

Honey shrugs. "People fear what they don't understand. That's human nature." She glances at me, then she shifts her attention back to the water again. "He didn't come to town much, but when he did, he made people uncomfortable.

That was the real truth of it, Grey. He had these strange eyes. He made people nervous, the way he watched them. And that was enough to put folks on edge whenever he came around."

"Did he have a family?"

Honey nods. "I knew his mama and daddy a little. They were bayou folk. Good people. Kept to themselves. But they both passed on a lot of years before that business with Ember and Orli."

"Did he have anyone else?"

"What does it matter?" Honey asks. "He's been gone a long time now."

I'm trying to make sense of that photo. Those familiar eyes.

"What about a wife?"

"Not that I knew of." Honey keeps her focus on the river.

"Kids?"

She shakes her head. "Let it go, Grey. No sense in dragging all that hurt up."

Honey slows the boat to a crawl as we creep out of the bayou and skirt along the edge of the river toward the dock.

"You don't believe Dempsey Fontenot killed Ember and Orli," I say. She'd told me as much on my first afternoon home. Hadn't she? Why hadn't I paid more attention?

"I never believed he did. No." Honey pauses for a second as the waves from a passing tug rock our tiny boat. I listen to them slap against the muddy shoreline. "And he didn't kill Elora, either, if that's what you're really wondering."

"Is that what you think?" I ask her. "Or what you know?"

She motions for me to toss her the docking rope. "That's what I know."

Once we get the boat tied up, Honey sends Bernadette home and asks me to watch the store for the rest of the afternoon, so she can go lie down. She says the heat is getting to her. Making her light-headed. But Honey's lived here her whole life. She doesn't notice the heat. I've never even seen her break a sweat.

I wander into the kitchen for a glass of water, but I end up trapped by my mother's haunted eyes. I can't stop thinking about them lately.

Her green eyes.

My green eyes.

Zale's blue ones. Like ice on fire. And Dempsey Fontenot's. Staring out at me from that newspaper article.

I spend the rest of the day waiting on customers and trying to read *The Tempest*. But I don't get anywhere. The story just doesn't hold my interest.

How could it?

Prospero's magic island has nothing on La Cachette.

Honey makes smoked sausage and corn bread for dinner, and she says she's feeling better. But she keeps looking at me like there's something she wants to say. Or something she wants to ask. She never gets around to it, though. The two of us spend the whole meal treading silence like deep water.

By the time we clean up, the sky is changing colors. But there's still a little bit of daylight left. I think about heading out to Li'l Pass. Like I told Zale I would.

I don't, though.

Because I keep seeing that newspaper photo of Dempsey Fontenot.

Instead I end up sitting at the kitchen table, trying to read some more of *The Tempest*.

And failing.

It's just about dark when I decide I need some fresh air. So I push open the kitchen door and step out on to the boardwalk behind the house. Something about the night makes me uneasy. It's too still. Too empty.

But I'm not afraid. Not really.

Not until I feel the goose bumps come up on my arms. That static charge in the air that tells me he's close.

"I didn't mean to scare you, Grey."

Zale is walking toward me out of evening mist. I see him in silhouette, backlit by fireflies. He's wearing a T-shirt this time. Faded yellow, the color of butter. Still no shoes.

"You didn't scare me," I tell him. But that's not quite the truth.

Fear licks at my insides. And my stomach is full of rocks.

His thrumming electricity pulses through my brain like a drumbeat. It starts my whole body tingling.

"You didn't come," he says. "I wanted to make sure you were okay."

His eyes are so beautiful. Warm. And kind. That easy, relaxed feeling rises up inside me.

But then I think about of those other eyes. The ones in the newspaper. And I tense up again.

Zale is watching me.

"You know you don't need to be afraid of me, right?"

I nod.

But I don't know that. I don't know that at all. How could I know that?

Suddenly I wonder what I'm doing out here.

There are things out here. In the almost-dark. Everybody says so. Why the hell am I standing here talking to a strange boy? A boy I don't even know.

A boy with Dempsey Fontenot's ice-fire eyes.

I should play it safe. Head inside. Lock the door.

I should. But I don't.

I can't.

"I found a picture," I whisper. "Of Dempsey Fontenot. And he – his –"

The night steals my words.

Zale is still standing down below me. Bare feet planted in the soft mud.

"It's okay," he promises. "You don't need to be afraid of him, either, Grey."

"He was –" I can't think straight.

"He was my daddy," Zale finishes for me. "But he's been dead a long time. Since dat summer."

I wish I could make sense of what he's saying, but it's all so fuzzy.

My fear is crumbling away like the edges of the riverbank, and all I want is to sink into that warm, peaceful feeling. But instead I struggle back to the surface so I can find the words I need.

"What he did –"

Thunder rumbles long and low off in the distance, and Zale corrects me.

"What dey say he did."

"I don't understand," I tell him.

There's cotton at the edges of my brain as thick as the dark at the edges of the sky. I try to push it back so I can think clearly. I need to know what happened all those years ago. I sit down cross-legged on the edge of the boardwalk, and Zale climbs the steps to sit beside me.

"I don't remember much of it." He leans back on his elbows to study the thick clouds that have rolled in out of nowhere, blocking out the twinkling stars. "I never saw those little girls in the water. But folks came around real early one mornin' and found dem dere, in the pond out behind our cabin. Drowned."

"Who came and found them there?" I'm trying to remember how the story goes.

Zale shrugs. "Town folks, that's all my mama ever said. I don't have any memory of that part. I just remember the fire."

Somewhere, way off in the distance, a single bolt of lightning reaches down from the sky to strike at the ground like a snake.

And I feel fear creep back in on me.

"My daddy wasn't even home that mornin'. He was off huntin'. It was just me and Mama and –" He chokes on something. Swallows back some deep hurt. "And all of a sudden, dere was fire everywhere. And smoke. So my mama grabbed me up, and we ran. I can still feel the heat of the flames."

"Nobody even knew he was married," I say.

In all our nightmares, the monster never had a wife.

Or a child.

Zale shrugs. "I don't imagine they ever were. Not on paper, anyway."

He pauses for a minute, and the air around us is more charged than ever. I hear the sharp crackle of it. My fingers brush one of the copper nails along the edge of the boardwalk, and I get a zap that's almost painful.

"I remember the two of us running through the bayou," he goes on, "her hand clamped over my mouth to keep me from yellin' out. Mama said they'd kill us, sure, if they were to find us."

"So you left," I say.

He nods. "Knocked around some till we ended up down in Florida. And I never heard her so much as mention my daddy's name again."

I think about that newspaper article. "But they've been looking for him. All these years. They're still looking for him."

Zale turns those ice-blue eyes on me, and for the first time, I notice the deep sadness in them. "Well, they're lookin' for a ghost, then."

"You don't know that, though," I tell him. "Not for sure."

When he sits up, his shoulder brushes against mine. And there's that little tingle. It feels so good. Not sharp, like the bite of the charged copper.

"He never came for us." Zale lifts his face toward the sky. "I don't care what dey told you about him, Grey. He was a good man. If he'd been alive, he would have come for us. My mama and me." I hear the heartbreak in his voice. Plain as anything. Real. And true. "He would have come for us. No matter what."

All these years people have said it was Dempsey Fontenot who burned the cabin to the ground. He lit it up like a bonfire, they told us, before he ran off for good.

But now Zale is telling me that was a lie.

And if that was a lie –

what else was a lie?

"You don't believe he did it," I say.

"Killed those little girls? No. I know for sure he didn't." More distant thunder. The hair on my neck stands up again. "My daddy was a gentle man. He never hurt a solitary soul."

"Did Elora know?" I ask him. "Who your daddy was?"

He nods. "I told her the truth, just like I'm tellin' you now. But Elora said it didn't matter. She told me everyone has at least one secret that'll break your heart."

That's such an Elora thing to say that I actually hear the words in her voice. Not Zale's.

"I'm glad you know the truth," he adds. "I shoulda told you soon as I met you, but I didn't wanna scare you off." He looks at me, and there's something different in his eyes. Something almost shy. "I been lonely, I guess."

"That's why you came back here," I say. "To find out what happened that night." And Zale nods.

"After my mama passed, I hitchhiked all the way from Everglades City. Did a little work here and there on the way. Picked up a little money to get me by. Been camping out back there, at the old home place, ever since."

I shiver in the summer-night heat.

"You've been staying back there? At Keller's Island? Alone? All this time?"

He nods. "Bought me a tent and an old flatboat off a guy up in Kinter. It's beat all to hell, but the motor's good. And I settled in. Started poking around. Doing some diggin'. To see if I could find out the truth. To see if I could find him, maybe. If there's anything left of him to find."

"You want to know that bad?"

Bad enough to live out there for months? In the bayou? All alone?

"He was my daddy," Zale says. "Wouldn't you wanna know what happened?"

"I'm not sure," I tell him. I'm thinking about my own mother. That photo with the haunted eyes. And about whatever Case did to Elora. "Maybe not knowing is better." Zale shakes his head.

"Knowing is hard," he says, "but it's a thing you can survive. The not knowing will kill you in the end. It's the secrets that fester."

A breeze moves through, and I hear the tinkling of wind chimes.

"How do you keep a secret in a town full of psychics?" I ask him, and light flashes bright inside those ice-fire eyes.

"You tell the truth," he answers. "At least part of it."

I turn and run. Bare feet pounding. Splashing.
As fast as I can go. And I don't look back.
I don't want to see. I don't want to know.
I don't want to remember.

15

It's full dark by the time Zale and I say goodbye.

"I'll tell you the same thing I told Elora, Grey. I'm not askin' you to keep my secret. That's too big a burden. If you need to tell about me, I won't do anything to stop you."

I think about that, but then I shake my head. "You're safe with me."

He told me the truth. And he didn't have to. He could have lied. Stayed hidden.

I look down at Elora's ring on my finger.

He didn't have to give me back that piece of her, either. He could have kept it for himself.

Zale smiles with obvious relief.

"You're safe with me, too," he says. "I promise you that."

He reaches for my hand and gives it a quick squeeze before he disappears, and my heart races with the energy of his touch.

I stand up and grab for the wooden railing outside the kitchen door to steady myself, but something bites at me and I draw back with a hiss. It's too dark to see, but I feel a long splinter lodged under the skin of my palm. I figure I better get on inside and let Honey dig it out, so it doesn't end up getting infected. But when I open the kitchen door, I hear Honey upstairs, laughing on the phone with her sister. And that could be a while. So I head back to my bedroom to find Case's Saint Sebastian medal in my underwear drawer.

That's one huge secret I can't let fester any more.

As soon as Honey gets off the phone, I'll show it to her. And she'll know what to do.

I wrap the little medal back up in the tissue and stick it in my pocket, then I go out to the front steps to wait.

Only someone is already out there. Waiting for me.

Hart's curls are wild and tangled, and his shoulders are slumped. He's staring out at the river as the smoke of an exhaled cigarette lingers above his head in the yellow porch light. Honey would kick his ass from here to Kinter and back if she caught him smoking on her front steps, but judging by the looks of him, he probably doesn't care.

It makes me jumpy to know that maybe he was sitting right here, just on the other side of the house, while Zale and I were out back.

I slip off Elora's ring and hide it in my pocket like a stone before I drop down to sit beside him. I feel my secrets, huge and heavy.

If I fell into the river, the weight of them would pull me straight to the bottom.

I know Hart can feel them, too, but he doesn't say anything. He just keeps his eyes on the river as he shakes out another cigarette and lights it up. I watch him pull the smoke into his lungs and hold it for a long time before he finally blows it out.

"I don't know what to say," he tells me. "About last night. I just –"

My cheeks burn. "Forget it," I mumble. "It doesn't matter."

I feel the dull throb of the splinter lodged deep in my palm. The beginnings of heat and redness.

Infection.

"Don't say that, Greycie. It matters." Hart flicks away ash and puts the cigarette to his lips again. "It's just, everything's all fucked up." He tips his head back to exhale words and smoke at the same time. "I'm all fucked up."

We sit there together for what feels like a long time. Silent. And if he can feel anything from me at all, I hope Hart feels how much I love him.

After a few minutes, he gets up and walks across the boardwalk to stand on the dock and stare out at the wide, rolling water. He doesn't even smoke. He just lets his cigarette burn all the way down until it becomes a column of ash and finally goes out in his hand.

He's burning himself to the ground.

The air moves, and Evie's wind chimes ring out like voices. They sound like whispered secrets.

And warnings.

I get so lost in their musical murmuring that the other voice doesn't register at first. Not until I see Hart turn around with his jaw set tight.

And there's Case, standing not five feet away from him.

Jesus.

Where the hell did he come from?

"You hear me? We gotta settle dis, Hart." When I get to my feet and cross the boardwalk, Hart moves to put himself between Case and me. "I didn't do shit to Elora. And you know it." The look in his eyes makes it clear that Case is itching for a fight.

And Hart is happy to give him one.

His muscles coil, and I grab for his arm. But it's too late. He launches himself at Case without a word, and they both go down. Hard. Spilling across the dock. While I watch. Frozen.

They trade blows – all fists and elbows – as they roll together on the white boards. They growl and snarl. Two mad dogs going after each other. If Honey were here, she'd turn the hose on them, like she used to do with the mean old hounds that Evie's uncle, Victor, kept out behind the house.

I hear a screen door slam, and Evie appears beside me on the boardwalk. I wonder if she was watching us again. Spying on Hart and me from her bedroom window.

I reach to put an arm around her, and Evie presses herself against me, halfway hiding behind my back. Every time Case lands a punch, I hear her react with a pained little yelp, and when he somehow scrambles to his feet and kicks Hart hard in the ribs, she muffles a scream.

Hart manages to get to his feet, too, still holding his side, and he grabs Case by the neck with one hand, slamming him back against a wooden post so hard I feel my own teeth rattle inside my skull. But then Case shoves him backward and they both lose their balance and go down again, rolling toward the edge of the dock.

Toward the roped-off rotten place and the long drop to the dark water below.

"Hart!" I call out his name in a panic.

That's when Evie pulls away from me. "Stop it!" she hisses. And at first, I think she's talking to Hart and Case. But then she crouches down low with her hands over her ears. "Leave me alone!" Her voice is desperate. "You're lying!" Eyes clamped shut. "Stop it!" she wails over and over. "Stop it! You're a liar!"

And I know then she's talking to somebody else. Someone I can't hear.

More feet behind us. I look over my shoulder as Mackey, Sera, and Sander appear out of the shadows. They must have come from Mackey's place, toward the upriver end of town.

"Shit!" Sera's eyes flicker from Case and Hart to me and finally to Evie, crumpled up in a heap on the ground. "Shit. Shit. Shit." She motions to Sander, and he goes to Evie and pulls her up to her feet, so he can wrap his arms around her.

Mackey looks back toward the houses lining the boardwalk. But there's no point. This time of night, everyone is safe inside dozing in their recliners. Windows closed. Curtains drawn. Big window-unit air conditioners humming and rattling. TVs blaring.

Nobody is coming out to stop this.

Hart and Case grapple and roll. Punching at each other. The sound of boot heels against wood. Blood spraying across white paint.

Then Hart gets his hands around Case's throat. And he doesn't let go.

That's when I know they really will kill each other if someone doesn't put an end to this.

And I don't want to watch anyone die. Definitely not Hart. And not Case, either.

Not even after what he did to Elora.

"Hart!" I yell his name again. "Stop it! You're gonna kill him!"

Hart's crying now. Sobbing and grunting. Totally out of control. And it scares me. He flips Case over on his back, and he's slamming his head against the dock over and over, choking him.

"Hart! Please!" My voice sounds hoarse, and I realize that I'm crying, too. I didn't even know it. "Stop!"

Hart glances in my direction, and then I see him look down at Case, red-faced and gasping for air.

"Don't," I tell him. "It won't bring her back."

Hart lets go then. He stands up and stumbles backward. He has the same look in his eyes that he had last night. After we kissed. Like he doesn't know where he is or how he got here.

Case scrambles to get his feet under him. Even in the moonlight, I can see the marks on his throat. But he's not ready to call it quits. He takes a step toward Hart, and Evie screams again.

"Case," I shout. "Stop! I know what you did! I found it! I found your medal!"

I reach into my pocket. Denim rubs against the throbbing

splinter in my palm, but I ignore the pain and dig the medal out for them to see.

Hart and Case both freeze. They're breathing hard. Soaked. Dripping sweat and blood.

"What the fuck, Greycie?" Hart sounds sick. Like he's having trouble talking around whatever is rising up in his throat. He's looking at me like I just stabbed him in the gut.

"Where'd ya get dat?" Case demands. He takes a step toward me, but Hart grabs him by the shirt and yanks him backward. I wrap my fingers tight around the medal.

And I feel that throbbing pain again.

"It was on the floor in Honey's shed," I tell him. "Where you dropped it. The night you killed Elora. When you stole that old black trunk to put her body in."

Hart's eyes go wide. And I've never watched anyone drown before, but that's what the look on his face makes me think of. "Jesus Christ, Greycie."

Behind me, I hear four identical gasps as Evie, Mackey, Sera, and Sander all realize what's happening here.

"You found out she was planning to run off with someone else," I say. "She sneaked away that night. To meet him. While everyone was playing flashlight tag. And you found out about it somehow. Only you couldn't let her go. So you killed her."

The truth sounds so terrible, flung out into the night air like that.

"Hell no!" Case turns and spits a broken tooth on to the dock. "Fuck dat!" His red hair is matted with blood, and one eye is already swollen shut. "Dat ain't what happened."

Hart shoves Case to the ground. He lies there, sprawled out in front of us while Hart towers over him. "Then you tell me what did happen." Hart gives him a hard kick in the ribs, and we all wince. "Before I kill your sorry ass." His voice breaks, and he chokes hard on tears and blood. "What happened to Elora that night?"

"I don't know," Case insists. He clutches his side and sits up, wiping at his destroyed face with the back of his arm. "I told everybody dat. I been sayin' it all along."

"Then why did I find your medal in Honey's shed?" I ask him. "With Elora's blood on it."

"Oh, God." It's Mackey behind me. "I think I'm gonna puke."

Hart's staring at the medal in my hand. He sways a little on his feet, but he doesn't go down.

Evie's breathing changes. She moans and sucks in air with a rattling, hitching wheeze. Covers her ears again.

And I feel bad. Because none of them were prepared for this. They didn't know it was coming.

"What the hell, Case?" Sera's sharp voice cuts through the chaos. Her river-sand-and-copper braid swings behind her back.

"It ain't my fault. Dat's where Wrynn lost it is all." Case starts to stand up. But Hart gives him another good kick. He groans and rolls on to his side. "Only she didn't tell me about it till it was months later. I swear."

"Wrynn?" Hart's face is really swelling up. His bottom lip is busted wide open. And it makes the word come out thick and twisted.

Case nods. "Wrynn told me she found my medal dat night. Lying right here. On dis dock." He manages to sit up, then he wipes at his face again. "Goddammit." Now Case is the one who's crying, big tears that make tracks down his cheeks through the smeared blood. "I loved 'er, you buncha assholes!" He glares at Hart. At all of us. "Since we were twelve years old, I fuckin' loved 'er." He pins me down with his eyes. "You know dat's right, chere."

And maybe I do, but loving someone doesn't mean you won't hurt them.

A heavy fog is rolling in off the river, and it wraps us all in thick, wet misery.

"Wrynn told me she saw da rougarou go after Elora dat night. Now, maybe dat's true, and maybe it ain't." Case shrugs. "But she said she picked up dat medal. After." He points a swollen purple finger in my direction. "And den she got scared. She's just a kid, right? So she went and hid in Miss Roselyn's shed. And dat's when she dropped Saint Sebastian. Only she didn't tell me till later."

"So you came back for it," I say, and Case nods.

"Been lookin' for it all summer.

"Because you knew if anybody found it, it'd make you look guilty."

Case shakes his head. "I came back for it 'cause Wrynn wanted it. Little Bird loved Elora, too." He stares us all down. Like he'd just as soon throw us in the river as look at us. "And dat medal is the only thing of Elora's she had." His voice quivers, and he turns his head to spit more blood. Then he struggles to his feet. "You all ain't gotta believe me. But I swear to God, I didn't kill my girl."

"She wasn't your fucking girl," Hart snarls through clenched teeth.

Case puffs up like a pissed-off bullfrog, but then he deflates right in front of our eyes. Like somebody stuck him with a pin. "I didn't kill her, Hart," he says. "I never touched a hair on her goddamn beautiful head. I swear dat on my mama's life."

The two of them stare at each other for a long, silent minute while the rest of us stand there holding our breath. Waiting for one of them to throw the next punch.

"He's telling the truth." Hart's voice is so quiet, I almost don't hear him.

"But –" I start.

"Dammit!" Hart turns and kicks an old wooden crate as hard as he can, sending it skittering across the dock and crashing into the river. We hear the splash. "I said he didn't do this. I feel it clear now."

"Hart –" I reach for his hand, but he flinches away from my touch.

"Don't," he growls.

Then he stalks off down the boardwalk toward his house, leaving the rest of us reeling. And he doesn't look back.

Evie wails and tears herself away from Sander to take a few steps after Hart, but Sera puts out a hand to stop her. "Let him go, Evie. He'll be okay."

And I'm relieved. Because it's not Case. He isn't the one. But I'm also lost, because . . .

if it wasn't Case ...

   and it wasn't Dempsey Fontenot ...

      and it sure as hell wasn't a swamp werewolf ...

then who killed Elora?

"Hart's been wastin' all dis time talkin' shit about me." Case's voice is low and wounded. "And I ain't never hurt nobody. Y'all shoulda know'd dat." He looks at us, one by one. But nobody meets his eyes. "Hell. Hart shoulda know'd dat." Case turns and spits. More blood. "That asshole got one thing right, though. Elora wasn't my girl. Not any more." The bitterness drips out of his mouth like the blood drips from his swollen nose. "I told you dat, Grey. You find whoever it is she was runnin' around on me wit', and I bet you find who killed 'er." He turns to go.

"Case, I'm sorry, I –"

His words cut me open. "I don't need your fuckin' sorry. I need to know what happened to Elora."

"Me too," I tell him.

And then I let him go. Because there's nothing else to say.

The five of us who are left look at each other. Evie's wind chimes are whispering again.

"Who was Elora in love with?" I ask.

But all I get are blank stares and shrugs. I look around the little group.

"Was it you?" I ask Mackey.

"Me? Nah." Mackey shakes his head. "It was never like that between Elora and me."

"Who, then?" I turn to look at Sander. "You?"

He looks at me, surprised, and shakes his head. Then he

pushes those sand-and-copper waves out of his face, so I can see his eyes, and he blinks at Sera like there's something he wants her to tell me.

"Sander likes boys," she says, just like she's telling me the sky is blue. And it's clear I'm the only one out of the loop on that.

Why are there so many holes in what I know about the people I'm supposed to know best?

Why haven't I been paying attention?

Suddenly, I wonder if Zale was telling me the truth this morning. When he said he and Elora weren't in love. The thought makes me nauseous. Because I believed him so easy.

But what if he's the one?

"If Elora was in deep with anybody," Sera is saying, "it was probably some guy from upriver. One of the Kinter boys she was always messin' around with. Somebody like that."

Great.

That could be any of a hundred guys.

I turn my attention to Evie. She's burrowed into Sander's chest. Her hair covers her face, and she's still crying softly. "Evie," I tell her. "If you know something. Or if you're hearing something. Voices or –"

"I don't," she sniffs. "I'm not."

"If you're hearing Elora –"

"Stop it!" she wails, and Sera shoots me a dirty look. "I'm not!"

"Please," I say. Evie looks so much younger than almost seventeen. She looks like a little girl. Terrified and lost. And it makes me feel awful. I make my voice as gentle as possible. "I need you to tell me the truth."

She pulls away from Sander and looks at me.

"Just leave me alone, Grey. There isn't any truth to tell." Her arms are wrapped tight around her chest. "Why can't everybody just leave me alone?"

Victor's voice slices through the fog. Thick and slippery with alcohol. He's calling from their front porch. "Evangeline! Where you at? Git yur ass in here, girl!"

I see Evie flinch at her uncle's words.

"It's okay, Evie," Sera soothes. "Everything's gonna be okay. Come on." She slips her arm around Evie's shaking shoulders. "Let's get you home, sè."

Sera and Sander practically carry a still sobbing Evie back toward the boardwalk with Mackey trailing behind them. He looks back over his shoulder to give me a sad smile.

"You get on to bed, Grey." Mackey's voice is kind, but his eyes are worried. "It's not safe out here this time of night."

Then the dark gobbles them up.

And I'm all alone.

I head back across the boardwalk to the light of Honey's front porch. I'm still clutching Elora's good luck charm. Case's Saint Sebastian medal. I sit down on the steps, slick with damp, and stare at that rust-colored smudge on the back.

My best friend's blood.

Evie's wind chimes start to sing again, soft this time. And I think maybe I hear my name whispered in the fog.

"Grey?"

I should go inside. The whisper comes again, over the tinkling of all those chimes. "Grey?"

The hair on my neck stands on end.

"Elora?"

But it's Wrynn who steps out of the shadows. She comes to sit beside me on the steps. Mosquito bites dot her skinny legs like a bad case of measles, and her long red hair is heavy and wet. She's still wearing that dime on the CheeWee-stained string around her neck.

Her face lights up when she sees the medal in my hand. "You found it!" she squeals. "I wanted it back so bad. And Case couldn't find it for me. But you did." I let her take the little silver charm from me. If Case didn't kill Elora, then I guess the medal doesn't mean anything. Besides, I figure Elora would want her to have it.

Wrynn notices the splinter in my palm. It's raised and angry-looking. Bright red and hot as fire. She runs her finger over it, and I suck in air through my teeth.

"It hurts," she says, and I nod. Tears prick at my eyes, but I blink them back.

Everything hurts this summer.

Wrynn takes her own palm and lays it over mine. Her touch is soft and cool. And when she pulls her hand back, the splinter is gone. I trace the spot where it should be, and the skin is unbroken.

Perfect.

I remember Honey telling me once that people used to call on Wrynn's grandmother – Ophelia's mama – when they were sick or hurting. Because she had a gift for easing a fever or making broken bones whole, just by laying on a hand.

Psychic healing.

I stare at my palm in wonder.

"I tried to do it to Elora," Wrynn whispers. "But she was already gone. And I cain't fix gone."

"She was dead," I say, and Wrynn nods. Her eyes are solemn. She rubs at the little saint's medal. Elora's good luck charm.

"When I came back, she was."

"What do you mean, when you came back?"

"I saw dat rougarou snatch her by da arm and open up wide, like he was gonna eat Elora right up. All dem sharp teeth showin'." She shivers. Scoots closer to me on the step. "So I got scared and took off. Hauled for home. 'Cause I sure didn't wanna see dat. Left Elora dere all alone with him." Wrynn sniffs. "And I'm awful sorry I did it. But den I got to thinkin', maybe I could help 'er. So I went on back."

"But she was already dead."

Wrynn nods again. "I was too late, Grey." She points a skinny finger toward the dock. "Elora was layin' right dere all bloody. And no heart beating in her chest. Not a bit of life in her no more."

I close my eyes against the image, and Wrynn goes on.

"I tried to fix 'er. Only I couldn't." She shakes her head. "Cain't fix dead. But I found dis lying dere beside her." She holds up the little medal. "So I kept it."

"Then what?"

She frowns. "I heard him comin' back."

"To get her body," I say, and Wrynn nods.

"So I went and hid. In Miss Roselyn's shed. Only . . ."

She stops, too afraid to go on. But I know her story isn't finished.

"Only he came in there, too, didn't he?" I ask her, and Wrynn nods again. Her whole body is shaking, and she's chewing at one dirty fingernail.

"I stayed hidden way back in one corner till he was gone. And I was so quiet, Grey. More quieter than a mouse. I didn't even breathe."

"He took something, didn't he?" I suggest. "From the shed. He took a big old trunk. A black one."

Wrynn nods one more time and closes her eyes tight against the memory of whatever she saw that night. Her words come out in a terrified whisper that makes me wonder how I could ever have believed she was just making up stories.

"Then I took off. But I dropped my medal somehow. Couldn't tell nobody, though. Not for one hundred and one days."

"Because of the curse," I say.

"I don't wanna be no rougarou."

"Then you told Case."

More than three months later.

Wrynn nods and opens her eyes. "Only he couldn't find it for me." She lays her head on my shoulder, and I feel her sticky little hand in mine. "But you did."

"Wrynn," I tell her. "Listen to me. This is really important. You have to tell me who killed Elora. Who did you really see that night?"

She sits up to look at me, confused. "You know who it was, Grey. I told you."

"Who killed Elora, Wrynn?" I grab her by her skinny shoulders and give her a hard shake. "Tell me the truth!"

The sound of my own voice scares me, and I guess it scares Wrynn, too, because she stands up and pulls away from me. When she steps out on to the boardwalk, the moon illuminates her big eyes and her pale skin so that she almost glows. Goose bumps cover her head to toe.

"Just tell me!" I beg her. "Please!"

"I already told you," she whispers. "It was da rougarou."

Whatever she knows, I'm not getting it out of her. At least not tonight.

"You better get on home," I say. "Case is hurt bad. He might need you."

Wrynn stares at me. "Daddy and the boys are out night fishin'. Way down at Sawdust Bend. Nobody but me and Mama home tonight."

She starts off down the boardwalk, but before the darkness swallows her up, she turns back to look at me.

"Dat ol' rougarou? He's a shape-shifter, sure enough. So you be careful, Grey. He may come right up on ya. Might sit down real close. Maybe even hold your hand. And you won't ever know it till you see dem teeth."

Wrynn turns and disappears into the night, but her words float back to me like the sound of wind chimes.

"And by den, it's too late. You're already dead."

My head bounces against his shoulder as he carries me through the storm. And I stop fighting then.

I turn my face up toward the sky and wait for the rain to drown me. Death in the water. Like Mackey said. What does it matter if the water swirls and bubbles up from below or if it falls from the sky? Water is water. And dead is dead.

16

The next day is Friday, and I make Mackey bring me his high school yearbook.

"I thought she killed herself," he tells me when he stops by the Mystic Rose that morning to drop it off. "Threw herself in the river, maybe." Mackey glances over his shoulder, nervous. "Hart doesn't like us to say it. But that's what I thought."

He has on basketball shorts and worn-out tennis shoes, and he reaches down to slap away a huge fly that lands on his shin.

"I figured that's why she ignored my warning about death in the water." His eyes settle on the stack of flyers by the register. The ones with Elora's picture. "Because she already knew she was gonna die."

When he leaves, I flip through the yearbook and try to compose a list of every boy I ever heard Elora mention.

Dalton Guidry
Jamal Tilman
Evan Richard

Matteo Arredondo

And on and on.

But it feels hopeless, because there were lots of older guys she ran with, too. And I don't have all the names. Besides, who's to say she didn't meet someone totally new since last August?

I know she had at least one new friend.

I add Zale's name to the list.

Erase it.

Add it again.

Cross it out.

The truth is, it could have been any boy south of New Orleans and east of Lafayette.

After lunch, I step out on the porch for some fresh air. Evie's put up a bunch of new wind chimes. I hear them ringing, even though I can't feel any breeze to speak of.

I wave when I catch her watching me from her bedroom window. But she pulls the curtains. So I don't get to ask again about what happened last night.

Why she freaked out. Whose voice she's hearing.

Not that she'd tell me anything.

We stay busy in the shop all afternoon, and after dinner I try to sneak out to meet Zale, but Honey wants to start teaching me the tarot. Now that we know I have the gift, she says, I might as well learn how to use it.

"Don't fear the Death card," she tells me when the bone-white face shows up in my first reading. "It doesn't represent physical death. The skeleton riding horseback foretells the end of something less concrete."

But I can't stop staring at those hollow eyes set deep into a grinning skull.

"You know, Sugar Bee," Honey says, "as spiritualists, we celebrate life by embracing death as a natural part of the cycle."

"What happens when the death isn't natural?" I ask her.

"Ah." Honey reaches over to pat my hand. "That's another thing altogether."

That night, when she goes to sleep, I take the tarot deck and sit on my bed for hours. Shuffling. And reshuffling. Sorting the thick deck into three equal piles.

Past.

Present.

Future.

Just like Honey showed me.

But I don't find any answers in the cards.

The next day is Saturday, and Honey gets Bernadette to mind the store so the two of us can take a day trip up to New Orleans. I know she's trying to distract me. But it doesn't work. Because I keep seeing Elora.

On Basin Street and Canal Street and Toulouse Street, beautiful girls catch my eye. Girls with long dark hair and mirrored sunglasses and laughter that sounds like improvised jazz. I see Elora in the crowd at Café Du Monde and among the street artists in Jackson Square.

But when I look again, it's never her. And my heart squeezes.

On the drive back down to Kinter, Honey tells me family stories about my great-grandparents and my grandfather. Great-aunts and great-uncles. Some distant cousins.

But she doesn't tell me about my mom.

She doesn't tell me any more about Dempsey Fontenot, either. Not even when I come right out and ask.

She just sighs and says, "Our eyes are on the front of our heads for a reason, Grey. Let the past stay where it belongs."

Then, when we get home, she goes straight into the kitchen and starts chopping up the holy trinity.

Onions.

Green peppers.

Celery.

A time-honored Louisiana recipe for ignoring hard questions.

The evening heat is unbearable. But the weather isn't nearly as oppressive as the silence.

Or the secrets.

So I pull on my mud boots and head out toward Li'l Pass, almost without realizing where I'm going.

When I get there, Zale is already waiting for me on top of the old trailer. Just like he knew I was coming. I think about what Case said after that fight out on the dock. About Elora's murderer.

You find whoever it is she was runnin' around on me wit' and I bet you'll find who killed 'er.

Fear tickles at me like a little spider walking across my skin, and I wonder one more time whether Zale was telling me the truth about him and Elora being just friends.

But then he looks up at me, and there is so much honesty in his eyes. I don't see any shadowy corners where he could hide a lie like that. So I pull off my boots and crawl up to sit next to him in the purple light.

"Hi," I say.

Somewhere a chuck-will's-widow begins its evening song, and a chorus of frogs decides to sing backup. The bayou is coming to life all around us.

And I suddenly feel shy and awkward. Like I don't know what to say next. But then he smiles at me, and there's so much I want to tell him.

I start with the fight between Case and Hart.

The bloody Saint Sebastian medal. Elora's good luck charm. How I thought Case was the one. And how Hart says he isn't. How he can feel the truth of that now.

So we're right back where we started.

"Did she ever tell you about anyone else?" I ask. "A new boyfriend?"

But Zale shakes his head. "Even that last night I saw her, when she told me she was leavin' town, she never said who with."

We sit together in the falling dark while the electric air dances around us. I see the energy coming off Zale in waves that look like heat rising up off the highway. The flies are biting at me something awful, but I never see one land on him.

"Honey says people didn't like your daddy because he was too powerful." He doesn't ask who Honey is. Just like he didn't ask who Hart is. Or Case. And it makes me wonder how much Zale knows about us.

About all of us.

"She says people were afraid of him. That he could bring

storms." He's studying me with those fire-and-ice eyes. "You can do that, too, can't you?"

"Do you know what *Zale* means?" he asks me. I shake my head, and he gives me a big grin. My heart skips a beat. Or three. "It means 'strength of the sea'. I was a hurricane baby."

It still feels so strange just sitting and talking to Zale like this. But it feels right, too. And that seems strange itself, until I remember that he's one of us. One of the Summer Children.

Just like Elora. And all the others.

Like Hart.

For a second, I think about those dark curls. And my fingers itch. I remember the way Hart laughs, deep in his throat. How he used to tease me. And I get overwhelmed with missing him.

The way he used to be.

The way we used to be.

But then that feeling fades away, and this beautiful fog rolls in to take its place inside my head. And I'm grateful.

"A huge storm blew in the night I was born," Zale is telling me. "Moved right across Keller's Island. My daddy tried to hold it back, but it was too strong for 'im. He couldn't stop it comin'. And my mama couldn't stop me comin.'"

"You were born into the storm," I say, and he nods.

"I wasn't two minutes old when the wind took our little shack. Blew it clean away. Sucked me right outta my mama's arms."

A couple stray clouds are scattered across the sky, but when Zale waves his hand, they roll off. Just like he shoo'd 'em away.

"When dey found me, I was lying in a big old mud puddle.

Safe and comfortable as you please. Storm raging all around me, except right dere where I was. In that little bubble, my mama said there wasn't even breeze enough to move the little curl on the top of my head."

"The power of the sea and the sky," I whisper. Just like Honey told me.

We're sitting so close together. I feel the static charge of his shoulder barely brushing mine. The two of us stay out there at Li'l Pass and talk for a long time while the sky turns velvet black and the stars blink on like Christmas lights.

And we do it the next night, too.

And the night after that.

And that's how it goes for weeks.

Those terrifying flashes of Elora keep coming, but I don't learn anything useful. It's like I swim and swim and swim against the current, but I never make any progress. The river just sweeps me farther downstream.

Hart drifts further away from me, too. And I miss him so much. My fingers still long for those curls sometimes, but he doesn't come around any more. I see him plenty. Standing on the dock staring at the river. Or sitting at the end of the boardwalk, watching Willie Nelson down at the gator pond. But there might as well be a hundred miles between us. His busted face heals up, but he loses weight. His cheeks are sunken and his eyes are dark. I'm watching him blow away, just like the ash at the end of his cigarette. I ache for him. But I can't reach him. I try once or twice, but as soon as I mention Elora he shuts down. Pushes me away. "Don't," he warns me. Like he can't stand to so much as hear her name. "She's gone. What does it matter?"

Evie's distant, too. Sometimes I catch her watching me from her bedroom window, but I don't see much of her. She finally comes over on the Fourth of July to sit with me on the front steps of the bookstore and watch people launch fireworks off the river dock. We eat ice cream sandwiches, and she lets me French braid her hair. "Have you seen Hart lately?" she asks, and I shake my head.

"Not really."

She looks at me like she thinks I'm lying. "But you guys are together, aren't you?"

I hear the hurt in her voice, and I wonder how much she saw between Hart and me that night a few weeks back. My birthday. I caught her watching us from her front porch. But now I'm wondering if she saw what happened before that. Down at the old pontoon boat.

That kiss.

"No," I reassure her. "We aren't together. It's not like that between us."

I don't tell her the real truth of it.

That Hart's too messed up to be with anybody right now.

"It doesn't matter anyway," she says, and it gets quiet. Except for the bottle rockets and the Roman candles. I want to ask her about the night of the fight. What happened to her out on the dock. I still need to know if the voice she was hearing was Elora's.

But I don't get a chance, because she makes an excuse to leave.

After that, she only comes out to hang more wind chimes.

Case is still pissed, and I don't blame him. We don't cross paths much, but when we do, he scowls at me. His face is all healed up, but Hart left him with a missing tooth and a pretty good scar over one eye, and I imagine that every time he looks in the mirror, it reminds him that we all thought he was capable of murder.

Even Wrynn stays hidden. Sometimes I look up in time to see her disappear around a corner. Or behind a tree. Her long red hair gives her away. So I know she's out there. But she doesn't come in close. And I wonder if she's more afraid of the rougarou or of me.

The rest of us still hang out, of course. Sometimes it's a bonfire out at Sera and Sander's place. Or passing around a couple beers in the clearing behind Mackey's house. Maybe even a little bit of weed, if someone has it. But with Elora gone and Case avoiding us, plus Hart missing in action and Evie always being a no-show, things are weird. We try our best to act normal. We laugh as much as we're able to. Listen to music. Tell stories. Occasionally, if Sera has enough to drink, she'll make out with Mackey. Just a little bit. Or sometimes we'll all pile up on someone's couch and watch an old movie. But the truth is, whenever we're together, I spend all my time counting heads. Just to make sure nobody else has disappeared.

During the days, I keep busy helping out in the Mystic Rose. I reprice the essential oils and dust the healing stones. Then I alphabetize all the books.

I study palm-reading guides and let Sander do my star chart.

I stare into mirrors. Burn sage, like Sera tells me to. Sleep with a piece of clear quartz under my pillow. Because Honey says it will bring me clarity. I even try one of those new yoga DVDs.

But none of it helps.

So I run.

A couple times a week I badger Mackey until he takes me up to Kinter with him. To the high school track. We lace up our running shoes, and I run until my lungs are on fire and my legs fail.

I run until my brain switches itself off.

Until Mackey puts a hand on my shoulder and tells me it's time to go home.

But no matter how fast I go, I can't catch up to Elora.

Or my mother.

Sometimes, when Honey isn't watching, I stop in the kitchen and study that photo on the wall. I try to imagine what kind of deep power the young woman with one hummingbird hair clip might have possessed. I close my eyes and reach for her, but my mother has never seemed so far away.

By the middle of July, I've pretty much given up on ever finishing *The Tempest*. But I'm still holding out hope that, somehow, I'll figure out what happened to Elora. Because if I leave here not knowing anything more than I know now, I figure I might as well be dead myself.

The temperature has become truly suffocating. The bayou loves the heat, though. Honey's roses wither. But the wild things thrive. Cattails and rousseau cane grow tall and thick along the edges of the boardwalk. Someone cuts them down when they threaten to take over. But they come right back. Taller. And thicker. Vines rise out of the muck to twist around the pilings, reaching up to tug at the white-painted planks that blister and peel in the unforgiving sun. Mold and rot creep in around the edges. And the smell of decay is overwhelming. By midday the air is so thick that it's like trying to breathe wet cotton. We stay inside during the worst of it, but even on high, the AC can't keep up. It makes us all slow and cranky. And I find myself watching the clock each day, counting the hours until the sun goes down and I can escape to join Zale back at Li'l Pass. Because when I'm with him, at least I feel like I can breathe a little easier.

We meet up most every evening when the frogs start to sing and the light begins to change. The two of us sit back there on the rusted-out trailer and talk until it gets too dark to see each other any more.

Mostly we talk about Elora. I tell him how the two of us used to share dreams sometimes. How we'd go to bed curled up together under Honey's quilts, and then both wake up at the exact same moment, having dreamed the exact same thing.

Zale tells me how no one had ever listened to him the way Elora did, without judgment or expectations. How he'd started to feel like a ghost, but the way Elora saw him – heard him – made him feel real again.

And it feels so good just to be able to breathe Elora's name out loud to someone. It feels like keeping her alive, maybe. In some small way.

"What if I never find out the truth?" I ask Zale one night. "Elora was everything to me. How do I go on living just the same? Like nothing ever happened?"

With summer more than halfway over, the thought of ever caring about trips to the mall or scheduling college visits . . . or even running track again . . . seems impossible.

Zale takes my hand, and electricity sparks between our fingers. He spins Elora's ring three times. Like making a wish.

"You don't go on living just the same," he tells me. "You have to go on living in a completely different way."

And that's the first thing that's made sense to me in a really long time.

We talk a lot about his daddy, too, and Zale always gets quiet when we come to the morning his mama pulled him from the flames and ran with him through the bayou. Her hand clamped tight over his mouth.

The same morning folks pulled Ember and Orli from the drowning pool.

"All those memories are filled with smoke," he tells me. "But my daddy wasn't a murderer. That's a thing I can say for certain."

So I try to let my old fear go. To think of Dempsey Fontenot as something other than a killer. To picture him the way Zale paints him in the stories he tells. But it's hard, because it's a really strange thing to find out the monster under your bed was never really a monster at all.

And at first, it seems like we need each other, Zale and me, so we can help solve each other's mysteries. But somewhere during those long, hot weeks, something changes. And we start talking about so many other things.

Because maybe we just need each other.

He tells me more about growing up in Florida. How his mama taught him the names of all the wetland plants, which ones you can eat and which ones are good for healing. And I tell him about why I love to run. How it makes me feel. The freedom I find in it.

And it feels so good to talk to someone. Really talk to someone.

About things that don't hurt.

And about things that do.

Night after night, we sit out there until the sky goes inky and the owls start to call and I know I'm late for supper. And then some.

But I never want to go in. Because being with Zale makes me feel like maybe I'll be okay. And the whole time I'm with him, I drink up that peaceful, slightly fuzzy feeling like it's cold, fresh water. And I'm dying of thirst.

More and more often, he'll hold my hand. Or brush against my arm. On purpose. And I'll feel that little shock of electric current. That tiny zap. Skin on skin.

One night he's telling me a story about the first time he ever tasted ice cream, and he puts a gentle hand on my bare thigh. Just for a second.

And I almost pass out from how good it feels. It makes me curious. Maybe even a little excited.

And that's a bit of a distraction, but it's not enough. Because as the summer wears on, I can't ignore this idea that something is coming. It's not a psychic vision or anything like that, but with every day that passes, I feel it building.

Gathering around us.

Something that nobody can stop.

Something that's even bigger than Zale's search for his dead father or our questions about what really happened to Ember and Orli thirteen summers ago.

Bigger than the mystery of Elora's murder, even.

Something with the power to sweep us all away.

I feel his hands around my neck. Squeezing. Choking. Holding me down in the mud and the water while the last bit of life drains out of me.

17

It's August 6 when I first hear it on the radio. But I know before that. When I wake up that morning, the air is different. Thicker. But also more alive. The bayou has started to breathe.

It's waiting.

"Storm warning," Honey says when I walk into the kitchen for breakfast, and she jerks her head toward the radio sitting on the counter. The weather guy tells us that a tropical depression has formed over the Bahamas, 350 miles east of Miami, Florida. But that's an awful long way from La Cachette, so Honey isn't paying much attention. She's too busy rolling out dough for biscuits. It makes me uneasy, though. I'm supposed to have three weeks left, but if it looks like things might get bad, Honey will send me home early.

But then the ten o'clock boat comes, and the weather forecast gets forgotten. It's a busy Sunday morning, and I spend most of my time ringing up sales. Then I rearrange the shelves of incense and organize the meditation CDs.

Every time I look down at my ring finger, though, or touch the little blue pearl hanging around my neck, I remember that I only have one mission this summer.

Figure out what happened to Elora.

And I know that I'm failing at it. Failing her. And now I might be running out of time.

I think about that latest vision. Strong hands around my throat.

Around Elora's throat.

The certainty that I'm going to die in the mud.

I feel Elora's panic rise inside me until I drop the meditation CDs and they scatter across the floor. And I have to start all over.

None of the flashes I've seen make sense.

Did Elora drown? Like I did that night on the bathroom floor?

Or was it the cold metal of a gun cocked behind her head that sealed her fate?

Click.

Or did someone steal her life with their bare hands? Fingers tightening around her windpipe?

How many ways are there to die?

Evie scampers across the boardwalk to sit with me on the porch for a little bit that evening after dinner. She's nervous and fidgety. Paler than usual. Her hair is wet and matted, so I go inside to get a brush, and she crouches on the steps between my feet while I work out the tangles.

It isn't long before Sera and Sander join us. And then

Mackey. Almost like something had pulled us together in the fading light. That used to happen all the time when we were kids. One of us would be outside somewhere. And then another of us would just show up. And another. And another. Until we were all there. Carrying on and horsing around.

But nobody has much to say now. We're all lost in our own thoughts.

"There's a storm comin'," Evie finally announces.

"Nothing to be afraid of," Sera says, and I know her words are meant to reassure us all. Not just Evie. "It probably won't hit here."

"I'm not afraid," Evie answers. "I hope it does come."

"You okay?" Mackey asks her.

"Everything's different." Evie frowns. "I thought things would stay the same." A breeze stirs, and her wind chimes come to life. There must be close to fifty of them now, made out of everything from seashells and Mardi Gras doubloons to old soup ladles and metal pie plates. The noise is enough to wake the dead, and her house has become kind of a tourist attraction. She chews on a broken fingernail. "I just wanted things to stay the same."

"I know," I say. "I did, too."

"Me too." Mackey sighs.

"Yeah," Sera says, and she reaches for her brother's hand. "We all did."

When they all leave, I trade my flip-flops for boots and grab a flashlight, then I head down the back steps into mud. Zale is already waiting for me back at Li'l Pass. Shirtless and smiling.

Worn-out jeans rolled up to his knees. He's been fishing, he tells me. His hair is windblown, and his skin is warm from the sun. He smells like sweet grass and pine trees, and when I crawl up to sit beside him on the trailer, I slip my hand into his, almost without realizing it.

Zale looks just as surprised as I am, and I blush. Flustered and embarrassed. But then then he grins. Doesn't let me pull away.

And that little zing makes me giddy.

"I was hopin' you'd come out tonight," he says, and he nods toward the river. "Look at that."

In the distance, the lights are coming on along the boardwalk, and La Cachette looks like an ocean liner sailing the vast, flat sea of the bayou.

"I remember comin' out here with my mama sometimes," Zale tells me. "When I was real little. Just this time of evening. To see the lights."

His voice is washing me clean. That flash of Elora that came to me earlier is fading. I can't feel those squeezing fingers on my neck any more. I need him to keep talking, so I ask a question.

"What was your mama like?"

This incredible light comes over Zale's face, and I feel all my worries blow away in the evening breeze.

"My mama was the softest soul. Folks called her Elsie. But her name was Elsinore. Her people were from Tennessee. Snake handlers. She used to tell me that my granddaddy could charm an angry rattler just by looking him in the eye. Soothe him so peaceful you'd think that snake was drunk. He'd stand up to preach a sermon wearing two or three of 'em draped around his shoulders like neckties. And none of 'em ever bit him."

It's the most I've ever heard Zale say at once, and I let his words roll over me in waves.

I realize now that I can hear a little bit of Tennessee drawl mixed in with that slight Acadian echo.

Sweet tea and gumbo.

The music of it is intoxicating, and it melts into the night air like the calling of the birds and the wind through the tops of the cypress trees.

"My mama's dead, too," I say. It's the first time I've mentioned my mother to him, and I feel the ache of her loss in a way that I haven't for a really long time.

Zale squeezes my hand, and the hurt eases some. He waits. Leaves me an opening. But I'm not ready to tell that story just yet.

"My mama had the same talent as my granddaddy," he goes on. "A gift to quiet the nerves and calm the soul. Only with her, it wasn't just snakes. She had that same way with people."

Zale is still talking. Telling me more about Florida. And about his mama. But I'm still thinking of my own mother. And her gift. Whatever deep magic she might have possessed.

I wish so much that I could remember her more clearly. I've tried so many times to conjure up the sound of her voice. Or the way she smelled. And sometimes I can, just for a few seconds. My memories of her are all so sketchy, though, because my mother might have died when I was eight years old . . . but she was gone a long time before that.

It scares me, not being able to remember her.

"You know the magic way Elora laughed?" I ask, and Zale turns to look at me. His ice-fire eyes burn so bright in the almost-dark. "What if I forget that someday?"

Zale lets go of my hand, and I miss that electric connection. But then he slips his arm around my shoulders and pulls me against him. I'm not expecting that, and the tingle makes my heart beat faster.

"Tell me something you want to remember," he says. "About Elora."

I have no idea where to start, so I pick the first memory that pops into my head.

"When we were in eighth grade, we both picked out the very same dress for our schools' homecoming dances. Me up in Little Rock, and her down here. And we never even knew it until we exchanged pictures that next summer. And there we were dressed just alike. The same shoes, even." Zale smiles, and I go on. "That sort of thing happened all the time. We'd give each other the same book for our birthdays. Send each other the same card for Christmas."

"Tell me something else," Zale says, and he holds me a little closer.

"When we were seven, we made up our own language. Just for the two of us. We spoke it most of a full year. Created a written alphabet and everything." I laugh out loud, for the very first time all summer, and it feels good. But strange. "Everybody said it was annoying, us talking gibberish all the time. Only it wasn't gibberish to us. We knew exactly what we were saying."

I like thinking about how much fun Elora and I always had together.

Instead of how much I miss her.

Or how she died.

I look up at Zale, and he's just watching me. "There's magic in your laugh, too, Grey. You know that, right?"

"No." I shake my head. "Elora was the special one."

"That's exactly what she told me about you," he says, and the thought of that stuns me. "She said you fed off each other's light."

Two flames lit from the same match.

Zale tightens his arm around me again. That constant hum is making me feel a little drunk. So I lay my head against his shoulder. Just to see what happens. I almost laugh again when that tingle moves across my scalp, like fingers through my hair. I can't help wondering what it would be like to kiss him, the way I kissed Hart. How would that buzz feel against my lips?

Frissons.

The good kind.

"I wish I could put into words what it's like," I say. "Being that in tune with another person. Never having to explain what you're thinking or feeling, or what you need, because the other person just knows you inside out. Being able to have a whole conversation without saying a single word." I sigh and settle in closer to Zale, let myself lean deeper into the throbbing ache of Elora's absence. I don't push the hurt away. I just let it come. "That feeling of having half your soul walking around inside someone else's body. It's the most powerful thing in the world, that connection."

I want him to understand that kind of love.

And that kind of unfathomable loss.

"You don't have to tell me," he says. "I know." I look back up at him, confused. "I had a twin, too. A brother." He takes a deep breath, like someone about to dive deep underwater. "His name was Aeron."

Was.

For a second, I can't think. I don't know what to say.

Then it all makes sense.

"There were twelve of us," I whisper.

And Zale nods.

I should have known it.

Twelve is the number of completion. The closing of a circle. The end of the cycle.

Twelve months in a year.

Twelve hours in a day.

Twelve tribes of Israel.

Twelve-bar blues.

Twelve babies born one long-ago Louisiana summer.

I have so many questions, but I wait. Quiet. My head feels fuzzy. Strange. Like when you wake up from a nap and you can't quite get your bearings.

"It was early mornin' when the cabin caught fire. Barely gettin' to be light out. My daddy was off huntin'. But my mama and me – and Aeron – we were all there. Asleep. And it burned hot. Fast. The whole thing went in a flash."

The wind picks up, and I hear it moaning through the Spanish moss.

"My mama woke up and grabbed me. But she couldn't get to Aeron. He was scared. Wouldn't come out. Huddled up in the corner. Behind a wall of fire. And the whole place was ablaze. Mama knew that if she didn't get me outta dere, she'd lose us both."

Thunder rolls, and lightning brightens the sky in a quick burst. Like the fast flicking of a light switch. I shiver against Zale, and I feel the electric current of his memory. It surges through him and flows right into me. I suck in my breath from the shock of it.

The pain.

"So we ran and hid. Didn't have anything left. Didn't know what to do. Couldn't get back to the cabin to find –" He hesitates. "We never even knew if anybody was decent enough to bury him."

The misery in his voice is enough to break my heart.

It hits me hard how every single one of us – everyone in the whole wide world – is walking around with missing pieces.

I'm not the only one with holes.

"And then we hid out there for a while, but my daddy never came lookin' for us. So mama knew dat meant he was dead, too. And it was just the two of us from then on out."

"Why didn't you tell me before?"

He shrugs. "Guilt, I guess." Then he tosses his long blond hair out of his face and looks at me. His eyes are hurt so deep. I look past the aching beauty of them to see the scars underneath.

And it's almost like looking in a mirror.

"I've lived my whole life torn up that I was the one she grabbed that night." He chokes, and I can't help myself. I reach up to touch his face. The softness of his hair. Everywhere my fingers make contact, I feel those little zips and zaps that steal my breath away. "So I never told anyone about Aeron." He looks at me. "Not even Elora. But he's a big part of why I came back here. I thought if I could find my father, and my brother, it would feel almost like saving them. Like I could put them to rest, finally. And Mama, too."

There were twelve of us. I'm trying to work out the equation of our lives. Four of us gone.

Dead.

Murdered.

One whole third of our original dozen.

The two of us sit with the silent weight of that for a few minutes. Zale is trailing his fingers up and down my arm, leaving little sparks of pure white energy everywhere he touches my bare skin.

"You ever think maybe they're connected?" he finally asks. "All our mysteries?"

"Are you saying whoever killed Ember and Orli killed Elora, too?"

It was such a long time ago.

"Maybe," Zale says. "Maybe not. But what if it's all tied together somehow? Ember and Orli. My father. Elora." He focuses those eyes on me, and they pull at my soul like magnetic north. "It's something I've been thinking about a lot."

It reminds me of a line from *The Tempest*. Before I stopped reading.

What's past is prologue.

I think the words inside my head, and Zale's ocean-deep voice comes right back to me, like an echo. Or a seashell held to my ear.

"We have to go back to the beginning, Grey."

Later, Zale walks me back to the boardwalk. But he stops me in the shadows. Before I reach the wooden steps.

"I almost forgot," he says. Then he smiles at me and pulls something out of his pocket. "I've got somethin' for you. Found it in the dirt, back at the island. I saw it winking at me in the moonlight." He reaches out to touch my cheek, and I lean into that magic tingle. "I just thought it was so pretty." His eyes glow with that fire that comes from somewhere deep inside him. He grins, and I think maybe I even see him blush a little. "I guess it reminded me of you."

I feel myself falling. Like I'm riding one of those drop rides at an amusement park. That exhilarating, breathtaking rush toward the ground.

Zale opens up his palm, and my heart forgets to beat. I'm caught. Staring transfixed at the little thing in his hand.

I tell myself it can't be what I think it is.

A delicate silver hair clip. One single hummingbird.

"It was a little tarnished," he says. "But I shined it up." I can't form any thoughts as he brushes back my bangs and slides the clip into my hair. "It suits you," he says. "Something beautiful. For a beautiful girl." He leans in and brushes his lips against my cheek. The barest whisper of a kiss.

And then he's gone.

I stand there, stunned, until I finally convince my feet to move toward home. When I slip in the kitchen door, I stop to stare at that picture of my mother and me.

There I am with my watermelon-pink sundress.

And there she is with those haunted eyes.

And that one hummingbird hair clip.

In my bedroom, I dig around until I find the one she's wearing in the photo. The one I've always kept. Then I slip the other one out of my hair. The one Zale found in the dirt back at Keller's Island.

I hold them in my palms. And they're perfect twins. Exactly the same, down to their hand-painted eyes.

I bury them both in my underwear drawer, so they can keep each other company.

And I try not to think about what it might mean.

I drag Sweet-N-Low out to do his business, then I take a long shower and try to sleep.

But I can't.

Because I keep thinking about what Zale said. Back to the beginning.

And no matter what happens with the weather, I figure Evie's right. There's definitely a storm coming. Because if we start digging around in thirteen years' worth of tangled secrets, who knows what we might find?

The sound of his voice makes me wish
the mud would hurry up and do its job.
I want it to suck me down and down and down
and then cover me up for good,
so there's nothing left of me for him to find.

18

When I wake up the next morning, Honey is listening to the radio while she does her crossword puzzle. She points me toward some muffins that Bernadette brought over. The storm that's now 230 miles east of Miami has strengthened. And they've given it a name, the weather guy says.

Tropical Storm Elizabeth.

I see Honey glance up from her puzzle to listen. But she doesn't seem too worried. Yet. That's still a long ways off. Besides, people here are no stranger to hurricanes. Even big ones. Every so often, a monster one blows in and the storm surge floods everyone out. Sometimes the boardwalk gets ripped apart and the houses wash downriver. Then they rebuild. And the tourists come back. Like it never happened.

I was two years old when Katrina turned this whole area into part of the Gulf of Mexico. That was the last really bad one. I don't remember anything about it, but I know we spent almost a year living up in Shreveport with Honey's sister, waiting for things to dry out, while folks down here pulled fishing boats out of snapped-off trees and La Cachette got put back together from scratch.

It's a slow day in the shop, so there's nothing to stop me thinking about Zale. That moment he slipped my mother's lost hummingbird into my hair. And what he said before that.

How maybe all the mysteries are connected.

After dinner, I open the front door to sneak away for a bit. I want to head out to Li'l Pass before it gets too dark. I need to ask Zale more about that hair clip.

Where exactly he found it.

But Evie is waiting for me on the porch. She's perched up on the wooden railing, her eyebrows pinched together in a worried frown.

"You're gonna leave, aren't you?" she asks me. "Because of the storm."

"I don't know," I tell her. "I might have to. If things get bad."

I see her chin quiver. "Are you gonna take Hart with you?"

"What? No," I say, and I move to sit beside her on the railing. "Of course not. Why would I take Hart?"

She looks down at her chipped toenail polish, and I hear her sigh. "'Cause he's in love with you." Her voice is barely a whisper. "Isn't he?"

Her fingers reach for her hair, and she starts twisting a long white-blonde strand around and around and around. Evie's always seemed so much younger than the rest of us. More immature in a lot of ways, I guess. But this summer, it's like she's aging backward. Every time I see her, she seems more like a lost little girl.

She's evaporating.

Just like Hart.

"No." I shake my head. "I told you, Evie. He isn't. Hart barely even talks to me any more."

She nods, but she doesn't say anything. I look over my shoulder at her wind chime collection, and I don't see any new ones. "You still making chimes?" I ask her. But she doesn't answer. "Evie?"

"I guess not." She won't look at me. "They don't really help any more." She draws herself up tight. "I hear her all the time now."

My stomach drops, and I tell myself to go easy.

"Elora?" I try to make my voice sound casual. Like it's nothing, this conversation we're having. But I fail miserably. "It's her you're hearing, isn't it? That's why all the wind chimes. To try and drown her out."

Evie nods. Just barely. And my heart races inside my chest.

"I'm so tired, Grey. She won't leave me alone. Not even for a minute."

I take a deep breath. Will myself not to cry. "Oh, Evie. I know that has to be hard. But Elora must trust you, right? That's why she's reaching out." Evie looks away from me, out toward the river, but I keep pushing. "There's something she wants you to know, isn't there? Something about what happened to her."

"I'm scared, Grey." Evie's words are so quiet I can barely make them out. "I don't know what to do. I'm so scared."

"Elora needs you, Evie." My voice is shaking now. "She needs us. Even if what she says is scary, you have to –"

Evie's creations start ringing and clinking. The tinkling sound of them fills up the air.

"Oh, God." She clamps her hands over her ears, and I freeze. "Please stop," Evie whimpers. And I don't know if she's talking to me or Elora. But if she's talking to Elora, it won't do her any good. Evie's brain is like a psychic radio, not a telephone. She can hear spirits, but she can't communicate with them.

"Are you hearing her right now?" I ask, and Evie nods.

I listen so hard for Elora's voice. I know it better than anyone. But I don't hear any words whispered in my ear, and it hurts to think that maybe Elora's still angry at me. That maybe that's why she's chosen Evie. Instead of me.

"What's she saying?" I plead. "You have to tell me. We have to tell someone –"

Evie blinks fast. I reach for her hand, but she hops down off the railing and skitters away from me, like a little crab.

"Oh, God. You can't tell, Grey," she begs. "Not anybody." Her voice is a tightened piano string. "Please!"

And then, before I can say anything else, she whirls around and hurries down the steps and across to her house. I hear the screen door slam.

I manage to get to my feet, but I keep my hand on the wooden railing. I don't trust my legs. They've turned to mush.

I look around for my mud boots, so I can head out to Li'l Pass. I need the warmth of Zale's electric touch.

But just then, Honey calls me in to help her fold some laundry.

A lot of laundry.

And then it's too late. Too dark. So I take the tarot deck and crawl up on to my bed. I'm hungry for answers. But over and over, I pull the blue-robed High Priestess.

The keeper of secrets.

Guarder of mysteries.

Ruler of a future as yet unrevealed.

Honey says the High Priestess is a sign that things around you are not what they appear to be.

Eventually, I end up falling asleep with the cards scattered across my sheets and Evie's wind chimes still whispering in my ear.

I manage to get up at a reasonable time the next morning to help Honey in the bookstore, but I can't focus on anything except Evie's revelation. And Zale's gift. My mother's hummingbird come home to the nest. So I make a million little mistakes. I drop a whole tray of tiny glass bottles, and they shatter into a zillion pieces. I forget how to make change and get the cash drawer all screwed up.

Honey keeps the radio on all day, and late that afternoon someone breaks in over the music to tell us that Elizabeth is now officially a hurricane, about to make landfall north of Miami. Seventy-five-mile-per-hour winds. Category 1.

The news makes me look up, but it's still not my problem.

I've got a category 5 shitstorm on my hands right here at home.

By five thirty, when Honey flips the sign on the door to CLOSED, I'm a complete mess. I make it through dinner, and then I help Honey clean up before I escape outside.

I figure I'll head out toward Li'l Pass. Toward Zale. But I don't. I can't.

Something stops me.

All day I've been thinking about the tender honesty in Zale's eyes. The flicker of his lips against my cheek.

And about his twin. Aeron. Lost in the fire.

How he swears his father couldn't have murdered Ember and Orli.

My mother's hummingbird hair clip cradled in his hand.

It's all too much. I don't know what any of it means. I don't know what anything means any more.

So I choose the devil I know instead and swing toward the downriver end of the boardwalk. In the direction of Hart and Elora's house. And the old pontoon boat. I don't really expect Hart to be there. I don't even know if I want him to be. We've hardly spoken in over a month, not since the night he almost killed Case.

He is there, though. And I know it before I get to the end of the boardwalk. His cigarette is like a smoke signal. I freeze and consider turning back. Because I don't know if I want to have this conversation. But it's too late. My feet on the boards have already given me away.

"You might as well come on down," he says. "I fixed the ladder."

I sigh and slip off Elora's ring before I climb down into the boat. Then I take my usual spot on the broken seat, and the two of us just sit there in silence. Trying to not to look at each other.

"Well, Greycie," Hart finally says as he stubs out his cigarette on the heel of his boot. "I'm glad we had this little talk."

And that sounds almost like the old him. It makes me smile. A little.

"You been okay?" I ask. But his only answer is a hollow laugh. "I've missed you."

"Yeah," he says, and lets out a long breath. His voice is full of rusty hinges. Like these are maybe the first words he's spoken in days. Or weeks. "I guess I missed you, too, Shortcake."

"I'm sorry I didn't tell you about Case's medal," I offer. "I should've told you as soon as I found it."

He looks up at me then, studying me with those familiar hazel eyes. It's startling how much weight he's lost just since the beginning of the summer. His cheekbones are sharp, and he looks paler than I ever remember seeing him.

"So why didn't you?"

I shrug. "I guess I couldn't stand to see you hurt any more."

His jaw hardens, and I realize I've said the exact wrong thing.

"I don't need you to protect me, Greycie."

"I know," I tell him. But I'm not sure he's right about that.

"Is that what you came down here to tell me?" he asks. "That you're sorry for keepin' secrets?"

"Not just that."

Hart raises one eyebrow at me and pulls out another cigarette. "Then you might as well spill the rest of it."

"She talks to Evie," I blurt out. "Elora. She whispers in her ear."

"Shit." Hart flicks open the lighter, but his hands are shaking too bad to get the cigarette lit. "What does she say?"

"I don't know. Evie won't tell me. But whatever it is, it's got her all freaked out." I look down at my empty finger. Where Elora's ring should be. "I wish she'd talk to me instead."

He flicks the lighter closed, and his flame goes out.

"What if she said things you didn't wanna hear?"

I don't know how to answer him, so I change the subject.

"She's in love with you, I think." Hart stares me. "Evie."

"Nah." He shakes his head. "She thinks she is. Maybe. That's all. 'Cause of what I did for 'er."

"What you did?"

"To Vic." Hart grimaces, then he runs one hand over his face and sighs. Deep. He sounds as exhausted as he looks. "That piece of shit was beatin' her black and blue."

"Oh, God." My stomach turns. "Evie told you that?"

"She didn't have to. I could feel it, Grey." Hart puts the cigarette to his lips. Then remembers it isn't lit. "I could fuckin' feel it. That fear of hers. And the pain. Thinkin' nobody in the world cared if that bastard killed 'er."

"Jesus, Hart."

One more wound that wasn't his, but that cut him just the same.

"And this whole town knew it, too. Not just me. You didn't need a psychic gift to see those bruises." Hart tries to light the cigarette again, and this time he makes it work. He sucks in smoke like oxygen. "Only nobody said a word about it."

Psychic Capital of the World or not, people down here still live by a certain kind of code. You don't get mixed up in what goes on behind closed doors. That's the way it's always been.

Honey used to tell me, *Worrying about other people's business is just one-man gossip.*

"You have no idea how messed up she was last winter," he says. "Evie. She was comin' apart at the seams. Poor kid. And there's Bernadette, too damn scared of her own shadow to say a word to her own asshole brother. Probably thought Vic'd start in on her again if she did." I just stare at him, openmouthed. "Fuck, Greycie. Everybody knows how he's always treated her."

I think about Bernadette. Her downcast eyes, and the shawls she wears, even in the summer heat. Hart's gone dark, and I know he's thinking about his own mama. How she suffered all those years at the hands of his daddy.

"If Vic had started in on Evie," he goes on, "maybe Bernadette at least figured she'd get some peace. Or maybe she was just afraid." He twists his neck, and I hear the bones crack. "Either way, she sure as shit wasn't ever gonna put a stop to it. And I couldn't really blame her for that."

"So you did."

For the first time in my life it occurs to me that, while I'm up in Little Rock most of the year, their lives all keep going on down here. In ways I'll never really understand.

Hart shrugs. "I went over there one night back in January. Took the shotgun. Same one my mama used. Pinned Vic up against the wall. Right in his own livin' room. Told him I had a killer's blood flowin' through my veins and that I'd blow his goddamn brains out if he ever so much as laid a finger on Evie again. Or Bernadette, either." He takes a long drag off that cigarette. "I said they'd be pickin' bits of his skull out of the wallpaper for the next ten years. Like we did my old man's."

"Oh, Hart," is all I can think to say. No wonder he's Evie's hero.

He rakes his fingers through dark, tangled curls and breathes out smoke like a dragon.

"I don't think he's touched either one of 'em since."

"You're lucky he didn't shoot you," I tell him. Vic keeps a bunch of old guns lying around, and he almost always has a pistol on him.

Hart smirks. "He was drunk as a skunk. Never saw me comin'."

Something horrible occurs to me. "Do you think Victor could have had something to do with whatever happened to Elora? Maybe as a way to get back at you?"

That would make so much sense. What if the secrets Elora is whispering in Evie's ear are all about Victor? Evie's own uncle. What if that's what she can't stand to hear?

Hart shakes his head. "I thought about that, believe me. And I sure as shit wouldn't put it past him. But Vic was up at bingo in Kinter that night. Came back on the same boat as Mama and Leo. And that was after midnight."

He gets up and moves toward the front of the boat to stare out at the gator pond. Hart's shoulders are slumped. And in the fading light, I barely recognize him.

"It was a good thing," I tell him, because it seems like he needs to hear it. "What you did for Evie."

He's quiet for a minute, then he says, "It wasn't just the

bruises. Vic got busted last fall up in Kinter. Parked at the bayou docks. Had a girl in his car not much older than Evie, even. She was barely seventeen, I think."

"Jesus."

Hart sucks in smoke again. "I just wanted the bastard to know I was watchin' him, you know? That I was watchin' Evie. And that I'd fuckin' kill 'im if he ever . . ." His voice trails off.

"You did a good thing," I say again. "You're good, Hart."

He turns back to look at me the way he used to sometimes when we were kids. So tender it could kill me. This is not the Hart that put a big old bullfrog in my bed the summer we were ten. Or the Hart that teased me relentlessly for being afraid of spiders. This is not even the Hart that kissed me once when we were both thirteen.

Or again when we were seventeen.

This Hart is the one that picked me up and carried me back to Honey when I tripped on a tree root out at Li'l Pass and nearly split my head open the summer we were both eleven. The Hart that used his favorite T-shirt to soak up the blood and told me awful knock-knock jokes the whole walk home, just to keep me calm.

"I'm so sorry, Shortcake," he tells me. "I'm sorry for this whole goddamn summer. You shouldn't be mixed up in any of this." He drops his cigarette butt and grinds it out in the bottom of the boat. "Elora didn't want you anywhere near all this shit. The kind of stuff that goes on down here. That's why she pushed you away last year."

"Because Victor was beating the shit out of Evie?" That

doesn't make sense. As awful as it is, that kind of stuff happens everywhere.

Hart shakes his head. "She didn't even know that then. Besides, that's just the tip of the iceberg. The part that's visible." It's dark now, but there's enough moonlight for me to see the look in his eyes. And it scares me. "There's so much more. This whole town is . . ."

Poison.

Hart squats down and reaches for my hand. "You shouldn't be here, Grey." He wraps his fingers around mine and squeezes hard. "If anything ever happened to you, Elora would never forgive me." His voice breaks, and I watch him struggle under the weight of unbearable grief. And guilt. "I'd never forgive myself."

He doesn't say anything else. But he doesn't stand up and move away, either. And I feel that old pull. So strong. So familiar. It's such a deep part of me, that longing for Hart. I know it so well. Like the feeling of the boardwalk under my feet.

Or the sound of Elora's laugh.

There's a kind of comfort in the timeless ache of it. Something about it that makes sense.

I reach out and run my fingers over his cheekbones and his jawline, like I'm trying to memorize the map of him. I see him flinch. But he doesn't pull away from my touch.

All I want in the whole world is for him not to hurt any more. And for me not to hurt any more.

Hart shuts his eyes and leans in closer. I can feel his breath on my lips.

So I kiss him. And he kisses me back. We kiss each other

so hard and so deep that it's like we've both been snakebit and we're trying to suck out the poison. Like we need to draw out each other's pain.

We kiss each other like it's a matter of life and death.

Tongues and teeth.

Hands.

I hear him moan my name, and the sound of it vibrates against something deep inside me. I try to speak his name out loud, but it gets all tangled up on my tongue.

Hart presses his lips against my ear, and the heat of his mouth makes me half-wild. "Shhhhh," he murmurs. "You don't have to talk, Greycie. I feel you."

The night is so hot, and we melt so far into each other, that I'm not sure whose arms or lips or searching fingers are whose any more.

Hart stops and pulls his shirt off over his head, then he turns and spreads it out over the cushion of cypress needles in the bottom of the boat. I pull my tank top off, too, then he scoops me up off the seat to lay me down.

For just a second, I think about Elora.

How she lost her virginity right here in this very spot. With Case.

And I wonder if the old pontoon boat will be the spot for me, too.

If my story will be an echo of hers.

The way it always has been.

But then Hart is on top of me. And I'm not thinking of anything any more.

Not even Elora.

Or Zale, with his ice-fire eyes and his electric touch.

All I'm thinking about is Hart.

How I wish I could press kisses to all the broken places way down deep inside him. All the sore spots I know I'll never be able to reach. But I can't. So my mouth finds his collarbone. His jaw. The hollow at the base of his neck.

Hart decides to pick up the pace, and I don't complain when he fast-forwards to the part where he awkwardly tries to unbutton my shorts and slide them down my legs. But they get all tangled around my ankles when I try to kick them off. And Hart laughs. It's a low, genuine chuckle deep in his throat, and when I hear it, I fall absolutely head over heels in love with him all over again.

For like the ten millionth time in seventeen summers.

That moment slips away like river fog, though, and Hart presses himself hard against me. I reach down to touch him through his jeans, and he hisses. I feel his teeth at my neck. Sharp. Not kissing me any more. Biting. Nipping. Pulling at me. Eating me alive.

Devouring me.

His breath is ragged and whiskey-thick. He pants in my ear and growls my name as he slides a rough hand under my bra.

From his side of the pond, Willie Nelson grunts and bellows at us, like maybe we're the noisy neighbors keeping him awake.

I fumble with the buttons on Hart's jeans, but I can't get them undone.

His tongue moves over the edges of my teeth, one hand

tangled in my hair, as he yanks his fly open. I hear the metal buttons scatter across the bottom of the boat.

He shoves his own hand down the front of his jeans, and I feel him moving against me as I open my mouth wider for him. Denim rubs at my thighs, and the weight of him steals my breath.

I tug at the waist of his jeans, trying to pull them down, but he won't let me.

"No," he says. "Don't. I just need –" But then my mouth finds his neck again, and his words become meaningless syllables as his hand keeps working.

"Fuck!" I feel all his muscles tighten before he goes limp in my arms.

And that's it.

It's all over.

Whatever it was that pulled us toward each other drifts away like mist.

Or cigarette smoke.

Hart helps me up. He slings his T-shirt over one shoulder before he shakes the cypress needles out of my tank top and hands it back to me. I turn it right side out and pull it over my head before I tug on my shorts.

He straightens up his jeans. Mutters something about the buttons. And how late it is. Tries to laugh again.

Fails.

Then he walks me home. He doesn't hold my hand, but he does manage to mumble, "Night."

Nothing more than that. And even that is more than I can force out.

When Hart leaves, I reach for the doorknob. But Evie suddenly appears out of the shadows on her front porch. She looks so small, and she moves so silently in my direction that I mistake her for Wrynn at first. But then the moon catches that white-blonde hair.

"You lied to me," she whispers. "You told me Hart didn't love you." Her chin quivers, and the misery in her voice is more than I can bear tonight.

"He doesn't. Evie –"

She comes a few steps closer. Her eyes are the color of river fog.

"Please don't take him away, Grey." She reaches for my hand. Squeezes hard. "He's the only good person left in this whole place." She bursts into tears. "You don't understand. You don't know what he did for me. He saved me, Grey. If he leaves –"

"I do know, Evie." She stares at me. Mouth open like a door off its hinges. "Hart told me what he did. For you."

"He told you?" Her words are a terrified whisper. Evie blinks. Gives her head a little shake. She lets go of my hand. Takes a step backward. And I see her shiver.

"You don't need to be afraid," I tell her. But she's still frozen. "Vic won't hurt you any more. Or your mama."

Evie kind of melts, and I pull her close to wrap her up in a hug. She clings to me like I'm some kind of life preserver. She's the closest thing I've ever had to a little sister. And I wish so much that I could keep her safe.

From Victor. And men like him.

From this place.

From the hurt of loving someone who won't ever be capable of loving her back. At least not the way she wants.

But I can't protect her from any of that. So I hold her and stroke her hair while she cries. I breathe in the sweet summertime scent of her. And I promise her over and over that Hart isn't going anywhere. That he loves her.

That I love her. So, so, so much. That everybody loves her. That everything will be okay. That's we'll always be here for each other.

Finally, Evie runs out of tears, and she pulls away from me to wipe at her face. Then she kisses me on the cheek before she tiptoes back toward her own front door. She gives me a sad little wave, and I see her mouth the words *I'm sorry, Grey* before she vanishes inside.

I feel like I'm in some kind of a daze. I slip into the Mystic Rose and ease the door closed behind me. Then I wander into the kitchen for a drink. Sweet-N-Low whines at me for turning on the light, but I ignore him. I'm staring at that photo again. The one of me and my mom.

I lift the frame off the wall. It's been there so long that the wallpaper underneath is brighter than the rest of the kitchen. It's like a time warp. The little apples are still red instead of faded pink.

I fold back the metal clips that secure the cardboard backing, then I pull out the photograph. The Scotch tape holding it in place is old enough that I barely have to tug on it. I rehang the dusty frame and carry the photo into my bathroom. I turn on the light and lean in toward the mirror.

Then I hold the picture up next to my own face.

The woman's haunted eyes don't match the innocent eyes of the little girl in the picture.

But they do match the eyes of the older girl in the mirror.

My mother and I have finally become twins, after all.

I take the photograph to bed with me and lean it up against the framed picture of me and Elora on my bedside table. Then I stare at it for a long time before I flip off the lamp and somehow drift off to sleep listening to Evie's wind chimes.

It's hours later when something wakes me up. I sit up in the dark, and for a second, I'm not sure why I'm awake. Then I hear it again. A tapping sound. Barely loud enough to register.

I turn my head toward the window and almost jump out of my skin when I see the shape on the other side of the glass. But then I hear the whisper, and my fear is replaced by a strange sense of déjà vu.

"Greycie," Hart pleads. "Let me in. Please."

For the second time in seventeen summers, I slide open my bedroom window and let Hart come inside. He climbs right over the top of Wrynn's little collection to stand staring at me in the moonlight. Dark curls. Strong back. Broad shoulders.

Hollow eyes.

A month's worth of stubble.

He starts to tremble. "I'm sorry," he says over and over. "I'm so sorry, Greycie. I'm so sorry. Oh, God. I'm so fucking sorry."

I take him by the hand and lead him to my bed. I spread back the blankets, then I slip off his boots and pull him under the covers with me. I wrap my arms tight around him. Like that night when we were five.

But he won't stop shaking.

"It's okay," I whisper again and again. But we both know nothing's okay.

"The hurricane made landfall." He spits the words out through chattering teeth. "Elizabeth. In Florida. Eighty-mile-an-hour winds. Two people dead so far."

"Shhhh," I soothe, and I run my fingers through his beautiful hair.

"Falling trees," he tells me.

I press my lips against this forehead. His skin is ice cold. Like a corpse.

"Hart –"

"I just wanna know, Greycie. I need to know what happened. I miss 'er so bad."

The tinkling of wind chimes grows louder and louder until it seems to fill my little bedroom with its fragile sound.

"Me too," I whisper.

And I know for sure then that what I told Evie was true. Hart isn't in love with me. Not like Evie meant. Need isn't love. Loneliness isn't love. And pain isn't love. Even if it's shared.

Hart notices the picture on my bedside table. The one of me and my mom. He reaches over to pick it up. There's just enough moonlight to see the young woman and the little girl on her lap.

He studies the photograph with dark eyes.

"Can you do it, too?" he finally asks me. His voice is low

in my ear. Hushed. Like we're whispering shared secrets. Only I don't know what he's talking about.

"Can I do what?"

"Leo told me that your mama could start fires. With her mind. He said he'd seen her do it. Once. A long time ago." Hart's stopped shaking. Finally. "Can you do it, too?"

I freeze. Cold under the covers.

"Because if you can, Greycie, you should burn this whole fucking town right down to the mud."

I let him carry me all the way back to the boardwalk. He doesn't say a word. And I don't, either. What do you say when you know you're about to die? I don't think I have any last words in me.

Hart is gone by the time I wake up. I sit up and swing my feet to the floor, but I don't get out of bed. Instead, I take the picture off my bedside table and hold it to the light streaming in the window. Hart didn't have any details about what he said my mother could do. The power that she had. Just a vague story Leo told him once when they were out fishing.

Maybe a tall tale to pass a long, hot afternoon.

But maybe not.

The hiding place draws power. It always has. The original group of spiritualists and seekers came down in 1887 from somewhere in upstate New York. They were tired of being run out of town after town by church people, and they were looking for a place where nobody would bother them.

Except the dead, of course.

So here came the psychics, wading into the swamp with their crystal balls and their tarot cards held high.

Honey's great-grandmother was one of them.

Elora's and Hart's families are both descended from that founding group, too.

Even before that, though, the runaway enslaved and the Creole people, along with the Houma and Chitimacha and others who shared these swamps, used to tell stories about this area. The Acadian settlers, too. Strange things happened here, they all said.

I think about Case and Wrynn. Bilocation. And the gift of healing.

And Zale. The power of the sea and the sky.

But if my mother had some gift like that – some deep power, like Sera said – I've never known anything about it.

And I certainly didn't inherit it.

I get dressed and wander into the kitchen to find Honey sitting at the table. She dumps a spoonful of sugar into her coffee and stirs as she listens to the radio.

Someone from the National Hurricane Center reports that Elizabeth has emerged from this side of the Florida peninsula, and that she's strengthening as she crosses the Gulf of Mexico's warm waters. In only a few hours, winds have increased to over one hundred miles an hour. She's a category 2 now.

Honey keeps stirring, and the radio station goes live to a press conference where the governor of Louisiana is declaring a state of emergency ahead of the storm's predicted arrival here.

"I'm not leaving," I say as I sit down across from Honey with a bowl of cereal.

She sighs. "Grey –"

"We don't even know what's going to happen yet. Give me a

little while longer," I beg. "Maybe it won't be bad." I'm stirring my cereal around, but I haven't made myself take a bite yet. "I can't leave. Not until I know what happened to Elora."

"Sugar Bee, in the end, not everything is knowable." Honey takes a small sip of her coffee. "Even for those of us entrusted with the gift of sight."

"This isn't the end," I tell her. "And this is knowable. I feel it."

Honey studies my face for a long minute before she nods. "One more day. But I won't take chances with your safety. If it looks like we're going to take a direct hit, you're going home."

"I already am home," I remind her.

All that morning and afternoon, we stay busy in the bookstore. I spend the whole day helping clueless people pick out decks of tarot cards and incense and books on astrology. I even sell that ugly Himalayan salt lamp.

Case's mama, Ophelia, comes in to pick up some herbal tea and to talk to Honey about the storm. It's the first time I've seen her all summer, and she gives me a big hug. It makes me ashamed of the way I treated Case. The things I was ready to believe about him, just because I was desperate for an answer. I can't help but wonder what he told her about his bashed-in face. That missing tooth. I imagine her laying a gentle hand on his cheek, to make the bleeding stop.

Wrynn hides behind her mama, just peeking out at me through that long red hair of hers. I see her snake out a skinny, freckled arm to snag some peppermints from Honey's candy dish. But she doesn't say a word. And I'm glad. I can't stand to hear any more rougarou talk. I have too much on my mind as it is.

All day, I keep waiting for an opening to bring up what Hart told me last night.

About my mother.

It's late afternoon when I finally get my chance. There's a lull between customers, and I jump right into the deep end. I figure I don't have time for wading.

"What was my mother's gift?"

Honey glances up from her word search to give me a strange look. Her earrings are dangly stars, and she has a bright purple scarf tied around her head. "You know she could see colors."

"You mean auras," I say. "People's energy, or whatever."

"That's right," Honey tells me. "We're all made up of energy. And that frequency creates a field around us. Different energies show up as different colors."

"Like grey."

"I know it's not the most exciting color in the world, Sugar Bee." I roll my eyes. Honey says her own aura is pink. "But grey is symbolic of a long spiritual journey. It means you're an old soul. You've traveled a long path in this life. That's something to be proud of."

"Right." I've heard all this a million times. "But could she do anything else?"

Honey looks at me for a few seconds. "We are all of us capable of so many more things than we know, Sugar Bee. Beautiful things. And terrible things."

The bell over the door jingles, and a trio of stunning girls washes in on a wave of laughter. One of them has gotten engaged, and they're looking for a reading. They want to know, should she marry DeShawn? Or hold out hope for something better?

Last summer, Honey would have made an appointment for them to see Miss Cassiopeia, Romance Counselor. But Becky has had her sign flipped to CLOSED since I got here, so Honey leads them to the alcove in the corner and pulls the curtain. Things get busy again after that, and she never offers me any more information. And I never get another chance to ask.

But I can't stop thinking about it. Because there's an idea forming in my head. And I hope like hell I'm wrong.

After dinner, I go to my room and pull out those twin hummingbirds. I weigh them. One in each hand.

Beautiful things.

And terrible things.

My pixie cut is too short for hair clips to look right on me, but I sweep my bangs back on each side and slide the hummingbirds into my hair anyway. Then I don't even bother to put on boots. I just set off into the bayou in my flip-flops, before I have time to chicken out and change my mind. I don't get very far before I have to slip my flip-flops off and carry them. And then I'm barefoot. Mud up to my knees. Just like Wrynn.

And Zale.

He's already waiting for me out at Li'l Pass, and the first thing I say when I see him is, "I need you to take me to Keller's Island."

"Okay," he says. He's staring at those hummingbird hair

clips. Both of them. And I see the questions burning in his ice-fire eyes. But he doesn't ask them. He just takes my hand in his, and I feel that tingling warmth course through me.

I leave my flip-flops sitting on top of the old flatbed trailer, and we trudge side by side through the long grass and the mud. And we don't say much. At least not out loud. But every so often, I hear the sound of the ocean. Like a seashell held to my ear.

Zale has an old flatboat hidden down at Holbert's Pond, about a half mile south of our spot at Li'l Pass. He pulls the rip cord, and the ancient motor coughs and sputters, then comes to life with a cloud of black smoke.

As we head out into the bayou, I glance back over my shoulder, and the lights along the boardwalk get smaller and smaller until they disappear behind us.

And then there's nothing but dark stretching out as far as I can see.

Keller's Island is a little bit of forested high ground that sits way back in the bayou. It's surrounded by deep water on three sides. Ringed with bald cypress trees at the edges and thick with huge live oaks in the center.

When we were growing up, after what happened to Ember and Orli, the older kids would go back there to party sometimes. It was a deserted place for them to get drunk and smoke weed and hook up in the dark. A spot to scare the daylights out of each other with real-life ghost stories.

But not for us. Not for the Summer Children.

We left it to the dead.

Even when we got big enough to do our own partying, that

place was off limits. We used to skirt wide around there when we were out in our airboats and ATVs. We'd point out the tree line. Whisper what happened there. Tell the story. Say the names like a ritual.

But we only went there one time.

To Killer's Island.

Hart took us all there the summer we were fourteen. We were supposed to be fishing, but he convinced us to take a detour on the way home. Some kind of sick field trip to see the place where all our childhood nightmares were born.

It was bright daylight when the eight of us stood there together behind the ruins of Dempsey Fontenot's burned-out cabin and stared at the pond where Ember and Orli died, but it still scared me so bad I couldn't sleep for weeks. I felt uneasy all the rest of that summer. I couldn't seem to wash the mud of that place off me, no matter how hard I scrubbed.

Now the idea of visiting there in the dark makes me sick to my stomach.

The journey doesn't take long by boat, and pretty soon I see the dark outline of tall trees standing sentry against the night sky. The closer we get, the bigger they get.

And the smaller I feel.

We fly back through the bayou toward that thick stand of trees. But really, we're flying back through time. All the way back to where this whole thing started, maybe.

Thirteen summers back.

To the beginning of it all.

What's past is prologue.

Zale runs the boat up into the shallow water, then hops out to drag it to shore. He takes my hand and helps me out, and I gasp from the shock of his touch. I wonder if that will ever wear off.

I hope it doesn't.

We hike through the thick woods and thicker dark, ducking low-hanging branches dripping with Spanish moss and dodging thorns that grab at us like fingers until we reach the tiny clearing at the center of the little island.

When we step out of the trees and into the moonshine, we're standing right behind what's left of the old Fontenot cabin. Dempsey lit it up like a bonfire, they always told us. I've heard that story so many times. Burned it to ashes before he cleared out.

After he drowned Ember and Orli and left them in the pond to rot.

Now, thirteen years down the road from that horrible summer, there's not much left to mark the spot. No monuments or memorials. No little white wooden crosses. Just a pile of fire-blackened logs.

My eyes adjust, and I look around the clearing to see signs of life.

A tiny tent leans at the edge of the tree line. A few belongings are scattered around. A bedroll. A razor lying on a rock. There's a fire ring. And a cooking pot with no handle. A discarded can of beans lies nearby, and a homemade fishing pole leans against a tree.

I take all that in. Because I can't stand to look at the spot where Zale's own childhood nightmares were born.

The bones of the cabin where his twin brother died.

Aeron.

Number twelve.

I don't want to look at the drowning pool, either. I'm trying not to imagine Ember and Orli. White dresses billowing out around them. Trailing blue ribbons the color of a cloudless Louisiana sky.

Fish nibbling at their staring eyes –

swimming in and out of their open mouths.

I don't want to know what they looked like when they pulled them out of the water.

Faces gone. Limbs swollen black.

But somehow I do know.

Zale is silent. I feel him watching me. Waiting. Curious. And I don't know if I can do what I need to do. I'm not sure I have the strength.

The deep power.

But I have to try. Because it's the secrets that fester.

I let go of Zale's hand and slip the little silver hummingbirds out of my hair. I hold them tight in my fists. Then I close my eyes and think about my mother. I don't move. I stay so still so long that my legs become cypress trees, rooted deep in the soft ground. I become part of the landscape of the bayou. Like the saw grass and the water hyacinth and the duckweed.

And then I open my eyes.

Zale doesn't move. He doesn't talk. I don't even hear him breathing.

I wonder if he's still there. I hope he is. But I can't turn my head to see, because I'm staring at my mother. Not inside my head, like a dream. But standing right there in front of me. Flesh and blood.

She isn't looking in my direction, though. Her green eyes are fixed ahead. Focused toward the cabin. She's beautiful. Young and slender. Radiant in the grey predawn light. But the look on her face is fierce. Determined.

There's an explosion of light, and my mother smiles.

Satisfied.

I see the orange glow of the fire reflecting off the little silver hummingbirds clipped in her long hair.

Two of them.

And then I feel the heat.

I smell the smoke as real as anything.

But it's all silent. No voices. No crackle and snap of flames.

Dead still.

The smoke fills up my nose and burns the back of my throat, so I turn away.

Away from the cabin.

Away from my mother.

Away from the other woman. The one who runs right by me as she slips unnoticed out the back of the inferno, clutching a little blond boy to her chest.

My eyes come to rest on the stagnant pond. The drowning pool. Two small shapes float side by side in the center of all that black water.

Firelight on white dresses.

Blue ribbons like the strings of a kite.

And just for a split second, I hear voices. Like someone turned the radio up.

All the way.

Angry shouting.

The noise of a crowd.

One person is sobbing.

Someone else is screaming.

The next thing I know, that's all gone and I'm on the ground. Zale is holding me. Calling my name. Hugging me to his chest. Everywhere our bodies touch, there's that tingle. He helps me to my feet, but I'm unsteady, so he keeps a hand on my elbow.

I open my fingers to stare at the little silver hummingbirds, and I know I have to tell him the truth. Even though I don't want to. Because we're all bound up by our secrets.

And that has to stop with me.

"My mother," I whisper. "She's the one who started the fire."

Overhead, there's a crack of thunder and a flash of lightning so loud and so bright that I'm temporarily deaf and blind. My ears ring and I see spots. A surge of electricity rips into my elbow and up my arm to slam straight into my chest. It's a white-hot burning. Immediate and violent. Like nothing I've ever felt before. I cry out in pain, and the force of the jolt knocks me backward. I land in the mud at the edge of the drowning pool, and I just sit there with my hand over my racing heart, gasping for breath. My muscles are cramping, and my vision is blurry. Everything tingles. And there's a strange metallic taste in my mouth. Thunder rolls again. The power in it makes me shake.

"I'm sorry," Zale tells me. "I didn't mean – I'm so sorry, Grey."

"I need to go home," I whisper.

Zale holds out his hand to help me up, but I hesitate. I'm still struggling for breath. "It's okay," he tells me. "I promise."

So I let him help me to my feet, but I'm too weak to stand. He scoops me up like I don't weigh anything at all, and I wrap my arms around his neck. Zale's skin is warm and soft. Alive with energy.

It's fully night now, but he never stumbles. He carries me out of the woods and down to the edge of the water. But he doesn't say a word. And then we're in the boat.

Killer's Island fades to black behind us.

Zale is taking it slow because of the dark, navigating the shallow channels with a sureness that Hart and Case would be hard-pressed to match. Like he's lived here all his life.

Like he belongs.

"Are you sure?" he finally asks me.

"I saw her."

"What about my father? Did you see –"

"No," I say, and I reach out to brush my trembling fingers through his blond hair. "I'm sorry."

We leave the boat at Holbert's Pond again, and I don't bother to go back to Li'l Pass for my flip-flops. I'm not as weak as I was, so I insist on walking. But Zale keeps his arm around my waist, and the buzz of that contact keeps me warm. He walks me all the way back to the boardwalk. Right up to the steps this time. He refuses to leave me alone in the dark.

We stand there staring at each other for a few seconds,

then Zale pulls me to his chest. I feel his lips brush the top of my head. It's so good. That tingling closeness. And his heart beating against mine. There's so much I want to tell him, but I can't find the right words. I don't know how he can even stand to touch me, after what my mother did.

When he knows what she took from him.

"Grey," he whispers, "look at me." And he tilts my face up toward his. "Whatever your mother did, you're not responsible for it." I nod, but I'm not sure I believe him. His eyes are dark blue now. Like the night sky. "Did I hurt you bad? Before?" I shake my head, and he lets out a breath of relief. "I'm glad." He lays a hand on my cheek. Little zips and zaps. Harmless. "I'd never mean to hurt you, Grey." His eyes flash in the dark. "You know that, don't you?"

"Of course," I tell him. "You'd never hurt anyone on purpose."

He's so gentle. More summer rain than lightning storm.

"I know," he says, and the wind picks up. "But sometimes people get hurt anyway."

Thunder rumbles low across the bayou.

Zale leans in close, and I think maybe he's going to kiss me. Really kiss me.

But he doesn't. He just whispers in my ear. Four words of absolute truth.

"There's a storm comin.'"

Then he disappears into the shadows, and I climb the wooden steps to the boardwalk. But before I go inside, I stand on the front porch of the Mystic Rose and watch the river for a really long time while I listen to the night singing of Evie's wind chimes.

Elora is standing right beside me.

Out of the corner of my eye, I can just almost glimpse her dazzling smile. That long dark hair. If I just turned my head a little . . .

But I don't turn my head. Because what if I'm wrong?

Across from me, on the dock, someone has put up more safety ropes. The rot has been spreading all summer. One whole side is blocked off now.

I turn and pull open the front door of the bookstore. Not locked. Of course. It's never locked. There's no crime to speak of in La Cachette. Never has been.

Unless you count arson, I mean.

And kidnapping.

Murder.

I close the door as softly as I can and twist the bolt behind me.

All the lights are off in the house, but I hear the radio playing in the kitchen. "Louisiana Blues." I tiptoe in to get a glass of milk, and Sweet-N-Low stirs on his pillow. His collar jingles, and he whimpers in his sleep.

I open the fridge, and light spills across the linoleum floor. A weather update breaks in over the music, and I pause to listen.

"The National Hurricane Center is predicting that Elizabeth will become a major storm by the time it reaches the central Gulf of Mexico." The voice on the radio is almost breathless with excitement. "The eye is now four hundred and sixty miles southeast of the mouth of the Mississippi River. Everyone in the listening area is urged to prepare for an extreme weather event."

The announcer goes away, and the harmonica comes back. Blues guitar.

And that's when I hear my name. I freeze, afraid that – somehow – the shadow of my dead mother has followed me home from Keller's Island.

But when I turn around, Honey is sitting at the kitchen table, all lit up in the refrigerator's glow. She has on her old pink robe. Curlers in her hair. And I wonder what she's doing down here. Sitting at the table. Listening to Muddy Waters moan "Louisiana Blues" into the dark.

But then I see the picture in her hand. The one of me and my mom. The one I left on the table beside my bed.

The one with the haunted eyes.

Honey looks down at the photo, then back up at me.

"Sugar Bee," she says, "we need to talk."

*My chest aches and I can't scream any more,
even if I wanted to. Not that there's
anybody to scream for.*

20

I close the fridge door and start to flip on the overhead light. Then I remember I'm barefoot. With mud up to my thighs. So I leave the light off and sit down across from Honey at the kitchen table.

"Didn't you want some milk?" she asks, but I shake my head. She's quiet for a second, staring at the photograph in her hand. "Lots to do tomorrow," she eventually says. But she doesn't take her eyes off the picture of me and my mom. "Gotta get the plywood up on the windows. Move everything from the bookstore up to my bedroom, in case the water gets high."

I nod.

"Leo said he'd help us out. Hart, too," Honey tells me. "Soon as they get their own place ready."

I haven't seen Hart all day. Not since he crawled in my window late last night. And the mention of his name makes me anxious.

"Your dad called this evening," she goes on. "I told him

I'd take you up to Shreveport with me when I leave day after tomorrow. He'll pick you up there."

So that's it, then. One full day left. Not nearly enough time to untangle all this mess.

I stand up and push my chair back.

"Grey. Wait." Honey finally looks at me. "Sit a minute. Please."

Heavy dread settles in my stomach, and it pulls me back down into the chair.

"I know you have questions," she says. "Now that you're growing up, I know there are things you want to know." She looks down at the picture again and sighs. "Need to know. About your mama. And I haven't been great about giving you real answers."

"My mother could start fires, couldn't she?"

Honey stares at me like I hauled off and slapped her. I didn't mean to blurt it out like that. But everything seems so urgent now.

"Your mother could do a lot of things, Grey. I don't know what all talents she had. I don't even think she knew. She was still figuring it out."

"But she burned down the cabin back at Keller's Island. Didn't she? Dempsey Fontenot's cabin."

Honey nods reluctantly. "She did."

"Did she know about the little boy? Aeron?" The stricken look on Honey's face almost makes me back down. But it's too late for that. "The one she killed?"

"How do you know about that?" Honey's voice shakes. But she holds that picture steady in her hands.

"Does it matter?" I ask. "What kind of person does that?"

Honey wilts right in front of me. "She didn't know he was in there," she says, and it's like she's aged ten years in ten seconds. "She didn't know."

"Why did she do it?"

"You don't know how angry this whole town was, Sugar Bee. The grief. How it tore us all to pieces when those babies went missing."

"Ember and Orli." I whisper the names like an old prayer.

"You weren't old enough to know how deep it shook people," Honey goes on, and I see her shudder. "Finding those sweet girls out there. Like that."

"But that little boy . . ." I say. And Honey nods.

"But that little boy," she repeats.

"How could she live with it?" I ask. "Knowing she killed a child?"

And when Honey doesn't answer, I realize that's a stupid question.

Because, obviously, she couldn't.

Honey looks down at the photo again. Then she hands it to me, and I stare down at those haunted eyes.

"She tried to do the right thing, Grey. After." Honey pauses to look at me. "She went back and buried him. Did you know that?"

I shake my head. "Where?"

"Back at Keller's Island. There's a big old two-trunked cypress tree that grows off to the edge of the clearing. She put him there. At the base of it."

"You should've told me," I say, and suddenly I'm so angry at her. Honey sighs. Her sadness fills up the whole kitchen.

"You're right, Sugar Bee." She reaches for my hand, but I pull it back. I'm not ready to forgive her for keeping all this from me. Not yet.

"Did she kill Dempsey Fontenot, too?" I'm making wild leaps with nothing to back them up. But we're short on time, and I'm getting desperate.

The radio station signs off for the night, and the harsh buzz of static sets my teeth on edge. "No, Grey." Honey sighs. "Your mother didn't kill Dempsey Fontenot."

"Are you sure?" I ask, and I feel relief wash over me like floodwater. At least I won't have to break that news to Zale.

"I am," she tells me. "That's a thing I can say for certain." Honey gets up and turns off the radio. No more static. But the tinkling of wind chimes moves in to fill the silence.

"Who did, then?" Honey doesn't answer me. "Somebody here did. Didn't they?"

"It was a long time ago," Honey starts. And I am so sick of hearing that. I push myself to my feet.

"I'm not eight years old any more. You need to stop protecting me."

"Grey, please. It's late and –"

"I need you to tell me what happened!" I've never raised my voice to Honey. Not ever in my whole life. Until now. "Please!" This desperate need to know is threatening to consume me. If I can't know what happened to Elora – if I can't put that mystery to rest for myself – then at least let me put an end to Zale's years of wondering.

"Grey –"

Sweet-N-Low is sitting up on his pillow now, looking back and forth between me and Honey. He's almost deaf, but even he can hear this. I'm not giving up, though. Not this time.

"You said he was innocent. You told me you never believed he killed Ember and Orli. Now tell me the rest of the truth! Who killed Dempsey Fontenot?"

"I don't know!" Honey's standing at the sink with her back to me. Her hands grip the edges of the counter like she's afraid to let go. "I don't know, Grey. I never wanted to know. And that's the truth. I used to be afraid that I'd hear from him. From Dempsey." She pauses. "That he'd reach out to me. Tell me who it was. And I didn't want that knowledge."

"He never did, though."

Honey shakes her head, and I hear her take a deep breath before she goes on. "What happened to those two little girls – then to that poor boy – and to Dempsey Fontenot, too – it's like a stain. On all of us. And this town will never be able to wash it off." Her shoulders droop, and she turns back to face me. It hits me how old she looks. Did that happen this summer? When I wasn't paying attention?

"Well, who killed Ember and Orli, then?" I ask. "Can you at least tell me that?"

Honey sighs. "I don't know the answer to that. I wish I did. There are a lot of unanswered questions. But most of us have learned to live with the holes."

"That's such bullshit," I say, and Honey pulls her robe a little tighter around her shoulders. Like she's cold.

"None of that has anything to do with you, Grey. I never wanted you to find out about any of it. Ever. That's why I didn't put up a fight when your daddy wanted to take you up to Little Rock. I figured the less time you spent here, the better. I wanted you away from all this." She puts her hand over her heart, like she's trying to stop it from bleeding. "I wanted to keep you safe."

"Who was keeping Elora safe?" I ask her. "Or Evie. Or Hart. Or any of the others?"

Who was there to keep Zale safe?

Or Aeron?

"Oh, Sugar Bee." Honey reaches out for me, but I take a step back, and she looks so hurt. "I don't see how that old business could possibly have any connection to Elora, if that's what you're thinking."

"Jesus!" I'm crying now. The angry kind of tears that always make me shake. "You don't know that! How could you possibly know that? What if it does have something to do with what happened to Elora? What if it has everything to do with what happened to Elora?"

For a second, there's only the sound of my rattled breathing. And the jingling of Sweet-N-Low's collar as he scratches his ear.

And, of course, the damn wind chimes.

"Plywood's out in the shed," Honey finally tells me. "Let's you and me drag it out first thing tomorrow, so we're ready when Leo gets here to board up the windows."

She kisses me good night and heads upstairs to bed. And I just stand there. Stunned. Because I know Honey loves me. And I know she wants to protect me. Keep me safe. I get that.

He squats down next to me. "Don't run!"
he shouts. "There's no point."

21

When Honey wakes me up before sunrise the next morning, I've barely slept at all. And the first thing I hear is the ringing of wind chimes.

But the first thing I see – feel – is that flash of Elora. Someone squatting low beside her.

Don't run.

I can't see a face.

There's no point.

I feel the weight of the words on my chest.

And I can almost hear the voice.

Almost.

But not quite.

I know I'm getting closer to whatever happened to Elora out there in the bayou, though. I just need a little more time. And that's something I don't have.

I struggle into some clothes and pull on my boots. Honey and I barely say two words to each other as we drag the big pieces of plywood out from the shed. One for every window.

I don't point out the missing black trunk.

And she doesn't notice it.

We turn on the radio again over breakfast and catch the tail end of another weather update. Elizabeth's winds have reached 115 miles per hour, making it a category 3 storm. A hurricane watch has been issued for all of coastal Louisiana, and evacuations are beginning. We've got less than sixty hours, the announcer tells us.

"We'll get everything tightened down today and head out first thing tomorrow," Honey says. But I can tell she's worried. She glances in my direction as she spreads strawberry jam on toast. "I should've sent you back to Little Rock days ago."

And I'm sure she means because of the storm. Mostly. But also because she could have avoided that whole scene last night.

We spend the morning carrying all the shop merchandise upstairs to Honey's big bedroom. Other than the big furniture, everything from my room has to go up, too. And the kitchen. Assuming the whole house doesn't blow away or get swept downriver, it's the flood that will do the damage. The stilts and the raised boardwalk protect us from high tides and even normal river flooding. But it won't be enough to keep our houses dry if a monster hurricane puts this whole area under twenty-five or thirty feet of water.

After lunch, Leo and Hart come and board up the windows for us. They carry the heaviest stuff upstairs and take down the swinging sign out front so it won't rip loose in the wind. I try to talk to Hart a couple times, but he doesn't have much to say other than "hold this rope" or "hand me that screw gun".

All up and down the boardwalk, people are tying down their boats and securing their property as best they can. Every so often, they stop work to mop their sweaty faces with soiled handkerchiefs and squint up at the perfect blue sky. I hear them whisper the names out loud in snatches of overheard conversation.

Rita. Camille.

Andrew. Betsy. Audrey.

Katrina.

Katrina.

Katrina.

Then back to work. No time to waste. Everybody is busy.

Even Victor. He's crawling around up on their roof checking for loose shingles, and I think again about how we all let Evie down. And her mama, too.

All of us except Hart.

By suppertime, we're about as ready as we're going to get. Honey and I eat fried bologna sandwiches at the kitchen table while Sweet-N-Low paces around the house on his stubby little legs, trying to figure out where all our stuff went. I figure he thinks we were robbed while he was asleep.

Being inside with the windows covered is making me seriously claustrophobic. Even with the AC running, it's like what happened between Honey and me last night has sucked all the oxygen out of the house. So I head out to the front porch to sit on the steps to stare at the river. You'd never even know a storm was brewing. It's a gorgeous evening. Clear with a good strong breeze to dry your sweat and keep the mosquitoes away.

To keep those chimes singing.

I was hoping to see Evie. I want to hug her goodbye. Make sure she's okay. And now that we're all evacuating tomorrow, I need to try one more time with her. To see if maybe she'll spill whatever secrets Elora has been whispering in her ear.

But Evie is nowhere to be seen. It isn't long before Sera and Sander and Mackey show up, though. At least our magic still holds. Still draws us together. The four of us huddle on the front steps of the Mystic Rose, exhausted from a long day of trying to get ready for the kind of storm you can't really prepare for.

"It's gonna be okay," Mackey says, more to himself than to us, and Sander gives his shoulder a squeeze. "Right?"

"No way to know," Sera answers. "There are some things you just can't say for sure."

That reminds me of Honey's words the other morning.

Sugar Bee, in the end, not everything is knowable.

But maybe she was wrong.

"How do you learn to control your gifts?" I know my question seems to come out of nowhere, but I've just realized I may not have another chance to ask them. At least not for a long time.

Sera just looks at me. "Grey," Mackey starts, "are you –"

But Sera cuts him off. "You don't learn to control 'em. You learn to live with 'em. You make space for whatever abilities you have. And you make damn sure to keep some space for yourself. If you can." She reaches over and lays her hand on mine. "If you're lucky." Sander is studying me, and his eyes look sad. "You fight as hard as you can every single day to never let yourself get lost."

I think about Hart, sinking so deep in the things he feels.

Of Evie. Drowning in what she hears.

And my mother, so swept up in her own power that she lost herself for good. First, when I was four, in the grey dawn behind Dempsey Fontenot's cabin. Then again in the dark of her own bedroom, when I was eight years old.

I vow that I won't let that happen to me.

When the others leave, I catch sight of Case and Wrynn out on the river dock.

It's been a long time since his fight with Hart, but I figure I still owe Case a real apology, so I cross the boardwalk in their direction.

"Hey," I say. Case is squatting down, examining the rotting wood. He scratches at the white paint with one fingernail to reveal the decay underneath. Then he stands up to look at me. "I just wanted to say –"

"Sorry?" He turns his head to spit into the river. "Or goodbye?"

"Both. I guess."

He smirks at me with one side of his mouth.

"Well," he says. "Guess dat 'bout covers it."

I don't know what else to tell him.

Case looks at me for a few seconds while Wrynn fidgets beside him.

"You know what made Elora so special?" he finally asks. His voice is low and gruff. Threaded with heartache. Like a Cajun ballad. "She made us all think dat she loved us best. Didn't she, chere?"

And I guess that's true.

"I gotta get on home," Case says. "Lots to do. We're clearin' out come mornin'. Before da storm hits."

"Take care of yourself, Case," I tell him.

"Yeah." He nods and runs a hand through that red hair. "And you take care a you, okay?"

He starts off down the boardwalk and Wrynn looks up at me, blinking.

"Be careful, Grey," she warns. She's all wide eyes and sun-pink cheeks. "Da rougarou, he don't care 'bout no storm. He'll eat you up, just da same."

Then she turns and runs after her brother. I head back to the front porch and change into my mud boots before I start for Li'l Pass.

There's nobody waiting for me at the trailer, so I kick off my boots and crawl up on top to sit cross-legged and watch the sun set.

La Cachette looks different somehow. All I see now is how small it is. How dwarfed the boardwalk looks, compared with the Mighty Mississippi stretched out behind it, ready to swallow it whole.

I feel the hair on my arms and neck react to his presence, but I don't turn around. I don't have to. I know he's there.

"I didn't mean to scare you, Grey."

It's an old joke between us now. He knows I'm not afraid of him.

"I have to leave tomorrow," I say as he crawls up to sit beside me. "I'm going back to Arkansas. It's over." I choke on the words. "I'll never know what happened to Elora."

I failed her. My twin flame.

Zale reaches for my hands, and I feel that tingle. My sorrow starts to evaporate, and that strange calm comes over me. It's like slipping into a hot bath at the end of a long day. I let him wrap his arms around me and pull me against his chest. That zing makes me shiver. He's warm and alive and beautiful. I breathe him in. Sunshine and cypress.

And it feels so good. He feels so good. I feel so good when I'm with him.

I can still feel the hurt of Elora. Not even Zale can make that go away. But his gentle touch makes it bearable somehow.

I think about Hart. How I love him with everything I have. How I always will.

Whatever that means.

But Hart is like the outgoing tide. If I hang on to him, he'll pull me farther and farther out to sea, until we finally drown together.

When I sit with Zale, though, even during the storm, I can see lights on shore.

"I'm sorry, Grey," he soothes. "I know how much you loved her. And I know how hard it is not knowing. Believe me."

I pull away from him a little, so I can see his face.

"There's something else I have to tell you. Something about your brother."

I see the fire of curiosity in Zale's eyes, and I feel it in his skin. Sharp enough to sting. But not hot enough to burn.

"You know where he is," he says, and I nod.

Zale's energy surges again to mingle with mine. Suddenly I'm breathless.

"There's an old cypress tree, back at Keller's Island. At the edge of the clearing. It has two trunks. You know the one I mean?"

"That's where I found the little hummingbird, Grey. Off in the dirt there."

"That's where my mother put Aeron. At the base of that tree."

Zale exhales into the night. The sound of bayou wind through tall grass. Then he pulls me tight against him again.

"Thank you, Grey," he whispers. And when he presses his lips to the top of my head, I let myself breathe out, too.

Finally.

My first real exhale since Elora went missing.

Because at least someone is found.

"I'm so sorry I couldn't help you find your father," I tell him.

If only we had a little more time.

I can almost feel the answers hanging in the thick night air.

I look up so I can see Zale's eyes. The intense blue of them. I reach out and run my fingers through his blond hair, then I lay my palm against the side of his face, and I can feel the dampness of his tears.

He's crying.

I run my thumb over the ridge of his cheekbone, and I'm rewarded with a series of little sizzling jolts. It makes me laugh in surprise. I can't help it.

Zale grins and holds me even closer.

The last night of a strange summer cut short by a churning monster.

Some secrets revealed. But others still buried deep.

"There's still so much I don't understand," I tell him. "About what happened to Elora."

And about what happened here thirteen summers ago.

"I feel like the real story is all tangled up with the lies," I say. "And I can't tell what's true any more."

"It's all true, I think. And none of it's true." Zale is tracing slow circles on my palm with one finger, and the little zips and zaps have me mesmerized. "So it becomes a kind of poem."

"Are you leaving tomorrow?" I ask him. It hadn't even occurred to me to wonder where he'd go. What he'd do when Elizabeth comes roaring into the bayou like a runaway freight train.

Zale shakes his head. "I still need to find out what happened to my father. And I need to know how dis all started. I need to know who put Ember and Orli in the pond behind our cabin."

I stare at him. There's a massive hurricane heading our way. This whole place will be flooded out. Storm surge halfway up the tallest trees. Twenty, maybe thirty feet. Or more.

"Can you –"

He gives me a little smile, and those ice-fire eyes light me up with their shine.

"I can't stop the storm comin'. But I'll be okay. I promise."

He's a hurricane baby, I tell myself. A boy born with all the power of the sea and the sky. And I know it's not my choice to make. But I'm scared for him.

Zale reaches out to tuck a piece of hair behind my ear, and I tremble.

"Don't be afraid, Grey," he tells me. "There are some things only the storm can teach us."

I'm waiting for the bullet to split my skull in half.
For the force of it to knock me face-first
into the water and the mud. But I never feel it.
I only hear the shot.

Zale walks me back to the boardwalk, but we don't say goodbye. We don't need to, he says, because we'll see each other again. Instead, we just stand in the shadows for a few long minutes, soaking up each other's light.

"You told me you saved each other," I remind him. "You and Elora. I know you fished her out of the river. But you never told me how she saved you."

He pulls me close, and the hum of his body against mine leaves me struggling to get enough air. I feel light-headed. But it's so good.

"She was my friend," he tells me. "And dat's really all there was to it. But it was enough."

And I know exactly what he means.

Zale looks down at me, and I reach up to run my fingers through his hair. I want to kiss him. But I don't. I'm afraid to. I'm scared that if I kiss Zale the way I kissed Hart – if I feel the tingle of his lips on mine – I won't be able to turn and walk away.

By the time I climb the sagging wooden steps to the boardwalk, a smothering fog has rolled in off the Mississippi. Evie's wind chimes ring out in the dark to welcome me back to the hiding place. It's late. Almost midnight. But I can't make myself go inside.

Those chimes are so loud in my head.

And in my heart.

Their song starts me thinking about Elora again. How I never got to say goodbye. I spin her ring on my finger. Three times. Like making a wish. Like blowing out the candles on a pink birthday cake.

And just for a second, I feel her so real. She's right behind me. If I just looked over my left shoulder, I'd see her.

I know it.

It's my last night in La Cachette this summer. Maybe ever. So I decide to do something I've been wanting to do since I first got home.

I turn away from the Mystic Rose and hurry down the boardwalk in the direction of Elora's house, dodging the places where long grass has started to grow up between the wooden planks.

And the spots where the white paint is worn away.

The slick black rot at the edges.

Leo told Honey that they weren't planning to put their own plywood up till tomorrow morning, so I know I'll be able to get in.

It only takes me a few minutes to reach my destination, and I hold my breath as I creep on to the porch that wraps around the front and sides of the house. Elora's window is toward the back, on the bayou side, and it never occurs to me that it might be locked. Sure enough, when I put my palms against the glass and push up, the window slides open without a sound.

I don't even stop to think about what I'm doing. I just throw one leg over the windowsill and climb in, like I've done it a million times before.

Because I have.

Hart was right about it being a disaster, and I'm grateful to Becky for not cleaning it up. For leaving it lived-in. Like something vibrant and laughing only this minute bubbled over and spilled across the floor in an explosion of glossy magazines and discarded tank tops and shiny tampon wrappers and colorful socks.

I wonder if they haven't packed it all up yet, or if they're just going to abandon it. Let the storm surge take it all. Sweep it out to sea.

Wash the room clean.

I sink down to sit on the shaggy yellow rug. I'm afraid to sit on the bed. I know it squeaks.

I close my eyes and breathe in Elora. She's been gone almost six months, but it still smells like her in here. Orange-vanilla body spray and cotton candy lip gloss. It's too much, and I turn to bury my face in the lilac flounces of her ruffled bedspread. The one we picked out together on a shopping trip up to New Orleans with Honey.

I remember how, the night my mother died, I'd been inconsolable. How I'd wailed with misery until, out of desperation,

Honey had carried me down here to Elora's house, and Leo and Becky had let her slip me into bed with a sleeping Elora. How, still half asleep, she'd reached for my hand and anchored me. Stopped my free fall.

Something down inside me twists and tears loose, squirming in my stomach like that dying snake on the end of Case's frog gig. But I can't cry. I don't have any tears. Just this awful feeling of wanting Elora so much that the weight of it threatens to pull me right through the floor and into the bottomless mud below.

Why didn't I try harder to make things right between us last summer? Why didn't I ask what was really going on with her? Why couldn't I give her what she needed from me? I should have said, "It's okay if things are changing. It's okay if you need some space. You know I'll always be here." Instead I lashed out. Made things worse. Drove the wedge in even deeper.

How do I forgive myself for that?

How do I ask Elora to?

When the hurt finally lets up a little, I get to my feet and take one last look around the room. I don't know what I was hoping to find here. Other than the faint scent of Elora. Some kind of last-minute clue, maybe. But I don't even know where to look.

Then I remember the secret spot. A place that only Elora and I know exists. A loose piece of paneling in the corner behind the bed. When we were kids, we hid our best treasures there. Bottle caps. Glitter pens. Plastic rings we got out of the quarter machine at the grocery store up in Kinter. And later, love notes we wrote to boys who would never read them and lists of faraway cities we planned to visit.

Someday.

I wedge myself into the little space between the bed and the wall and sink down to my knees. Then I feel around for the loose paneling and pry it away slow and easy, so it doesn't make any noise.

I feel around inside our hiding hole, and there's nothing but a folded piece of notebook paper. When I pull it out and open it up, a simple gold bracelet spills into my hands. I carry it to the window and hold it to the moonlight so I can get a better look at the charm dangling from one end. A single tiny heart inlaid with a red stone.

Red for passion. Red for sensuality.

Red to get a fire going, if you know what I mean.

When I turn it over in my fingers, Elora's name is engraved in fancy cursive on the back. It's exquisite and delicate and breathtakingly lovely. And not at all something Case would ever pick out. Not in a million years.

Zale said Elora was waiting for someone that night. She sneaked away while everyone was playing flashlight tag. Left them out in the storm, searching and calling her name.

I take another look at the notebook paper the bracelet was wrapped in, but there's only one word handwritten there in dark blue ink.

Soon.

That's all it says. Definitely not Elora's loopy script. Plain printed letters. They're distinctive, though. The *S* leans forward at a sharp angle, and the double *o*'s are odd-looking. Tall and elongated. More egg-shaped than round.

Soon.

"Who bought you this?" I whisper the words out loud to the ruffled bedspread and the yellow rug, then I wrap the little bracelet back up in the notebook paper and tuck it into my pocket.

I replace the loose paneling and inhale once more. A deep lungful of Elora. Then I climb back out the window like the worst thief ever. I haven't taken much. Just a little love token and the faint whiff of orange-vanilla body spray still clinging to my skin. I slide the window closed, and I freeze.

Cigarette smoke hangs thick in the wet air.

So I know he's there before I hear his voice.

"You shouldn't be out here, Shortcake. Don't ya know there's a hurricane comin'?"

When I'm dead, then what? Will he leave me here for the gators? Toss me in the river like trash? Will they find me floating facedown in the drowning pool? Like Ember and Orli? Or maybe he has something even worse in mind.

23

Hart lights up another cigarette, then he sucks in smoke and holds it for a long time before he blows it out. He's got me in the hot seat, and he knows it. He ashes the cigarette and cocks his head to one side. "You wanna tell me what the hell you're doin', Greycie?"

"I just needed to be in her room. So I could say goodbye."

"Damn." Hart shakes his head. "We don't even know how to tell the truth to each other any more, you and me." He turns and walks toward the end of the boardwalk. And I follow him. Like always.

He's carrying a big pair of bolt cutters in his other hand. He gives them to me, then he hops down into the pontoon boat with the cigarette between his lips. The water hyacinth has grown so thick, it must be choking the old boat half to death. The purple flowers are pretty. But it's invasive. It can suffocate a pond when it takes over. Block out the light. Steal all the oxygen.

I sit down on the edge of the boardwalk, and Hart motions for me to hand him down the bolt cutters, so I do. He cuts the chain on the boat, then he climbs back up the ladder to sit beside me.

"Things get as bad as they're sayin', I don't want it smashin' against the boardwalk. Might take the pilings out."

He finishes the cigarette and tosses the butt down into the bow of the boat. I focus my eyes on it for a few seconds, to see if I can get the cypress needles to light.

To see if I have any of my mother in me, I guess.

But nothing happens.

"You leavin' tomorrow?" he asks, and I nod.

We listen to the night music for a while. Even the frogs sound worried. Like they know what's coming.

"I'm not evacuating," Hart finally tells me. "I decided I'm gonna stay and ride it out."

So that's his plan. Suicide by hurricane.

"Becky's never gonna let you do that," I tell him. "That's stupid. She'll get Leo to drag your ass on the boat."

He laughs. "I'd like to see him try."

"Hart –"

"I can't leave her here." His voice is so twisted up that it's almost unrecognizable. "I was supposed to look out for 'er. I can't leave her here all by herself."

It hits me that maybe Elora was lucky. She disappeared all at once. But Hart's been disappearing a little bit at a time. Every time I see him, there's more of him missing.

I reach for him, and he lets me wrap my fingers around his. He doesn't say anything for a few seconds. And then I realize it's because he's staring at my finger.

At the little blue pearl.

I try to snatch my hand back, but it's too late. He's got a death grip on me. Hart's mouth is open and his eyes are dark. He can't look away from the ring.

"Where the hell did you get that?"

"I found it. Just now. In her room." I hate myself for the lie, but I can't think what else to tell him.

"Bullshit," Hart whispers. "You're lying to me." He pulls his gaze away from my hand and looks up into my face. And I see the exact moment my own fear settles behind his hazel eyes. "You're afraid." He breathes. And my chest rises and falls. "I can feel it." We both shiver. Mirror images of each other. But I can't make myself say anything. Hart tightens his grip on my hand, and I wince.

"Somebody gave it to me," I admit.

"Who?" My brain stalls out, and Hart loses patience. He clamps down on my hand even harder. I yelp and try to pull away again. But it's no use. He's so much stronger than I am. "Who gave it to you?" he demands.

"You're hurting me," I whimper. But he doesn't seem to care.

"Elora loved that ring. She never took it off her damn finger. If somebody had it, they stole it off 'er after they killed 'er."

"No." He's getting things all wrong. But I don't know how to fix this. "It's not like that."

"For fuck's sake! Stop playin' games and tell me the truth, Greycie!" Hart's voice is rising. There's a frantic undercurrent to his words. And it throws me off balance. "Tell me where you got it!" His eyes are wild, and I wonder if the panic I see in them is his. Or mine. Or if it comes from both of us. "Please!"

"Zale gave it to me." I spit out the truth. And then I wish immediately that I could swallow it up again.

Hart is staring at me. Confused. "Who the hell is Zale?"

"He's Dempsey Fontenot's son."

Hart's reaction is instant. He lets go of my hand and recoils like I sucker punched him. "That's not possible," he stammers. But I tell him he's wrong, and his face turns to ash in the moonlight. "You need to tell me the rest of it, Grey. Right now. No more secrets."

"Okay," I agree, and I rub at my sore fingers. "No more secrets."

So I finally tell Hart all about Zale. Starting with how I saw him outside my window. That very first night I was home. And once I get started, it all comes out so fast. In such a breathless rush. Like water over a spillway.

Secrets over the dam.

I tell him everything Zale's told me. All about how he met Elora. How they saved each other. How she gave him her ring as a friendship token. That night on the dock. Right before she disappeared.

The night she sneaked away during a game of flashlight tag to meet her secret love.

Hart looks like he's going to be sick, but he doesn't interrupt me.

I tell him about what Zale remembers of the night their cabin burned, too. Thirteen years ago. How his mother carried him through the dark.

And how I know now that my mother was the one who started the fire.

I end with how Zale came back here to find Aeron. His twin. So he could lay him to rest.

And to find out what really happened to his father.

"Holy shit." Hart tries to light another cigarette, but he fumbles with it and drops the lighter in the muck.

I explain that Zale was a hurricane baby. A boy born with all the power of the sea and the sky.

Just like Dempsey Fontenot.

Hart laughs an ugly laugh. It's nothing like the sexy chuckle that used to make me swoon. "Like father, like son," he mutters. "Isn't that what everybody says?"

I tell pretty much the whole story, right up through tonight.

But I never mention how Zale's touch makes me tingle. Or how his skin feels against mine. How I wonder what it would be like to kiss him.

I do tell him how Zale says Dempsey Fontenot didn't kill Ember and Orli, though. And I guess that's about all Hart can take.

"Jesus Christ, Greycie. Stop it! Just stop it! Listen to yourself for a minute!" Hart runs both hands through his tangled hair like he wants to pull the curls out. "They found them on his property. Not ten feet from his goddamn back door. And everybody knew he was a freak."

"Honey doesn't believe he did it. She says –"

"I don't give a flying fuck what Miss Roselyn said!" he roars. He's suddenly on his feet, and I'm still sitting on the boardwalk, with my legs dangling over the edge. I'm afraid to move. Hart's never yelled at me like this.

"Zale wouldn't lie to me." My voice is so quiet. Like Evie's. It gets lost. Swallowed up by the night sounds.

Hart looks at me like I've lost my mind.

"He wouldn't lie to you? Jesus! You gotta be fuckin' kiddin' me, Grey! He wouldn't lie to you? Listen to yourself! Everybody fuckin' lies!"

Not everybody.

Not Zale.

"Goddammit, Grey! This asshole blows in here and fills your head with all kinds of bullshit, and you take every word that falls out of his mouth like it's the gospel truth?"

I open my mouth to argue. But then I close it again.

My mind is racing. I want to tell him that's not what happened. But I can't.

Because what if he's right?

"Fuck!" Hart whirls around and kicks a metal bucket that's sitting up on the boardwalk. I duck and it goes flying over my head. I hear it land in the mud, and there's the unmistakable growl of a pissed-off Willie Nelson.

"Don't you get it?" Hart's dark eyes are glowing with rage. It scares me. He's got the same wild look he had that night he almost killed Case on the dock. "He's the one, Greycie! Your fucking secret boyfriend in the woods!"

"I never said he was –"

But I know he can feel it.

"He's the fucking one!"

My head hurts. Everything hurts. And I'm so tired. "What do you mean, the one?"

Hart drops to a crouch right beside me. His breath is hot and angry in my face.

"He's the one who killed Elora."

"No," I say. I'm shaking my head. "No way. That's not true." It can't be true.

I'm panicking. I shouldn't have told him. I should've known that's what he'd think. Where his mind would go. Because Hart doesn't know Zale. He doesn't know how gentle he is.

How beautiful.

He's never seen the aching honesty in his eyes.

But I have.

And I've felt it in his touch.

"Listen, Greycie. Just listen. This guy, he meets Elora. Like you said. And they strike up this secret friendship. Right?"

"Stop it." I'm pleading with him. "It's not true."

"And she doesn't tell a soul. Nobody. Not even me. Then . . . what . . . a month later . . . *bam*. Elora's dead." He runs a hand through his hair again. Those curls. "Missing. Whatever." He looks at me, waiting for some kind of response. But I don't know what to say. "Don't you think that's fuckin' weird?"

"I –"

Hart doesn't give me a chance to form a whole thought. "Don't you get it?"

"Get what?" I ask him.

"You're next."

I remember Honey's old warning.

The lightning hunts us.

She's been telling me that forever. Since I can remember.

"Don't," I say. "Don't say that. You're wrong." I feel Zale's gentle hand on my cheek. His strong arms carrying me to his boat. "If he came back here to find out what happened to his father, why would he want to kill Elora?" It doesn't make sense. "Why?"

"Come on." Hart yanks me up. I yelp and try to jerk my arm away, but he's too strong. And he's already dragging me down the boardwalk after him, like I'm some kind of rag doll.

"What are you doing? Hart! Stop!" He ignores me. His grip on my arm is crushing, and I'm barely able to stay on my feet as I trail along behind him. "Slow down! You're hurting me!"

My feet get tangled in a thick vine that reaches up through a crack in the wood to grab at me. I lose one of my boots, but Hart doesn't wait for me to get it back on, and I have no choice but to keep stumbling along.

Like Elora. That night. Out in the bayou.

He hauls me all the way down to the Mystic Rose, but he doesn't head toward the front porch. Instead, we end up out on the river dock. Hart lets go of my arm, and I look down at his finger marks. I rub the bruises I can already feel forming under the skin.

"What the hell?" I demand. "What's wrong with you?" But he grabs me again and clamps a hand over my mouth.

Evie's wind chimes are ringing in my ear. Frantic and frenzied.

"Shut up," Hart whispers. "Just shut up for one goddamn

minute. I have to show you something. And I need you to be quiet. Okay?" There's something in his voice that makes my blood run cold.

I nod, and Hart takes his hand away. He glances up toward the plywood-covered windows along the boardwalk, then he ignores the DANGER sign and ducks under the safety rope.

I open my mouth to tell him to be careful – to watch out for the rotten places – but he's already moving crates. A tall stack of old wooden boxes. They've been there a million years. So long that they've become a permanent part of the dock. And behind them there are five or six big oil drums. Huge fifty-five gallon barrels. Everything is piled up with rotten fishing nets and old crab traps and rusting anchor chains.

I want to remind Hart that stuff is dangerous. That's what we've been told our whole lives.

Stay away from all that old junk out on the dock.

Don't play around there.

It's dangerous.

It takes him a while to move enough stuff to get back to the barrels.

"Come 'ere," he says. But I'm rooted to the spot. Hart looks up at me and sighs. His eyes go soft. "Shit. Greycie. I'm sorry. About before. I just need you to see this. I don't know any other way." He motions for me to come toward him. "I need you to understand how seriously fucked up this all is. 'Cause you have no idea what you've gotten yourself into. With that boy. And I need to make sure you believe me. I need –" He looks down toward the barrels. "I need you to be safe."

I duck under the rope and take a few heavy steps toward Hart. He grabs my hand and pulls me toward the barrel in the center of the mess. I stand and watch as he tries to pry the lid off, but it's stuck tight. "Goddammit," he mutters, and he digs around for his pocketknife. He pulls it out and flips it open to start working around the edge of the barrel, like he's opening a can of paint. It takes him forever. And the whole time he's trying to get that barrel open, I don't breathe.

When Hart finally gets the top pried loose, he slips his knife back in his pocket. "Ready?" he asks, but there is no way for me to answer that question.

He wrenches the lid off the big black barrel, and the smell hits me. Like something that's been dead a really, really long time. I cover my mouth and my nose, but I can't see anything. It's too dark. He jerks his head, motioning for me to come closer. So I use every bit of strength I have left to make my feet move those last few steps.

And then I peek inside.

Moonlight bounces off something white. Long finger bones. And a skull. A faded overall strap with a brass button. That's all I see before I scurry backward, gagging. Hart has to grab me by the arm again to keep me from backing right off the dock into the water.

"Hey. Easy," he warns me. "It's all rotten."

But I don't know if he's talking about the wood we're standing on, or what's in the barrel.

"Is that –?"

Hart nods. "Dempsey Fontenot."

I sink down to sit on one of the wooden crates while Hart puts the lid back on the barrel and restacks the boxes and junk all around it. I close my eyes and take deep breaths, trying to keep from throwing up.

"He's been here all these years." The words taste slimy in my mouth.

Every time I sat on the front steps of the Mystic Rose, I was looking right at him.

Jesus.

All those nights Zale sat here on the dock with Elora, his father was right there.

Close enough to touch.

My stomach rushes into my throat, and I jump up and lurch toward the edge of the dock. I fall to my knees and vomit into the river. Hart is instantly beside me. He grabs the back of my tank top tight in his fist. And he hangs on. "Hey," he soothes. "You're okay. I gotcha." I feel his other hand in my hair. And the tenderness of it makes me choke. "Just breathe, Greycie."

When it's finally over, he digs a wadded-up tissue out of his pocket and hands it to me, so I can wipe my mouth. Then he helps me back to the crate and sits down next to me.

I hear him sigh, and I know he's wishing for a cigarette. But he dropped his lighter in the mud back at the gator pond.

"Ember and Orli have been missing three days," he starts. "No sign of 'em anywhere. Sheriff can't find hide nor hair of 'em."

"Like Elora," I murmur. And Hart nods.

"Just like that. So the search party decides to go check out at Keller's Island again. 'Cause everybody knew Dempsey

Fontenot wasn't right. The way he looked at people." He pauses to glance at me. "So they all head out there. My mama and daddy. Your mama. Bernadette. Leo. All the parents. Victor, even. Everybody in town, really."

"Honey?" I ask, and Hart shakes his head.

"Miss Roselyn didn't want anything to do with that. At least that's how Leo tells it." Hart digs around in his pockets until he finds another lighter. He holds it up like a trophy before he shakes out a cigarette and lights it. Then he goes on.

"And it's real early when they head out there. Not even dawn yet. But they find Ember and Orli. Sure enough. Floating there in that pond. And Sheriff had already been out there, but Dempsey Fontenot must have had 'em hid somewhere. Cause there they are. Drowned." He pauses for a second to breathe in smoke. "And people kind of lost their minds, I guess. They wanted to hang him right there. String him up from one of those big old live oaks. They yelled for him to come out of that cabin, but he wouldn't."

"He wasn't in there," I say, and I think about Zale's mama. Waking up to all that. Her there alone. And two little boys to protect.

"So everybody got worked up, and things got out of control. People were swept up in that moment, you know?" He ashes the cigarette. Hesitates. "And that's when your mama lit it up." Hart looks at me. "That's the story, anyway. Burned it to the ground just by casting her eyes on it."

"How do you know all this?"

He shrugs. "I've heard it in bits and pieces over the years.

A little from Leo here and there. Even Vic told me part of it one night when he was drunk off his ass." He inhales smoke again. "A man will tell another man shit like that. If he's fucked up enough."

"Do the others know? Sera and Sander? Case? And Mackey? Does Evie know?"

Hart shrugs and exhales. "We've never talked about it. But I imagine some of them probably know some of it. Or at least suspect it."

"Did Elora know?"

"She did." Hart flicks his wrist, and ashes scatter across the dock. "I told her back at the beginning of last summer." He pauses to put the cigarette to his lips again, and I get impatient waiting for him to exhale. "That's a big part of why she was tryin' to drive you away."

"From her?"

Hart shakes his head. "From here. No matter what else was going on between the two of you, she didn't want you comin' –"

"Why the hell didn't she just tell me? Why didn't anybody ever tell me?" I'm so angry that everybody's been keeping me in the dark. "This is my home, Hart!" I glance up at the houses along the boardwalk and lower my voice to a pissed-off whisper. "Have you guys been laughing at me? All this time? Because I'm so stupid? Because I don't know? Is that it?"

"Whoa." Hart puts out the cigarette under his heel. "Hold up, Greycie. It's not like that."

"Well how is it, then?" I feel like the world's biggest idiot. The only one at the party not in on the joke.

"Elora didn't tell you because she didn't wanna give you that secret to keep. She didn't wanna put that burden on you. That guilt that comes with knowin' what happened down here." He runs a hand over his face. "Shit," he mutters. "What happens down here."

"I could have handled it," I tell him. "She never gave me a chance."

"Because that kind of shit changes you. You know what I mean? It messes you up. For life. You can trust me on that." Hart sighs, and the sound of it is as deep and muddy as the Mississippi. "You keep saying this is your home, Greycie. But it isn't."

"Yes, it is!"

Hart growls at me in frustration.

"No! It isn't! You got out. You left." I open my mouth to argue again, but he shuts me down. "No. Wait. Just fuckin' listen." He rakes a hand through his curls and looks over at me. "Dammit, Grey. You were out of all this shit. Away from it. And sure, you'd come back summers. But you didn't live here. You weren't ever here long enough to let the stink of this place soak into you."

"That's not my fault! I wanted to be here. You know how bad –"

"Stop it! Are you even hearing what I'm saying? We were glad you got away from all this." He gestures around. To the dock. And the boardwalk. The big black barrel. "We loved you, Grey. Shit!" He grits his teeth like something hurts him. Way down deep. "We love you," he says. "Elora, especially. It almost killed her, cuttin' things off with you last summer. Lettin' it end that way. For a long while, I didn't know if she'd survive it. But you were gonna come home. Turn eighteen and come back to this. And she loved you too fuckin' much to let that happen. And me! God. Greycie. I love you so much. But all of us. Every goddamn one of us. We all fuckin' love you." He pauses to catch his breath. "So, you wanna know why we never told you any of this? We never told for the same reason Miss Roselyn never told you. Because we love you. And we want you to be okay." His voice splinters like rotten wood, and he swipes at his eyes with the back of his hand. "One of us needs to fucking be okay."

My mouth is hanging open, but I can't seem to make it work. I don't have the will or the words to respond to that, so I sit there for a few seconds in silence watching Hart search his pockets for another cigarette. When he lights it up, I study the slow burn of the paper.

And that reminds me of my mother.

"What happened next?" I whisper. "After the fire?"

Hart gets up and walks toward the side of the dock. Toward the rotten, crumbling edge.

"They left it still smokin'. Figured that was it, I guess. They thought Dempsey Fontenot was in there and that he was dead. For sure. So they came on home."

"But that wasn't it. Was it?"

Hart shakes his head, then takes a few long drags off his cigarette before he goes on. Like he needs to prepare himself for whatever he's about to tell me.

"He showed up right here. On the boardwalk. Dempsey Fontenot. That very same evenin'. About nightfall."

I keep my eyes on the dark river so I don't have to look at Hart the way he is now. All hollow and scarred.

"And I was there for this part," he says. "Nobody had to tell me about it. I actually saw it happen. I remember it firsthand." He finishes the cigarette and tosses it into the current. "Dempsey Fontenot blows in here that night like a hurricane. Bellowing like a wounded boar and carrying on like a wild man. And people start coming out to see what the ruckus is. So my daddy, he takes me with him. Just for the fun of it. He wants me to see, I guess. For whatever fucked-up reason. And Dempsey, he's screaming about how they killed his kid. Murdered his baby. That's what he kept yellin'. Burned him alive, he said. And nobody would've believed it. Because nobody had any idea. About the wife. Or the son." He corrects himself. "Sons, I guess."

"Twins," I say. "Like Ember and Orli."

And Sera and Sander.

Elora and me.

Hart nods. "Only we didn't know that. Shit. I never knew it until tonight. But he had the one kid, Greycie. The little boy. He actually had the kid with him. Had his body." He stops and looks at me. "What did you say his name was?"

"Aeron."

"Aeron," Hart whispers. "I never knew his name. But I knew he was my age. Four years old."

"Number twelve," I tell him. And Hart nods again.

"And Dempsey Fontenot is standing on the boardwalk holding this dead kid. Screaming bloody murder. And this kid is . . . all burned up. You know?"

"And you saw that?"

"I didn't just see it. I could feel it. I could feel that pain." He shakes his head. "Strong enough to make me piss my pants. Right there where I was standin'."

Evie's wind chimes are whispering in my ear again.

"And that's when the storm kicks up. Out of nowhere. I remember the rain. Buckets and buckets of cold rain. Huge waves on the river. This impossible flash flood on a clear evening. And the lightning and thunder. It was unreal. You could feel that electricity in the air. Strong enough to stand your hair up on top of your head."

"The power of the sea and the sky," I whisper. And Hart nods.

"I've never felt anything like it. That kind of power."

I shiver and wrap my arms around my chest. I'm thinking of those flashes I've been getting. Of the night Elora died.

The wind.

And the rain.

I remember what Hart said about that night. A raging storm came out of nowhere.

Like father.

Like son.

"Lightning hit a couple big ol' trees. And they went up." He snaps his fingers. "Like that. Wind took the roof clean off Bernadette and Victor's place." Hart stops and digs through his pocket for another cigarette. But there isn't one. So he curses under his breath and goes on. "But it's the hail I remember most. Huge, jagged chunks of ice crashin' out of the dark. People runnin'. Screamin'. All bloody. And there's Dempsey

Fontenot standing in the middle of it all holding that dead kid, lookin' up at the sky and grinnin' like the devil himself."

Where was I while all this was going on? I wonder. Inside, I guess. With Honey.

Safe.

I don't have any memory of any of it.

Hart shrugs. "And that's when somebody shot him. Blew a hole in his chest big enough to drive a four-wheeler through. And it all stopped. The wind and the hail. Lightning. The rain. All of it. And things were so wild. But I saw who it was. I saw who was holding that shotgun." Hart turns and pins me down with a hard stare. "And you wanna know who it was? It was Leo, Grey. Leo. Elora's daddy is the one who killed Dempsey Fontenot. You think that's a fuckin' coincidence?"

Hart is wrong. He has to be.

"Why Leo?" I ask, and Hart shrugs.

"Why not Leo? Somebody had to put a stop to it, didn't they? Before Dempsey Fontenot tore the whole damn town to pieces."

"Did Elora know that?" I ask. "What her daddy did?"

Hart nods. "I told her that part, too."

"But Zale couldn't know it." I feel like I'm falling. Grabbing for solid ground. The edge of the cliff. A tree root. Anything. But all I get is a handful of air. "How could he possibly know that? He wasn't even there." My head is spinning.

My whole world is spinning.

Not Zale.

Please.

Not Zale.

I wanted an answer. But I didn't want that one.

Hart tips his head back and laughs. He throws his hands up and gestures at the boarded windows. "How could he know that? Are you for real? Jesus. I don't know, Greycie. It's the Fucking Psychic Capital of the Goddamn World. You tell me how he knew it." He looks me dead in the eye. "Maybe Elora told him herself. You said they were friends, right? She was keepin' that from all of us."

Hart's words are suffocating me. I stand up and try to get a deep breath.

But I can't.

Hart points at the black barrel.

"So right there's why your new boyfriend would wanna kill Elora. Why he was probably plannin' to kill you, too. Hell, Greycie, maybe he was gonna pick us all off one by one. All the Summer Children. That's some real-life Shakespearean drama, right there. Sins of the father and all that shit."

"But Zale really doesn't know," I protest. "He doesn't know what Leo did. He doesn't know any of that. He's been looking for his father this whole time. He didn't even know what my mother did, until I told him."

Hart shakes his head. "Why the hell do you believe a thing this guy says? What kind of power does he have over you? We've been dickin' around since you got here – tryin' to figure out who might want Elora dead – comin' up with nothin'. Jesus Christ. And you've been sittin' on the answer since literally day one?" He shakes his head, like he just can't make sense of it.

"And you never breathed a word of it? Not even to me?"

I can't stand the hurt on his face, so I look away.

"Any more secrets?" he asks.

I shake my head.

"Right," he scoffs. "Me either."

Some kind of line has been crossed. And I know that it can't be uncrossed. Things will never be the same between us.

My head is still reeling. I'm sick and dizzy, trying to come up with a reason I never questioned a single thing Zale said. Why I took him at his word, right from the very beginning. Why didn't I ask more questions? Push him for more details.

Any details.

Then I remember what Zale told me about his mother. How she had a gift to calm the soul and settle the nerves.

With her, it wasn't just snakes. She had that same way with people.

All those times he made me feel safe but hazy. Slightly drugged. Or drunk. Peaceful. But off-kilter. Like I couldn't think straight.

Did I let him do that to me?

Had I let him soothe and charm me with magic eyes and an ocean-deep voice and a touch that took my breath away?

That tingle of bare skin against skin.

So that I never saw the danger? Like a cottonmouth hidden in the weeds.

The wind has picked up, and Hart's curls blow around the edges of his eyes. Elizabeth is coming for us. She'll be here . . .

soon.

The word reminds me of that one-syllable love note.

"I found something," I say. "Tonight. Hidden in Elora's room."

Hart's staring at me. "We tore that room apart lookin' for clues. Me. Mom and Leo. Sheriff. The boys from the state police. None of us found shit."

"You didn't know where to look," I tell him. And he laughs that dead-sounding laugh again.

"What'd you find?" He's eyeing me warily. Like I'm a strange animal he doesn't quite trust.

I pull out the piece of folded notebook paper and hand it to him. "Zale must have given it to her," I say. And I feel so stupid. I look down at the water, so Hart won't see the pain in my eyes.

But I know he feels it.

Hart unfolds the paper and stares at the delicate gold bracelet with the tiny charm. That little red heart. And the one-word love poem.

Soon.

The odd slanting *S* and those two egg-shaped *o*'s.

A fierce wind blows across the dock, and chimes ring out like alarm bells.

Hart's face goes hard again, and he looks out toward the river. I follow his gaze, but there's nothing to see. Without saying a word, he wads up the paper and pulls his arm back. Then he pitches the note and the bracelet as far as he can out into the dark river. And I cry out, because it feels like watching the last little bit of Elora vanish from my life forever.

"Why did you do that?" I'm close to tears. Everything seems so unfair. "It didn't belong to you!"

"It didn't belong to you, either."

"You're an asshole!" I tell him. And I mean it. "Maybe I wanted to keep it."

"Why?" Hart turns his back on the river. "Get yourself another souvenir. The guy who gave her that obviously didn't turn out to be the person she thought he was."

Maybe that's true. But maybe none of us are the person we think we are.

"You don't know that Zale –"

"Zale killed Elora, Grey." My heart races and my knees feel weak. "There isn't any other answer. And you know it now as well as I do. He's the missing piece in all this. He killed her because Leo killed his father. And he was gonna kill you, too." Hart crosses to me and puts his hands on my shoulders. "For what your mama did that night at Keller's Island."

"This whole town covered it up," I whisper, and Hart nods. But I still can't really believe it. "All these years."

"That's the problem, Greycie." Hart's jaw is set, and I see the veins throbbing in his neck. "That's always been the problem with this place. It's too damn easy to cover things up down here." There's something in his voice I can't put my finger on. Something still unspoken. "All that black water."

I think of the bayou stretching back toward Killer's Island like a dark and shallow sea. How it washes over everything.

Conceals all our lies.

Our sins.

And our twisted roots.

How it drowns us all. One way or the other.

"But this is where it ends." Hart's voice is strangely calm now. His words are careful. Even. "You need to get to bed. Honey'll have you up early in the mornin'. Gotta get out before the storm hits."

"What about you?"

He grins at me then, and if I wasn't already terrified, I am now.

"I'm goin' huntin' tomorrow. Back at Keller's Island."

Hearing him say it makes me feel sick. Something burns in the back of my throat.

"What if you end up dead?" I ask him. "Like Elora."

Because if Zale doesn't kill him, Elizabeth will.

Hart shrugs. "What if I do?"

We duck back under the safety rope, and he walks me up to the porch. He promises he'll see me in the morning. To say goodbye.

And he reminds me to lock the doors. The windows. Double-check them all, he says.

Because the rougarou is on the prowl.

Then he's gone.

When I turn to head inside, I think maybe I catch a flash of movement in Evie's darkened bedroom window. I freeze and watch for a few seconds, but nothing moves again behind the glass. So maybe I imagined it.

In the kitchen, Honey has left the radio on and Sweet-N-Low is listening to the weather. Hurricane Elizabeth is still strengthening. Winds up to 145 miles an hour now. Category 4.

A killer storm.

The eye is three hundred miles south of us, and she's cutting a path due north. Straight toward the mouth of the Mississippi River.

La Cachette is going to take a direct hit. No one here is safe. Not in the hiding place.

Truth is, none of us ever have been.

It's dark and slippery. And the blinding rain makes it hard to see. A few times, he almost loses his footing, and I think maybe we'll both go down. If we do, would I have the strength to get back up and run?

When morning comes, Honey gets the boat ready, and the two of us make a dozen trips between the house and the dock, loading up things she can't stand to leave behind.

Each time I step outside, I'm trying not to look at those big black barrels.

Especially the one in the middle.

Instead, I focus on that latest flash of Elora, and I try to work out if those are Zale's arms carrying her though the storm. I wish I could see his face. Or even feel that tingle.

So I'd know.

For sure.

Because I still don't want it to be true.

"Have you seen Evie this morning?" Honey stops me on a trip back inside, and I shake my head.

"Why?"

"Bernadette says they've been looking for her for a while." Honey frowns. "Can't imagine where she's got off to, today of all days." She shakes her head and tells me not to worry. "I'm sure she'll turn up."

But I can feel it. Something's not right.

The National Hurricane Center says we're less than thirty-six hours from landfall. As of this morning, all of coastal Louisiana is under a mandatory evacuation order, so the rest of the morning is one long goodbye.

Sera.

Sander.

Mackey.

We stand on the dock and cling to each other. Fret about Evie. Cry. Start to leave. Then stop and do it all over again.

Sera pulls me close to whisper in my ear. "Get the hell away from here and be happy, Grey. That's what Elora wanted for you. That's how you do right by her. You understand?"

I don't have the words to answer.

Sander kisses my cheek, and for a second, I think he's going to say something. But he doesn't. At least not with words.

I look around our little group, and I feel the loss of them so deep already. Evie should be here. And Hart. Case.

And Elora.

Ember and Orli.

We should all be here for this goodbye. Together. All the Summer Children.

I don't let myself think about Zale. Or Aeron.

"I love you guys," I say.

We hug some more. Cry again. Make big promises. Swear to keep in touch. Always. No matter what.

"Good luck with track next year," Mackey tells me.

"You too," I say.

"My school's gonna be underwater for a while." He tries to laugh. But he can't pull it off. None of us can. "Guess I'll have to join the swim team."

We all just stand there for a few seconds. I'm holding Sander's hand. Nobody wants to be the first to go.

But Mackey's brother is telling him to hurry up, and Delphine is shouting at Sera and Sander in Creole.

So it's time.

"Forget about La Cachette," Sera whispers as she gives me one last hug. "*Laise tout ça pour les morts.*"

Leave all that for the dead.

Then I go back inside for another load of stuff, just so I don't have to watch them leave.

When I come back out, Honey is standing on the dock with Bernadette and Victor. And for once in his life, Vic doesn't sound drunk. Just pissed off. "Goddammit," he says. "I've looked everywhere for that stupid little bitch."

Honey gives him a hard look and slips her arm around Evie's crying mama. "She'll turn up, Bernadette. She can't have gone far."

Victor throws an old duffel bag into their beat-up flatboat. "Yeah. Well, I ain't got no more time to wait. Y'all see that girl, you tell her we went on up to Monroe." He turns to his sister. "Get in the boat, Bernie. Evangeline can take care of her own damn self." Nobody moves, and Vic hisses again. "I said, get in the goddamn boat, Bernie."

"Bernadette," Honey starts, but Evie's mama just shakes her head and gets into the boat with her brother.

"We gotta get on up to Kinter," she mumbles. "Get the truck and head up to Monroe. Like Vic says." Victor gets the motor going, and black smoke billows across the dock. "Storm's comin' in." There's no expression on Bernadette's face. She's gone all blank. *I'm sorry.* She mouths the words to the crowd as their boat pulls away. But I don't know who she means them for.

Honey shakes her head and pats my shoulder before she gets back to work. Evie's bound to show up any minute, she says. There are men out looking for her right now. And then somebody will take her up to Kinter with them. Get her on the shelter bus to Monroe. See that she's taken care of.

But I know time is running out.

I catch sight of Hart sitting on the steps of the Mystic Rose, and I know he purposefully skipped out on the painful goodbye with the others.

I walk over and sit down beside him.

"He took her," Hart tells me. "Evie."

"That's ridiculous," I say. "You don't know that."

But all morning, I've had this horrible feeling. It isn't like Evie to go off alone.

"Me and Leo, we've been out lookin' for 'er for hours. Since sunup." Hart stares down at his boots and runs a hand over his face. "She's gone, Greycie. Vanished."

Honey yells at me from the dock. She wants me to take one last walk through the house.

Hart follows me inside as I move from room to room. "I told Mama and Leo I'm not goin' today," he says. And I stop to stare at him. I didn't believe him when he said it last night. I figured he was out of his head. Or talkin' big. "I told 'em I wouldn't leave here without Evie. That I'd stay and track her down. There's a chance she's still alive. At least right now."

His voice echoes in the emptiness.

"Leo says their company has a big supply boat still out in the gulf. It's tryin' to get in, though, so it can beat the storm up to New Orleans. It'll be comin' up this way tomorrow mornin', just ahead of landfall."

"No way." I shake my head. "That's cutting it too close."

"Leo already radioed the captain, and they're gonna make a quick stop here. To pick up Evie. They'll get her someplace safe. If I can find her."

The radio is still broadcasting weather updates from the kitchen. A reporter tells us that Elizabeth is a Category 5 hurricane now. And she's only 225 miles from the mouth of the Mississippi.

"What about you?" I ask him.

Hart shakes his head. "I told you I'm not going."

"Don't be stupid, you have to –"

Hart shuts me down. "I'm not leaving here."

"Sugar Bee!" Honey is yelling at me from the front porch. "We gotta get on the way."

"I'm staying with you," I tell him, and he shakes his head.

"The hell you are."

"Just until tomorrow morning. To help look for Evie. Then I'll get on that boat. I promise."

And I'll make sure he's on it, too.

No way I'm leaving him behind.

Hart opens his mouth to tell me no again, but Honey charges in holding Sweet-N-Low. "We have to go, Sugar Bee. The wind's really picking up."

"I'm not going," I tell her. "Not right now." She stares at me, confused. "I'm staying behind with Hart. To find Evie." Hart's opens his mouth, but I grab his hand and squeeze hard. "We've already lost Elora. I'm not losing Evie, too."

And there is no way I'm letting Hart stay here to die.

"Evie will be fine," Honey argues. "There are people looking for her right now. They'll find her. She'll be okay."

"Evie isn't somebody else's responsibility," I say. "She's my responsibility. And Hart's."

Hart stares at me with those hazel eyes, and for the first time in a long while, they look like the eyes I've known my whole life.

"Grey's right," he says. "Evie's one of us, Miss Roselyn. We oughtta be the ones lookin' for 'er."

"Grey," Honey starts. "I've got people already loaded in my boat. Waiting. They're counting on me to get them up to Kinter and –" I don't let her finish.

"My mother killed herself because she couldn't live with the guilt of what she did."

Honey's face crumples. She looks like she's at least a hundred years old. "She didn't know about the little boy, Grey. I told you that."

"I know," I tell her. "But it was that regret that killed her. And if I leave here without finding Evie, the same thing could happen to me."

"There's a big supply boat comin' in tomorrow mornin'. Just ahead of the storm," Hart says. "Carrying evacuees from the offshore oil rigs. Headin' up to New Orleans. And I promise you, Miss Roselyn, Grey will be on that boat. I give you my word. Leo's already got it all worked out."

Honey looks back and forth between Hart and me as Sweet-N-Low starts to whine in her arms.

"You can meet her up in New Orleans, tomorrow afternoon," Hart tells her. "And the two of you can still get out before the worst of it hits."

"Weather will be bad by then," Honey says. "Roads will be clogged."

"We'll make it," I say.

Honey knows she's fighting a losing battle. "You two make sure you're on that boat. You understand? Come hell or high water."

"We'll be on the boat," I promise. "All three of us." And I squeeze Hart's hand again.

Honey sighs. "I'll meet you at the Coast Guard station in New Orleans. Tomorrow afternoon. And we'll hightail it up to Shreveport. Hart, you tell your mama we'll take you up with us. Evie, too."

"Sure," Hart says. "Okay."

We walk Honey outside, and Hart takes Sweet-N-Low and gets him settled in the boat. Then he gives him a good scratch behind the ears. "Good luck, old boy," he says.

"Look at me, Grey." Honey lays her hands on each side of my face. "After your mama died, I wanted to protect you. So I hid things. And that was wrong. I'll tell you anything else you want to know, whenever you're ready. No more secrets. Not between you and me. Not ever. I promise."

"You can tell me tomorrow," I say. "On the drive up to Shreveport."

"Tomorrow." She nods. "I'll tell you tomorrow."

Honey hugs me tight, and I tell her I love her. Then Hart helps her into the boat, and she and Sweet-N-Low start off toward Kinter with a load of grateful passengers. I stare after them until they take the cut into the bayou.

"Come on," Hart says when we can't see them any more. "No sense wastin' time. Let's you and me head out to Keller's Island. See what we can find."

I trade my flip-flops for mud boots before I follow him down the wooden steps to where he's parked the four-wheeler out behind Honey's shed.

I climb up behind Hart and try to swallow the bad taste in my mouth. But it doesn't go away. When we splash through Li'l Pass, I glance back over my shoulder. I'm looking for the reassuring white gleam of the boardwalk, but all I see is swamp. And, to the south, those wispy storm clouds twisting at the edges. The outer bands of the storm.

It's a long, miserable ride out to Keller's Island, and it seems like hours before the thick trees finally rise up to greet us. Hart stops the noisy four-wheeler a half mile or so back, then he grabs his rifle off the gun mount and we slog the rest of the way on foot. By the time we reach the ring of cypress trees that marks the edge of the island, I'm soaking wet and covered head to toe in mud.

We push our way through tangles of honeysuckle and wild blackberries, and Hart moves in front of me as we get closer to the clearing. He takes the rifle off his back and lifts it to his shoulder. Ready for whatever.

Ready for Zale.

We barely breathe as we inch our way toward the cabin. Toward Zale's campsite. I've been so focused on helping Honey get things ready for the storm. Plus worrying about Evie. I haven't dared to let myself think about Zale. But now those blue eyes take up all the space in my mind.

"Maybe you're wrong," I whisper. "Maybe whatever's happened to Evie doesn't have anything to do with Zale." Hart doesn't respond. "Maybe whatever happened to Elora didn't have anything to do with him, either."

Hart stops and turns on me. "You're in love with him."

I'm not prepared for his words. Or for the look on his face.

"That's nuts," I say. "I don't even know him."

Not really.

Hart shakes his head. And I remember who I'm talking to.

"Lots of people fall in love with monsters," he tells me. "Only they don't realize it until it's too late." Hart's dark curls are plastered to his forehead, and his shirt is soaked clean through with sweat. But he still looks cold. Like there's some part of him that can't quite get warm. "My mama did." He's standing there in front of me, words seeping out of open wounds. "Elora sure as hell did."

"Hart –"

"I guess you did, too."

He turns and heads farther in, and I can't do anything except follow him and wonder if he's right.

It's all for nothing, though. Because there's no trace of Evie at Keller's Island. And there's no trace of Zale, either. Even all his stuff is gone. We search every square inch of high ground.

Nothing.

Not even a left-behind can of beans or the remains of a campfire.

The only thing that proves Zale was ever there is a strange little grave at the base of a two-trunked cypress tree.

Someone has pulled away the thick vines and brambles to expose the dark earth underneath. And there's a small wooden marker with a name carved into its surface.

AERON

The gouges in the wood are deep and angry. Rough.

Full of splinters.

"Why didn't he kill me, if that's what he wanted to do?" The question keeps running through my mind. All those times we were alone. Totally isolated. No one would have ever known what happened to me.

Just like Elora.

"I don't know." Hart is staring down at the grave, and some of the harshness has gone out of his voice. "Maybe he needed you."

"Needed me for what?"

Hart looks up at me, then back down at Aeron's resting place. "To help him find what he was looking for."

I kneel down in the soft dirt and slip the little silver hummingbird out of my pocket. The one Zale found right here. In this spot. I grabbed it when Honey and I were loading up the boat. Now I press it into the soil at the base of the handmade marker, and when my fingers make contact with the ground, I feel a hint of that familiar tingle. It's so faint. But it's there.

I whisper that I'm sorry.

When I stand up, Hart is watching me. "You're not the one who killed him, Greycie." I nod, but my seams are starting to separate.

"Fuck," Hart mutters. "Goddammit." He reaches out and pulls me against his chest. He wraps me up in his arms, and I feel myself let go. Really let go. Suddenly I'm sobbing.

For Elora.

And Evie.

For Hart and me.

And for Zale.

For my mother.

And Dempsey Fontenot. Thirteen years rotting away in a black oil drum.

For Ember and Orli, lost so long ago I can barely remember them.

And Aeron. Who I never got to know at all.

Hart holds me, and he doesn't try to stop me crying. He just keeps one hand on my back and one hand tangled in my hair while he lets the pain bubble up out of me and soak right into him, the way my tears are soaking into his shirt.

He stands there and absorbs it.

Feels it.

All of it.

Without flinching.

And when I'm finally out of tears, he looks down at me and says, "Don't take on that weight, Shortcake. That guilt over what your mama did. All those years ago." His voice is low in my ear, and the gruff sound of it fills up some of my cracked-open places. "If you do, you won't survive it. Trust me."

We head back to the four-wheeler and spend the rest of the afternoon searching the bayou for Evie. And Zale. But there's no sign of either of them anywhere. And the longer we look, the darker Hart's mood gets.

Just like the clouds to the south of us.

And I'm not a psychic empath like he is, but I know he feels like he's failing Evie. Letting her down.

Same as he did Elora.

I know it for a fact, because that's exactly what I'm feeling, too.

It's almost nightfall when we finally head back to the Mystic Rose for some food and to gas up the four-wheeler.

The weather is changing fast now.

The pressure keeps dropping, and the air feels different.

Hart and I sit on the kitchen floor and listen to the radio while we try to eat peanut butter sandwiches washed down with a couple warm beers that Leo left behind.

The National Hurricane Center is calling Elizabeth a "potentially catastrophic" storm. They predict storm surge flooding all along the Gulf Coast. Another Katrina, they warn us. Expect large-scale destruction to property and significant loss of life.

But even with Elizabeth practically knocking on our front door, it's the hurricane brewing inside Hart that really scares me.

He's silent, and he barely touches his food. He just stares off toward the kitchen window, like he's looking out into the bayou. But the window is all boarded up.

There's nothing to see.

"Evie's already dead," he finally tells me. "Just like Elora. That's what I'm thinkin'. He killed her, and then he got the hell outta here ahead of the storm."

I push my sandwich away. I can't eat it. The peanut butter sticks in my throat and keeps me from swallowing.

"Zale's not afraid of the storm," I remind him. "He wouldn't run from a hurricane."

"Then he killed her and he's holed up somewhere. Hiding."

"We don't know that," I tell him. "We don't know anything."

Hart shrugs and drains the last of his beer. "Knowing is seriously overrated."

I barely recognize the guy sitting across from me. He's skin and bones.

All hollowed out.

And sunken in.

It hurts me to look at him. But he's not dead. Yet.

"I need you to come with me in the morning," I say. "On the boat. If we find Evie." I swallow hard. "Even if we don't –"

Hart shakes his head. "We've been over that."

"You have to get out of here, Hart. For good."

"There isn't any good in me," he mutters.

"That's not true. Just come with me," I plead. "I'll help you. We can –"

"Look," he says, "I'm glad you stayed, Greycie." Something catches in his throat, and he washes it down with a swig of beer. "I'm grateful to have you here. With me. Tonight." He tightens up his jaw. Gives his head another shake. "But my mind's made up."

"Hart –"

"Drop it," he snarls. There's a warning in his voice. But I don't listen. Not this time.

"All you have to do is get on the damn boat."

He laughs that sad half laugh, and it makes my heart ache for the other version. That familiar throaty chuckle that crinkles his eyes up at the edges.

"I can't do that. That's why I'm in this mess to begin with. I don't belong out there. With all those people."

"What happened to you?" I ask him, and he stares at me. But I've finally reached my breaking point with him. "You think it'll be hard living out there, so you'd rather die here? Is that it? Fuck all of us who love you." I take a deep breath. Try to hold myself together. "All of us who need you."

"You don't get it," he says.

"I do get it. Nobody else matters. You don't care about

anybody but yourself." My voice is rising like floodwater. "You're a coward, Hart. That's all it is. Jesus! When did you get to be so pathetic?" I scramble to my feet, shaking with rage and grief. "You're spineless! Elora would be so ashamed of you!"

Hart lunges in my direction, but I shrink back, out of the way. He grabs his beer bottle and throws it against the wall behind me. The shattering glass gets my full attention, and I freeze.

"You think I want it this way?" he roars. He's boring holes through me with his eyes, and his breath comes in furious, ragged puffs. "You don't know shit, Greycie!" He wipes his mouth and runs a hand through his hair. Then he drops his voice to a low growl. Clenches his fists at his sides. "You don't know half of what I've seen. The things I've felt. Things that would rip your guts out and send you huntin' a shotgun to put in your mouth. Things that live inside me every fucking minute of every miserable day." His words are Category 5. I struggle to stay on my feet. "You don't know me, Grey. You never have." He shakes his head. "Nobody does."

"I know that if you don't get on that boat, Hart, I'm not going to, either." My whole body is trembling. "And then we'll both die here. And it'll be your fault. You want that on you?"

He snarls and takes a step toward me. I scurry backward, but he keeps on coming. He backs me up clear across the room, until I'm pinned against the wall.

"You're leaving in the mornin', Greycie. I made a promise to Miss Roselyn. And I owe it to Elora. She wanted you safe. Out of here. Away from this place." He leans down until we're nose to nose. "And if I have to carry your ass on to that boat, kicking and screaming, and hand you over to the captain, I will. Hell, I'll knock you unconscious if I have to. So don't you fuckin' test me."

"Hart –" I can't stand this. I reach out to lay a hand on his chest, but he pulls away and glares at me.

"I'm heading back out to look for Evie." He practically spits the words at me. "You stay here. In case she comes back." He grabs his rifle and a flashlight. "And keep the doors locked. Because your goddamn boyfriend is still out there somewhere."

He jerks open the front door and slams it behind him. The whole house shakes with his anger.

And then I'm all alone.

My ears ring with deafening silence.

And then the clanking of wind chimes.

I let go of the boardwalk piling and throw myself headlong into the wind. It knocks me sideways. I skitter and claw at the boards to keep from ending up in the water, but I manage to right myself and keep plowing forward.

That flash of Elora hits me as soon as Hart is gone. I grit my teeth against the terror of that moment. My twin flame fighting the storm to stay on her feet.

I get up and lock the door, then I sit and stare at the empty room. The AC is still rattling in the window, but it feels like there's no air left in the sealed-up house. From the kitchen, I hear the weather announcer giving the latest update.

Twenty-four hours till landfall.

Hurricane Elizabeth is still moving north, targeting the Louisiana coast. A weather buoy out in the gulf is already reporting fifty-foot waves.

Fear gnaws at me with sharp teeth.

What if the supply boat can't make it in?

I tell myself it's already safe in one of the lower river passes, anchored down and ready to head on up this way at first light.

But there's no way to know that for sure.

I'm feel myself spiraling and I don't know what else to do, so I dig *The Tempest* out of my backpack and read until midnight.

But when the final act ends with everyone safe and forgiven, I throw the book across the room and scream at the walls.

Because that feels like cheating.

And then there's nothing to do but wait.

Pace the floor. Count the little faded apples on the kitchen wallpaper. And wonder. Drive myself wild with worry. Wait some more. Until I finally fall asleep on the cold linoleum.

It's hours later when I wake up. 4:32 a.m.

I wonder if Hart has found Zale.

Out there.

In the wild dark of the bayou.

I think about Evie. How terrified she must be. If she's anything at all any more.

I stand up to stretch my aching back, and suddenly the radio turns to static. A low white-noise hum.

The overhead light flickers. Then dims. Then goes blazing bright. And dims again.

The hair on my arms stands straight up, and I hear my heart hammering in my ears.

I creep to the back door to crack it open and peer out into the night. But there are no ice-fire eyes burning in the shadows.

A gust of wind sweeps into the kitchen. It rips the knob from my hand and flings the door wide open.

Evie's chimes whisper my name. They call me outside. Like an invitation.

So I step out on to boardwalk behind the house. Almost like I'm dreaming.

Hart would tell me not to. But Hart isn't here.

There's a forgotten hammer lying on the back step, from when we put the plywood over the windows, and I pick it up and wrap my fingers around the handle.

I pause to search the dark again for bright blue eye-shine. Like looking for a gator in a black pond. I tighten my grip on the hammer. But I still don't see that icy glow staring back at me from the edges of the swamp. I know he's close, though, so I tiptoe around the side of the house until I can peek around the corner and look toward the dock.

And there he is, blond hair blowing in the moonlight. Looking out at the water. Standing not five feet away from what's left of his father.

I freeze, but it's too late. Zale turns to look back, and I'm caught in his fire-and-ice gaze. He raises a hand to wave at me, and it's like the movement wipes me clean. My fear slips away, and calm settles on me like a cool sheet in the summertime. It pulls me out of hiding, and I stand in the middle of the boardwalk staring at him, the hammer still dangling from my hand.

"I didn't mean to scare you, Grey."

"What are you doing here?" I ask him.

He smiles at me.

Those eyes.

"I wanted to make sure you were safe."

But I'm not safe, am I? Not with him here.

Everything is so confusing.

I push back at the fog that's blanketing my brain. I can't let him work that magic on me.

Not tonight.

I wriggle out of that peaceful feeling like I'm shedding wet clothes.

"Where's Evie?" I demand. "What did you do with her?"

Zale looks confused. "Evie?"

"You took her," I say. "Like you took Elora." The look on his face is proof that he didn't see that coming. "Is she dead?" I push. "Did you kill her, too?" My stomach is all tied up in writhing knots. Like a nest of snakes. "The way you killed Elora?"

The sudden electricity in the air is enough to stand my hair on end. Across the river, lightning scatters sparks like the Fourth of July. Thunder rumbles, then cracks sharp.

"I never hurt Elora," Zale protests, and I hear the hurt in his voice. "I wouldn't –"

"That's a lie." Anger bubbles up inside me until it overflows so hot I'm afraid I'll melt into the boardwalk. "You made her fall in love with you. Then you promised her you'd run away together. You told her to sneak away and meet you that night. On the dock."

"Grey –"

"And then you killed her instead."

"I didn't." His voice is low. Calm. But mine is rising fast.

"You were the last one to see her alive," I accuse. "You told me that yourself!"

"I never hurt her," he tells me. "Elora was my friend. Until I met you, she was my only friend." He looks so genuinely lost. "I didn't think I'd ever be able to trust anyone. But Elora proved me wrong. I loved her, Grey. Same as you did. Why would I kill her?"

Zale takes a step in my direction, and the light in his eyes dims when I move away from him.

"Grey? Why? Why would I kill Elora?" He takes another step toward me, offers me his hand. "Grey. Why?" I need him to stop talking. I need him not to come any closer. "We saved each other. I told you that."

I take another step backward.

"Tell me," he says. "Why would I do that?" He reaches for me again. "Why?" I can't take this. He has to stop. "Why?"

That last word echoes off the river.

"Because we killed your father!"

Zale freezes as the wind moans around him. He doesn't move. He doesn't say anything. I wait for the flash of lightning. For the roll of thunder. But there's nothing.

Just bewildered silence.

And sudden, terrible cold.

"What do you mean?" The question is so quiet. So deep. So utterly real. "Who killed my father?"

"Elora's daddy."

Zale staggers backward, like I shot him in the chest. The way Leo shot Dempsey Fontenot the night this all started.

"But really it was the whole town," I say. "All of us."

"Tell me what happened, Grey." Zale sinks down to sit with his back against a wooden crate. But I can't stop staring at the black barrels behind him. "Please," he begs. And I hear a lifetime's worth of unanswered questions underneath those words. "He was my father."

Zale's pain and confusion float between us like fog. They're genuine.

Real.

I feel the truth of that every bit as clear as Hart would be able to, if he were here.

Zale doesn't know about what happened on the boardwalk. On that dark summer evening. After my mother set the fire to the cabin back at Keller's Island. And if he doesn't know what Leo did . . . then it's not a motive for revenge.

For murder.

And if Zale didn't kill Elora, he didn't take Evie, either.

Hart was wrong.

He was wrong.

About all of it.

I think about the calm, peaceful feeling that Zale gives me. And I know it's nice. It feels good. That fuzziness. But I realize it was never why I trusted him. Not really. Because that feeling never lasted long, and I could push it away if I tried.

I trusted him because he gave me so many reasons to. At first, because Elora had trusted him enough to share our special words with him. And because he cared enough to give me back Elora's ring, when I didn't even know he had it. But then, because of the way he treated me. His patience and his gentleness. The way he was honest with me, over and over, when he could have fed me easy lies.

I recognized the blazing sincerity in his gaze.

Felt the burn of truth in his touch.

Why did I ever doubt him? Why did I doubt myself?

I drop the hammer and move to kneel beside Zale as he reaches for my hand.

His fingers are like ice in mine. There's no spark. No warm tingle. The flame has gone out inside him.

"Grey," he whispers. "Please. I need to know."

So I repeat the story Hart told me last night. I tell Zale how Dempsey Fontenot showed up on the boardwalk after the fire, cradling the body of his dead child. How he rained down fury on the crowd that gathered to gawk at him. Hailstones the size of grapefruits. And how Leo – Elora's daddy – blew a hole in his chest.

How they hid the body.

Right here in the heart of La Cachette.

The hiding place.

And how they all kept the secret. Every single one of them.

All this time.

When I'm finished, it's quiet for a long while. Zale drops his head to his hands and sits with the crushing weight of the truth on his shoulders.

"Where?" he finally asks me. "Where did they put him?"

I stand up and duck under the safety rope to pick my way through the stacks of crates and the rotting fishing nets. I work my way around the broken crab traps and the rusting anchor chains until I'm standing next to the middle barrel. I lay my hand on top, and Zale gets to his feet and makes his way through the scattered junk to stand across from me.

"Do you want to open it?" I ask, but I'm relieved when he shakes his head.

"You're sure he's really in there?" He raises his eyes to meet mine.

"Yeah," I say. "I saw him myself."

Zale takes his hands and lays them on top of the barrel alongside my own. I feel that faint tingle. Like the little mound of earth back at Keller's Island.

The moment feels solemn. Almost like a eulogy.

"Did Elora know?" he asks me. "About what happened to my father?" I nod, and Zale looks hurt. I know he's wondering why she kept it from him.

But I think about that little grave out at Keller's Island, and I understand why. Because even when the secrets we hide in our pockets aren't our own, the weight of them can still be enough to drown us.

Zale is studying my face. "Thank you for this, Grey."

"I didn't know," I tell him. "You have to believe me."

"Of course I believe you," he says, like there could never be any doubt. Like he trusts me completely.

And I feel like shit again for letting Hart convince me that Zale could be a murderer. Or that Case could, either, for that matter. I should have known better. I did know better, deep down. But my whole life, Elora has been my candle. And Hart has been my North Star. I've always depended on their light to guide me. It never occurred to me I had the power to push back my own darkness.

"What are you going to do now?" I ask.

"Go get my boat. Take him home," Zale tells me. "Lay him to rest. Next to Aeron."

"Let me help you," I offer. "I have to leave in a couple hours, but –"

He shakes his head. "This is something I need to do alone."

And I understand that.

Zale takes my hand and walks me back across the boardwalk to the Mystic Rose. With the people all gone, it's hard to ignore the peeling paint and the sagging boards. The weeds and thorny vines pushing up through the holes and all the little broken places.

He stops at the front steps, but I lead him around the house. To the kitchen door in the back. I need to put some distance between our goodbye and the bones of his father.

"Be careful," I tell him. "The storm –"

"I'll be fine," he reassures me. "And if you need me, I'll be here."

We lock eyes, and that feels like a promise

"My daddy wasn't a monster," he says. "He didn't kill those little girls."

"I believe you," I tell him.

"And your mama wasn't a monster, either. People do terrible things when they're hurtin'." He lays a hand on my cheek. "Doesn't make 'em all bad."

I nod, and something inside me loosens up.

Seems like, every time I'm with Zale, I come away just a little bit healed.

I let him wrap me in his arms and pull me against him.

"And Elora and I weren't in love," he whispers. "Not like you mean. Not like that."

We stand there for a few minutes, all tangled up in each other. And I start to feel that humming current again. It gets stronger and stronger until Zale's white-hot energy is coursing through both of us.

Everywhere his body touches mine, I'm suddenly so alive.

Wide awake.

And when I look up toward his face, his eyes blaze down at me bright blue.

Evie's wind chimes sing out like tinkling laughter. It's a familiar sound. Magical.

I reach up on my tiptoes to pull Zale's mouth toward mine. Not because I'm hurting and I need the pain to go away. But because he makes me happy. And I need that to last a little bit longer.

I am so unprepared for the sensation of kissing him, though. So completely unprepared.

When our lips meet, it's the lighting of a fuse. Zale is soft and sweet, but thrumming with barely contained electricity. Little zaps to my front teeth. The roof of my mouth. *Zip.* Shock after shock after shock that makes it hard to keep breathing. My legs are shaking. And Zale's hands are at my waist.

My wide-open heart skips and jumps. It stops hard. Then races.

And when I finally feel his tongue against mine, it's the completing of a circuit. We hum and vibrate together like our bodies are tuned to the exact same frequency.

That buzz erases everything that hurts and all the things

that scare me, at least for a few minutes. I pull him even closer. And I stop fighting the way he makes me feel.

Eventually, we have to stop so I can catch my breath. Zale bends low to whisper in my ear.

"There's magic in you, Grey."

And for the first time ever, I almost believe that.

The sky is turning light in the east. But off to the south, there's a solid wall of black. It's the light in the sky that scares me, though. Not the dark.

"You have to leave," I tell him. "You need to get out of here."

He smiles at me. "I'm not afraid of the hurricane. I was born into the storm. Remember?"

"I know," I tell him. "But you need to be afraid of Hart. He's got a gun, and he's convinced you killed Elora." Fear grips me all over again. "There's a supply boat coming this morning. I'm gonna make him leave with me. But if he finds you, he'll kill you." My heart is being split right down the middle. "He's messed up right now. Half out of his mind. But he's not a bad guy, he just –" Thinking about Hart makes it all hurt again. "Elora was everything. To both of us."

"I understand." Zale reaches out to run his fingers through my hair, and I lean into the tenderness of his touch. "You have to love deep to grieve deep like dat."

I nod and swallow hard. "That's why Hart went back to Keller's Island that night. When Elora disappeared. Even though he knew your father was dead. He needed to feel like he was doing something. You know? He needed to look absolutely everywhere. Even if it didn't make any sense."

Zale stares down at me, and something flickers through his eyes. "Grey, Hart never came back to Keller's Island the night Elora disappeared."

"He did," I argue. "He said he came back here and got the four-wheeler. Then he drove out there. He told me he ended up covered in bug bites."

Zale shakes his head. "I was there the whole night, Grey. I went back there right after I saw Elora on the dock. And Hart never came around. If he'd come poking around back there, I'd have known it." The wind is ripping at the shingles on the roof, and the sound of them flapping is like a flock of birds coming home to roost. "Nobody came around looking for Elora that night. Nobody at all."

I yell his name as loud as I can.
Somehow I make myself heard over the raging of
the storm. He looks back over his shoulder at me.
His mouth falls open in surprise. And mine does,
too. Because he isn't human. Not any more.

26

When Zale leaves, I stagger back inside. My head is heavy. My stomach, too. Like they're both full of mud.

Why would Hart lie to me?

I slump in a corner and pull my knees up to my chest. I miss Zale already. I need that energy of his. My whole body aches. I'm confused. And I'm so bone-tired. The kind of exhausted that comes from fighting and fighting and fighting.

And losing.

And losing.

And losing.

How long has it been since I slept? Really slept.

Days?

Weeks?

Months?

And that's when that flash hits me. Elora yelling into the storm. I scratch and claw at it. I grab it and dig my fingernails in. Try to hang on long enough to see something useful.

But I can't see her face.

And I can't hear whose name she's screaming. I only feel the sound tearing its way out of my throat.

Her throat.

My eyes burn.

So I close them. Just for a second.

And somehow, I fall asleep like that. Huddled up against the wall.

When I wake up, Hart is standing in the doorway. Watching me. And there's no Evie.

"You didn't find her."

"No," he says. "Looked all night. Not a trace of 'er."

My chest constricts, and the next words come out all pained. "Did you find him?"

Zale.

Hart shakes his head. "I didn't find shit."

I let myself take a deep breath. Because that means Zale is probably safe. At least for now.

Hart looks at me in disgust, so I know he feels my relief.

I want to ask him about what Zale told me. How he said that Hart never showed up at Keller's Island that night. Back in February. And how that doesn't make sense. Because it's one of the very first things Hart told me.

But I can't figure out how to ask without letting Hart know that Zale is the one who gave me that information. That he was here just a few hours ago. That I kissed him in the gathering storm. And telling Hart any of that seems like a really bad idea.

So I convince myself it's a misunderstanding. A mix-up. Some kind of confusion.

Things must have been so wild that night. With the wind and the downpour. And Elora disappearing.

It's seven o'clock in the morning. The supply boat should be here soon.

I hear rain pounding the roof.

I rub the sleep out of my eyes and follow Hart into the kitchen. The radio is still on. Twelve hours till Elizabeth blows into Plaquemines Parish. That's what the announcer is saying. But he warns that we're already getting intense bands of precipitation and gale-force winds. Waloons they call them down here.

"What are we going to do?" I ask. "About Evie?"

It just about kills me, thinking maybe she's out in this.

Alone.

"Nothing we can do," Hart says. His voice doesn't sound like his at all. There's nothing in it that I recognize. "Like I said, she's already dead. I'd bet my life on it."

I come so close to telling him that we both know his life isn't worth much at this point.

But I don't.

"It wasn't Zale," I say. "He didn't –"

"It doesn't matter now." Hart's voice sounds like he's talking from the bottom of a well. "It's all over. We're never gonna know what really happened that night."

"But –"

"Boat'll be here soon," he goes on. Like he's telling me what's for breakfast. "It'll blast the horn three times. Once you hear that last one, you better get your ass on board. Because there won't be a fourth."

He turns and heads out the front door. And I stumble after him.

The boardwalk is uneven. Groping vines push the wood aside so the planks look like a smile with missing teeth.

I yell Hart's name, and he whirls on me. His face is twisted up with rage. He stands there breathing hard. Battling the wind and the rain.

"Jesus, Greycie! Get the hell outta here and let me be!"

"I can't leave you here to die," I yell at him.

"The hell you can't!"

"Hart, please! Don't do this! Don't give up like this. I –"

"Shut up!" he yells at me, and he rakes his hands through his wet hair. Pulls hard on his curls. "Dammit! Will you just shut up?" He's sputtering at me. Choking on rain. "Jesus. Greycie. Please," he begs. "Just shut the fuck up."

We stare at each other.

The rain stops suddenly as the squall moves off. But the air hangs thick and heavy between us. We stand there dripping.

"You were right," he admits. "About what you said. About me." His hands are shaking as he pulls out a soggy, bent cigarette. It's almost broken in half, but somehow he gets it to light, despite the whipping wind. It's a hurricane miracle. Then he sucks in smoke before he exhales a long, uneven breath. "I'm a goddamn coward."

A gust slams into me from behind. It feels like getting hit by a truck.

"I didn't mean it," I tell him. "I was angry. And scared."

"Jesus, Grey. I know that. But you were still right."

Hart turns and makes his way toward the end of the boardwalk.

And I follow him.

Again.

Hart's curls are blowing wild, and his T-shirt catches the wind like a sail.

He stops and stares down at the gator pond. The old pontoon boat has drifted across to the other side. I wonder where it will end up, once the water really starts to rise.

I wonder where all of us will end up.

"Hart," I plead. "Don't do this. Please come with me." He just stares at the water. "For your mama's sake." I see him flinch when I mention Becky. "For my sake. We can still be okay."

He just shakes his head and takes a long drag off that broken cigarette.

"Maybe in our next life."

I look at Hart and realize he's just as gone as Elora is. He's not going to get on that boat. No matter what I say or do. I can stay here and die with him, or I can go on living. Without him. Those are my only two choices.

"You need to get on down to Miss Roselyn's," he tells me, and he flicks his cigarette down into the mud. And the rising water. "Stay close to the dock. Boat's bound to be here any minute. Be ready. They won't have time to wait. Three blasts –"

"I know," I say. "There won't be a fourth."

There's no way I can possibly tell him goodbye. Not Hart. So I wrap my arms around him and hold on tight. I want him to feel all the things I can't say. Deep down, I'm still hoping maybe that will be enough to save him.

But it isn't.

"Get outta here, Greycie," he tells me. "Get on down to the bookstore." He has to peel me off him. "Go on now. I promised Miss Roselyn you'd be on that boat. And I don't wanna have to show up at some damn séance to apologize for lettin' 'er down."

"You're not a coward," I tell him. "You never have been."

He smiles at me. It's an almost-Hart grin. And it hurts so much I think I might drop dead. Right there on the spot.

"Just 'cause you're psychic now, Shortcake, don't go thinkin' you know everything." His smile disappears. "There's a lot of shit you don't know still."

Hart looks back out toward the gator pond, and I know that if I don't go now, I won't be able to. So I turn and run for home. My foot finds a broken place in the boardwalk, and I go sprawling. But I get back up and keep moving. I tell myself Evie will be waiting on the front porch. That we can still make it out of here together, the two of us at least.

But she isn't there.

I grab my backpack from the kitchen and sit on the steps of the Mystic Rose to wait for the boat. I try not to think. And I try not to be afraid. Of Elizabeth. Or of whatever happened to Elora. And Evie. Or of what's going to happen to Hart. And Zale.

I just watch the big waves on the river. And I wait. I wait a really long time. The rain comes and goes as those bands of squalls move through. The wind blows so hard that it drives the rain sideways. I move back off the steps to sit against the front door. I still get wet. But I'm already soaked, so who cares.

By noon, I'm in full panic mode. The wind is unbelievable. It forces me back inside the bookstore. I crouch by the door and peek out to watch the storm peel shingles off houses all up and down the boardwalk. I listen to the water slap against the dock.

And there's still no boat.

Elizabeth is only seven hours away. The storm surge is already sneaking in. The water has crept up past the high tide mark. And it's rising fast. Soon it'll be over the river flood markers. I think of Honey waiting on the dock up in New Orleans. She won't leave there without me. If anything happens to her, it'll be my fault.

That's when I start to cry.

A few more hours trickle by.

Five or six times I think I hear a boat horn. I leap up and run out on to the porch. The wind and rain bite into me.

But there's never anything there.

I search for the shine of Zale's bright blue eyes. And I don't see that, either. And I wonder where he is. He promised he'd be here when I needed him.

And I need him bad.

By late afternoon, all I can do is rock back and forth on my hands and knees on the floor of the Mystic Rose while I tell myself how stupid this all was.

How I'm going to die here. Just like Hart.

It's around four o'clock that afternoon when the back door

crashes open with a bang. I run to see what happened, and Hart stands dripping in the middle of the kitchen, wild-eyed and breathing hard. Furious. "What the fuck are you doing here?" he demands. "You were supposed to get on the goddamn boat!" He looks like he wants to kill me with his bare hands.

"The boat hasn't come yet," I tell him. And as soon as I say it, I know the truth.

We both know it.

It's too late.

The boat isn't coming. Something must have happened. They couldn't make it in.

Just then, there's a voice from the front porch. "You still here, chere? Where you at?" And I know it's Case. But I also know Case and his whole family went up to his memaw's place in Georgia.

They're long gone.

Hart follows me into the front room. And sure enough, there stands Case. And he has Wrynn with him. When she sees us, she ducks behind her brother and cowers in fear.

"What the hell are you doing here?" Hart thunders.

"We came lookin' for Evie. Just to see if we could spot 'er. Bernadette called my mama from da shelter up in Monroe. Carryin' on 'bout Evie gettin' left behind. And I knew couldn't nobody get down here to check on 'er by road or river." He glares at Hart. "So dat's what the hell I'm doin' here. Brought Little Bird with me." He puts a hand on Wrynn's head. But she buries her face against her big brother. "In case Evie was hurt or somethin.'"

"You're too fucking late," Hart announces. "Evie's dead already."

"No, she ain't," Case tells him. "We found her." He ruffles Wrynn's hair. "Little Bird did. She's back at Li'l Pass, holed up in that old clothes dryer."

My heart leaps, then twists. Because even if Evie is alive now, she won't be for long.

"How did you know where she was?" I ask Wrynn. But she won't answer me. So Case does.

"Wrynn said she seen Evie hidin' in dere before."

Hiding from Victor, probably. God. How many times did we all fail her?

All of us except Hart.

"She wouldn't come out for me," Case says. "She's bad scared." He shakes his head. "Couldn't get her to come out for nothin'."

I turn toward Hart. "She'll come out for you."

"If I get her outta there, can you take her back with you?" Hart takes a step toward Case. Wrynn cringes and whimpers. "Her and Grey both?"

Case shakes his head. But I already knew it.

"I can bring Wrynn, 'cause she has a bit of that gift, too. Same as me. But it's like I told Evie's mama; I can't bring nobody else. It just don't work like that." He looks at me. "I wish it did, chere."

"You've gotta go get her anyway," I tell Hart. "At least with us all together, we have a chance. If the water doesn't get too high, we might make it. Up on the second floor. Or on the roof."

"Fuck!" Hart turns and puts his fist through the wall of the bookstore. We all jump. Wrynn gives a little shriek and starts to cry. "Goddammit." He kicks at the baseboard, but then he grabs a flashlight and storms out the front door, leaving it wide open and banging behind him.

Wrynn is full-on sobbing now. She has Case's T-shirt balled up so tight in her fists that she's about to pull it off him.

"Evie'll be okay," I soothe. "Hart will take care of her. I promise." But that just makes Wrynn cry louder. "You need to get her out of here," I tell Case. "Get her somewhere safe."

"Wish I could get you somewhere safe, chere." Case shakes his head. "That's sure a thing I wish I could do." His voice gets extra deep. "For Elora." Wrynn is still trembling. She wipes snot on the back of Case's shirt. "You want me ta come back? After I get Little Bird home? You want me ta be here with you when . . ." He stops. But I know what he's getting at.

"Thanks," I tell him. "But Hart will be here. And Evie." I try to fight my rising panic. "We'll be together. And there's nothing you could do to help us anyway." Case's face twists up, but he nods. "Let Honey know that I love her, okay? And that I'm sorry about . . . about everything."

Case nods again. "I sure will, chere. Y'all look out for each other. Ya hear?" He wipes at his face with the back of his hand. "I ain't giving up on ya. We'll get somebody down here to see 'boutcha, soon as this blows through."

Then he turns and heads out to the front porch.

He doesn't say goodbye.

I crouch down low to talk to Wrynn. "Hey," I tell her. "Thanks for finding Evie for us."

She looks at me, all red-faced and puffy-eyed. "Don't let it get ya, Grey," she pleads. Her voice is a terrified whisper. And at first I think she means the hurricane. Elizabeth. But then she says, "Da rougarou." I reach out and run my hand over her stringy red hair.

"Don't worry," I tell her. "I won't."

But she grabs my hand and squeezes so hard it hurts. "You promise me, Grey," she begs. "Please! He's gonna get Evie, sure. 'Cause Case told him right where she's at. But when he comes back here, don't you let him get you, too. You fight with everythin' ya got."

She turns and runs to follow Case outside, but when I step through the front door after her, they've both already disappeared.

I manage to make it back inside before my legs go out from under me. I lean against the wall and slide down to sit on the bare floor.

The house shakes as the wind moves around the corners with a high-pitched keening sound that makes me shiver.

It's howling.

Like a bayou werewolf.

I think about the way Wrynn acted when she saw Hart.

That terror in her eyes.

He's gonna get Evie, sure. 'Cause Case told him right where she's at.

I find the little blue pearl around my neck.

Twist Elora's ring around my finger.

My hands are shaking when I reach for my backpack.

I pull it across the floor toward me and unzip the front pocket. I'm looking for that photograph of Elora and me. Our tenth birthday. The pink sheet cake. Or the sketch Sander did of the two of us. I just want to see her face.

I need to feel less alone.

But the first thing I find is that birthday card from Hart. The one in the purple envelope. Folded in half. And water-stained.

The one I never opened.

I pull it out and unfold it. Then I stare at my name scrawled in pencil across the front. I trace the letters with my finger before I break the seal and pull the card out of the ruined envelope. Because I need to remind myself who Hart is. Who he's always been.

The front of the card features a dancing pig in a pink tutu. She's holding a can of beer in one hand and throwing a peace sign with the other.

IT'S YOUR BIRTHDAY! GO HOG-WILD!

And there's a handwritten note on the inside.

Happy birthday, Shortcake. Sorry this year has been so shitty. You deserve a better party. Hope you get to celebrate in style sometime soon. Love, Hart.

And that's when the hurricane hits.

Category 10. At least.

Soon.

I stare at the word. That slanting *s* and those two egg-shaped *o*'s leap right off the paper to lodge themselves deep in my throat. They make it impossible to breathe.

Soon.

A one-word love note.

An unfulfilled promise.

A delicate gold bracelet with one tiny charm.

A single

   perfect

     red

       heart.

That's when I know for sure.
And knowing feels unsurvivable.
Whatever he might do to me tonight –
even if he kills me – it can't be
worse than this terrible knowing.

It's unbelievable – wrong – to think of Hart and Elora together. Like that. They aren't really related. Not by blood, anyway. But still. It's like finding out grass grows from the sky and rain falls from the ground.

I feel upside down.

Betrayed.

And I couldn't even say if I'm jealous of Elora for what she had with Hart.

Or if I'm jealous of Hart for what he had with Elora.

Either way, I don't want it to be true.

But there's no denying that *s* and those *o*'s.

Soon.

That word ricochets inside my head like a bullet.

Soon Elizabeth will be here.

Soon La Cachette will be underwater.

Soon we'll all be drowned.

I shove the card in my backpack and zip it up tight. And I tell myself I'm being ridiculous. So what if Hart and Elora were in love? It doesn't mean he's a murderer.

Only I can't get over the fact that he lied to me about going out to Keller's Island that night. And if he wasn't out there, what was he doing while everyone else was searching for Elora out at Li'l Pass?

I think about how he tried so hard to convince me that Case was guilty. And then Zale.

And about the way Wrynn looked at him.

Like she was face-to-face with a monster.

He's gonna get Evie, sure. 'Cause Case told him right where she's at.

Oh, God. I lean back against the wall and hope like hell I don't pass out.

Because I think I finally know what Elora has been whispering to Evie from beyond the grave. She's been saying that Hart is the one who killed her.

That would explain the wind chimes.

All Evie's jumpiness this summer.

Because there's no way she would want to hear that. Not about Hart. Not with him being her knight in shining armor.

The dead? They lie. Just like the rest of us.

And – shit! – I'm the one who told Hart that Elora was whispering secrets in Evie's ear. So now he knows that she knows. If Hart kills Evie, it's all my fault.

I have to do something.

Now.

Because *soon* Evie will be dead.

Soon Hart will be back.

I jump up and run into the kitchen to pull on my boots and grab a flashlight. Hart's got a good head start on me. He's probably back at Li'l Pass already. And maybe it doesn't matter anyway. If we're all gonna die. Maybe nothing matters.

Except it does.

Because there's a difference. I don't want Hart to kill Evie back there in the swamp. If Evie and I fight this storm tooth and nail, and we end up drowning together, that's still better than whatever happened to Elora.

That's not what really drives me out into the hurricane, though.

Not deep down. Not in the bottom of my soul. It's the hope that maybe I'm wrong.

Please let me be wrong.

I have to be wrong.

I jerk open the kitchen door, and the wind knocks me backward. It's late afternoon, so it shouldn't be dark yet. But it is. It isn't raining at the moment, though, and that's something.

I lean into the wind and start down the wooden steps into the bayou. And I immediately sink up to my knees. It's like walking on the bottom of a lake. Every time I take a step, water rushes in to fill my footprints.

Erasing them.

Like I was never there at all.

It's slow going. I keep having to stop and pull my boots out of the mud, and I have to skirt around some low-lying places that are already covered by high water.

When I finally get back to Li'l Pass, there's no Hart.

No Evie in the old dryer, either.

Nobody at all.

I long for the warmth of Zale's electric touch. For the calm of his ice-blue eyes.

I turn in a slow circle to peer through the thickening dark.

But I'm utterly alone.

Then I see it. Sudden movement in a cluster of scrawny trees and twisting undergrowth on the other side of the Li'l Pass.

A floating ball of light.

An old fear claws at me.

Because now I'm hunting fifolet.

The water is way up in Li'l Pass, but it's not flooded yet. I splash across and pull myself through the mud on the other side. Then I push into the thicket. Thorns tear at my arms and legs as I move deeper into the center.

And suddenly there they are. Trapped in my flashlight beam.

Hart is standing over Evie, and she's the one he's attacking, but I feel his hands around my neck, too. I know those hands so well. I've felt them on my skin. It isn't hard to imagine them

– rough and strong and familiar –

Squeezing.

Choking.

Holding me down in the mud and the water while the last bit of life drains out of me.

"Hart!" I yell his name as loud as I can. Somehow I make myself heard over the raging of the storm. He lets go of Evie and looks back over his shoulder at me. His mouth falls open in surprise. And mine does, too. Because he isn't human. Not any more.

His eyes glow with rage. They're animal eyes.

His teeth are bared.

Sharp.

He's panting.

All fangs and claws.

Wrynn was right all along. For just a second, I see him the way she must have seen him that night. In the moment he first became the rougarou.

And that's when I know for sure. And knowing feels unsurvivable. Whatever he might do to me tonight – even if he kills me – it can't be worse than this terrible knowing.

Then I hear the boat horn.

One blast.

One last chance.

I'd given up on anything that felt like hope.

"Run!" I'm yelling at Evie, but I don't know if she can hear me. "Boat!" I'm pointing in the direction of the boardwalk and screaming my throat raw. "Go!"

She looks at me. Then at Hart. Hesitates. And I shriek at her again. "Evie! He killed Elora! You know that! Get out of here! Go!"

Hart is staring at me. He looks dazed. Like I hit him over the head.

Evie scrambles to her feet and gives Hart one last look, then she takes off. Running like the dickens. But I don't move. And neither does Hart.

We're holding each other hostage.

The wind is merciless. It's like being hit with a two-by-four. Over and over and over. I grab one of the spindly little trees and hang on. But I don't take my eyes off him. I can't. Because there's nobody else left in the whole world now. It's down to just the two of us.

Him.

And me.

A second blast of the boat horn cuts through the wind.

I hang on as long as I can, to give Evie a few more seconds' head start, then I let go of the tree and take a few steps back. Away from Hart.

Because this is where everything ends. We both know it now.

And that's when the rain finally comes again.

The sky splits open and it comes all at once. It comes in buckets.

Rivers.

The kind of rain that washes away the blood and carries away the evidence.

No clue. No trace.

No goodbye.

All those visions. Those strange flashes.

I didn't understand what I was seeing. I had it all confused.

It was never Elora running through the storm.

It was always me.

How could I not have known that?

I freeze. Terrified. Struck by my own stupidity. Because I've seen all this play out before. I know what's coming.

I just don't know how it ends.

Not yet, anyway.

"Don't, Greycie!" Hart shouts at me, and he picks up his flashlight. "Don't run!" His voice is pleading. But I do it anyway. I turn and run. I run like I have someplace to run to. Even though I don't. I run like there's somewhere to go. Even though I know there isn't. "Fuck!" I hear him howl. Then he takes off after me.

He's tearing through the brush behind me. Breathing hard and calling my name. Even with the wind and the driving rain, he's all I hear. So I push myself faster.

We break out on to the wide-open flats, and I feel him closing in on me. There's nowhere left to hide, except inside the dark. So I turn off my flashlight and let the blackness eat me alive.

I see the glow of his light, and I zigzag to stay out of the beam.

And now we're playing flashlight tag. Like they were that night. The old rhyme jeers at me.

Run and hide.
Hide and run.
I'll count from ten, then join the fun.
Say a prayer and bow your head.
If my light finds you, you'll be dead.
Ten, nine, eight, seven, six, five, four, three, two, one.
Ready or not, here I come.
I'm Dempsey Fontenot.
You better run.

I kick off my boots. They're slowing me down. Then I swallow the panic along with the rain and keep running.

Blind.

Arms stretched out in front of me. Hoping not to feel anything.

Hoping if I do feel something, it won't be him.

Not him.

Not him.

Please don't let it be him.

I hear the third blast of the boat horn, and I'm trying to work out if Evie's had time to make it to the dock.

Something grabs my ankle – cold, wet fingers – and I scream and go down hard. I hit the mud like it's concrete, and it forces every bit of air out of my lungs. My chest aches and I couldn't scream any more, even if I wanted to. Not that there's anybody to scream for.

I kick at the hand at my ankle and realize it's just a twisting root. But I don't have the strength or the will to get up.

Slicing rain stings my skin like a thousand tiny knives. The mud is pulling at me.

Sucking me down.

If I don't do something now, this is where they'll find my body.

I wonder if Elora kept running.

Everything feels so surreal. Like watching a movie I've seen before. Only I was half asleep the first time. Not paying attention.

Now I'm wide awake.

I hear Hart calling my name. The sound of his voice makes

me wish the mud would hurry up and do its job. I want it to suck me down and down and down and then cover me up for good, so there's nothing left of me for him to find.

But then something thick and slimy moves against my leg. And I'm on my feet before I have time to think about what it might be.

I stumble again when I hit water, but I don't go down. Li'l Pass isn't so little any more. There's no jumping it now. The water is up to my knees, and I fight the current to stay on my feet.

I see the bounce of his flashlight beam, and I hear Hart yelling my name again. Over the wind and the rain and the rushing water. And I'm not completely sure if I'm hearing him outside my head.

Or inside.

"Greycie," he pleads. "Where are you? It's me. Please." His voice is broken, hoarse and bleeding. Like his throat is ripped open. Like all of him is ripped open. And I can tell he's crying. But I don't call back. I can't let him find me.

Because if I do, he'll kill me.

Just like he killed Elora.

Hart's flashlight beam cuts through the dark again, and I drop down to my hands and knees in the middle of the storm. In the middle of Li'l Pass. My mouth is barely above the water, and I dig my fingers and toes into the mud to keep from being swept away.

The feeling is familiar, and I remember, too late, what happens next.

How I drowned the first time.

On my bathroom floor.

The bayou is flooding out. Water runs over my back and swirls around my ears. Deeper and deeper. I try not to breathe it in. But I have to breathe. I gasp for air and water rushes in instead. I'm coughing and gagging, and every time my body cries out for oxygen, all I get is water.

Panic stabs at my insides. It slices me up and leaves me in ribbons. I can't see. I can't think. I can't breathe. I can't –

My throat is on fire. The water burns my lungs like I'm sucking in gasoline.

I lose my grip on the mud, and I feel myself being pulled along with the torrent. Tumbling. Spinning. Arms over head over knees or elbows. Mud in my nose. My mouth. My eyes. There's nothing to grab on to. Nothing solid in the whole world.

And then it all goes black.

Peaceful.

No more fear.

Until –

Hart hauls me up by my arm – like I'm a catfish he's pulling out of a pond – and I come roaring back to myself. I fight against him. I kick and I claw and I bite. I spit rain and mud and curse words. But he's too strong, and there's not enough life left in me. I'm choking. Fighting to breathe. Out of the water but still drowning.

"Goddammit, Grey." He gathers me up in his arms. "Just stop."

My head is pounding, and it bounces against his shoulder as he carries me through the storm. I vomit bucketfuls of water on to his chest. And I stop fighting then. I turn my face up toward the sky and wait for the rain to drown me.

Death in the water.

Just like Mackey said about Elora.

What does it matter if the water swirls and bubbles up from below or if it falls from the sky?

Water is water.

And dead is dead.

And when I'm dead, then what?

Will Hart leave me here for the gators?

Toss me in the river like trash?

Will they find me floating facedown in the drowning pool? Like Ember and Orli?

Or maybe he has something even worse in mind.

Maybe, right here at the very end, I'll finally find out exactly what he did with Elora.

28

Hart carries me all the way back to La Cachette. Then he sets me down gently. On the edge of the boardwalk. Right above the gator pond.

In the middle of a hurricane.

"Hang on!" he yells at me. And I wrap my arms tight around the piling. He squats down next to me. And I know exactly what he's going to say. "Don't run, Greycie!" he shouts. "There's no point!"

He ducks and sprints for the front porch. And all I can do is watch him. I squint against the rain as he messes with the gas generator. It takes him a few minutes to get it going, but eventually the huge floodlight on the side of the house comes on. I blink and hide my eyes. It's like the sun coming up in the middle of the night.

Hart races back in my direction. "What did you do with her?" I shout. "Just tell me where she is!" I think I'm crying again. And maybe he is, too. The rain makes it impossible to say. "That's all I want to know!"

But he doesn't answer.

He just kicks off his boots. Then he rips off his soaked T-shirt. And his jeans. The wind picks up his discarded clothes like they're made of tissue paper. It whisks them away into the dark. And Hart stands there for a second. Almost naked. With the rain coming down in solid sheets and the wind tearing at his bare skin.

Then he starts to climb down into the gator pond. The water is already high. Over the bottom few rungs of the ladder. Water hyacinth clogs the surface. But Hart ignores the weeds and the muck and dives into that muddy pit. I try to scream his name, but the wind snatches the word and shoves it back into my mouth so I choke on it.

This is all new. I never saw this part. So I have no idea what's going on.

Or what happens next.

I watch Hart's head disappear beneath the surface of the water, and I imagine Willie Nelson's jaws clamping down on his chest.

Teeth.

Nothing but teeth.

Teeth piercing skin. Then muscle. Then bone.

Hart comes up to take a breath and dives back down again. He's down there a really long time. And I figure Willie Nelson really did get him. But then his head breaks the surface, and this time he's pulling something toward the edge of the pond.

Something heavy.

He struggles with it in the water, and I think he'll probably drown. But he doesn't.

I watch as he hauls it up on to a bit of muddy high ground near the bald cypress tree, and I know what it is even before I see it.

The missing black trunk.

I cling to the boardwalk piling, shaking, as Hart opens it up. I half expect a grand flourish and a *ta-da*, like he used to do when we were little kids. Back when he was magic.

But there's only beating rain.

And crushing wind.

The emergency generator keeps shining. False moonlight on dark hair.

Hart's curls plastered to his forehead.

Elora's.

Spilling over the lip of the trunk.

And I know now why my mind couldn't show me this part. Why it kept this part hidden. Didn't let me peek.

I thought I was empty, but I lean forward and vomit into the water and the wind.

Over and over and over. I vomit until I've turned myself inside out.

"Greycie?" Hart sounds far away. Not distance far. Time far. He sounds five again. Terrified. Confused. Like when he came knocking on my window.

The first time.

And the second.

Only this time, I can't open the window and let him in.

Because he's the rougarou. Finally come to rip me to shreds.

"Why?" It's the only thing I can get out. "Why did you kill her, Hart?" I'm choking again. On the rain. And the words.

"I didn't!" he shouts. "I didn't, Greycie! I swear to God!" He sinks to his knees in the mud, surrounded by a half-dozen cypress knees poking up out of the earth like witnesses. "You have to believe me! I didn't kill her!"

I can't stop staring at Elora's dark hair spilling out of the trunk. I can't see that. I have to get away.

I have to be away.

From that.

I pull myself up to my feet, then I let go of the boardwalk piling and throw myself headlong into the wind. It knocks me sideways. I skitter and claw at the boards to keep from ending up in the water, but I manage to right myself and keep plowing forward.

And I don't take time to look over my shoulder.

I'm hurdling gaps in the boardwalk. Hungry-looking holes that nip at my ankles with splintered teeth. I kick at the grabbing vines.

If I can just make it home . . . maybe.

Maybe this hurricane won't be as bad as they think.

Maybe the house won't blow down.

Maybe it won't wash away.

Maybe I won't drown.

Maybe Zale will come for me.

Elora is dead.

Hart killed her and dumped her in the gator pond.

But maybe he won't kill me.

Maybe I'll live.

I look toward the dock, but there's no boat. Upriver I can barely make out the lights of something big. A huge commercial supply boat. Churning north. Slow and steady. Trying to get ahead of the storm. Evie isn't anywhere to be seen. And I tell myself she made it.

She had to have made it.

I run into the bookstore and slam the front door behind me. The electricity is off, but the flashlight in my pocket still works. I flip the dead bolt and hurry to the back door to do the same. Then I stand in the middle of the floor, dripping and sucking in great gulps of oxygen. Grateful to be breathing air again instead of water.

Until I look around.

In the kitchen, the apple wallpaper peels like the skin of a snake. It's grey. Stained. Molting away from the walls. Rain drips through cracks that spread across the ceiling like spiderwebs. And in the corners, thick vines push up through the linoleum floor and stretch out toward the plywood-covered windows.

I shut my eyes against this haunted-house version of home.

But when I open them again, nothing has changed.

I back out of the kitchen and start up the stairs, toward Honey's bedroom. When the storm surge comes, that's where I'll need to be. But a horrible creaking, groaning noise stops me in my tracks.

The wind is trying to take the roof.

The Mystic Rose shudders and sways under the attack.

I freeze for a second, listening to the house do battle with the hurricane. There's a cracking, splintering noise from up above, and I back slowly down the stairs.

I head toward my little bedroom and lock the door. I try to ignore the water stains that cover the sagging ceiling. And how the walls are fuzzy with mold. The way the floor feels spongy and rotten under my feet.

I just sit in the middle of the empty room. In the dark. And I wait.

For Hart.

Or for Elizabeth.

And I wonder which one will get me first.

The storm sounds like nothing I've ever heard in my life. I feel the walls shake. The roar of the rain is deafening. I cover my ears. Tell myself this is the worst of it.

Even though I know it isn't.

I close my eyes and think about Zale. The electricity in his kiss.

The power in his touch.

How he makes me feel.

How he said he'd be here if I needed him.

There's another groaning sound. Splintering wood. I shine my flashlight toward the window. Elizabeth is pulling at the plywood. Ripping it away from the glass. One last sharp crack and the job is done. The wind takes the plywood and I scream.

But then there's a face outside.

In the dark.

And I realize Elizabeth didn't take the plywood.

Hart did.

I scream again and scramble back toward a damp corner as he smashes the window and climbs inside. The curtains Honey made me get sucked out to flap in the storm, and Wrynn's shiny little collection gets scattered. Paper clips go flying. Bottle caps roll across the floor.

And Hart never stops to count them.

But he doesn't come for me. He doesn't eat me alive. He just collapses in the middle of my bedroom floor. Blood runs down his arms from where he sliced himself on the glass.

"I loved her, Grey!" he shouts. He repeats it over and over and over until the words become strangled sobs. "I loved her! God. I loved her so fucking much!"

The hurricane has followed him inside, but I somehow manage to find my voice. "I loved her, too!" I yell. "But I didn't kill her!"

"We didn't mean for it to happen. But it did." Hart is all blood and tears and rain. "And we couldn't tell anybody. 'Cause what would they have said? What would Leo have said? And my mama? And Case? Shit. Sera and Evie and all of 'em."

All of them.

The Summer Children.

What would we have said?

"That's why things felt so weird last summer. Between the two of you. She was afraid you were gonna find out. About her and me. That you'd see it. Because she never could hide things from you."

It makes sense now. That gulf between Elora and me last

summer. Her sneaking around. Keeping me at arm's length. That change in our dynamic. A shift I could feel but couldn't put a name to. Why didn't I dig deeper? Try to find out what was really going on?

"I would have done anything for her!" I shout. "And for you! You could've told me!" But even as the words come out of my mouth, I wonder if I mean them.

Hart shakes his head. "We couldn't tell anybody! But at least we could have that one perfect thing. That secret. Together. Just for ourselves." He pounds his fists against my bedroom floor. "And, fuck, that was something! That was enough to make all the other shit bearable."

"Why, then?" I pull myself up, because I have to know. "Why did you kill her? If you loved her so much?"

Hart recoils like I'd laid into him with a baseball bat. "I'm tellin' you I didn't kill her, Grey!" He's still on his hands and knees in the middle of my floor. "We met up that night on the dock. While everybody else was out searchin' for 'er. That was the plan all along. To finally get the hell out of La Cachette. We'd decided months before that. Because what you said to her at the end of last summer, about how she'd never get out of here, that scared her. Bad. How you said she was gonna die here."

It's almost more than my heart can take, hearing my own awful words out loud again. How could I have said those things to her?

To Elora?

"So we were finally gonna go. And Elora had been so messed up after you left. After she had to let you go. Like that. But when

I finally said we could leave, she was so happy." Hart's voice cracks. "She was so fucking happy, Grey." I remember what Zale said. About how she didn't need the river any more, and I wonder if that's why. Because she finally saw the light at the end of the tunnel. "That's why she sneaked off. We were supposed to be runnin' away that night. Together."

"Then what the hell happened?" I demand. "How did she end up dead?"

"I backed out. Couldn't do it. Couldn't leave. I was too chickenshit. And Elora called me on it." He looks up at me. "Just like you did."

"You didn't have to kill her, Hart!"

"I didn't! Just fuckin' listen to me! Jesus!" He's shaking all over. "We fought about it. And it was bad. Really, really bad. I just lost it. I yelled at her. Threatened her. Probably scared her half to death. I was so worked up. You know?"

I hear the creaking and groaning of the roof again. Like the wood can't stand to listen to this any more than I can.

"Mostly, I was just pissed at myself for being such a fucking piece-of-shit coward. I didn't have the balls to leave, but I knew she was gonna go either way. Sooner or later. And I couldn't stand the thought of being here without her, either. What would be left for me here? Without Elora."

"What's left for any of us here without Elora?" I choke on my own fury. "You took her away from all of us! Just so you wouldn't have to let her go!"

"No! Grey! Please!" Hart sits back on his heels to look up at me. "Listen. She was so freaked out. And she stumbled, tryin' to get away from me. Got 'er feet all tangled up and went down. So I grabbed her by the arm and yanked her up. I didn't mean to hurt 'er. But, God, I was half out of my mind. Angry. And afraid. Just outta control. And the way she was lookin' at me – So I grabbed 'er. That's all. But the look in her eyes when I did it –"

I wince, remembering Wrynn's terrified whisper.

I saw dat rougarou snatch her by da arm and open up wide, like he was gonna eat Elora right up. All dem sharp teeth showin'.

"And that's when I left!" he goes on. "I knew I had to! I walked away. Left her there. Standin' on the dock. And she was sure as shit alive. Pissed as hell. Yeah. But not even hurt. I swear it!"

I have no idea what to believe any more.

I can't tell truth from lies.

But why tell lies at the end of the world?

"I went home. And I tried to figure out what to do. I paced around. Calmed down some. And it wasn't fifteen minutes later when I went back." He's wailing now. "I was gonna tell her I was sorry! More than sorry! That I'd go. That we'd make it work. That I loved her. And I didn't give two shits about anything besides that!" The next part comes out all chewed up and mangled. "That I didn't wanna stay here and become my fucking father!"

Right then the rain stops.

Abracadabra.

Like magic.

And the wind stills.

It's suddenly dead calm outside my broken window.

And dead quiet inside my bedroom.

I hear the crunch of broken glass under Hart's knees.

"And that's when I found her. On the dock." His voice is barely a whisper now. "Beat all to hell. Skull bashed in. Just crushed. Face nothin' but pulp." He gags on the words. "You couldn't even recognize her." I slump against the wall. "Somebody tore into her with one of those old anchor chains. Blood everywhere. All slippery and red in the rain." I'm trying not to picture it the way he says. "And she was gone, Greycie. She was already gone."

I can't be in the room with him. With that image. I unlock my bedroom door and head for the porch. But Hart gets up and follows me. Outside, a thick tangle of brambles smothers the front of the bookstore and the weathered front steps slouch against each other, trying to catch their breath.

Nothing moves. There isn't so much as a ripple on the surface of the river.

Even Evie's wind chimes are silent.

Then moonlight breaks through the thick clouds, and the bugs start to sing again. And the frogs. They think it's all over.

But it isn't over.

Not by a long shot.

We're inside the eye.

"I'm the one who put her in the trunk, though." Hart's voice barely manages to cut through the thick air. "I'm the one who put her in the pond."

"Why?" I turn around to face him, and I'm looking at a stranger.

Someone I don't know.

"Hart, why? If you didn't kill her? Why?"

It's the ultimate betrayal, stuffing her in that dark box and leaving her there to rot in that filthy pond outside her own bedroom window. While all the rest of us lost our minds with worry. Wondering.

It's worse than killing her, maybe.

Hart sinks down to sit on the ruined steps, but I just stand and stare at him.

"Why?" I demand again.

"I panicked," he says. "I wasn't thinking straight. I didn't think at all. I just did it." He looks bewildered. Like he's talking about something someone else did. "I figured if it all came out – the two of us being together – like that – I'd be the first one they'd come after."

"Why?" It's the only word my brain still knows.

"Nobody'd ever believe she was alive when I left her and dead when I came back, not fifteen minutes later. They'd all think I did it." He looks toward the big black barrels out on the dock. Doesn't seem to notice that there's one missing now. "And I guess I knew where I'd end up."

"Why wouldn't anyone believe you?" Nothing he's saying makes sense.

"Because I'm the son of a killer."

"Stop saying that. Your mama isn't a killer, Hart. She was defending herself. And you."

He shakes his head. "I'm not talkin' about my mama. I'm talkin' about my daddy."

I take a few stunned steps backward.

"Ember and Orli." I breathe their names into the silence, and Hart nods.

"He drowned 'em. In an old bathtub out behind our place. All filled up with rainwater. And then he left 'em there to rot in the heat. Covered up with a blue tarp." He wipes at his face with bloody hands. "Till he had a chance to get rid of 'em."

The sudden stillness is suffocating. My brain stutters. Stalls. Like a car engine that won't turn over. "Why?" It's the only word I can get my mouth to form any more.

"I guess he'd got bored torturin' my mama. And me. Needed some new blood, maybe. Somethin' he could take a little further. He was on the hunt that summer, I think."

"How long have you known?" I ask him.

"Since the day he did it," he admits. "I saw 'em. Right after. He made me look at 'em. Eyes wide open. Starin' up at nothin'. Said if I ever told, he'd do the same to me."

"Why?" That kind of cruelty is impossible to imagine. "Why would he want you to see that?"

Hart shrugs. "Same reason he killed 'em in the first place, I guess." He takes a deep breath. "So he could feel my fear. So he could get off on it."

"He was an empath, too," I say. "Like you." And Hart nods.

"Only he fed off pain. And terror. That shit was like honey to him. It got to be where he was addicted. Like an alcoholic. He needed it more and more." Hart presses the heels of his palms into his eyes, like he's trying to erase what he saw all those years ago. "And he couldn't kill my mama. Or me. Not without people pointin' the finger at him. So when he saw Ember and Orli all alone on the boardwalk that mornin' . . . all tied up with blue ribbons . . . like they'd been gift wrapped just for him . . ."

Hart is telling the story. But it's like listening to an audio recording. He isn't here.

Not really.

All that's left is a stranger with an empty face.

"Later, he made me help move 'em. Woke me up one night real late and we took 'em out to Dempsey Fontenot's place. Dumped 'em in the pond there, for everybody to find the next mornin'."

"And you never told anybody?"

Hart shivers, and I remember that he's sitting there in his boxer shorts. Soaking wet. And bleeding all over. He's lost so much weight. He's just skin.

And bones.

"I told one person." He runs his fingers through those perfect curls, and I'm gutted. "I told my mama. But not till a little while later."

Blood and brains all over the kitchen wallpaper.

"But this whole town knows," he goes on. "Only they all wanna carry on actin' like it was Dempsey Fontenot. 'Cause of that barrel out on the dock. And that little grave back at Keller's Island." Hart shakes his head and rubs at the smeared blood on his arms. "They all know what my daddy did, though. What we did."

In the hiding place, nothing is a secret.

And everything is.

"You were four years old," I remind him.

"He made me help carry their bodies, Greycie. Those little girls I'd played with. Dead. And me not any bigger than them." Hart starts to look for a cigarette. Force of habit. Then he realizes he doesn't have one. That he doesn't even have pockets. "He didn't need my help. He just wanted to fuck with me. That was part of the fun for him."

"You felt them," I say.

"I feel them," he corrects me. "Every single day. What Ember and Orli felt, it's stuck inside me. And what Dempsey Fontenot felt. And Aeron. What Elora felt." He's staring out at the river. "What your mama felt. And my mama." He turns back to look at me. "What you felt when you thought I was a murderer. And what you're feeling right now. That's all part of me. I can't shake it off."

"Hart." I whisper his name, and I wish I could make myself touch him. I want to. But I can't. "Is that why you're so ready to die?"

He shakes his head. "It's the water that makes me wanna die."

Evie's wind chimes start to sing again. Real quiet at first. A soft tinkling sound. Gentle.

Hart gets up and walks out to stand on the boardwalk. And I follow him. The planks are warped. Loose. I feel them shifting under our feet.

"What about the water?" He won't look at me now. And those wind chimes ring out louder. And louder. "Hart. What about the water?"

The air is full of ringing and clanking.

"What Mackey said." Hart's watching the river roll by, just like it's a regular summer night. "Death in the water. If I'd known that, I never would have put her in the pond."

"Oh, God." My stomach lurches again. "You think maybe she was still alive."

He turns back to face me, and I'm not prepared for his eyes. "She was dead, Grey. I swear she was already gone."

"But what if she wasn't, Hart?"

I imagine Elora. Coming to in that dark trunk as the cold water rushes in. Clawing at the wood. Choking on blood, first, and then on water.

Hart nods. Those wind chimes are so loud. It's like they're screaming at me.

"But what if she wasn't."

We stare at each other.

"What do you think happened that night?" It's the only question left. I think about what Hart said. Elora with her skull bashed in. "Who did that to her?" Maybe it doesn't even matter any more. But I can't let it go. Not even now.

Suddenly the rain comes again like someone turned on a faucet. It falls in sheets that blow sideways as the wind roars back to life. The worst of Elizabeth will be coming for real now. The storm surge. We don't have long. I grab Hart's hands just to keep from being blown away, and he shouts something at me that I can't understand.

"What?" I yell, and he tries again.

"Evie!" he shouts. "Fuckin' Evie!" But that can't be right. I must have misunderstood what he was trying to say.

Hart pulls me hard against his chest so he can shout right in my ear. "I didn't know! I never felt it from 'er! There was so much other stuff to feel. And I was so mixed-up. But she told me, Grey! She told me the truth tonight! Back at Li'l Pass!"

I remember that scene in the trees. Hart's hands around Evie's neck.

And that's when I hear it. Finally. That sound I've been wondering about since I heard it that first time in my bedroom, so clear it made me turn my head and look over my shoulder.

Click.

The cocking of the gun. Just behind my head. There's so much noise. Rain and wind and the thumping of my heart. But that single metallic sound echoes louder than any of them. It's the flipping of a light switch. *Click.* And everything else fades to black.

I untangle myself from Hart and turn around slowly. And she's standing right there pointing one of Victor's old pistols at me.

Everyone's baby.

Evie.

That white-blonde hair is plastered to her head, and her painted-on eyes blink against the rain.

"He was gonna leave, Grey!" Her voice is a high-pitched whine. I can barely hear it above the wind. "She was gonna take him away from here! I overheard them talking about it!"

"Oh, Evie." I thought my heart couldn't break any more. But I was wrong.

I think about Elora, whispering in Evie's ear from that dark, wet trunk at the bottom of the gator pond.

She hasn't been murmuring warnings.

She's been shouting accusations.

The storm surge is pouring into the bayou, and the water is rising fast. It's already spilling across the tops of the wooden planks. Huge waves crash against the dock.

Another few minutes and the boardwalk will be underwater.

Then the whole town will be underwater.

"I didn't mean to kill her," Evie whines. "I just needed Hart to stay! He saved me, Grey. He saved my mama!"

"I know."

"And I was so scared after. I was hiding there on the dock, and I didn't know what to do. And I saw Wrynn come and try to save her. But she couldn't." Evie makes a horrible sound, like she's being torn apart by the storm. "And I was so sorry."

"It's okay." I take a step toward her.

"But then Hart came back. And I saw what he did. For me. How he put her in that trunk and took her away. To protect me. And I thought he loved me. I thought –"

"We all love you, Evie." One more step in her direction.

"No! That's a lie!" Evie stops me with a shake of her head and a finger on the trigger. Behind me, I hear Hart suck in his breath. "Now you want to take him away with you!"

"I don't!" I soothe. "I'm not."

"I won't let you," she warns me.

The air around me changes, and another figure appears out of the darkness and the rain at the edge of my vision.

He promised he'd be here.

Zale holds out his hand and I start to go toward him, but Evie screams at me to be still. Not to move. She puts the gun against my head and I freeze. She's shaking hard. Half-blind from the rain. Confused and scared and fighting the wind to stay on her feet.

I feel the water swirling around my ankles.

"Let Grey go!" Hart's shouting at Evie. "Let her go, and I'll stay here. I'll stay with you. I swear!"

There's an awful splintering, cracking sound as the rotting river dock gives way. It crumbles and collapses and disappears into the raging water rising around us.

The revenge of the river.

"Let Grey go, Evie!" Hart shouts again. "I won't leave. I promise. It'll be just you and me."

Evie chews on her lip. She moves back and forth on one foot. In that Evie way she has. And I think maybe I can't stand this. Maybe it would be better to die with them.

But then she nods and lowers the gun. And Hart pulls her into his arms.

"Go!" Hart's voice is the crack of a whip.

But I can't move.

"Now, Greycie!" He screams at me over the tempest. "Go!"

I turn and run toward Zale. Bare feet pounding. Splashing. As fast as I can go. The boardwalk tilts at an awkward angle. The pilings on one side are sliding deeper into the muck. I feel it sinking underneath me. A climbing vine grabs me by the ankle. Tries to pull me into the flood. I tear myself loose. But

I don't stop. And I don't look back. I don't want to see. I don't want to know. I don't want to remember. I'm waiting for the bullet to split my skull in half. For the force of it to knock me face-first into the water and the mud. But I never feel it. I only hear the shot.

And then another.

Zale grabs me by the hand, and that electric touch gives me life. We run together toward the end of the boardwalk. Toward the little flatboat he has waiting there. I freeze at the edge. Standing over the flooded-out gator pond. I'm looking for the black trunk. But it's already vanished.

Elora is already gone.

Taken away from me first by Evie.

And then again by Hart.

And finally by Elizabeth.

Zale squeezes my hand. We're standing on the boardwalk in fast-moving water up to our knees.

We're standing in the middle of the river.

And, just for a second, I hear a musical laugh carried on the rain like a zydeco waltz. I finally let myself look over my shoulder, but there's only dark water.

I know she's there, though. I can feel her. Right behind me.

And I know I'm strong enough to face the storm.

So I let Zale help me into the tiny boat, and then he yells at me to get down. I hunker in the bottom and close my eyes tight. I hear the engine roar to life, and then we're moving.

And it takes me a minute to realize.

I don't feel the rain any more.

And I can't feel the wind.

Not even enough wind to move the hair on the top of my head.

When the boat stops, we're bobbing on gentle little swells. Everything is peaceful. Quiet. And I start to sit up.

But then I catch a glimpse of towering waves. Jagged lightning. A dark and violent sky.

Zale takes my face in his hands.

"Whatever you do, don't look at the storm." He wraps me in his arms, and I feel him surge through me. More powerful than ever. "You're safe. I promise. Just keep your eyes on mine."

But I couldn't look way from those fire-and-ice blues, even if I wanted to.

"I didn't mean to scare you, Grey." His ocean-deep voice settles over me like a quilt.

"You didn't," I whisper.

And the world is perfectly calm when he kisses me.

After, though . . . somewhere in my mind . . . I see a massive wall of water slam into La Cachette. It finds the hiding place and swallows it whole in one big gulp.

Like a sea monster.

And Zale holds me tight as I scream.

) EPILOGUE (

We never went back. After Elizabeth.

No one did. Except maybe Willie Nelson.

La Cachette is under thirty feet of water now. It's a permanent part of the river, and the Summer Children are scattered.

Six of us alive.

And six of us dead.

I never went back up to Little Rock, either. Dad drove my stuff down to Shreveport and Honey and I set up shop in New Orleans. We have a little bookstore on Royal Street. The Grey Rose. I'm a student at Tulane, too, and that keeps me pretty busy, but I help out as much as I can.

Full-time college student.

Part-time psychic.

It's a strange life, and I love it. But my soul is still wet.

So tonight, I follow St. Ann Street all the way down to the park, where I can stand above the Mighty Mississippi.

And I face south.

Toward La Cachette.

I touch the blue pearl hanging around my neck. Spin Elora's ring on my finger.

Three times.

Like making a wish.

And I long for the slow roll of the tides beneath my feet.

The crackle of electricity in the air.

But I'm nineteen now. And it's been two summers.

I find a spot to sit. An empty bench in a crowded city. If I close my eyes and breathe in the river, I can almost imagine myself home.

It's strange to think that the water flowing by below me will eventually make its way down to the hiding place. It will slip over the polished skeleton of the boardwalk. And the bones of the Mystic Rose.

It will wash over what's left of Hart.

And Evie.

Whatever remains of Elora.

Dempsey Fontenot.

And Aeron.

I murmur their names to the river.

Spark their memories like a candle.

Because we were all flames lit from the same match.

And I'm the only one still burning.

So much has changed. It's like Zale said. I've had to go on living in a completely different way. But I do know for sure now that there is magic in me. Not the kind my mama had. That beautiful, terrible power. But the kind that comes from walking through a storm.

And making it out the other side still breathing.

It's getting late and the sun is sinking. I should be heading home for dinner. I stand up to go, but something stops me.

A sudden change in the air.

It hums and snaps like a living thing. Dances against my skin.

I hear the echo of my name. Ocean-deep. And, when I turn around, those fire-and-ice eyes stop my heart from beating.

Zale grins at me. Holds out his hand. And I whisper the words out loud.

"It's okay. I'm not scared."

) ACKNOWLEDGMENTS (

I've spent most of my life working in the theatre, so when I first started thinking about writing, it seemed like such a solitary art. It didn't take me long to realize how wrong I was. So many people have a hand in bringing a book to life that, in the end, it's just as collaborative an act as putting on a play.

First and foremost, I need to thank my family. My mother and father raised their three children in a house where books and words were a part of our daily lives from the very beginning. My mother, Anna Myers, is the author of many wonderful middle grade novels, and my father, Paul Myers, was a poet. Their examples meant that, when I did decide to start writing, I knew it was actually a thing real people could do. Thanks especially to my mother, whose absolute faith in me prompted me to give this a try. And to my son, Paul, who wasn't a bit surprised when I told him I was writing a book, because that's just what people in our family do. Thanks also to my sister, Anna-Maria Lane, for always being up for a phone call or a lunch date when I needed a break, and to my brother, Ben Myers, an exceptional Oklahoma poet whose writing continually inspires me. My whole extended family deserves to be mentioned here, but I want to specifically to list my cousin, Becky Kephart, who is one of the most genuinely enthusiastic cheerleaders anyone could have, and our friend Lela Fox, who isn't actually related to us but definitely deserves to be counted here among my family. Thanks to all of you for everything!

Thank you to my agent, Pete Knapp, who first read this book over the Fourth of July weekend, even though I didn't really believe him when he said he would. Pete, I'm blown away by your passion for great stories, your clarity of vision, your kindness and generosity, and your absolute dedication to the authors you work with. To everyone else at Park & Fine, thank you! I can't imagine a better literary home. I especially want to mention the foreign rights team, Abigail Koons and Ema Barnes.

A huge thank-you to my wonderful editor, Ruta Rimas at Razorbill, who saw from the very beginning what this story could be. Your enthusiasm for this book was unmatched. You made this whole process so easy and seamless, and this nervous debut author is eternally grateful for your guidance, your expertise, and your patience.

Thank you to so many other wonderful team members at Razorbill and Penguin Young Readers who made this possible, including Casey McIntyre, Felicity Vallence, Kaitlin Kneafsey, Gretchen Durning, James Akinaka, the wonderful marketing and sales teams, and all the rest who work behind the scenes like Jayne Ziemba and Abigail Powers, and Kristie Radwilowicz, who designed the gorgeous cover.

I owe a huge debt to my critique partners turned best friends and brunch buddies – Tiffany Thomason, Brenda Maier, Catren Lamb, and Valerie Lawson – who have read this book so many times they can quote it by heart now. You are amazing and I love you! Thanks also to the entire Margarita Night gang who have kept me going with the promise of good food, good conversation, and lots of laughter every Wednesday evening; to all the members of SCBWI Oklahoma; and to the other authors in my incredible debut group, The 21ders. I couldn't wish for more supportive communities to be a part of. Thanks also to everyone at the Philbrook Museum of Art, the most beautiful place in Oklahoma and the best place ever to work!

Last, I want to send all my love to the STAGES theatre kids who taught me so much over the years about friendship, passion, loyalty, bravery, and found family. I was working on revisions for this book when we lost our beloved Caitie very suddenly and much too soon, and so much of that grief and loss made its way on to these pages. I know she would have had to read this story with all the lights on, but I also know she would have loved it anyway . . . because she loved me. I'm so grateful to Caitlin's grandmother, whom she called Honey, for dragging a crying seven-year-old into my theatre twenty-four summers ago and changing our lives forever.

In closing, I'd be remiss if I didn't thank my college boyfriend, Garrick, who first introduced me to the bayous of south Louisiana all those years ago. He probably won't ever read this, but if he does, I'd like him to know that my alligator obsession endures.

Look out for the next
thrilling novel by
Ginny Myers Sain,
coming in 2022 . . .

FIVE TEENAGERS WITH NOTHING IN COMMON. THROWN TOGETHER BY AN ACT OF TERRORISM.

'Heart-rending and utterly gripping' – Kat Ellis, author of *Harrow Lake*

THIS CAN NEVER NOT BE REAL

SERA MILANO

CAN'T SURVIVE THE NIGHT WITHOUT EACH OTHER.

When it comes to horror movie
the rules are clear . . .

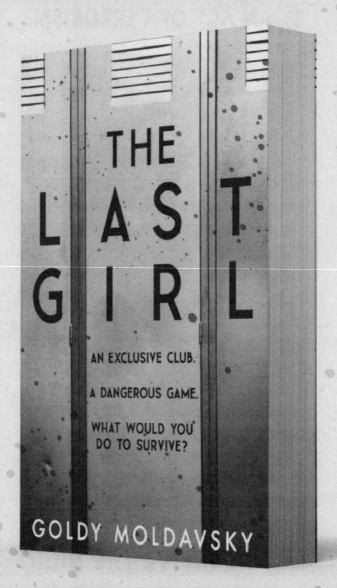

THE
LAST
GIRL

AN EXCLUSIVE CLUB.

A DANGEROUS GAME.

WHAT WOULD YOU
DO TO SURVIVE?

GOLDY MOLDAVSKY

Break them and it's game over